THE CAGE

THE CAGE

Quintin Jardine

HEADLINE

First published in Great Britain in 2023 by
HEADLINE PUBLISHING GROUP

1

Cataloguing in Publication Data is available from the British Library

Hardback ISBN 978 1 0354 0297 7
Trade Paperback ISBN 978 1 0354 0299 1

Typeset in 12.5/16pt Electra LT Std by Jouve (UK), Milton Keynes

Printed and bound in Great Britain by Clays Ltd, Elcograf S.p.A.

Headline's policy is to use papers that are natural, renewable and recyclable
products and made from wood grown in well-managed forests and other controlled
sources. The logging and manufacturing processes are expected to conform to the
environmental regulations of the country of origin.

HEADLINE PUBLISHING GROUP
An Hachette UK Company
Carmelite House
50 Victoria Embankment
London EC4Y 0DZ

www.headline.co.uk
www.hachette.co.uk

This book is dedicated to Dr Harry Bennett, of PAEP, Edinburgh, who sees everything and helped me do the same.

Acknowledgements

To the real AJ.

To my friend Dave, who makes a brief appearance disguised as a swan and with a career change.

To the proprietors of various East Lothian hostelries, who receive friendly mentions.

To the lovely Frida Teixidor Hoverstad, who makes great tomato toast, and is a queen with oysters too.

To her brother-in-law, my friend Nicola.

To my grandkids, Mia and Rex, for continuing to motivate me.

Welcome back, Spike Thomson.

To Anne, for introducing me to new cultures, and for showing me a way forward.

One

Noele McClair flexed her shoulders, adjusting the chest carrier in which Matilda, her six-week-old daughter, was soundly asleep.

'Is she too much for you?' her mother asked anxiously, following in her footsteps.

'Nah, we're good,' she promised. 'I need to do this, Mum; I have to keep in shape, post-pregnancy. I didn't after Harry was born, and I suffered for it. I put on so much weight that when I looked in the mirror I thought I was still up the duff. Also,' she added, 'it's a lovely day, so let's the three of us take advantage of it.'

The grassy path on which they were walking widened into a small clearing, flat enough for a wild camper to have pitched a tent. The man, who was dressed in a Levi Strauss sweatshirt and khaki shorts, was sitting on a folding chair in front of the open flap, frying bacon and eggs. Inside the tent two sleeping bags could be seen, disturbed. He nodded a greeting as they passed in front of him. Noele kept walking, but Sue McClair stopped, for a chat and possibly for a breather.

'Good for you,' she told him, 'using a primus stove rather than lighting a fire. I wish all of you did that.'

'It's how I was trained,' he replied. 'I pitch here a lot. It's next to the Nature Reserve but not part of it. We're bird watchers,' he added, with a self-effacing grin. 'My partner's gone to find the showers; I'll do hers when she gets back.'

'Well, enjoy your breakfast, both of you,' Sue said, 'and your birds. If you have any bread left over feed it to the birds.'

'You're not really supposed to do that,' the camper said. Then he smiled. 'But they won't tell anybody, so . . .'.

She set off to catch up with her daughter and grandchild, who were hidden from sight temporarily by the undulations of the terrain before her. As she reached a crest she saw them, a hundred yards ahead, Noele cutting across the edge of the golf course then taking the path that led up to the bench, to the seat on which they customarily paused to take in the view. It had been five days since their last outing; time they had devoted to helping Harry, the baby's half-brother, into his school routine with the start of the autumn term.

'Is it to do with Covid and staycationing, do you think?' Sue asked as she took her place on the bench. Noele had removed the carrier, and was holding it in front of her with its base on the ground. 'This increase in the number of wild campers?' she continued.

'I suppose,' she said. 'Maybe we just didn't notice them before.'

'Mmm. Maybe not, but we sure do now. They're all right, I suppose, as long as they behave responsibly and clean up after themselves like that chap. I hear the woods behind Yellowcraig can be bad sometimes.'

'Bears, shit, and all that . . .?' Noele murmured.

'What?'

'Never mind.' Sue's sense of humour was slow to engage.

'When your maternity leave is over,' she asked, suddenly, 'are you really going back to work?'

Her daughter stared at her. The stare became a frown, but its target was unaware of it as she bent to fuss over Matilda, who was showing signs of stirring.

'Well?' she persisted.

'Well what?' Noele retorted.

'Are you going back?

'Of course, I'm going back, Mum,' she exclaimed. 'I'm a single parent with a new baby and a son who's only halfway through primary. I don't have a choice.'

'Couldn't you work from home? I know that some other officers were doing that during lockdown.'

Noele stifled a spontaneous laugh as Matilda stirred, momentarily, in the carrier. 'Mother,' she chuckled, 'I'm a detective inspector. I'm part of a Serious Crimes Unit. They're not going to bring the crime scenes to me.'

'But what about Mattie?' Sue McClair persisted. 'Harry's no bother, and as you say he's at school for much of the time, but a baby, that's a whole different kettle of fish. I don't know if I could cope with that.'

Noele grinned. 'Among bad analogies that gets very high marks, but it'll be okay; you won't have to breast-feed her. Mum,' she continued, 'I wouldn't dream of asking you to look after a baby on a daily basis; the thought never even occurred to me. You've got your own life, especially now that your new man Duncan's on the scene. Look, by the time I go back to work, Mattie'll be eight or nine months old. She'll go to a child-minder, full-time, until she's old enough to start nursery.'

'A full-time child-minder? That'll be expensive.' She paused. 'I could help, I suppose . . .'

'I can afford it,' her daughter retorted, cutting her off. 'A DI's salary is over fifty K, and Terry's life insurance took care of the mortgage, remember. Nobody's going to suffer.'

'But what about your house? It's fine for you and Harry at the moment, and the baby, but as she gets older . . .'

Noele eased herself on to the left side of the bench, finding an area free of bird droppings. 'Well . . .' she said, drawing the word out, 'the thing is . . . I will be moving, but I'm not quite sure where. It'll still be in Gullane . . . I wouldn't take Harry out of the school . . . maybe one of the new houses, but I have to take care of some stuff to do with Matthew's estate before I can focus on that. Thing is, Mum,' she explained, 'under Scottish law, Matilda's entitled to half of her father's estate.'

Matilda Reid McClair was the product of a very brief liaison between her mother and Matthew Reid, a man thirty years older. He had died before the birth, never aware that he was to parent. His will had named another police officer as his heiress, Karen Neville, the daughter of Reid's long-dead best friend and his unofficial niece.

Sue's eyes widened as she gasped. 'But that'll be a . . . Matthew was well off, wasn't he?'

'Maybe not as well off as people might imagine,' Noele countered, 'but yes, he was comfortable, let's say.'

'You too? Are you entitled?'

'Don't be daft, Mum. Of course, I'm not; we didn't cohabit. My God, I only slept with him once.'

'Will you have to go to court? It won't get messy, will it?'

'Hopefully not. Karen's not only the beneficiary of Matthew's will, she's the executor. As such, she had legal advice. As a matter of fact, it was Karen that approached me about the situation.'

'Did she ask for DNA proof?' Noele was not taken aback by the question. She knew well enough that her mother was sharper than she appeared to others.

'No, but her lawyers did, and it's been provided. I've instructed

4

Paris Steele, my solicitors in North Berwick, to liaise with them and reach a simple agreement. When it's sorted, whatever Matilda inherits will go into a trust fund for her that'll be managed by Euan, my financial adviser. I'm not going to touch it, not at all. I won't even tell her until she's old enough to get her head round the idea.'

'Wouldn't it help towards your new house?'

'Absolutely not!' Noele declared. 'That'll be completely separate. I'll probably go for one of the houses they're building close to the school. I've got my eye on the site . . .' Her voice faded in mid-sentence, eyes narrowing as she gazed past her mother.

'What is it?' Sue asked.

'Down there.' Rising to her feet, she pointed towards the green L-shaped fence that served as a safety barrier on the twelfth tee of the golf course. It was the longest of three on the par five hole, sited on a small piece of flat land above a sheer hundred-foot drop, and used only for club competitions. 'Look just to the right of the fence, the cage thingy,' she exclaimed, her voice rising, 'then down at the shoreline, on the rocks. Can you see it?'

Her mother turned to follow her pointing finger, but shook her head. 'I can't see that far away,' she admitted. 'I think my cataracts are beginning to affect my long vision. What is it?'

'That might be "Who is it?", Mum.' Reaching down, Noele found the clasp of the baby harness and snapped it loose from her leg. Slipping free of the straps, she passed the drowsy Matilda to her grandmother. 'Look after her,' she ordered. 'I need to get down there.'

She jumped from the bench back on to the well-worn track; her left foot slipped momentarily on a small gravel patch but she steadied herself, walking more carefully, but still with purpose. The way ran between the partly fenced rectangle and the forward tee that was used for regular play. As she passed by, her movement distracted one of a group of three golfers as he steadied himself to drive, but she was unaware of his glower or his hiss of exasperation as she pressed on. Ahead of her, a huge concrete cube, an immoveable relic of the Second World War, marked the start of the descent towards the shore. The natural path was steep and it was narrow; one slip and she might have tumbled to the beach below, but she made her way carefully down until finally she felt the soft sand beneath her feet.

A high pillar of rock rose vertically on her right, the outcrop on which 'the cage' stood; it was red, in contrast with the horizontal grey stone for which she was headed, and was a barrier blocking her way. She picked her way around it, but saw only another rugged rocky obstacle, topped with brown seaweed waiting to be washed by the incoming tide. Finding footholds, she climbed up and on to its flat surface. She scanned the surrounding area, but saw nothing. Doubt crept over her. She was sleep-deprived from the frequent night feeds that Matilda still demanded. Had her eyes been playing tricks? Puzzled, she jumped down on to damp sand, moving backwards towards the waterline but gazing upwards until her mother came into view, still sitting on the bench, holding Matilda, who had been released from her carrier. Frowning, she looked around, questioning herself ever more. Maybe it was time for an eye test. Until, finally . . .

Her gaze fell on a calf-length brown boot. It protruded from what she realised was a V-shaped wedge, formed by two ancient slabs of stone that had been ground over millennia by the force of pounding waves, rising four or five feet above a rock pool, from which, on the edge of her vision, she saw a small crab crawl.

Noele found new footholds and levered herself upwards, to stand once again on the smooth surface. She moved towards the fissure, picking her way carefully, mindful of the treacherous clumps of bladderwrack beneath her feet, until finally she saw what had attracted her from high above.

She knelt on the edge of the space in which the object that had drawn her to it was wedged and looked down. The boot was worn by a man, but she knew at once that it, and its owner, had taken their last steps. Glazed half-open brown eyes stared upwards but saw nothing. She lay flat and reached down into the crevice, checking the neck for a pulse that she knew she would not find.

Her second realisation as she brushed the dead man's clothing was that it was dry, her third was that he was still warm. The unvoiced assumption that she had made from above was wrong. This was no drowning victim brought in by the tide; he had died on shore, within the last hour or two. In that moment all of her training and professional instincts kicked in. Detective Inspector McClair took out her phone, activated its camera and began to record video with an audio description.

'The casualty is male, most likely in his thirties, forty at the oldest,' her commentary began. 'He's wearing denim cut-offs and a sweat shirt. There are signs of an injury on his left temple; there's blood but not much. I'm guessing that he was walking on the rocks in the wrong footwear, slipped and fell in there, smashing his head on the way down and sustaining a fatal injury. Except . . . hold on.' She zoomed the camera. 'He's got spurs on,' she said. 'Those are riding boots. So where's his helmet? Or wasn't he wearing one? And where's his horse?' She paused. 'Unless the boots were all that was handy when he decided to go out for a walk. Still . . .' she murmured.

Stopping the recording, she stood, her camera and her eyes scanning the mile-long beach. She knew that horses were often exercised there, particularly when the tide was out, but there were none in sight. Switching off the phone, she looked around. 'Gotcha!' she murmured. Down on the sand, just beyond the rock pool, she spotted a riding helmet, its strap unfastened. From her vantage point she zoomed in and took a still photograph. 'No doubt now,' she murmured. 'Carelessness costs lives, you poor man. If that helmet had been secure when your horse got spooked and threw you, you might still be alive.' She sighed. 'But why the hell did you forget it for me to find you?' Noele McClair had seen more than enough of violent death, personally and professionally.

Turning her attention back to her phone, she found a number in her directory and called it. She had expected a constable or sergeant to answer and was surprised when Ronnie Hill, her successor in the Haddington office that she had left to go back to CID, picked up himself.

'Station Inspector,' he said, cautiously. The number was a direct line, listed only in internal directories.

'Ronnie,' she replied. 'It's Noele McClair.'

'Noele,' Hill exclaimed, obviously relieved. 'I thought you were on maternity leave. How's the bairn?'

'I am, and she's fine. Right now she's with my mother. I'm on the rocks at the west end of Gullane beach, standing beside what appears to be a fatal accident victim. He's male, thirty-something likely, and he's wearing riding gear. His injuries suggest that he's been thrown by his horse and cracked his skull on the way down. You'll need to get uniforms and some sort of recovery vehicle down here, and I suppose a doctor to formally certify death. You need to do it sharpish though. The tide is on the way in, and I'm not about to haul him out of where he is, not on my own. I've shot some video at the scene. Give me a mobile number and I'll forward it to you.'

'Okay,' Hill replied, fully engaged. 'Can you stay till we get there?'

'It looks as if I'll have to. It isn't busy, but there are punters about on the beach, and potentially there'll be golfers up above who can see him too. We don't want a crowd scene developing.'

'Have you got any idea who he is? You live thereabouts, don't you, Noele?'

'Yes, I do, but I've never seen him before. He possibly has ID in a pocket but I'm not in a position to access it.'

'Would the horse no' give you an idea who he is?' her colleague chuckled, grimly. 'Do they have to wear identification like dogs?'

'Who knows? When you find it, you can interrogate it,' she said. 'It's bolted. In the meantime, Ronnie, please get some people here, now.'

Two

'Is there any chance that you recognise him, Dr Michael?' Inspector Hill asked, more in hope than expectation. 'Could he be one of your patients?'

"I suppose he could be, if he's local,' the GP replied. 'We have thousands of people registered with us. But if he is,' she added, 'he's not one who's ever consulted me. I've never seen him before.'

'That's a pity,' the inspector sighed. He had driven directly from his office, and had arrived before any of his patrol officers, beating the doctor to the scene by only a few minutes. 'He doesn't appear to have any means of identification on him, unless there's a wallet in the back pocket of those shorts. I was hoping . . .'

'Sorry,' she said. 'All I can tell you is that he's male and he's dead . . . although these days we have to be careful attesting to the gender,' she added in a whisper, with a conspiratorial smile. 'The likeliest cause of death is a fractured skull sustained in a fall, but only a post-mortem examination will tell you for sure. I assume he'll be taken to the mortuary in Edinburgh.'

Hill shrugged. 'That would be the norm, unless he goes to the Royal Infirmary, that being closer. I'm expecting a pick-up vehicle, but I don't know where it's coming from. To be honest I'm more concerned about how they'll get him off the beach.

And ourselves for that matter,' he added, eyebrows raised. 'The tide's risen even since we got here. I doubt that they'll want to carry a body bag over the rocks.' He glanced up, towards the green fencing. 'They might have to carry him up the path Noele McClair used.'

Dr Michael's eyebrows rose. 'Noele found him? Now she is a patient of mine, but I haven't seen her since she had the baby. That's a good sign, by the way,' she added. 'We don't get involved with new-borns unless there's a problem. The community nursing side do that. Is she still here?' she asked, looking around.

'No, she left as soon as I arrived. She's still on leave, obviously, but even if she wasn't, an accidental death's my department, not hers.' He glanced at his watch, with a show of impatience. 'I wish the mortuary vehicle would hurry up. We've been lucky in that this spot's away from the main beach, but places like Gullane all have Facebook news groups. The word will spread for sure.' As he spoke his mobile sounded. The doctor watched him as he took the call. He sighed as he listened; it was clear to her that his office was his comfort zone, anywhere else being an inconvenience.

'Tell them we're attending an incident in Gullane beach,' she heard him say, 'and that we'll issue a statement in due course. The usual crap.' He paused. 'Yes, it's a fatal, but don't bloody tell them that!' He ended the call. 'Press Office,' he explained to the doctor as he pocketed his phone. 'Pardon my French, but they get to me. I must have been right about Facebook; the *East Lothian Courier's* been on to them, and I'm sure that's where they'll have got it.' He sighed again as he eyed the incoming tide. 'If the wagon doesn't get here soon, this guy'll be under water.'

As he spoke, his police radio crackled into life. 'Ian Marshall for Inspector Hill. PC Black and I are on scene. The recovery van's here too. We're all down by the beach toilet block. How do we get to you?'

'From there you don't, Sergeant,' he replied, 'not directly. I'm right at the west end of the beach, near the start of the Nature Reserve.'

'I know where you are. What?' Marshall paused for a few seconds. 'Aye right, you do that,' Hill heard him say, and then, 'The driver of the recovery vehicle's a member here, sir. He says the best thing to do is for him and his mate to get a four-seated golf buggy from the pro shop and use that to get as close to the scene as they can. They've got a plastic coffin in the van; it'll go on the back seat of the buggy, and they'll use it to remove the victim. Black and I will be with you soonest.'

'Okay,' the inspector replied. 'By the way,' he added. 'If you see a horse on the way here, take it into custody!'

Three

'Yes,' Professor Sarah Grace said. 'I can fit a post-mortem in, late afternoon or early evening. But,' she added, 'I'd rather not have to go into Edinburgh. Can you have the victim taken to the Royal rather than the city mortuary? You can? In that case you're on.'

'Who was that?' her husband asked as she ended the call. 'Fiscal's office?'

'You got it in one.'

'From a crime scene?'

'No, it's an accident victim. Very close to here too. Male, appears to have been thrown from a horse on the beach and suffered a fatal head injury on the rocks.'

'Christ!' Sir Robert Skinner exclaimed. 'I probably saw him when I was out running this morning, about six thirty. There was a lone rider, on a bay horse; quite a big bloke in a sweat shirt and shorts. I was going east, he was going west. He gave me a wave, I waved back. It sounds as if I was waving him goodbye, the poor bastard!'

Sarah frowned. 'Did you recognise him? The fiscal said that so far he's unidentified.'

'I'm sure that I've seen him and his horse on the beach before,' he told her, 'around the same time, but I've got no idea who he is or where he's from. I don't think I've ever seen him with any other riders either.'

'Does that suggest to you he has his own stable, rather than keeping his horse in a livery like West Fenton or Archerfield, where the owners tend to go out in small groups?'

Bob shrugged. 'It doesn't suggest anything. All I can tell you is he's a good rider and it's a powerful beast; a horse, not a pony, a gelding, not a mare. Not the sort of animal to be walked in a neat orderly line. It looks not unlike a police horse. That sort of size.'

'How do you know so much about horses all of a sudden?'

'I don't really, but Paloma Aislado has one, remember, out in Girona.'

Sarah smiled. 'Does her father ride it?'

He returned her grin. 'God help it if he did. His feet would be dragging the ground, Xavi being two metres tall.'

'How is he?' she asked. 'Is there any sign of him wanting to come back as chairman of the company?' Skinner's friend Xavier Aislado was the owner of InterMedia, an international group as the name suggested, based in Girona, Spain. Its portfolio included the Scottish newspaper, the *Saltire*, which Bob had been brought on to the board of directors to oversee, a few years before. They had worked well together, and the group's UK interests had grown, until tragedy had intervened through the agency of the Covid pandemic. It had claimed Xavi's wife, Sheila, and he had withdrawn abruptly from the business world. Grief-stricken, he had asked Bob to replace him as executive chairman of the group until he was ready to return.

'Not yet,' he replied. 'I ask him every time I see him, and every time he says the same thing, that the company is better off with me in the chair.' He paused. 'All that said, though, he still takes an interest; not in the everyday running of the business, but in its shape and its future. For example, like all the other main global news organisations, InterMedia has a presence in Washington. You knew that already, but now . . . this is something I haven't told you . . . Xavi's asked the board to explore the possibility of a completely new start operation broadcasting within the US, in Spanish. There are plenty of Hispanic stations there already, but they're nearly all entertainment-based. We're talking about a cable news network. Hector Sureda, the CEO, and I are looking at the viability of a Hispanic equivalent of CNN.'

'Or Fox News?'

'God forbid!' He grinned, in unexpected contrast with his vehemence. 'That said . . . and don't breathe a word of this, because it comes from Hector; Xavi and I don't discuss it . . . his working title is *Noticias Zorro*.'

'Spanish for Fox News? Why not for real?'

'One, they would sue our arses off, two it would send entirely the wrong political message. They don't call the *Saltire* "The Scottish *Guardian*" for nothing. Speaking of which,' he said, picking up his phone, 'I must alert our news desk to the dead horseman on the beach.' He glanced out of the kitchen window as a movement caught his eye. 'Were you expecting Noele?' he asked, as her car drew up in her driveway.

Sarah frowned. 'No. And she usually calls if she's going to drop in,' she added.

'You let her in, okay? I must make that call to the news desk: plus, I have a Zoom meeting with the InterMedia department heads in a couple of minutes.'

'Including the Italians?'

'Yup.'

'Will there be subtitles?' she chuckled.

He shook his head, with a smile that revealed a hint of pride. 'No. We're doing it entirely in Spanish.'

'Yeah?'

'Yeah,' he repeated. 'After all these years of having a second home in Spain, I am finally fluent in the language at business level.' He left the room, heading for his small office, while Sarah went to the front door, anticipating the arrival of the visitor.

'Sorry for the unexpected visit,' Noele McClair began, as she entered. 'I'm not holding you back from anything, am I?'

'No,' Sarah assured her. 'I've got half an hour before I need to leave. A short-notice autopsy.'

'I guessed as much. There's a bit of gossip I must share.'

'So come on in. Where's Matilda?' she asked as she led the way to the kitchen.

'Sound asleep in her car seat . . . with the window slightly open,' she added. 'I gave her a top-up feed when I dropped Mum off. That'll be her off for at least a couple of hours. Is your Dawn with Trish?'

'Play-group,' she replied. 'Want a coffee?'

'No thanks, Sarah. I'm off that while I'm feeding. Water would be fine.

'Fizzy or still?'

'Bubbles if you have them.'

'So? The gossip?' Sarah exclaimed as she opened the fridge. 'It wouldn't involve a dead man on the beach, would it?'

'That's your short-notice autopsy?' Noele took the proffered water.

'Unless there are two of them. I've been booked to do it later on this afternoon, at the Royal.'

'Jeez, that was quick.'

'It's Friday, isn't it? The fiscal's office didn't want him to lie in the cooler over the weekend. But how did you know it was quick?'

'Because I found him. I saw him from the path above where he fell. We were just beside the cage. I left Matilda with Mum and went down there. Poor sod was well dead by the time I got there.'

'What about the horse?'

'How did you know about the horse?'

'Bob saw him when he was running on the beach. They were going in different directions so he didn't witness the accident.' She hesitated, considering the circumstances. 'Maybe,' she whispered, 'if Bob had been heading west too, he'd have seen it happen and been able to help.'

Noele frowned. 'No doubt you'll determine that when you examine him, but on the basis of what I saw, he wouldn't. The man's helmet came off in the fall and there was a head injury, not big on the outside, but obviously enough to kill him.'

'Nothing's obvious until I open him up,' Sarah said. 'I wonder why he was thrown?' she murmured. 'The way Bob described him he was a capable rider.'

'We'll never know for sure, unless a witness comes forward. I can only speculate that he took the horse too close to the rocks and that spooked it.'

'Was the horse injured?'

'Dunno. The culprit fled the scene, as they say. There was no sign of it when I got there.' Noele paused to sip her water. 'What time did Bob see him?'

'It would have been around six thirty. Normally he runs early; more often than not Jazz goes with him, but this morning he was alone.' She smiled, fleetingly. 'And there lies a story. Our younger son and a few of his pals had an end of summer barbecue at

Yellowcraig yesterday evening,' she added. 'They all cycled there and back, and Jazz was home later than he should have been . . . with a fat lip. When Bob quizzed him about it, he said there had been "an incident" . . . his words. You know that Yellowcraig is full of wild campers during the summer?' Noele nodded. 'Well,' Sarah continued, 'one of the girls in Jazz's group tripped over one of the guy ropes of a tent, pulling it out in the process. A man in his boxers came out yelling, demanding to know who had done it. Jazz said sorry, that it had been an accident, and he said, "Yes, well so was this." Then he grabbed him by the shirt front and hit him.'

'God,' Noele gasped, 'what did Bob do when he heard that? Get the car out and head for Yellowcraig?'

'He was going to, but Jazz said no, that he'd dealt with it. Bob didn't press him; he just said, "Okay, if that's how it played, get off to bed." A few minutes later I had a WhatsApp from the mother of the girl, thanking my son for standing up for her daughter. Apparently after he was hit, Jazz smiled at the fellow, said "This wasn't," and sank his fist wrist-deep in his belly. The guy turned into a pile of jelly, and that was all she wrote. His girlfriend stuck her head outside just in time to see it all.'

'Jesus, Sarah, Jazz is only twelve.'

'Forget "only"; you haven't seen him lately. He's always been a big boy and he's in a growing phase. He's been doing Judo since he was five, Taekwondo since he was eight and Boxercise with his Aunt Alex since he was ten. Plus he's his father's son.' She grinned. 'Are you going to report him for assault?'

'Of course not, but what if the guy does?'

'If he's that stupid, there will be eight witnesses saying it was self-defence. If anyone should make a police report it's Jazz.'

'Even if he doesn't,' McClair countered, 'Bob should get in

touch with Ronnie Hill at Haddington . . . if only to put his sighting of the dead man on the record.'

'He'll probably do that automatically, but I'll remind him,' Sarah said. 'It won't contribute anything to the investigation, but it does give me a starting point for the time of death. I'll call you once I've done the examination.'

'You don't need to. I'm on maternity, remember.'

'Maybe but you're still a cop. I've been married to one long enough to know that, once their curiosity is aroused, it's never satisfied until it knows the whole story.'

Four

'What about the horse?' Bob Skinner asked.

'It's been found,' Inspector Hill told him. 'A group of twitchers on the Nature Reserve came across it. It was distressed I'm told, but fortunately one of the people had some experience with horses and was able to calm her down.'

'Him.'

'Sorry, sir?'

'It's a gelding,' Skinner explained. 'It has no tackle, but it's still male. I'm no equestrian, but I've seen a few horses' arses in my time, so I know. How are you going it recover it?'

'I've asked for a horse box from our mounted unit to be taken to the scene.'

'Are you going to report it to the procurator fiscal?' he joked. He had known Hill from the inspector's earliest days in the Edinburgh force. 'You could charge it with leaving the scene of an accident.'

Hill laughed. 'How do you think the fiscal would react to that, sir?'

'We've both met a few who might have signed off on it. When I was chief constable in Edinburgh, I'd a letter from an MP complaining that one of his constituents had been kicked by a police horse during a disturbance at a football game, and demanding that disciplinary action be taken against it.'

'How did you handle that one?'

'There was CCTV that covered the incident. We looked at it and saw the constituent throwing what appeared to be pepper in the horse's face. We threw the whole fucking book back in his; he went away for three months.'

'I'll bear that in mind,' Hill said. 'Meantime I have officers calling round all the livery stables in the area, trying to identify the animal and its owner. We've still got no clue who the dead man was. If we don't track him down soon we might have to put his photo online . . . once he's been cleaned up at the morgue.'

'What photos have you got now?'

'I took a couple once the body had been extracted, and Noele did some video when she found him.'

'Send me the best of the stills, please Ronnie,' Skinner requested. 'I didn't recognise him when our paths crossed, but it was fleeting, and he was wearing a helmet. Let me have another look, on the off chance that I might have come across him some-where else.'

'I will do, sir. The livery stable trawl will probably lead us to an identity, but if you could help, that would be good.'

Five

Detective Superintendent Harold 'Sauce' Haddock raised his infant daughter Samantha above his head. 'How's your day been so far, wee one? Mine's been a proper bore.'

'Careful!' her mother warned. 'She's not long fed. She's liable to barf all over you.'

'You wouldn't do that would you, gorgeous?' he chuckled. Nevertheless he lowered the grinning child, holding her on his hip, as he leaned over to kiss his wife. 'And your morning?' he murmured.

'Rewarding,' Cheeky replied. 'I've signed up the bank I've been targeting; it's agreed to be a major contributor for the next five years. If yours is that dull you could always come and work for the foundation, as I keep telling you.'

'And as I keep telling you, you were born to do good things, and I was born to stop folk doing bad things.' He handed his daughter back to her mother. 'See you this evening; I'm off to charge someone with embezzlement.'

'That's a serious crime?'

'He's a solicitor: that makes it serious.'

'Could you tell him that if he gives the money to my foundation, he could be a hero rather than a villain?'

'And what would his defrauded clients say to that?'

'True,' Cheeky conceded. 'But maybe his defence counsel could portray him as a Robin Hood type?'

'Most of our judges would be on the side of the Sheriff of Nottingham; plus some of the folk he's stolen from might well be your clients as a result.'

'In that case charge him with all you can. See you later.' She smiled as he headed for the door.

Less than a year had passed since the sudden death of Cameron McCullough, the man after whom Cheeky had been named. She had called him 'Grandpa' for all of her twenty-nine years, unaware that he was in reality her father and that the wayward woman she had known as her mother was her aunt. She had inherited most of his considerable fortune, of which a little over a third had been held in Russia. With apparent, but actually accidental, foresight she had disposed of those assets six weeks before the invasion of Ukraine and had used the money to establish a charitable foundation for the relief of family poverty in Scotland. Its growth and its management had become a full-time job, for her and for a small executive team. They were charged with delivering aid to those most in need, while Cheeky concentrated her efforts on attracting donations and pledges from corporate and private contributors.

The late Cameron senior had been a hands-on businessman, with a wide range of interests and holdings, most of which he had sheltered within a trust. This had reduced the potential hit of inheritance and capital gains tax. It had left his heiress with three choices: sell everything, pick up the reins that he had held, or appoint an executive to manage and grow her holdings while she balanced her home life with her charitable work. She had chosen option three, recruiting a bright young woman from Stenton Provost, one of Britain's leading investment management houses.

Rosemarie Delday had been on a path to partnership with the firm, but had been attracted by the job description that Cheeky had laid out: 'Focus my holdings on creating and sustaining as many jobs as possible, rather than on increasing my wealth.'

As Cheeky's future career had taken shape, her husband had stepped up one more rung on the promotion ladder, to detective superintendent. He had been given operational command of serious crime investigation across Scotland, reporting to Assistant Chief Constable Becky Stallings. When he had been offered the post by Deputy Chief Constable Mario McGuire he had asked for time to think about it. The DCC was taken aback, but when Haddock had explained that he needed to consult his wife, he had agreed.

In fact, he had made an additional call to his one-time mentor. 'Do you think I'm ready, Gaffer?' he had asked. 'Or do the bosses think more of me than they should?'

'If they're over-rating you, Sauce, then so do I,' Sir Robert Skinner had replied. 'You've been fast-tracked since you were a detective constable. You must see that. There's no harm having friends in high places, but nobody's judgement's being coloured. You've been assessed on the basis of your job performance all the way along the line, but they've looked beyond that. There's lots of capable detectives in the police service, lad, but not too many natural leaders. You're one of those.'

'Thanks, Gaffer, but there's worries. I'll have oversight of Lottie Mann in Glasgow and Jimmy Nairn up in Aberdeen. How are they going to take it?'

'I don't know Nairn, but I do know Lottie. She's as good a detective as you are, but she's not the same leader. I think she knows it too. She'll be fine; she'll probably like having you as a sounding board.'

'That's good to hear,' he had said, 'but I want to be more than that. The broader my caseload, the more time I'll spend in the office. I worry about that.'

'As I did, Sauce. I spent a few years dreading the day of Jimmy Proud's retirement, knowing I would take over as chief constable.'

'When it happened, how did you handle it?'

Haddock recalled the laugh. 'You're not so new in CID that you don't remember. I turned up at every major crime scene, made myself a pain in the arse for the investigating officers, and I let my ACCs get on with the mundane shite. Take the job, son. Do what I did.'

Skinner's advice had been echoed by Cheeky, from a different viewpoint. 'You might be frustrated by the extra office work, but if it gets you home regularly and at a reasonable hour, so much the better. I need all the help I can get.'

Shelving his reservations, he had accepted the post and the promotion, after ensuring that he would continue to work out of his office in Edinburgh. Happily, his first weeks in post had coincided with a seasonal lull in serious crime across Scotland. 'Are you and Jimmy Nairn leaving stuff in your in-trays?' he had asked Lottie Mann, on a visit to her Glasgow office. 'Or have the bad guys finally been cowed by our fearsome reputation as crime-fighters?'

The formidable detective chief inspector had raised a heavy eyebrow. 'Sauce, the bad guys are cruising the Caribbean with their wives and weans, on Disney holiday liners. Everything fucking stops for the Glasgow Fair holidays!'

Six

'I'm sorry, Inspector Hill,' Marion Wayne said, her tone emphasising her regret, 'but I can't help you. I have twenty-seven horses stabled here. As we speak twenty-four of them are in their stalls. The other three are out with their owners . . . all of them ladies . . . probably on the old railway line and around the farm it goes through. And that's another thing; the majority of my owners and riders are women. The man you're describing, he isn't one of mine, and the way you say the horse was being ridden, that doesn't sound right either. I don't have hunters or show-jumpers here, just quiet, placid ponies and mares that are suitable for all the family members. They're walked, mostly, and rarely get above a trot.'

'Do you know any of the other stables in the area?' he asked.

'I'm familiar with all of them, but you're not ringing any bells there either. Sorry again. I really do wish I could help you. It's awful, I know, but riding accidents do happen. Rarely around here, though,' she added. 'There isn't a drag hunt with hounds within miles of Gullane, far less one that crosses the boundary of legality. That's where you'd be most likely to have a fatality. Your thinking is that the horse was alarmed by its surroundings?'

'That's one theory,' Hill admitted.

'That is possible,' Mrs Wayne agreed, 'but I know the area you're describing. I don't think it likely that an experienced rider would get into trouble there, and certainly not at low tide. Likely he'd have been walking his mount . . . but, not knowing the animal,' she admitted, 'I couldn't discount an accident.' She paused. 'Listen, my three owners should be back fairly soon. I'll ask them if your description matches someone that one of them might know. If any bells are rung, I'll get back to you.'

Seven

'What are you looking at?' Sarah asked, as she picked her car keys from the hook on the kitchen wall.

'What? Mmm, sorry,' her husband exclaimed, closing the image on his phone and returning it to his jacket. 'Your afternoon appointment, as it happens. Inspector Hill in Haddington is still struggling to identify him. I said I'd take a look.'

'And can you? Put a name to him?'

He winced. 'No, I can't. Yes, he's the rider I saw, but also . . . there's something niggling at me that I can't pin down. I don't know who he is, but somewhere at the back of my mind, there's a wee bell sounding.'

'Who took the pictures?'

'Ronnie Hill took them himself, once the body had been removed from the crevice it was stuck in. Noele McClair took some video earlier like any good officer would, but Hill said his is better.'

'Can I have a look?'

Bob grinned. 'You'll be seeing the real thing soon, but sure, if you want.' He took his phone from his pocket, retrieved the image and handed it over. He watched her as she studied it, intrigued unexpectedly by the frown that creased her forehead.

'I've seen him,' she murmured. 'I'm almost certain of it. Give me a minute and it'll come back to me.' In fact, the recollection took only a few seconds. 'Last time you and I were out for dinner at the Main Course. When was it?' she asked herself, then answered. 'At the beginning of July, it would have been. We had a side table, remember, as intimate as you can be in a ninety-seater restaurant. As usual you took the gunfighter seat, with the view of the door, with me looking towards the back. It was busy but I remember one particular couple, more by the way she behaved than him. They arrived just after us, both dressed up to the nines. He seemed entirely relaxed, but she was definitely ill at ease, more than a little nervous. She kept glancing around and towards the door . . . always a giveaway . . . and I thought, "There's something going on there. She's hoping nobody recog-nises her." I have a sense for these things.'

'As you keep telling me. "Suspicious Minds" is your favourite song. So?'

Sarah brandished the image. 'So, he was the guy,' she declared.

'Are you sure?'

'Ninety per cent. I remember facial features and he had a very well-defined jaw line . . . as does our accident victim.' She handed the phone back.

'If you're certain,' he said, 'you'd better tell Ronnie Hill.'

'You do it for me please, honey. I really have to shoot.'

'Aye, okay,' Skinner conceded.

As the front door closed behind her, he re-dialled Inspector Hill and related his wife's recollection. 'She has no idea who he was,' he said, 'but she's pretty much certain it was your man. I'd my back to them, so I can't confirm it, but Sarah's never wrong. First Saturday in July, it would have been. We were booked for eight, and Sarah said they arrived just after.'

'Right,' Hill declared. 'I'll ask the restaurant for a list of tables booked from seven thirty on. His name should be there.'

'Unless she booked the table,' Skinner pointed out.

'If she did, she might have reported him missing by now, or heard about the accident through social media and called us.'

'Maybe not, if Sarah's suspicions were right.'

'We'll still find him.' He paused. 'I suppose this means you don't know who he is, sir.'

'I don't,' Skinner admitted. 'And yet, I have this . . .' He stopped in mid-sentence. Had it been a video call the inspector would have seen his eyebrows rise dramatically. 'Yes! That's it,' he exclaimed. 'Ronnie, you know Witches Hill Golf Club, don't you?'

'Of course. The posh place just outside Aberlady that was built by the Marquis of Kinture on his own land, then sold to a Middle East investment group after he died. There was a murder there once, wasn't there? In the jacuzzi?'

'Spot on,' he confirmed. 'I play there occasionally; the Marquis, God bless and keep him, gave me a life membership. The new owners honoured it, but I only use it on the odd occasion. The last time I did was back in April when I took my boy Jazz for a round. I remember, there was a four-ball in front of us, with caddies; the sods held us up all the way round. They were still in the changing room when we got in, and one of them had the grace to apologise to me. He explained that his mate, his playing partner, had only just taken up the game and that he'd never been a golf club member before. The mate,' he said, 'I didn't speak to him, or ask his name, but now that I think about it, the dead man, it's him. I'm certain of it.'

Eight

Marion Wayne was hosing mud from the wheels of her pick-up, a frequent task even in summer, when she saw the group of three morning riders leave the narrow and potentially hazardous road and enter the field next to the stable block.

Most of her clients were long-term. She knew them well, and their horses even better. Iris Coffey for example, the oldest of the approaching trio: her Blackie was thirteen and had been at the stable for ten years, succeeding Iris's beloved old Mary, who had occupied the same stall for twelve before that. She was in her mid-sixties, the widow of a chartered accountant, and rode almost every day, in all but the most extreme weather. Frances Hilton, her regular companion, on Tess, was her best friend. The two had been schoolmates at St George's. A former teacher, Frances had come to the stable when she and her husband, a high-ranking civil servant, had moved to Dirleton from Edinburgh. They seemed to have a comfortable marriage. In their retirement he golfed and she rode.

The third member of the trio, Claire Hornell, was a new-comer. Marion knew that she lived somewhere beyond Aberlady and that she was married, with a pre-school child who attended a private nursery school close to the stables. She had been told that her husband was Royal Navy: 'an officer on some ship or other who tends to be away for months at a time,' Marion's friend, the nursery proprietor, had volunteered. Claire had dropped her daughter off that morning and had come to exercise Cassie, her pony, arriving a minute after the two friends, who had invited her to join them.

'All well?' Marion called out as Frances Hilton led the group into the stable yard. 'Your mounts look placid enough. You do know that it does them good to break sweat every now and again,' she added ironically. 'How about you Mrs Hornell? Did these veterans hold you back?'

'Claire, please,' the younger woman responded as she dismounted. 'No, they were very pleasant companions, and they're much better horse-women than me.'

'You can join us any time you like,' Iris Coffey told her. 'We're out most days.'

'Where did you go today?' Marion Wayne asked.

'Not very far,' her client replied. 'The customary route up the West Fenton road, then onto the new path, through the building site, the new houses, and then across to the farm and the old railway line. Finally, back here. No alarms, apart from a black Lab that was a bit bolshie, but its owner sorted it.'

'You didn't go down to the beach then?'

'No, not today. Why do you ask, Marion?'

'Apparently there was a riding accident there this morning. A fatality.' She paused, as if for emphasis. 'A police officer called me about it. He told me they don't know who the victim is yet. I can't place him myself from the description they gave, but I wondered whether any of you might. He was a man in his thirties, the inspector said, fit, fair hair, a confident rider according to someone who saw him earlier. He was riding a bay gelding, wearing shorts and a sweatshirt. The theory is that his horse threw him and he cracked his head on the rocks. Does he ring any bells with you?'

Frances Hilton shook her head. 'Not me, I'm afraid. Confident, you say? Sounds as if he was over-confident, poor chap.' She glanced to her left. 'How about you, Iris?'

Mrs Coffey shook her head. 'If you don't know him I doubt that I would.' She turned to Hornell. 'How about you, Claire?'

The younger woman was staring past her; she was pale-faced, her gaze distant. She shook her shoulders as if she was pulling herself back into the present. 'Me? No,' she exclaimed. 'I wouldn't know, how could I?' She grabbed her horse's rein, looking towards the stable. 'I'm sorry, I really must go. I have to pick up Poppy from nursery. See you again, ladies.'

Marion Wayne watched her as she led her mount away and the others followed. She watched her as she unsaddled, then stabled and fed her pony. From a distance she watched her as she slid behind the wheel of her Polestar, took out her phone and made a call. A minute later she saw her toss it on to the passenger seat, then bury her face in her hands, rubbing her eyes vigorously. She waited until Claire Hornell finally drove off, then reached for her own mobile and redialled her last caller.

'Inspector Hill,' she murmured as he picked up, 'Marion Wayne. I've spoken to my three lady clients. None of them could offer any clue to the identity of the dead man on the beach. Two of them, you can take that as gospel, but the third? Of her, I'm not so sure.'

Nine

Sauce Haddock sighed as he opened yet another update from Jimmy Nairn on his terminal. He liked Lottie Mann's reports, not least because there were fewer of them. The Glaswegian DCI understood that silence was golden as far as her new boss was concerned. It meant that her investigations were on course, that she was coping and that she was managing her workload, and continuing to break in her new detective sergeant. He had been moved on to Mann's team as a replacement for John Cotter, who had returned to his native Newcastle in a blaze of glory after taking the lead in solving a high-profile mystery, one whose repercussions were still being felt.

DCI Nairn's approach was a polar opposite. He briefed Haddock on a daily basis on every open investigation that he had. It occurred to the newly promoted detective superintendent that while Mann's approach showed her confidence that he had her back, Nairn's constant covering of his arse showed the opposite, and as such it was self-fulfilling.

In fact, Haddock was biding his time, assessing the clear-up rates and respective man-hour expenditure in each of the Scottish regions, including his own. When he was ready, in other words when he felt that he had extended enough rope, he intended to go to ACC Stallings with the proposition that Nairn be returned from CID to the administrative duties for which he was manifestly more equipped. Gazing at the latest tranche of pointless reports, Haddock smiled as he decided that the moment should be no more than a week away. He was still grinning as he answered an incoming call on his direct landline.

'Sauce,' Professor Sarah Grace exclaimed. 'You're still there. Good.'

'Professor,' he murmured, 'when you call me at four twenty-five on a Friday on my private line, one thing I know for sure. Good, it will not be. What's up?'

'I've stepped out for a moment,' she said, 'from an autopsy I'm performing on the body of an unidentified adult Caucasian male, age mid-thirties. He was presented to me as an accident victim, having fallen from a horse this morning on to rocks at the west end of Gullane beach and having sustained an apparently fatal head injury. With me so far?'

'Yes, Sarah,' he replied. 'Go on.'

'The initial assumption was justified,' she continued. 'The victim has a massive depressed skull fracture. He also has a catastrophic and un-survivable brain injury.'

'Poor bastard.' He smiled for a second. 'And you're telling me this, why?'

'Because,' she answered, 'I do like a mystery and because that's not what killed him. He had a fractured skull, yes. He had the massive brain trauma, yes. But, Sauce, the two were unconnected. When I removed the brain from the cranium, it was pretty much mush. When I looked further, I found a soft-nosed bullet lodged in the base of the skull, just behind the left ear. When I went back to the section I'd just taken off, I found an entry wound well above his hairline on the right side, one that I'd missed . . . understandably, because I had no reason to go look-ing for it. They brought his riding helmet here from the scene and when I looked at that I found a neat round hole. The project-ile spread out on impact, passed through the brain on a downward trajectory, destroying it as it went, until it found its resting place. I'm not a firearms expert but this is a rifle bullet beyond a doubt. Knowing what I know of the site, I'd say this man was shot by a sniper, positioned pretty near the spot from where Noele told me she saw the body. Sauce, I suggest that you secure that scene and get a forensic team there as quickly as possible.'

Ten

'First Saturday in July, you're saying? A table for two?'

'That's right,' Ronnie Hill confirmed. 'I'm told that they arrived just after eight. Would they have needed a booking that evening?'

'For sure,' the restaurateur replied. 'The Main Course is always rammed on a Saturday, I'm happy to say. Let me check for you, see if I can get you a name.'

'Thanks,' the inspector murmured. 'I'd appreciate that.'

'What's he done, this man?'

'Nothing, that I know of. We just need to put a name to him, that's all.'

'Okay, I won't press you. Although . . .' he paused, 'should I be worried about data protection?'

'I don't want his credit card details,' Hill said. 'I just want to know who he was.' He was aware of his error in the moment it was uttered.

'Oh. This wouldn't have to do with the beach incident this morning, would it? One of my waiters said he saw police activity down there.'

'Yes, okay, Mr Crolla,' he sighed. 'I'm trying to identify an accident victim. His horse is a useless witness.'

'I see.' The man's tone changed. 'I'll get right on it. I won't be a minute; just need to check the bookings for that date.'

Hill nodded, a gesture aimed at his office wall, turning in his chair to gaze at the street outside where the mid-afternoon traffic was building up. As he waited, he was alerted to an incoming call: on his line 'Number withheld' usually meant a colleague. For a second, he considered putting the restaurateur on hold but he came back on line.

'I've got two possibilities,' he announced, 'but really only one, because I reckon you'd have known Sir Bob Skinner. The other is a Mr Ayre, spelled A, Y, R, E. Table for two, eight p.m. First initial G, according to his credit card. It was one of these online banks, Moneze, if that's of any use to you. That was his first visit to us, but he's been back since then a couple of times. Once was midweek lunchtime, but he booked even then; always a table for two. Always the same couple. My head waiter, he's got a hell of a memory; he remembers them. A striking pair, he says; he was a tall good-looking guy, and she was a bit of a dish.'

'When you say "a couple",' Hill ventured.

'That's what my man says. She wore a big ruby-and-diamond engagement ring, and a wedding ring, he said. It sounds as if you've got some bad news to break. That's too bad. If it helps, they were picked up each time by the same taxi firm. AJ Private Hire, a local outfit. I've got their number if you want; this is it.' He dictated an eleven-digit mobile number, then repeated it. 'Give them a call and they should be able to tell you where they took them. Poor lady,' he added. 'Tough as it is, Inspector, I've got to tell you I'd rather have my job than yours.'

'Mr Crolla,' Ronnie Hill replied sincerely, 'if you ever change your mind about that, I'd be more than happy to swap. Thanks for your help.' He ended the call; as he replaced the phone in its cradle, he saw that he had a voice message awaiting his attention. He pushed the play button.

'Inspector Hill,' a youthful but authoritative male voice began, 'this is DCI . . . sorry, Detective Superintendent Haddock, Serious Crimes, Edinburgh. Call me back ASAP, please.'

'Fuck me,' Hill whispered. 'Why do I feel that my day's about to get longer?'

Eleven

'I know you're a busy man, Sir Robert,' James Wanjiru said, 'but you don't come here often enough.'

'To be honest, I don't like to impose,' Skinner admitted. 'The late Marquis made me an honorary member, but he's gone now, and his heirs don't own Witches Hill any longer. Your employers do. They were kind enough to accept that as a condition of purchase . . . even though I knew nothing about it, far less having asked for it . . . but I don't like to take advantage of their generosity.'

'It is not generosity, sir,' the chief executive insisted. 'The owners are aware of the reason Lord Kinture gave you membership and as far as they're concerned it is still relevant. Without your intervention this place could have crashed and burned in its first year. Besides, sir,' he added, 'you pay a subscription, just like everyone else,'

'Fuck's sake, James, stop calling me "sir". It's Bob, okay? Yes, I pay a sub, which you determine. I don't know but I suspect that it's a hell of a lot less than your high-roller members are paying.'

The Kenyan beamed back at him. 'You think? The fact is you are paying more per round played than most of them . . . another reason for you to come here more often . . . Bob. With your son,' he added. 'We don't have enough young people playing here, not by a long way.'

Skinner sighed and gave in. 'Okay, and thank you,' he said. 'But it's a digression. It's not why I'm here. I bear bad news. I believe that you may have lost a member.'

Wanjiru frowned. 'Indeed? Who? How?'

'Who, I don't know. How? He was killed this morning in a riding accident. The police have a problem though. They're struggling to identify him.'

'And yet you knew he was a member here? I don't understand.'

'I saw him this morning, just before he died. I don't know who he was, but I'm certain I'd seen him before and that it was here at Witches Hill. He stuck in my mind that day because he was a novice golfer. He was playing in a fourball that included a football pundit and a *Strictly* contestant. None of them had the courtesy to invite Jazz and me to play through, but the would-be dancer did apologise afterwards. The man in question was about the same size as me, but twenty years younger, fair hair, clean shaven, tanned. He was wearing Nike clothing that looked as if it had come straight from the pro shop. And, he couldn't putt to save his life, although in the event he could have been Brad Faxon and it wouldn't have helped him, the rest of his game being so dodgy.'

'I know who your *Strictly* contestant was,' Wanjiru told him. 'He's here just now, in fact. I left him in the bar. He had a tee time booked, but his partner didn't turn up. I wonder if . . .'

'Yes, me too.'

'Let me go and ask him.'

The chief executive turned and walked into the imposing clubhouse, leaving Skinner on the terrace. He checked his watch, chiding himself for undertaking a mission that he could, and probably should, have left to Ronnie Hill. When Wanjiru reappeared he was carrying a pale blue folder.

He opened it and displayed a photograph: male, fair-haired and smiling confidently.

'That's him,' Skinner murmured.

'His name is Gavin Ayre,' the chief executive said. 'He joined us at the beginning of February.'

'Who introduced him? Did he have a proposer and seconder?'

'Nobody; the truth is that's not strictly necessary. The owners want Witches Hill to be accessible, rather than being a cosy circle. Yes, one can be introduced by a member, but one can also apply directly. That's what Mr Ayre did. He approached me, and we had a telephone discussion. That led to a semi-formal interview and to his acceptance.'

'Who did the interview?'

'I did, with the chairman of our owners. It's become standard practice to do these things using a remote conference platform. I didn't actually meet Mr Ayre until he arrived to play his first round. By then he had paid a non-refundable registration fee of twenty-five thousand pounds and the full annual subscription for the calendar year, another twenty in his case. I had asked for a banker's reference in advance of the interview, of course,' he added.

'Which bank? Skinner enquired. 'Or would you rather not say?'

Wanjiru shrugged. 'He's dead so I don't see why not. The funds came from a Jersey bank account.'

'What else do you know about him?'

'His member file describes him as single. As for his address, it's simply shown as a plot number on a gated estate between Dirleton and Gullane.'

'Mmm,' Skinner mused. 'I know that layout, and what the plots cost. They could accommodate a house that would be big enough for an owner to have his own stable. How about his occupation?' he asked. 'Does the file say anything about that or don't you need to know?'

'He described himself as a property facilitator.'

'What the fuck is that?' he exclaimed

The chief executive smiled. 'Who knows?'

'How about his next of kin? Is anyone named in his file?'

'No, there's nobody listed. Mr Ayre was asked about his status at the interview but he said that he's alone; his parents are dead, and he has no significant other, as he put it.'

Skinner raised an eyebrow. 'Indeed? The lady he was with when my wife saw him at dinner a few weeks ago didn't sound insignificant, not the way she described them.'

'We don't intrude, Bob,' Wanjiru said. 'The truth is, our members can be whoever they like.'

He laughed. 'In that case, can I be Tiger Woods?' He paused, his smile disappearing. 'James, I'd suggest that you pass all this information on to Inspector Hill, at Haddington police office. He might have identified Mr Ayre through another channel by now, but it'll probably be useful to him regardless. Thanks for your help. I must be on my way.'

He shook hands with the chief executive and headed for the car park. He was halfway there when his mobile sounded.

'Well,' his wife exclaimed when he answered. 'Have I got news for you!'

Twelve

The face of the captain of Gullane Golf Club was lined with concern as he glowered at the roughly square area around the competition tee that had been marked off by yellow-and-black tape.

'This is difficult, Detective Superintendent!' Lee Sanders exclaimed. 'We have a competition this weekend, played off the back tees, and your people have declared that the twelfth's a crime scene. Is it really? Do you know what you're looking for?'

'Yes, Mr Sanders, we do,' Sauce Haddock replied, patiently. 'First and foremost, we're looking for a bullet casing expelled from a rifle that was used to assassinate a man on the beach this morning. As well as that, we're trying to establish the exact spot that it was fired from in the hope that we can gather any trace evidence that might help us identify the shooter; a hair, say, or even a thread or fibre from clothing. Anything, anything at all. Suppose he had hay fever and sneezed on a blade of grass, that could give us a sample of his saliva.'

'Or her,' Sanders countered, with a half-smile. 'We can't be too politically correct these days.'

'You're right. Maybe we're looking for a They.'

'Are you saying there might be two of them?'

Fuck me, Haddock fell just short of whispering. 'We're ruling nothing out at this stage,' he said. 'By the way, we'll need to speak to every one of your greenkeepers. If they've gone for the day, we'll need addresses.'

'You should take that up with the Club secretary,' the captain suggested. 'That sort of stuff falls within his remit. When will you be gone?' he asked. 'By tomorrow morning, I hope.'

'I'm not able to put a time limit on the forensic team, I'm afraid,' the detective replied.

'But surely . . .' Sanders paused, then added, 'Listen, officer, without naming names, I have some influence within the club. You understand me?'

Haddock felt the limit of his patience drawing near. 'Captain,' he said, calmly, 'my team will be here until they tell me they're done, I'm afraid. This is a murder inquiry and as such it takes priority over the invitation foursomes. You can play the twelfth off a temporary tee if necessary without it ruining your day; you know that as well as I do. As for your influence, if you're talking about Bob Skinner, I'm due to play in the event as his guest. I'm not looking forward to telling him that he might have to find a new partner, but he'll understand exactly why. Now, if you'll excuse me, I need to check on progress down there.'

He turned away and jogged down the slope towards the closed off square. Reaching it, he pulled on blue disposable overshoes before ducking under the tape and stepping into the area where half a dozen blue-suited technicians were working, combing through the scene inch by inch. One of them noted his arrival and stood.

'Detective Superintendent Haddock?' He nodded. 'Jenny Bramley, I'm the new head of the scientific support unit. Pleased to meet you.'

'Likewise. Is Paul here?' he asked, nodding towards her colleagues.

Paul Dorward was the son of Bramley's predecessor, whose fall from grace had caused a seismic reaction throughout the policing community in Scotland.

'No, he's not,' she replied. 'We've agreed that Paul will be confining himself to the lab for a while. He and I both felt that he shouldn't attend crime scenes in case his presence was noted by the media and became a distraction. The last I heard, the Crown Office was still in a debate with defence counsel about whether his dad is fit to plead or not.'

'That's right,' Haddock confirmed. 'Arthur has terminal pancreatic cancer. The prognosis indicates that he could die halfway through a trial. What does Paul think? Have you talked to him about it?'

'He hasn't said a word, and I don't know him well enough to ask.'

'Whatever, the last I heard was that if they don't set a trial date by the end of this month, there won't be one.'

'How will the murder victim's next of kin feel about that?'

He smiled softly. 'She's only a few weeks old, so I doubt that she'll be troubled by it. So, Ms Bramley . . .'

'Doctor, actually, Superintendent,' she corrected him, 'but Jenny will do just fine. Have you dealt with Mr Anxious up there?'

'Captain Anxious, please . . . and people call me Sauce. I've given up trying to stop them. I've explained to Mr Sanders he's going to have to live with your team for as long as is necessary. Forgive him, this is a bombshell for him. You're under no time pressure.'

'That's good,' Bramley replied, 'because this one could take some time. The greens staff here do a very good job. The most obvious firing position for the sniper is prone, behind that fence because the ground is absolutely flat there, but so far we can't find any trace of anyone being there. The ground is so firm and the grass is so well cut that there's no obvious sign of anyone having lain there.'

'How do you know the shooter was prone?' Haddock asked.

'Because I'm a shooter myself,' the scientist replied. 'It's my sport: rifle shooting. I hope to make the next Commonwealth Games team. On the basis of what I was told by your DS Wright when she called us out, that he was killed by a rifle bullet passing through his brain on a downward trajectory . . . that's not a shot anyone would attempt while standing. It's not a shot that many people could pull off either.'

'What are you saying?'

Bramley gazed at him for a few seconds. 'I came to this job from London,' she said. 'I worked on crime scenes there. As you can imagine, I was kept pretty busy. I may be, I probably am, telling you stuff you know already, but in my experience there are four types of homicide. There's manslaughter, culpable homicide to use the Scottish legal term, unintended killing. There's spur of the moment murder, for example, a domestic confrontation that goes way too far or two guys having a barney in a pub and someone produces a blade. There are what the media like to call gangland killings, sometimes over drug dealing, sometimes just over turf. Then there are contract murders. They happen when someone buys a professional hit. Even in London they were the rarest type. The effect was the same, someone dead on the floor, but I learned to identify them and separate them from the rest.'

'How?'

'By the complete lack of forensic evidence. A professional

assassin will leave nothing behind him. Tell me, Sauce, how many murders have you investigated where that was the case?'

'One,' Haddock replied. 'And yes, the perpetrator was definitely a professional.'

Bramley managed to smile and frown simultaneously. 'I think I know the one you mean. That one was unique, but it proves my point; a professional leaves nothing behind. I might be proved wrong, but I have a feeling that's what we're looking at here. Whoever the dead man on those rocks down there was, someone wanted him dead and may well have paid for it to happen.'

The detective nodded. 'Noted, but I still have to consider every possibility until I know it isn't. But, Jenny,' he added, 'haven't you missed out another type of homicide. Could this be a random act? There have been serial killers in Scotland before. What if this is another?"

'If it is,' Bramley murmured, 'then . . . excuse my Swahili . . . you have a real *kutania* problem!'

Thirteen

Spike Thomson smiled as his mobile screen lit up. He slowed the treadmill down to walking pace, paused the playlist on his earbuds, and took the call. 'Hello, Bob,' he said, his voice raised against the background noise of the gym. 'This is a pleasant surprise. It's well timed too, I've just finished my five K and was thinking about doing five more.'

'Bloody hell,' Skinner exclaimed. 'Are you running the London Marathon?' He had known the one-time radio presenter and impresario for many years, but as the former policeman's life had changed, they had seen less of each other.

'Not this year,' Thomson chuckled. 'I'm in rehab, breaking in my knee replacement. It's hard work, I'll tell you. Are all your joints still in working order?'

'So far. At least I think they are. I have a couple of training partners these days, and they keep me honest.'

'Who are they?'

'My sons, Nacho and Jazz. Nacho's twenty-one; Jazz is just breaking into his teens, but he's the pace setter. He humiliated his brother a few months ago, which was a good thing because it made Nacho realise he needed to work on his fitness. He's not with us full time, but when he is, we often run as a trio.'

'With you still in the lead?'

'That's not guaranteed,' Skinner admitted. 'Jazz has still got a lot of growing to do, so I rein him in, but when I let him loose we see his back and there's not much Nacho or I can do about it.'

'Maybe he could pace me,' Thomson chuckled, his voice reflecting his situation.

'Be careful what you wish for. Anyway, Spike, good as it is to compare athletic notes, that's not why I'm calling. I know that since you retired from the entertainment business you've been spending a lot of time at Witches Hill golf club.'

'Too right. More so since my knee op because they have no issue with me using a buggy.'

'You're a sociable guy so I imagine you mix with the membership while you're there.'

'Of course,' Thomson agreed. 'That's why they call it a club.'

'Does the name Gavin Ayre mean anything to you?' Skinner asked. He waited as his friend considered his question for a few seconds.

'I know a Gavin. Tall, fairish hair, probably in his thirties. I've seen him there a few times; even had a drink or two with him, but his surname never stuck. I'm bad for that; especially in a group situation. Could that be him?'

'That matches the description. Do you know much about him?'

'I know he's not Scottish. He was at my table at the Burns Supper last February, just after he'd joined. He thought that Tam O'Shanter was real, a historical figure. Poor old George Woodburn ripped the piss out of him about it. You knew George, didn't you? *Schadenfreude*, they called him, because of his delight at the misfortunes of his golf partners.'

50

'I remember him,' Skinner conceded. 'Why the past tense, though?'

'Did you not hear?' Thomson exclaimed. 'He walked in front of a tram, in Prague, a few weeks ago. He was there on a business trip. Gavin got the joke that night though. He was really cut up about George last time I saw him.'

'When was that?'

'It would have been last month, when I played my first full round after my surgery. He was looking for a game so he came out with me. He wouldn't get in the buggy, though. I did offer, but he said he was there for the exercise more than the golf. He's keen on the game, even though he's a novice. He told me he was thinking of having a short-game practice area with a putting green laid out in front of his house. He said he lives in one of the new places just west of Yellowcraig overlooking Fidra Island. I asked him what his wife would say about a golf course in the garden. He said he didn't have one so he could do what he liked.'

'What about his business? Did he say anything about that?'

'Yes, he did, when I asked him. He said he was in logistics. I've got to say, in my recent experience when someone tells you that, it's a polite way of telling you to mind your own fucking business, so I didn't press him for any details. Why are you so interested in him, Bob?' he asked. 'I thought you'd moved on from the detecting business.'

Skinner laughed. 'My new career's in press-and-broadcast media. It's much the same thing.'

'I suppose so, when you think about it. So why's the mighty *Saltire* newspaper interested in this guy. What's he done to attract its attention?'

'He's got himself killed, Spike. A few minutes after I saw him on Gullane beach, he came off his horse and never got up again.'

'Bloody hell!' Thomson exclaimed. 'Really?'

'Really. My wife did his autopsy this afternoon. She assures me he was dead before she began.'

Fourteen

'What you're telling me, Sauce,' Noele McClair said, 'is that I was looking at a murder and I wrote it off as accidental death. That's really made my day, not.'

'I would have thought exactly the same thing,' Haddock countered, gazing at her image on his phone screen. 'So did the best pathologist in the country until she found the bullet lodged inside the skull.'

'Still,' she persisted. 'I was a detective inspector at a crime scene and I took things for granted. I made a snap judgement without considering all the possibilities.'

'You were a new mum out for a walk with her baby. Listen Noele, if I'd been there and run through the possibilities, a professional hit by a sniper would not have been one of them. If the Gaffer had been running in the other direction and had found him, he'd have called it in as a fatal accident too.'

'What do you mean?' she exclaimed. 'How is Bob involved?'

'He saw him on the beach just before the . . . just before he was shot. He helped Inspector Hill identify him.'

'He did?'

'Yes, his name was Gavin Ayre. He lived in a new property on a gated estate, out beyond Muirfield golf course.'

'How did Bob know him?'

'He didn't. He'd seen him at Witches Hill, without knowing who he was, so he went there and checked him out. You know what he's like.'

'Do I ever. What do you do next?' she asked.

'We go through his house,' Haddock replied. 'But I'll leave that until the forensic team are finished at the crime scene. Monday, I reckon, we'll be in there.'

'Can I help?'

He grinned. 'Noele, you're on maternity leave. Your baby needs you.'

'And you need me too. You're stretched by my absence, and don't try to tell me otherwise. I'm not talking about coming into the office, or interviewing suspects. But there are things I could do online or on the phone. Sauce, this morning I laughed at my mother for suggesting I could work from home. I hate to admit it, but she's right. I'm here, and I'm available, so use me, please.'

Fifteen

'Nice putt, Spike,' Bob Skinner called out to his playing partner as their ball dropped into the hole. 'I'll try to leave you the same length on the next hole.'

'A tap-in would be better,' Spike Thomson replied, casually, as he strolled towards him from the eleventh green after recovering the ball. He glanced beyond his host, towards what would have been the twelfth tee on another day. 'What's going on over there behind the yellow tape?' he asked.

'It's a crime scene,' Skinner told him. 'The blue tunics are what the Yanks like to call CSIs.'

'A crime scene? What happened?'

'I told you. Gavin Ayre, the guy I asked you about.'

'Yes, I read about that in the *Saltire* yesterday, but given what you told me I thought it was just a riding accident. You and your reporters are slipping up.'

His friend smiled and shook his head. 'No, we're not. I only know because Sarah was involved.' He paused. 'Well, also because Sauce Haddock's the SIO, and he was supposed to be playing with me today. It's privileged information, so I couldn't share it. There's a press briefing at ten tomorrow when Sauce will announce that it's a murder investigation.' His smile returned.

55

'However, if you'd read the Sunday paper this morning you'd have seen a story about a forensic team working in Gullane Hill. I could let them know that much.' Glancing towards the temporary tee he saw that the match before theirs had yet to drive off. 'Come on,' he murmured. 'Let's find out how they're getting on.' He walked towards the taped off area, with Thomson following behind.

An enormous figure, his crime scene tunic stretched almost to bursting point, greeted their approach. 'No civilians allowed, gentlemen,' he boomed, but with a grin on his face. 'Morning, sir.'

'Detective Inspector Tarvil Singh, as I live and breathe.' Skinner returned his smile. 'Congratulations on the promotion, big man,' he said. 'Long overdue. It would have happened a fucking sight sooner if the politicians hadn't wished *Scot Squad* on us.'

Spike Thomson chuckled at the reference to the TV satire. His friend's dislike of the unification of Scotland's police forces was legendary.

'Have you got much more to do here?' Skinner asked.

'I think they're just about done,' Singh replied. 'Is that right, Jenny?' he called out as the team leader came towards them. 'Jenny,' he continued, 'this is . . .'

'I know who he is,' she said. 'Paul Dorward marked my card when we were called here. He said it was a racing certainty that Sir Robert Skinner would turn up sooner or later to find out what we were up to.'

'Or simply to meet you, Dr Bramley,' he countered. 'I heard about your appointment and I welcome it. New thinking and new ideas benefit any unit. Not to mention a change in leadership style,' he added. 'So, what have you got? Anything worthwhile?'

She held up a sealed evidence envelope. 'We have this. A casing from a seven-point-six-two sniper cartridge . . .'

'Fired by?'

'There are a number of possibilities. Whatever the shooter was most comfortable with. M24, Arctic Warfare, or possibly something custom made, since we're almost certainly looking at a pro. That may be the most likely, given the force with which the casing was expelled. It's taken us two days to find it, buried in the heart of a tuft of grass yards away from the likely firing point. I'm afraid we've found nothing else, though. I'm pinning my hopes on there being a recoverable DNA trace on the bullet.'

'The chances of that being slim or none,' Skinner forecast. 'A pro will have worn gloves to load the weapon and probably wiped the cartridge as well.'

'Did you ever have to investigate a hit like this, Sir Robert?' Bramley asked.

'I've seen one,' he replied, 'but there was no investigation required. The shooter didn't leave the scene. Well, he did, but in a box. Assuming we're right and there are no forensic traces on the bullet casing, could there be other markings to link this with other assassinations, here or in other countries?'

'I won't be able to answer that until we've had a look at it in the lab . . . that's assuming I'm asked the question officially,' she added.

'You will be.' He looked across at the tee, where their companions were waiting. 'We must be off,' he said. 'We have a competition to win.'

As they walked, Spike Thomson broke his uncharacteristic silence. 'Is that what happened, Bob?' he murmured. 'The guy was shot by a sniper, from up here?'

'That's what the evidence suggested. They've just proved it.'

'Jesus, how could anyone do that? Just snuff someone's life out in a second.'

'It happens all the time in warfare.'

'But this wasn't in warfare. It was a guy on the beach in the morning and . . .' He put the tips of two fingers to the side of his head.

'I know.'

'Who could do that? What sort of mentality would they need?'

'I could do it,' Skinner replied. 'Any firearms trained police officer could in specific circumstances . . . if there was a threat to life.'

'Have you ever done it?'

'I'm not going to answer that, mate. Firearms officers are trained, physically and psychologically, to use lethal force. If they're authorised at a scene and in their judgement it's necessary, they fire.'

'There's always room for error, though.'

'There is, and there have been fatal mistakes made; that can't be denied. But hopefully a lesson was learned from every one of those. And always remember, very few police officers in this country have ever fired their weapon away from the range. It's not like fucking *Blue Bloods*. Jesus, Danny Regan's kill count must be enormous.'

'And afterwards? The ones who do. How do they feel afterwards?'

'Traumatised. At least I hope they do. If they don't, they should never be given a firearm again. Even then . . .' Skinner's voice tailed off as he considered his own past and the things he had tried to banish from his memory without ever succeeding.

'What about the fellow who did . . . that?' Thomson asked. 'What will he feel?'

'Nothing. Nothing at all, other than the satisfaction of a job well done.' He forced himself back into the moment. 'Come on, mate,' he said briskly. 'You're up. Hit it left of the bunker,' he instructed as his partner pulled his driver from his golf bag. 'Left, you understand; don't leave me in it.'

Thomson nodded, took dead aim, and swung. The ball flew straight and true, until it stalled in the head wind and plummeted straight into the sand trap.

Sixteen

Ronnie Hill had been a fan of the Boomtown Rats, until a colleague explained that 'I Don't Like Mondays' was not about a disgruntled check-out girl at Tesco, as his older sister had led him to believe. He had gone off the band after that but held to the sentiment of the notorious song's title. The only saving grace, he thought as he sat behind his desk, was that he had not been required to attend Sauce Haddock's press briefing in Edinburgh.

When his phone rang, he was catching up on the reports from patrol officers on what appeared to have been an unexceptional August weekend everywhere but in Gullane, and briefly in Dunbar where a territorial dispute between rival groups of visitors from Edinburgh had been brought under control. He sighed as he picked it up.

'Inspector,' the desk officer said, 'I've got a Mr Crolla on the line from the Main Course restaurant. He says he'd like to speak to you. Do you want to take the call?'

'Aye, why not? Put him through.' He waited as the call was connected. 'Mr Crolla,' he murmured. 'What can I do for you?'

'It's about the thing we spoke about the other day,' the restaurateur replied, 'the man you were trying to identify.'

'Yes, thanks, that was very helpful. We have confirmed his

identity, if that's what you wanted to know. It'll be announced at a press briefing later on this morning.'

'That's good, but it's no' why I'm calling. His lady friend was here yesterday lunchtime. I thought you might want to know that.'

Hill straightened in his chair. 'We do indeed. That was good thinking, Mr Crolla. What can you tell me about her?'

'She was in with two other women and with three wee girls. From what they were saying the women are all parents at the nursery school up near Kingston. It was supposed to be a birthday party for one of the kids, but I suspect it was more about the three ladies havin' an away day . . . well, two of them anyway. The woman we're talking about, Mr Ayre's friend, she was pretty subdued. That would be hardly surprising, if she knew about him,' he added. 'The booking was in her name; it's Hornell, Claire Hornell. We asked for her phone number when she made the booking, so I can give you that too.'

Suddenly Ronnie Hill realised that Mondays weren't so bad.

Seventeen

'Detective Superintendent, you've had a forensics team working over the weekend on an area above where you say the body was found. Does that mean that he fell from there? Or that he was pushed?'

Haddock looked at the journalist over the top of the lectern in the makeshift briefing room in what had been the gym of the Fettes Avenue office when it had been Edinburgh's police headquarters. As he framed his reply, he wondered whether it had ever been used for that purpose since Bob Skinner's time.

'We don't believe so. The evidence suggests that he died where he was found.'

'Can you give us his name?'

'Not before he's been formally identified.'

'When will that happen?'

'When we find someone to do it. We're trying to locate next of kin, but so far without success.'

'But you do have a name?'

'We do.'

'And an address?'

'Yes.'

'Did you find anything significant there?'

'We haven't gone into the property yet. That will happen later today, now that the forensic team have finished their work at the crime scene.' Haddock paused and drew a breath. 'Ladies and gentlemen, that's all I can tell you for now. As soon as we can confirm the victim's identity, we'll do so through the press office. Meanwhile,' he continued, 'I'll repeat what I said earlier. I want to ask anyone who was in the vicinity of the twelfth tee on Gullane Number One golf course or on the beach between six and seven a.m. on Friday to get in touch with us. Dog walkers, campers, morning runners, wild swimmers, anyone; we need to talk to you. If you saw anything or anyone, however insignificant it might have seemed, we need to speak to you. We've already had significant help from one person, but we need more. Thanks and good morning.'

Picking up his phone and his tablet from the lectern, Haddock left the room by a nearby side exit, with Jane Balfour, the civilian press officer, following. As the closing door cut off the sound of shouted questions, he stopped. 'Thanks for that, Jane.' He frowned. 'I wonder where Jack Darke was, the *Saltire* crime guy that we don't like. The Costa del Sol, maybe.'

She smiled as she shook her head. 'No, haven't you heard? He's gone. His editor, June Crampsey, decided that his open animosity towards the Deputy Chief was compromising his objectivity so she told him she was moving him to the local government team. He resigned, and now he's claiming constructive dismissal.'

'Good luck with that one,' Haddock chuckled. 'Do you think he'll call DCC McGuire as a witness?'

'That I would love to see. I heard he's joining an online news outlet once his gardening leave's finished, so I'm sure we'll be seeing him again.'

'If your office gives him accreditation, we will,' he observed.

Balfour sighed. 'I doubt that we could refuse.'

'But you can take a while to consider his application. Okay Jane,' he said. 'I'm going back to my office to make a couple of calls, then I'm off to open Ayre's house with the forensic team. Hopefully we'll find a lead there that'll help us make a formal identification.'

'What if you don't?' she asked.

'If we don't, we might have to resort to his golf club. As it stands, the chief executive of Witches Hill is our best bet.'

'Will the Crown Office be okay with using someone who isn't a relative?'

Haddock smiled. 'I'm not sure I'm going to ask them. We'll speak later, once I've been inside Ayre's seaside palace.'

He made his way back to his office, taking a circuitous route to avoid crossing the path of any departing journalist. Leaning back in his chair and gazing out of the window, he opened his phone contact favourites, clicked on a name, and waited.

'Sauce.' Bob Skinner's voice was louder than normal. There was background noise, of vehicles and aircraft. 'You just caught me. The company plane's ready and I'm off to Girona.'

'Private jet,' Haddock laughed. 'That's the way to travel.'

'You should try it. Your wife can afford it.'

'She and I have had that discussion. I said no. How did you get on in the foursomes?' he asked. 'You and my replacement.'

'We tied third. Spike played very well; I missed a couple of putts or we could have won it. Never mind that. How are you getting on with your investigation?'

'To be honest, I'm looking for a couple of straws to clutch at. We know the victim's name but that's all. The rest's a mystery. I'm living in hope that we'll find stuff in his house that'll tell us everything we need to know about him, but I'm not counting my chickens. I'm not even lining up the eggs.'

'Having seen his member file at Witches Hill,' Skinner commented, '. . . which your team should do as well, for the record . . . I understand what you mean. There's something . . . two-dimensional about the man.'

'What would you have done so far that we haven't, Gaffer?' the detective asked.

'I'm assuming that you've already run his image and finger-prints through the criminal intelligence databases.'

'Yes, we did that on Saturday,' Haddock confirmed. 'And his DNA too, when we got the profile yesterday. He isn't on any of them; he has no criminal background, not even a parking ticket. I've still got to check the Passport Office and DVLA, but I'll do that once we've been through his house. I'm assuming that his passport and licence will be there.'

'How about Interpol? Europol?' Skinner asked. 'Have you shared what you have with them?'

'That's the next step, if I need to.'

'I have a feeling you will. How about the intelligence commu-nity? MI5, for openers? Sauce, this guy was important enough, or significant enough, for what looks like a professional hit to have been ordered. In your shoes, I'd be looking there, and probably in military intelligence too.'

'No stone unturned? Is that what you're saying?'

'Exactly. Now I must go. The pilot's making a performance out of checking his watch.'

'Fly safe, Gaffer.'

Haddock stood and turned, gazing through the L-shaped window. The view took in two schools. The car park of Broughton High was full and people could be seen moving from one block to another while the great grey looming bulk of Fettes College was silent on its perch above the police building. It followed the English academic calendar and its pupils were still on holiday. The contrast between the two reminded Haddock that in a few years he and Cheeky were going to have to make a choice. Would Samantha, and any siblings who might follow her, be educated in the state or private systems? The latter had been out of his parents' financial reach but all options were open to his children. They had discussed it already; in principle he favoured the public system, but he recognised his wife's concern that the offspring of a high-ranking police officer might have a lower profile in a private school. He looked up at Fettes, an extravagant blend of French and Scottish baronial architecture that he had always suspected of being deliberately intimidating, and murmured, 'But not there. Somewhere less grandiose, I think.'

'Sorry, Sauce, what did you say?'

Startled, he turned. Detective Sergeant Jackie Wright had entered the room quietly, while he was wrapped in his thoughts. 'Talking to myself, Jackie,' he confessed. 'What can you do for me, before Tarvil and I head for East Lothian?'

'I've just come off the phone with Gavin Ayre's bank in Jersey,' she said, 'but I'm not a lot wiser than I was before the conversation.'

Haddock stiffened slightly. 'They're not playing silly buggers, are they? If they try hiding behind client privilege in a murder investigation . . . I'll set the Crown Office on them if I have to, or the Justice Department at Westminster if that's what it takes.'

'No, no,' Wright exclaimed, 'it's not that. The woman didn't have any problem speaking to me, it's just that there was little or nothing she could tell me. The sterling account that was used to pay the fee at Witches Hill was set up two years ago. It's used for all his regular domestic outgoings; there are direct debits in place for the council tax, energy, Sky TV sub, and of course the nightmare that's BT . . . Tiggy Benjamin checked with them,' she added. 'It took her forever, as you'd expect. He has Halo Three broadband and a mobile, but no land line . . . apparently you don't need one but they don't rush to tell you that. As well as all those, there's a regular monthly payment of just over eight hundred pounds to a car-leasing company, occasional transfers to a cleaning company, and one-off payments to a gardening and landscaping firm based in Dunbar. Those go back a few months. Alongside those he also has a debit for an online bank called Moneze . . .'

'The one Inspector Hill said he used in the restaurant?'

'That's right; it's a Mastercard. I haven't tracked it down yet, but the monthly amounts are erratic; I suspect that's how he does his everyday shopping.'

'That's the only account he has in Jersey?' the superintendent asked.

'The only one that I can find,' Wright confirmed.

'Okay, so far everything you've described has been outgoing payments. What about movements in the other direction? Where does his money come from? What's the source? Who's his employer? His customers? His clients?'

'There aren't any,' she replied. 'There's nothing flowing into that account from any source in the UK.'

'He works offshore, as well as banking offshore? Is that what you mean?'

'No, boss. He doesn't appear to work at all. The Jersey account is fed by regular, large transfers from an account in Liechtenstein. Over the two years of its existence funds totalling just over eight million quid have been paid in.'

'What about the house?' Haddock asked. 'It's new, it was only completed at the back end of last year. And the plot it's built on: I know that itself cost a million and that would be before they put the services in.'

'I wasn't looking that far back,' she replied, 'only at his regular spending patterns. However,' she added, 'there are no mortgage payments. That means either Mr Ayre owned it lock, stock and riding stable, or he had a rich benefactor.'

'Bloody hell,' he whispered. 'The man's a mystery, right enough.'

Eighteen

For the first time in almost a year, Noele McClair felt content: her brief affair . . . be honest Noele, call it what it was . . . her one-night stand with a much older man, his disappearance, her unexpected pregnancy with its inevitable career hiatus, they had all combined to throw her off kilter, turning a confident professional into a confused woman, full of doubt about her future and full of trepidation about her ability to function as a single mother. She realised that her plea to Sauce to be allowed to take part in the Gavin Ayre investigation, albeit remotely, had been a cry for help, and she was grateful to her young boss for giving her the go-ahead. They both knew that with Tarvil Singh's promotion the team could have functioned without her. Haddock's acquiescence had been a favour granted, but also a statement that she still had a place as a senior member of the Serious Crimes team.

She gazed at her phone on its hands-free stand as the ring tone sounded, once, twice, three times, until it was replaced by a cautious male voice. 'Yes?'

'Mr Biggs?' she enquired. 'Gerry Biggs?'

'Yes, it's Gerry.' Caution gave way to assertiveness, with an edge of aggression. 'Who's this?'

'Detective Inspector Noele McClair, Edinburgh Serious

Crimes squad.' As she spoke Matilda let out a small cry as she lost her grip on the nipple from which she was feeding.

'Oh yes,' Biggs drawled, 'so how come I can hear a wean in the background?'

'I'm working from home,' she replied, as she moved her daughter from one breast to the other. 'We have a major inquiry so it's all hands on deck, even those on maternity leave. I've been given your number by Olbo Holdings; they say you've built on several of the plots they sold, specifically on one owned by a Mr Gavin Ayre.'

'Aye, that's right,' the builder confirmed enthusiastically. 'We did a good job for the guy; it's the best house on that estate. There was virtually no limit on the budget; he kept addin' extras until the job went up to over five million. He's the best client I ever had, that man. The stage payments all came through early, a rarity, I'll tell you. He treated us well and we looked after him. The job was finished a month early. He'll be enjoyin' livin' there.'

'Not any longer he isn't,' McClair told him. 'He was murdered on Friday morning.'

A gasp came from her phone's speaker. 'Seriously?' Biggs whispered.

'I'm afraid so. Look, we know very little about Mr Ayre, hence my call. In your dealings with him did he ever mention his family, say anything about his origins?'

'No, but he couldn't. I never met the man.'

'You didn't meet him?' the detective exclaimed.

'Never. I never even spoke to him.'

'You're telling me that you built him a five-million-pound home without ever clapping eyes on him? How did you get the job?'

'Competitive tender,' the builder explained. 'Us and two other contractors.'

'Wasn't there an interview before the contract was awarded?'

70

'Of course, but it was Tim Lloyd that handled it. Tim was the guy I dealt with from beginning to end.'

'Who's Tim Lloyd?' McClair asked.

'He was the architect on the project. It was his design we built; bloody beautiful it is. Tim and his firm represented the client all the way through. He was the go-to guy all along. If you want to know anything about Mr Ayre, you should go to him. Do you want his number?'

'Yes, please.' Matilda sighed against her chest, her feeding over, for that moment. 'Can you text it to me? I can't quite reach my pen.'

'Of course, Inspector.' Biggs drew a breath. 'If that's all . . .'

'It is for now. Thank you.'

She ended the call and waited. The promised text arrived less than a minute later, as she was making her daughter comfortable. With Mattie peaceful and secure in her crib, Noele opened the message and keyed the number into her phone. Before calling, she opened her laptop and entered a search for 'Tim Lloyd Architect'. Google took her straight to www.LloydandPrice.com. She opened the site and found a clean, crisp presentation for a two-partner Edinburgh business, with a statement of principles and completed project examples. She scanned the latter but found nothing suggesting that any of them might be Gavin Ayre's luxury home. Tim Lloyd's biography was concise; he was aged forty-seven and a graduate of Strathclyde University. His portfolio was a mix of commercial and residential projects but, again, with no link to Gavin Ayre.

Having put a face to the name she called the number Biggs had sent her, only to be sent immediately to voicemail and invited to leave a message. 'Mr Lloyd,' she began, after a tone, 'this is Detective Inspector Noele McClair of Edinburgh Serious Crimes squad. I need to talk to you about your late client, Mr Gavin Ayre. I'd be very grateful if you can reply to this message as soon as you receive it.'

She pocketed her phone and went through to her small kitchen. Her craving for a coffee was close to desperate, but she had sworn to abstain for as long as she was feeding the baby. Instead, she took a bottle of aerated water from the fridge. She was in the act of uncapping it when her ring tone chirped. 'McClair,' she announced crisply as she put the phone to her ear.

'Detective Inspector? This is Tim Lloyd, architect. Your message said my late client. What do you mean? Is Gavin dead?'

'Yes,' she confirmed. 'I'm sorry to tell you that he was shot dead on Friday morning.'

'God,' Lloyd murmured. 'I'm driving just now. I heard a news report at the top of the hour on the car radio, about the police announcing they're investigating the murder of a man they can't yet name. Then I had a call from my office, then I got your voice message and pulled into a layby to call you back. Are you telling me that was him they were talking about, that it was Gavin?'

'I'm afraid so. Were you and he close?' she asked.

'He was my client,' he said, 'but we got on, yes.'

'And you actually met, unlike Mr Biggs the builder and him.'

'Of course we did.'

'In that case, would you be prepared to formally identify Mr Ayre's body? We're having trouble finding someone to do it.'

'If it'll help and there's no alternative, yes, I'll do that. I'm not surprised by your difficulty. Gavin was a very private man. As I said, I got to know him reasonably well, but I can't recall him ever letting anything slip about his background.'

'How did the two of you meet?'

'He walked into my office one day, said that he'd bought a plot in East Lothian and was going to build a house on it. He told my partner Sue and me that he'd looked at our work online along with a few others and that we fitted the bill, so were we interested? Not just in designing it, he said, but in project managing the construction, because he worked internationally so he couldn't do it himself. We jumped at it of course, especially when he told us what the budget was. Up to five million construction, over and above our fees.'

McClair nodded, as if he had been in the room. 'Was he around much during the building?'

'Hardly ever,' Lloyd told her. 'He left me to choose the builder, which was good, for both of us. Gerry Biggs' company wasn't actually the lowest bidder; another contractor was marginally cheaper, but I had worked with both of them and factored reliability into the choice. A hands-on client might not have let me do that.'

'Did you get to know Ayre at all?' the detective asked. 'Beyond the professional, I mean.'

'Mmm,' he murmured. 'He visited East Lothian a couple of times, at weekends when there was no activity on site. On each occasion he turned up with no more than a day's notice. The second time, when the job was almost done, was the longest I spent with him. I took him up to my golf club . . .'

'Would that be Witches Hill?' McClair interjected.

'Yes, that's right. He said he'd never played the game, so I gave him an old driver from my locker and let him hit a few balls. He was okay for a beginner, so we played a few holes. The next time I saw him he was a member. We played a couple of months back with another couple of guys. He was desperately slow, though. In fact, we held up Sir Robert Skinner and his son for the last few holes. I was embarrassed by that; one of the other guys apologised to them in the locker room afterwards.' The architect paused for a brief moment. 'And yet,' he resumed, 'now that I think about it, in all the time I spent with him, I still didn't learn anything about him. Funny people we Scots, are we not? We have this phobia about being thought to be nosey . . . or maybe we're just inherently polite. Gavin didn't volunteer anything about himself, and I never thought to ask.'

'Was he Scottish?'

'I don't think so,' Lloyd replied. 'If his accent was anything to go by, he wasn't. It was transatlantic; that's how I'd describe it. But I'm almost certain he was Canadian.'

'Why do you think that?'

'Because of the way he said one word, "house". I've been to Ontario a few times. It took me a while to notice it but when they say the "ow" sound, it comes out Scottish. A lot of Scots migrated to Canada so it's natural, I suppose, if part of our accent's been assimilated.' He took a breath, 'Does that help you?'

'It might,' McClair conceded. 'It's another avenue for us. We're hoping that when we get into the house all our unresolved questions will be answered. My boss is meant to be putting a forensic team in there this morning.'

She heard Lloyd laugh, softly. 'How are they going to get in?' he asked.

'They're taking a locksmith, I suppose.'

'In that case he'd better be good. There are no locks as such. Entry's by keypad on every main door: to the house and to the stable too. That was Gavin's stipulation. It's a high-tech system with no keys. It can't be drilled out, and your standard police battering ram will just bounce off it. I don't see how you're getting in without the code.'

She sighed. 'That's bloody magic! We know nothing else about Mr Ayre so how are we going to get that?'

'You could try asking me,' the architect suggested quietly. 'The system was installed by a specialist firm from Switzerland: I was there when it was programmed. A pass code was needed and they asked me, so I used the first thing that came into my head. It's possible Gavin could have changed it but not without going through the installers, and to get to them he'd have had to go through me. "Could he have asked my secretary?" you might ask. Yes. "Would she have told me?" Certainly.'

'Is this where you tell me you've forgotten it?' McClair sighed.

'No,' Lloyd replied, 'but it might be where I have to ask my lawyer whether I'm at liberty to disclose it.'

'Which would take us to where we have to get a disclosure order from the Sheriff . . . or charge you with obstructing the police,' she added, with a light laugh.

'But my lawyer is expensive,' he continued, 'so maybe I won't bother asking him. Your people also need to know that there's an alarm system as well as the keypad entry; belt and braces. I used a local provider for that rather than one of the big boys; again, someone I know and trust, like Gerry Biggs. The control panel's just inside the door; you open the keypad then deactivate the alarm. To avoid confusion I set them up with the same code. It's the Queen's birthday . . . the late Queen, not the new one.'

'Which birthday?' she asked. 'Unlike the rest of the world she had two.'

'The real one,' Lloyd said. 'Not the official one where they troop the colour. But,' he paused, 'in the code, the numbers are reversed.'

Nineteen

'Six . . . two . . . four . . . zero . . . one . . . two,' Sauce Haddock
dictated. Detective Inspector Tarvil Singh keyed in each number
carefully, ensuring that his massive digit did not accidentally
press more than one number simultaneously. On the stroke of
'two', there was a click and the massive door swung open seemingly of its own volition.

'What does this level of protection say to you, big man?' the
superintendent asked as the pair, each wearing a disposable sterile tunic, stepped into a great airy hall, lit by a cupola above their
heads.

'It takes me right back to my earliest days in the police, bursting open steel doors in Pilton, going in fast and hard before they
had time to flush the drugs down the lavvy. I was always the guy
that got to swing the ram, because I could do the job in one go.
The rest took three or more, and by the time you got in you could
hear the cistern. It wasn't just Pilton either,' he added. 'There
were dealers in posher parts of the city than that but they all had
the steel door in common.' His laugh boomed, unexpectedly. 'I
remember once we got sent to the wrong address, a terraced
house in the New Town. I swung the knocker and the door just
splintered. It turned out that the owner was an advocate who'd

given a certain detective constable a hard time in the witness box. No prizes for guessing who was behind the bogus tip, but the bosses never could pin it on him.'

'Was it a name I might know?' Haddock enquired.

'Yes, but I'm not going to share it, just in case you go looking for him when you make Assistant Chief.'

The superintendent grinned. 'You're getting ahead of yourself, Tarvil.'

'No, I'm not and we both know it.'

'Maybe I don't want that,' he suggested, voicing a thought that had been occupying his quieter moments.

'Sure,' Singh laughed, dismissively, 'like my wife doesn't want to go to Barbados this Christmas.'

His movement triggered the alarm system. Quickly, Haddock moved to the control panel and silenced it with the deactivation code. 'Okay,' he said, 'you can bring in Jackie and the search team.'

The DI stepped outside and waved to Wright, who had been waiting in a seven-seater vehicle with six other officers. She led them into the house where they grouped together in the hall.

'Nine of us,' Haddock said. 'Enough for an efficient search. This isn't a crime scene, but we're dressed as if it was, and I want you all to behave that way. Don't rip the place apart, don't make a mess; leave everything as it was. We're looking for personal items that will tell us who this man was. Phone, computer, documents, business correspondence, personal letters, everything. If you find a birthday card, we'll want to know who sent it.'

'Do we think this guy was dodgy?' a constable called out. The man was a veteran; possibly as much as ten years older than the detective superintendent. The edge to his tone made it clear that he knew it.

'That would be, do we think this guy was dodgy . . . sir?' Singh's eyes were cold as he stared at the speaker. For all his size he was not an intimidating figure: unless he chose to be.

'We've got no specific reason to believe so,' Haddock replied briskly. 'But in my experience,' he paused for a beat, but it was enough to send a message, 'when someone reveals as little about themselves as Mr Ayre did, there are usually reasons beyond them being just naturally reclusive. But let's proceed and see what we find. Report everything to DS Wright; she's the coordinator. DI Singh and I will search the stable. We'd do the swimming pool as well,' he added, with a grin, 'but Tarvil can't swim, and if he fell in, I wouldn't fancy hauling him out.'

As the search team dispersed, the two senior officers stepped outside. The front of the house overlooked the wide Firth of Forth, through a stand of pines with trunks so tall and narrow that they would never obstruct the view. The stable was in a separate block, behind the house, located in such a way that it was out of the sight of the neighbouring properties from most angles. It had a pitched roof and high double doors that looked high enough to accommodate horse and rider.

'What would you call this lot, Sauce?' Singh wondered as he looked around. 'A villa? A mansion? A palace?'

'When you've spent that amount of money, you can call it anything you fucking like,' Haddock observed. 'As far as the planning authority's concerned it's a detached dwelling with an outbuilding and that's it.'

'Will you and Cheeky be moving into something like this?'

The superintendent stopped and looked, unsmiling, at his colleague. 'I'll say this only once, mate,' he replied. 'My wife inherited a fortune. I didn't. Its use, as it affects her, that's her business. As it affects us, that's a joint decision, but it will not involve a seaside gin palace, that's for sure. We'll do what's best for our kids. End of story.'

'Understood,' Singh said, quietly. 'I didn't mean to rattle your cage.'

'You didn't, don't worry about it.' As they moved on, he continued. 'Does anything strike you about the layout of this place?'

'Not really. What are you seeing?'

'It's minimum maintenance. Monoblock paving, sculptures, all sorts, but no grass. It's as if Ayre wanted as few people here as possible, gardeners, cleaners, what have you. It strikes me as an extension of his obvious obsession with privacy.'

'There's worse faults in a man.'

'Maybe, but why would you build something like this, when as far as we can see it's all just for him and his horse?'

'Dunno,' the DI said as they reached the stable. He beamed. 'Maybe he just loved his horse that much. It certainly seems that the animal's got a nice sea view.' There was a window to the left of the double entrance door. Through it they could see a wide padded stall, with a manger on one side, stretching back into the building.

Singh punched the code into the keypad on the right of the frame and once again the doors swung open, seemingly under power. 'More than just a stable,' he exclaimed as the two stepped inside. The horse's stall occupied less than half of the building. Behind it on the left, there was a changing room with built-in storage, a shower and, they saw through its open door, a toilet compartment with a hand basin. The space to the right served as a garage, with a separate up-and-over door. It housed three vehicles: a Land Rover Defender, a sports car and a Triumph Tiger motorcycle.

'That Land Rover would do me,' the big detective said. 'I've never been a biker, and no way would I fit in that two-seater. What is it, anyway?'

'A Lotus Emira, I think,' Haddock ventured. 'It's modest, compared to everything else we're seeing here. I was expecting a Ferrari or a Lamborghini.' He inspected each vehicle, finding nothing in either glove box, or in the door storage compartments. 'He trusted his security,' he noted. 'The keys are in them.'

Singh moved across to the changing section and opened the three doors. 'Riding gear,' he said, looking at a wardrobe section. 'Formal and waterproof. For the winter, I suppose.' Alongside were two smaller compartments. One held a few items of equestrian equipment: a tiny saddle, spare stirrups, a short whip. The other was mostly filled by towels. The DI lifted them out, but found nothing else save for a box; he opened it and saw spare keys, two lightning cables and an old sixteen-gigabyte USB drive, irrelevant in the modern era, Singh thought. 'Anything in the horse's stall, Sauce?' he called out.

'Hay and shit,' the superintendent replied. 'Large quantities of the latter. Let's be generous and say he was planning to sweep it out when he got back . . . only he never did. Tarvil, one thing occurs to me. We were assuming that Ayre lived here full time, but didn't the architect tell Noele that he worked internationally?'

'That's right,' his colleague confirmed, re-joining him.

'In that case, what did he do with the horse when he was away?'

'That's a bloody good question,' Singh agreed.

'We should get Inspector Hill to ask around. Come on, we're done here. Let's see how the team's getting on.'

The pair returned to the house to find Jackie Wright in the living room, with her back to them. The window was panoramic;

the sunlit view took in four islands including the massive Bass Rock. Beyond, the outline of Fife coastal villages could be seen. The scene appeared to be lost on her as she sorted through the items on a table. She turned at their entry. 'What we've found so far,' she said. 'His phone and an Apple MacBook Pro laptop, both password protected, obviously. There's an iMac desktop in a study just along there; we'll take that too.' She held up a watch. 'Rolex, platinum and diamond. One hundred grand, give or take?' she wondered. Then another. 'Breitling Aerospace. More affordable, my girlfriend has one like it. We have his wallet, containing two hundred and forty pounds in cash. Also a Moneze Mastercard and a debit card from his bank in Jersey plus an Amex gold card. Two airline club cards from British Airways and Singapore Air. We have his driving licence, obviously renewed recently because this address is on it. There's his passport, a new blue one, show-ing his date of birth; that's also the same as the old Queen, believe it or not, but only thirty-four years ago. There are no other per-sonal records that we've found so far. No birth certificate. I can't see anything that refers to any other family member.'

'How about photographs?' Haddock asked.

'There's nothing,' Wright replied. 'No photographs; none at all.'

'Fuck me,' he whispered. 'The Gaffer might be right.'

Singh frowned at him. 'What?'

'I spoke to Bob Skinner earlier on, just picking his brain. He suggested that Ayre might have been a spook. The way things are here we're being pointed in that direction. I might need to go back to him. He's part spook himself; he's still got contacts way out of my league, or even Mario McGuire's.'

'Does your average spook own a hundred-grand watch?'

'Whatever Mr Ayre was, there was nothing average about him.

We need, I need, to check out that avenue.' He turned back to the DS. 'Jackie, what else have they found?'

'Personal items. Shaver, toothbrush, gold cufflinks monogrammed "GA". Clothing, all of it designer stuff. And yet he didn't have a big wardrobe. He had two suits, two casual jackets, trousers, jeans, a big Barbour overcoat, a dozen shirts and a white tuxedo with black trousers. They're all top brands like I said, not mass market; no Marks and Spencer in his wardrobe, not even Charles Tyrwhitt.'

'Who?' Singh asked.

'Nobody you'd know about, Tarvil,' Wright shot back. 'They don't make your size. Come to think of it, who does?'

'Is there any good news coming?' Haddock wondered aloud.

'Maybe. There are some women's items in his wardrobe. Not much, underwear . . . feminine rather than just serviceable . . . including a thirty-six C-cup bra, a dress, a shirt, a pair of jeans, twenty-eight waist, a bikini bottom . . .'

'No top?'

'Sauce, he's got a private pool.'

'Why would she just wear bottoms? Why wear anything at all?'

'I can think of a reason, but it's not relevant. Point being, these are the only items we've found here that relate to anyone other than Gavin Ayre. Sauce, do you remember the first sighting we had of Ayre, when Professor Grace recognised him from being in that restaurant?"

Haddock's eyebrows rose, very slightly. 'Yes. He was with a woman, right?'

'Right. Well, we know who she is. Inspector Hill called me this morning with an update. Her name's Claire Hornell . . . Mrs Claire Hornell. She's been back in the Main Course with a group of mothers from a local nursery school. I don't know where she lives, but I do have her mobile number. I was going to call her when we were finished here.'

'Jackie,' he exclaimed, 'you are finished here. Get on the phone and call the lady. Make an appointment to meet her, but without telling her what it's about. She may have worked it out already after this morning's press briefing, but if not, break it as gently as you can. She's our only witness and we need her on-side.'

Twenty

Bob Skinner smiled as he looked out of the window of the InterMedia company aircraft. Its approach to Girona Airport took it over the old city, which he had always loved. There was something about the cathedral, overlooking its river, that reminded him of Notre Dame and the banks of the Seine. There was little architectural similarity and their two cities were vastly different, but each dated from the same era yet still stood proud and unbreachable, even if the French version had proved to be more combustible. He settled back in his seat as the Beechcraft continued its descent, closing in on the runway a few kilometres ahead.

He had been making the journey for well over a year, since his friend Xavi Aislado, grieving from the loss to Covid of his beloved wife, had stepped away from the family-owned media conglomerate and asked him to take the chair in his absence. Skinner had assumed the arrangement would last for only a few months, but there was no sign of Xavi wanting to return. At first he had felt inadequate, an alien imported over the heads of people who could probably have done the job better than he, but he had settled into the role. He understood the business from his time with its UK subsidiary, and realised that at the very least he was a useful sounding board for the people on the ground who drove it forward on a day-to-day basis. Xavi had been a journalist in Scotland before joining his brother in Spain, his friendship with Skinner going back to that era. He had been old school, running a business that was expanding into areas well beyond his expertise, but he had been an excellent strategic decision-maker. Skinner had discovered that he was too. He had reached the point at which he would be secretly disappointed if Xavi decided to return, rather than focusing on preparing his daughter Paloma to be his long-term successor.

The aircraft landed with barely a suggestion of a bump. 'Welcome once again to Catalunya, sir,' the pilot said through the small speaker as the plane began its taxi towards the executive reception area, where a police officer would be waiting to check his passport, another privilege he appreciated. It was turning off the runway when his phone sounded. He glanced at the name on the screen. 'Indeed?' he murmured. 'What can I do for you, Deputy Chief Constable,' he said as he took the call.

'Is that engine noise I can hear?' Mario McGuire asked.

'Yes, but we're on the ground.'

'Where?'

'Spain. We've got a board meeting tomorrow.'

'Can't you do all that stuff by Zoom?'

Skinner laughed. 'Those whose business is driven by communications technology are only too well aware of how insecure that can be. Besides, I like to be in the room with people. I can smell insecurity; you can't do that on screen.'

'Lucky you,' McGuire said. 'We'll be doing more of that Zooming from now on. Neil went up to Orkney and Shetland last week; tour of inspection, he called it. He had a couple of bumpy landings island-hopping and came back saying "Never again!" Conference calls will be standard practice from now on. That's only the start of it. Some fucking genius in technical support is suggesting that we use drones for routine surveillance and cut down on manned patrols.'

'Is that something you should tell a guy who oversees a national newspaper?' Skinner asked.

'Maybe not, now you mention it. Forget I said it.'

'Okay, but before I do, what's Chief Constable McIlhenney saying to the eye-in-the-sky proposal?'

'We're discussing it at a chief officers' meeting tomorrow . . . remotely, of course. I'm going to suggest that the things might as well be armed if they're up there. Think of the money we'd save,' McGuire laughed. 'We see a violent crime in progress, we could zap them before they leave the scene.'

'Have you ever thought of standing for Parliament? Some Tory voters would love you.'

'I might,' he conceded, 'if only to identify them and eliminate them.'

'An interesting concept,' Skinner observed, as the aircraft came to a halt. 'Now, before you're co-opted as Donald Trump's campaign director, is there a reason for this call?'

'Yes,' the deputy chief replied. 'Gavin Ayre, the mystery murder victim. Are you up to speed with the investigation? I know that Haddock still uses you as a sounding board. I'm fine with that, by the way,' he added. 'I'm doing it myself, right now.'

'Since you ask, I spoke to Sauce earlier on this morning. I suggested a couple of lines of enquiry, mainly about who might have ordered a professional hit, and why. I suggested he might broaden his investigation. How about you, Mario? Do you have anything in mind?'

'Well, based on the update Sauce has just given me, after going over the victim's place, I'm thinking . . . There's a layer of mystery around the man, secrecy almost, that can only be deliberate. Then there's the way his house was built, with a respectable local architect and straight-up unimpeachable contractors given pretty much free rein. On top of that, there's the movement of funds, serious capital, with no apparent checks or declarations . . .'

'Money laundering?' Skinner asked. 'Is that what you're suggesting?'

'Yes. What do you think?'

'It's a possibility,' he conceded. 'But if that's behind it, why close the laundry down by killing Ayre?'

Twenty-One

'You're sure you're happy to be having this discussion here, Mrs Hornell?' Jackie Wright asked.

'I suggested it, so I think you can assume that,' Claire Hornell replied, just a shade archly. She was a slender blonde woman; attractive, Wright acknowledged, although not her type. Her accent was possibly Yorkshire, the DS thought, although she did not consider herself an expert in English regional variations.

Hornell looked around the café. 'It's handy for Poppy's nursery school, I have to have lunch, and this is usually quiet on a Monday.'

And maybe you didn't want a police officer calling on you at home, the DS thought. A DVLA check had established that the woman was thirty-one years old and lived in Longniddry. Her husband was one Edward Anthony Hornell, according to the electoral roll.

'Can I take your orders?'

Wright looked up at the waiter. 'I'll have a baked potato with coronation chicken.'

'And I'll have the same but with tuna mayo,' Claire Hornell said.

'Your child?'

She patted the tray of the high chair. 'Poppy will share mine, thank you.' She waited for the man to retreat to the kitchen then continued. 'You're going to tell me Gavin's dead, aren't you?' she murmured.

'I'm afraid I am. How did you know?'

Her eyes moistened; the perceptive police officer, who had given the death message often in her career, saw grief but more. She read guilt, and something else. Might it have been relief?

'I was riding on Friday at the stable along the road there.' Hornell pointed, vaguely, westward. 'When I got back, the owner said something about a body being found on the beach. The way she described it, I just knew.'

'But you didn't think to call us?' Wright's tone was a little accusatory. Inwardly she chided herself.

'No, I couldn't,' she murmured. 'I thought about it, but decided "no". I mean it might not have been him and then . . . what . . .' She stopped, her mouth set in a firm line. 'Look,' she whispered, eventually. 'I'm married, happily married with a child. I just couldn't come forward.'

The detective sergeant nodded, recognising that an antagonistic witness would be no good at all. 'Yes,' she said, 'I can understand that. What does your husband do?'

'He's in the navy,' Hornell replied. 'He's the executive officer on an aircraft carrier, the *Prince William*. He's away a lot, always showing the flag somewhere. That's part of the problem, I suppose, why I was . . .'

'Vulnerable?' Wright suggested.

She nodded, with a small smile. 'That's a nice way of putting it. I'm not a slapper, you know. Gavin's . . . Gavin was . . . the only fling I've had since I've been married, but Eddie's been away for months, not for the first time, and I was feeling neglected.'

'How did you meet Gavin?'

'I was riding, early June it was, a Tuesday. Cassie, my pony, was a thirtieth birthday present from my dad. I keep her at Luffness because it isn't on a main road, but close to the beach. I'm new there, only just getting to meet people, so up until now mostly I've been riding on my own while Poppy's at nursery. I was on my own back then, walking Cassie through the woods beyond the new golf course, when I met Gavin on his horse, Winalot.'

'That's a funny name for a horse,' the DS observed.

'That's what I said, but Gavin said that Shergar had probably wound up in a dog-food tin, so he thought it was sort of okay. He said he was going to call it Pedigree, but he decided that was too tame so he went for Winalot instead. Anyway. That's how we met. Truth be told, I was lost at the time; literally, not emotionally,' she added. 'I didn't know how to get out of there. He led me down to the beach. The tide was very low so we were able to trot the horses, although he was holding Winalot back. It's a gelding; a big horse but Gavin was a big bloke. Afterwards he put me back on the road to my stable. When we were going our separate ways he asked if he could see me again, without the horses. I'd already said I had to pick up my child, but that didn't seem to deter him. I don't know why I said yes, but I did. So, I got a baby-sitter and we met for dinner in the Italian restaurant in Gullane two nights later, a Thursday when it was relatively quiet.'

She fell silent. Wright said nothing, asked nothing, waiting.

'So yes,' Hornell continued, 'we went back to his place. He'd come in a taxi. I hadn't been drinking so I was able to drive. Have you been there?' she asked.

'This morning,' the detective replied.

'Then you'll understand why I was surprised when I saw it. It's beautiful, like something you'd expect to find in Dubai but not in East Lothian. I told him as much. He showed me round; I was gobsmacked when I saw the pool, the gym, the sauna. I didn't mean to be bold, but I said, "Next time I'll bring a cossie." He looked at me, smiled and said, "Really?" And that was it, really. We didn't sleep together that night, but we met up on the following Monday on the horses and a couple of days later I got the baby-sitter again and went to his. We had a swim. No, I didn't take a cossie, and the rest you can take as read.'

'How long did the affair last?' Wright asked.

'It never stopped. We saw each other a couple of times a week all through the summer. We went back to the Main Course once, but I was a bit nervous. Even though I'm not known in Gullane, you never know who might see you. People go there from all over. Mostly I would just go to his place. Sometimes during the day when Poppy was at nursery, sometimes . . .'

The DS held up a hand, a warning that the waiter was returning with their meals. Hornell stopped in mid-sentence.

Poppy had been dozing in the high chair; the prospect of lunch revived her. The narrative was paused as the mother fed her child, before turning herself to what remained, no more than half of the baked potato and its filling. *No wonder you're slim,* Wright thought.

When she could see that Hornell was ready, the DS asked, 'When was the last time you were there?'

'Last Thursday. We'd agreed that I would go back tomorrow morning,' she added.

'How did you communicate?'

'We didn't really,' she said. 'We made arrangements and stuck to them. Yes, we exchanged mobile numbers, in case one of us couldn't make it, but we didn't call each other. A couple of texts, that was it. Look, Sergeant, we weren't in love or anything like that. He was an attractive, kind and charming man and he was very good in bed, but I wasn't going to leave Eddie for him, however bloody rich he was. Not that I was ever asked,' she added. 'Friendship with benefits, that was the extent of it. In fact, I was going to end it tomorrow. Eddie's due home in a couple of weeks, plus . . . Poppy's getting to the age where she's starting to notice things and remember them . . . things like having baby-sitters every week.'

'Of course,' Wright said. 'Mrs Hornell, I'm not being judgmental. The reason I need to speak to you is that you're one of only two people we can find who knew Gavin Ayre. The other was his architect.'

'Tim Lloyd?'

'Yes. Do you know him?'

Hornell shook her head. 'No, but Gavin talked about him all the time. He told me that Tim had designed and built the place for him. He said his lifestyle meant that he needed to have someone on the ground in charge of the construction.'

'Did he elaborate on that? His lifestyle? We're trying to create a picture of Mr Ayre. So far, we know nothing about him.'

'No, he didn't. In fact, he said from the start that the less we knew about each other the better. He didn't want to know anything about Eddie, he said, or guilt might kick in and ruin what we had.'

'Did he ever refer to his background at all?'

'No.' She frowned, briefly. 'I know he had a brother, but he didn't volunteer that, not really. I mentioned once that my younger brother, Jude's, twenty-first is this year. He said, "Is he all you have?" I said, "Yes", and he said, "Me too, but not the full shilling, a half-brother." But that was all; he didn't put a name to him.'

'Did he say anything about his business interests? Or about the source of the wealth that built his house?'

'No, nothing. You're making me realise, Detective Sergeant, that he was as big a mystery to me as clearly he is to you. The only time I asked him a personal question was the first time I was there, when he showed me round the house. I asked hm where all this had come from, what did he do? "Let's just say I've been lucky," was all he said, with a smile, mind you. He really was a nice man. It's tragic he should die in a stupid accident. Winalot really got his own back for that name. What will happen to him?'

'He's being taken care of,' Wright replied. 'But Mrs Hornell, there's something I have to tell you. Mr Ayre's death was no accident. He was murdered.'

Hornell's eyes widened; her tanned face paled. 'He was what?'

'He was killed. I'm part of a homicide investigation, and so far we have absolutely no leads. There's nothing in the house to give us a clue, nothing that we wouldn't have expected to find there, apart from a few items of your clothing, that is.'

The woman stared at her. 'My clothing?'

'Yes, we found female items in his bedroom.'

At least twenty seconds passed in silence as Claire Hornell considered what she had been told. When she was ready, she murmured, 'DS Wright, I swear that everything that I wore to Gavin's I put back on before I went home. Whatever you found there . . . it isn't mine.'

Twenty-Two

'Do you believe her?'

'I have no reason not to, Sauce,' Jackie Wright replied. 'She didn't try to hide anything, she was frank in her answers. When I told her that Ayre had been murdered I believe she was genuinely gob-smacked. If she'd even had a whiff of something shady about him she wouldn't have reacted like that; I'd have caught a flicker of it.'

'What about her background?' Singh asked. The trio were seated at the conference table in Haddock's room at the Fettes building. A fourth participant sat on the detective superintendent's right: Deputy Chief Constable Mario McGuire. His arrival had been unexpected; prefaced by a voice message on Haddock's mobile advising that he was on his way and would like to be briefed.

'Privileged, but not minted, I would say. They live in one of the new houses in Longniddry on the south side of the railway line, having moved from Gloucester four years ago. She told me that her dad has a metal bashing business . . . her descrip-tion . . . near Halifax in west Yorkshire. He pays the kid's nursery fees and her stable costs as well. She told me that long term her younger brother will inherit the business, so her father's making sure she wants for nothing.'

'And the husband?' McGuire asked.

'Lieutenant Commander Hornell, Royal Navy, like she said. His ship's on patrol in the Far East.'

'Trying to impress the Chinese, I suppose,' the DCC grunted. 'So,' he continued, 'she's been able to advance our knowledge of the victim by not one inch.'

Haddock shook his head. 'Not quite, sir, maybe by a foot or so. We know now that he's got a half-brother. Also, if we accept Mrs Hornell's insistence that the clothes we found aren't hers . . .'

'We can,' Wright interjected. 'Claire's a B cup at most, and those jeans, they were twenty-eight waist. She's no more than a twenty-four.'

'Okay,' he continued, 'so we know also that he has another girlfriend. We need to locate her. Tarvil, is there anything on his phone or his laptop to tell us who she is? If you've been able to get into them, that is.'

'No problem with doing that,' the Sikh DI said. 'I didn't even need the IT people to open it. His password on both was the same as the entry keypad. I don't know why he bothered. There was nothing there to protect. There were no contacts on his phone, and no history on it either, or on his laptop. The guy must have deleted everything on a daily basis. The only thing I found was an incoming call around the time we believe he died. There's a mobile number but the caller didn't leave a message.'

'How about his email address? Did he even have one?'

'Yes, it's G Ayre at gmail dot com. I've looked into that on both devices but, like I said, he's deleted anything that was there, and not just from the bin, from the history as well. I haven't looked at the desk-top yet, but I don't expect to find anything there.'

'Look at it, just in case,' Haddock told him. 'And pin down that incoming caller if you can.'

'Will do.'

The superintendent took a deep breath, straightening in his chair. 'Okay,' he said, 'let's consider where we are in this investigation. We have a man about whom we know little or nothing, the victim of what appears to be a well-planned professional assassination. Let's focus on that word "planned". Over the weekend we've had officers stationed at the beach car park in Gullane and near the crime scene, interviewing people and asking if they were in the area on Friday morning and might have seen the shooter. So far, we've drawn as big a blank as Gavin Ayre's CV. We need to widen the scope of our questioning and focus on that word I used earlier, "planned". Witnesses have told us that Ayre exercised his horse on the beach pretty much every day, at the same time. The shooter must have known that too, which means that he . . . yes Jackie, or she . . . must have observed Ayre for a few days before going, literally, for the kill. We need to widen our window in the hope that in the days leading up to the murder someone might have seen something helpful. I'll ask Jane in the press office to make a public appeal to that effect.' He turned to McGuire, seated by his side. 'Agreed, sir?'

The DCC nodded. 'For sure, Sauce. That's assuming that Ayre actually was targeted and that this wasn't just a random nutter with a gun. God knows, they're commonplace in America. If it was, there is every chance that he . . . or she . . . will do it again.' He paused. 'However, if I can make one suggestion. The female clothing that you found at Ayre's place: some people . . . my Paula for example . . . have the annoying habit of cutting off the labels from garments, the bits with the washing instructions on them. When you get them back from the lab, as you should tomorrow, if any of those are still on the items from Ayre's bedroom, they might also have barcodes that'll tell you where they were purchased and maybe, if you get really lucky, by whom.'

Twenty-Three

Noele McClair was changing Mattie when her ring tone demanded attention. She ignored it, letting it go to voicemail. When her daughter was settled once again she found a message from the architect, asking her to phone him back.

'Sorry I couldn't take your call, Mr Lloyd,' she said as they connected. 'A pressing matter demanded my attention. How can I help you?'

'It might be the other way around, Detective Inspector,' he said, but his tone sounded more positive than his words. 'I remembered something, something away from the norm about Gavin. When I installed the keypad entry for him, as I told you I used a specialist contractor. The job was an add-on, not something included in Gerry Biggs's quote. The firm offered me ten per cent off if I paid up front, so I did, then billed Gavin for the work once it was completed, up and running. He paid me by return, as he always did, but . . . that time the money didn't come from his Jersey bank. It was from another account with Sabadell, a Spanish bank, and he paid me in euros. The same number, but not sterling, so he was about ten per cent short, but Gavin was such a good client that I said nothing about the shortfall and took the hit. The truth is,' he confessed, 'I'd left off the discount from my invoice, since I'd funded the work myself for that short period, so I was only a few quid out of pocket.'

'That is helpful,' McClair told him. 'I don't know that bank,' she said, 'is it offshore too, like Jersey, or online?'

'No, it's conventional. There was an IBAN and a Swift code with the remittance. I'll copy them and send them to you. As I said, I hope it helps.'

'So do I,' she echoed. 'Mr Lloyd, thank you very much.'

The architect's text hit her phone less than three minutes later. By the time it arrived she was on her computer, running a search for the Spanish bank. Banco Sabadell was easy to find; it was one of the market leaders in Spain. She studied the information that Lloyd had sent her and was on the point of passing it on to Haddock, when she hesitated. What would he do? Pass it on to DC Tiggy Benjamin or another junior officer, who would in turn contact the Spanish authorities or the British consulate in Madrid to pinpoint the account. 'To hell with that,' she whispered. 'It might be below my pay grade, but I can make a couple of phone calls.' She returned to the bank's homepage, in search of a contact telephone number. Fifteen minutes later, frustrated and confused by its opacity, she called the commercial section of the British consulate in Madrid.

'Detective Inspector Noele McClair, Edinburgh Serious Crimes Unit,' she began. 'I'm looking for assistance.'

'Then should you not be speaking to the *Policia Nacional*?' a cut-glass voice replied. 'They're your official channel.'

'Maybe,' she snapped, 'but I don't speak Spanish and I don't have time for them to dig up a translator. I'm part of a homicide investigation, and I'm looking for a swift answer to a fairly simple commercial question. Are you going to help me or not?'

'Oh, very well,' the man sighed. 'What is it?'

'I'm trying to identify the location of a bank account. I believe it to have been held by a British national whose death we're investigating. We know very little about him and I'm hoping that his Spanish bank can help. I have the international bank account number, it's a Sabadell account, and I need all the information they have on the owner.'

'Give it me,' he said. 'I'm a Sabadell customer myself. They've probably closed for the day, but I'll call my account handler and see what she can do. Give me your details and I'll get back to you. I see that you're calling from a mobile. I'll need an office number so that I can verify your *bona fides*, your good faith, that is.'

McClair had studied Latin in her final year at high school; she fought to restrain an acid retort. Instead she spelled out the IBAN and added the direct line number of her unit at Fettes. 'Once you've checked me out, call my mobile. I repeat, it is urgent.'

Twenty-Four

Darkness was descending and the Crime Campus was silent as Paul Dorward looked up at the approaching figure. 'Boss,' he exclaimed. 'I thought you'd have been away home by now.'

'I couldn't do that,' Bramley replied. 'Not with you slogging away here in the lab. And stop calling me "Boss". My name's Jenny. How are you getting on?'

'That's me done with the clothing Edinburgh sent us,' he told her.

'That's good. They want it back, soonest, I'm told. If you can package it all up, item by item, I'll arrange for a car to take them all through tonight. Did you get anything from them?'

'The garments are almost an evidential desert,' Dorward said, 'apart from two finds. I've got a semen deposit in a pair of knickers that I'll be able to process. The obvious conclusion is that it's Ayre's but I'll confirm it. And also, the swimming garment, the thong thing, that has a plastic liner in the . . . the . . .'

'Gusset?'

'That's the word . . . but I've been able to extract from it a single black pubic hair, complete with follicle. I'm going to assume it's female,' he added, smiling. 'That will let me confirm the claim by their witness, Ayre's lady friend, that it doesn't belong to her. I'm in the process of profiling the swab she provided.'

'If you do get something from the hair,' Bramley, observed, 'and the owner's on a database, it might even tell the investigating team who she is . . . but let's not raise anyone's hopes. Good work, Paul. I haven't said this, but I really am glad that you decided to stay with us.'

Twenty-Five

Tiggy Benjamin held up the bikini bottom. 'What do you think of this, Sarge?' she asked Jackie Wright. 'Size medium, it says.'

Her colleague frowned. 'I'd hate to see small,' she said. 'Whoever wore that must have had some extreme waxing . . . or wasn't bothered. That would barely cover my minge and I wouldn't say I was outsize. You'd better not either,' she added.

The young DC laughed. 'I wouldn't dare!' She had found her colleague intimidating in her early days with the Serious Crimes Unit but gradually, as her confidence grew, she had come to like her more and more. Wright's humour was deadpan, but it was never far from the surface.

'How are you getting on with those clothes anyway?' she asked. 'Have you made any progress towards finding their wearer?'

'This thing's my last hope,' Benjamin admitted. 'The other things had all been washed so often that any identifying marks were unreadable. The half bikini, though, that's pretty much new. The barcode is still readable.'

'How will you go about tracing it?'

'I have to start with the manufacturer. The brand is Bershka. Ever heard of it?'

'Not quite my scene, Tiggy.' Wright paused. 'But I do know

there's a branch in St James's Quarter. My other half mentioned it. It's the sort of place she would shop. I'm more of a Millet's girl myself. Why don't you get yourself up there now, show it to the manager and check where and when it was bought? They should be able to give you a rough idea from that code.'

Benjamin checked the time on her phone display. 'Ten to ten. Do you think they'll be open by now?'

'If not, they will by the time you arrive. On you go downstairs and I'll get a patrol car to take you up there.'

Wright was as good as her word. When Benjamin reached the entrance a police vehicle was waiting, with a constable at the wheel. 'Your taxi awaits,' the man said gruffly.

The DC guessed that he might have been fifteen years her senior, possibly even more, an old lag filling in the days until his retirement on a plump old-style pension. 'Will I sit in the back?' she responded, eliciting a grunt from the driver as she took the seat beside him.

'Been in CID long?' he asked, finally breaking his silence as they passed Edinburgh Academicals rugby ground.

'Since the year before last,' she replied. 'I was in uniform in East Lothian before that. That was my first posting after college.'

'How long were you there?'

'Three years.'

'Nowhere else?'

'No, that was all.'

'High-flyer then,' he said, with a cynically raised eyebrow.

'I wouldn't say so.'

'That's a quick move to CID,' he observed, 'and that's usually a sign.'

'Would you be saying that if I was a male officer?' Benjamin countered.

'Hey,' the PC chuckled, 'don't go "Me too" on me. I'm just sayin'. I never had a sniff at plain clothes, but most of the guys my age that did had to wait a minimum of eight years. That was in the old force, mind; and it was mostly guys. It's a different world in the new set-up. More opportunities, I suppose, if you're prepared to travel. But even without that, it's a lot easier for you young ones. Look at that boy Haddock. He's what? Thirty-odd and he's a detective super.'

'He's my boss,' she told him. 'He's brilliant.'

'He was Maggie Rose's protégé if I remember right. I was at the West End when she was there. He was so far under her wing he probably smelt of her deodorant. They said he was Skinner's boy too, like the new chief, big McIlhenney, was. I remember him too, in CID, him and his mate McGuire, the DCC now. They were wild bastards, those two. They were good though, I'll grant them that. Still, I never thought either of them would rise that high. Skinner's Army; that's what we called them when I was your age. That's three of them made chief constable now; Martin, Rose and McIlhenney . . . but everybody knows McIlhenney's only there because McGuire didn't want it.'

'What did you think of Sir Robert?' Benjamin asked.

'Big Bob? He was all right; no, he was better than all right. He was a good bloke, but fucking terrifyin' if you got on the wrong side of him. I was surprised when he walked away, but I can see why now. He runs the *Saltire* newspaper, doesn't he?'

'And a lot more,' she said.

'Who's your DI?' the driver asked, suddenly.

'Noele McClair,' she told him. 'She's the reason I'm in CID, to be honest. She was my boss in uniform in Haddington. When she was pulled back in, I asked, no, I begged her to take me with her, and she did. She's on maternity leave just now. DI Singh's my line manager just now, I suppose.'

'The big Sikh? I think he was moved to CID because they couldn't find a uniform to fit him.' He paused. 'McClair,' he murmured. 'Isn't she the one that's husband got . . .'

'Ex-husband,' the DC corrected. 'But yes, she's the one.'

'So, if she's on maternity leave, and she's single like I heard, who's the . . .'

'That's her business, don't you think?'

'Aye, maybe so but . . .'

'No buts,' Benjamin said, as they approached York Place. 'Just drop me here, thanks. It'll be easier for you if I walk the rest. That way you won't get caught up in the Picardy Place traffic.'

'I don't mind taking you right into the car park,' the driver insisted.

'Just drop me here,' she repeated.

'Okay, if you say so.' He drew up, opposite the Scottish National Portrait Gallery.

She jumped out with a quick 'Thank you,' taking advantage of a gap in the traffic to cross the road, putting distance between herself and the inquisitive PC. She knew that the identity of Matilda McClair's father was the subject of much speculation in the office. A very small circle knew the answer to that question. She was one of them and had no wish to be suspected of leaking the secret.

Easing her way through the knot of pedestrians outside the gallery, she headed for Elder Street. She had visited the recently completed St James Quarter before, but had no idea where to find Bershka. Luck was on her side as she spied the sign quickly, not far from the entrance. She felt at home immediately in the place; the browsing customers seemed to be all female and in her age group, apart from a couple of teenagers and a few males, each with the anxious look of someone expecting an imminent hit on his credit card. There was a queue at the cash desk, and so she chose a woman who appeared to be the oldest of the shop floor assistants and approached her.

'Detective Constable Tiggy Benjamin,' she began. 'I'm looking for information about one of your products. Is the manager available?'

'At your service,' she said. 'Margaret O'Reilly. Which piece are we talking about?'

The young detective delved into her shoulder bag and produced the garment, in a clear plastic evidence bag. 'This one. I don't have the other part, I'm afraid.'

'That's not a problem,' the manager replied. 'We price the tops and bottoms separately.'

'Ideally I'd like to know who bought it, where and when.'

The woman winced. 'Ouch! I can't guarantee all three, but with a bit of luck I can get you a location and a time. Can I take it out the bag?'

'Of course.'

Benjamin watched as she removed the tiny garment, frowning as she peered at the information on the label.

'I can tell you right now,' O'Reilly volunteered, 'that it wasn't bought here. I think this is Spanish.' She held the clothing up, brandishing the code. 'You see that letter, T, beside the M? I think that means "size" in Spanish. Maybe it's Italian, but I don't think so. I'll need to go into the office and make a couple of phone calls. I might be a wee while, are you okay with that? I can get you a coffee.'

'No, I'm fine thanks,' the DC assured her. 'I'll just browse while you do that.'

The manager was gone for twelve minutes, time enough for Benjamin to have bought a jump suit, a T shirt and a biker jacket that she was sure she would regret the moment she left the store. She returned just as she was stepping away from the pay point. 'Let me see your receipt,' she said at once. 'I'll give you a discount.'

'Thanks, but that's okay,' the detective assured her. 'I don't think I'd be allowed to accept it, as I'm working.'

O'Reilly checked her watch. 'It's half past ten,' she pointed out. 'Time for Popmaster. Let's assume I'm Ken Bruce and you're on your tea break like most of the country.'

Benjamin smiled and handed over her till receipt. 'Let's do that. Before you went off you told me something,' she continued, 'didn't you?'

'I did. I've got you all three.' O'Reilly beamed, looking more than a little pleased with the outcome of her research. 'The item was sold on April thirtieth, in our outlet in a mall called Espai Girona, which is . . . believe it or not . . . in Girona, Spain. It was paid for with a Mastercard from a bank called Sabadell, but that's all they could tell me.'

'Wow!' the DC exclaimed. 'That's much more than I'd expected. Are you allowed to give me any more details? The card number for example.'

'That's all I've got, I'm afraid. For anything else, I think you'll have to ask in Spain.' O'Reilly frowned. 'What's this about? Can I ask you? Or aren't you allowed to say?'

'It's an ongoing investigation, that's all I'm allowed to tell you. But, I'm from the Serious Crimes Unit, if that helps.'

'Big time, eh? I hope I've helped you catch the . . . the perp, if that's what you call them. Meantime,' she continued, 'I'll get you that discount.'

Twenty-Six

As ACC Lowell Payne gazed at the face on his tablet, he found his mind dwelling on the continuing influence of Bob Skinner on a service he had left some time before. His own career had blossomed after his path had crossed that of the man who had been married to his wife's late sister. He had never met Myra but her daughter Alexis had been a regular visitor to her Aunt Jean during her student days in Glasgow, and still was.

Payne had been a sergeant in the cumbersome and unloved Strathclyde force at the time, locked at that rank for the rest of his career, he had assumed: then Skinner had become chief constable and everything had changed. Merit was identified and rewarded, and he had been a beneficiary. He had never dreamed of reaching command status, and yet he had, in the sensitive and at times secretive division that in the unified police service had replaced what was known as Special Branch in the former regional set-up.

When he looked at Sauce Haddock, the youngest of Skinner's many protégés, he saw himself, but with a difference. Payne knew that he had finally reached his ceiling; he expected the newly promoted detective superintendent to surpass it, possibly while he was still in the service himself.

'I've reached out,' he said, 'like you asked me to. The Security Service has never heard of your man Gavin Ayre. They've reached out themselves to other interests and nobody, anywhere, has his image, his DNA or his fingerprints on record. That's not surprising. I expect the General Register Office will come back to confirm that Gavin Ayre was born on the date on his passport, but that the original died in infancy. It's a flaw in the system that can still be exploited. You pull a birth certificate and use it to obtain a passport. It doesn't work with a driving licence though. You need to pass a test for that. Ayre's licence is a very impressive forgery. Your man's a ghost, Sauce.'

Haddock frowned as he looked at the figure on his own screen, confident in his tunic with his badges of rank on his shoulders. Most police officers over forty-five, and the younger ones who knew of the connection, believed that Lowell Payne would still be a uniformed inspector at best had it not been for his tenuous relationship to Bob Skinner. He was not among them. He recognised the ACC's sharp analytical mind, his ability to envisage every possibility in a developing situation and most of all his thoroughness. He had been raised to believe that while rank deserved automatic respect, the person who held it had to earn it. Payne passed muster with him on both levels, unlike his own line manager, ACC Becky Stallings, who had never in his experience made a positive contribution to any investigation. Most people in the HR department could do her job, and more efficiently at that.

'What's your thinking, Superintendent?' Payne asked.

'So he's Caspar, and the spooks don't know of him,' Haddock replied. 'But, suppose he was a spook himself, would they tell us?'

'A reasonable question,' the ACC conceded. 'My contact would, I'm pretty sure.' In fact, he had reached out to Clyde

Houseman who had been the MI5 presence in Scotland until a combination of circumstances had precipitated his recall to Millbank. Houseman had been his best conduit to military intelligence, who treated their secrets as personal property and were notoriously unwilling to share. 'Sorry, Sauce,' he said. 'I can't take it any further.'

Haddock sighed as he closed the connection. He was pondering his next move when there was a light knock at the door and Jackie Wright eased herself into the room. 'What have you got?' he asked. 'Something? Anything?'

'Maybe,' she replied. 'Benjamin's called me from St James's Quarter. She's established that the bikini bottom in Ayre's bedroom was bought in Spain, in a shopping mall in Girona.'

'That's something,' he conceded. 'Do we know who bought it?'

'That's the hard part. They've got the last four digits of a card number, but we'll need to involve the Spanish police to trace the holder . . . if that's even possible. What's the police force there?'

'Girona's in Catalonia,' Haddock said, 'so it's probably the *Mossos d'Esquadra*. They'll take their own time, if past experience is anything to go by. But,' he smiled, 'maybe there's an informal route we can try first. Give me all the information you have, please, and leave it with me.'

Twenty-Seven

'Paul,' Jenny Bramley said quietly. 'I saw from the sign-out book that you were here until midnight. I told you to take today off, not just this morning, yet here you are in the lab at lunchtime. You don't have anything to prove to me, you know.'

Paul Dorward met her gaze. 'If I thought I did, I'd be long gone,' he replied. 'And I did appreciate the day-off offer. My old man would never have done that. He wouldn't have been here until ten o'clock either, as the same book told me you were. But morning was enough, really. I wanted to see what the pube from Gavin Ayre's seaside palace tells us about the donor, if it tells us anything.'

'And does it? Will it help Haddock and his shoal?'

He grinned. 'Don't let him hear you say that. "Sauce" he tolerates, but only from those who know him well enough. Any other fishy gags get shut down.'

'I'll bear that in mind when I speak to him.' She took a breath. 'When I do, will I have anything to tell him?'

'Well, you won't be able to put a name to her, I'm afraid, not yet at least. Like Ayre, she hasn't shown up on any of the standard databases. I'm still waiting for European feedback.'

She frowned deeply. 'Pretty much what I expected you to say,' she sighed. 'Let's hope the clothing we sent back to Edinburgh gives them a lead to her.'

'Yes,' Dorward agreed, 'let's hope. But,' he continued, 'when you talk to Sauce, you will get his attention. Where did you say those garments were found?'

'In Ayre's bedroom, in the dressing area.'

'How many bedrooms were there?'

'Five, all en-suite.'

The ginger-haired scientist grinned. 'In that case, you might be triggering another investigation. Like I told you, there was a semen trace on a pair of the knickers you gave me. As I said, I ran a profile, and yes, it was Ayre's.'

'To be expected.'

'Normally, but . . . My dad always said never to leave a step untaken, one thing he did get right. So, when I got the completed profile on the female, I compared it with all the other DNA traces recovered from the scene, just two of them unknown, excluding careless police officers that I eliminated, and also with Gavin Ayre's, automatically. And guess what?' A wide smile spread across his face. 'She's his half-sister. I'm not a criminal lawyer, but still I'm pretty certain that counts as incest in Scotland. How about letting me call Sauce? I really would like to make his day.'

Bramley's beam matched his. 'Then go ahead. You've earned it!'

Twenty-Eight

Bob Skinner regarded it as one of life's ironies. He had spent thirty years anticipating the day when his daily commute would be a thing of the past, only to drift into a new one when his role in Girona required him to spend at least two or three days there every week.

His Spanish property was reachable, in the coastal town of L'Escala, a little under fifty kilometres from the InterMedia head office, but the traffic was a bind. Eventually he had taken a big decision, to spend most of the performance bonus from his first year in the chair on an apartment in the city, a duplex in a new-build seven-storey block. It was so close to the business hub that on occasion he and his senior colleagues would meet there, out of the melee that was inevitable in a building whose main activity was news and current affairs.

Street noise drifted upwards as he and Hector Sureda, the company's CEO, stood on the rooftop terrace, each with a beer in hand. 'It's exciting, Bob, is it not,' his colleague murmured, 'to be launching a business in North America. Did you ever go there when you were a cop?'

'A few times,' Skinner replied. 'Chiefly I was at Quantico, the FBI headquarters, on international exchanges, and as a lecturer a couple of times. I didn't go down too well there. The Americans don't like being told by a foreigner that much, no, most of their street crime can be blamed four square on the Second Amendment.'

'The age-old problem,' Sureda said. 'The right to bear arms.'

'Mmm,' Skinner grunted. 'But it doesn't define "arms", nor does it say a word about ammunition.'

'Is that where you would start to tackle it?'

'In an ideal world, yes, but that isn't the USA. It's insoluble. The way I see it, the gun lobby can't be overthrown. They have to live with that. To me the more dangerous part of the Second Amendment is the reference to a well-regulated militia. That opens the door to all sorts of hairy-backs.'

'Will the next presidential campaign focus on that, do you think?'

'It will be an element, for sure. And when it rises to the surface, Hector, what will be the editorial stance of *Intermedia Latino*, as you and the big man are proposing to call it?'

'I don't know,' Sureda admitted. 'We know the project has been Xavi's way of keeping in touch with the business with me taking it to you and the board, but that's a discussion he and I have not had. Maybe we should not take an editorial stance,' he suggested.

'How would that work?' Skinner challenged. 'We'll be running a news outlet. On present plans we'll open on the first day of next year, election year in the US. That will dominate the news agenda. We'll have programme anchors. We'll have expert opinion, guest input. How can we be neutral?'

'Those guests could be academics.'

'Academics are as polarised in the States as everyone else,' he countered. 'Look Hector, the people on our platform have to reflect the philosophy and morality of what we perceive our target audience to be . . . and what its owner believes . . . or you and he wouldn't have taken it this far.' He tilted his Corona bottle in Sureda's direction. 'Where are politics in America right now?' he asked. 'There's the incumbent in the White House, with an element in his party that's flat-out socialist, a cuss word to most of the electorate. There's the opposition party in the grip of the militant Right, the Proud Boys and such. But now, between them, there's the new guy, the independent. He's pitching himself as the voice of sanity, the man to rebuild moderate America. From what we hear and read he's gathering a lot of middle-ground support. Jesus, my wife is still an American citizen. She's a dual passport holder, as are our three kids, a long-term view we took when Jazz was born. Sarah says she'd vote for Silver, and I believe she's a pretty good benchmark.'

'But Bob,' Sureda intervened, 'as you know, the man is only an independent. There are dozens of those on the ballot at every election.'

'Yes,' Skinner conceded, 'but none of the others are attracting serious interest from the media and the voting public. This one is. Will he still be around on January one next year when *Intermedia Latino* goes live on air, assuming we get regulatory approval . . . that is? If he is, and polling significantly as he is just now . . .'

'Are you going to propose that *Intermedia Latino* should support him?'

'Not yet, but I am putting it on the table as an alternative to neutrality, which I believe is impossible in practice, or supporting the Democrats, which would be the natural home of the viewing audience we'll be trying to reach. Hector, you've been Xavi's man in developing the project. I'd like you to talk through the alternatives with him and bring a proposal to the board.'

'Could you not have that conversation, Bob?' Sureda asked. 'You talk to him all the time.'

'I talk to him about football, about art and about the price of cheese, but we don't talk often about board business. When I took the job I told him I wouldn't be his stooge. We're both very clear about that. By the same token he and I haven't discussed *Intermedia Latino*. So you need to do it, and it's time you did.'

The chief executive nodded. 'Yes, boss,' he chuckled. 'We will. Tomorrow, I promise. Now I must go.'

As he spoke Skinner's ring tone sounded. He glanced at the screen. 'Hector, I need to take this. See yourself out, okay?'

As Sureda left, he accepted the call. 'Sauce? What's up?'

'Are you still in Spain, Gaffer?' Haddock asked.

He held his phone high, away from his ear, for a few seconds. 'Very much so,' he said as he returned it. 'Can you hear the city in the background?'

'Yes,' the detective replied. 'Are you in your new place?'

'I am. It's just as well. My first-born daughter's in residence in L'Escala, with her friend Dominick.'

'Dominick Jackson? The psychologist? Are Alex and he . . .?'

'I don't think so. If they are, she's not going to tell me and I'm not going to ask. So why are you calling? Are you going to tell me you've made an arrest in the Ayre investigation?'

'Sadly no,' Haddock replied. 'But if he was still alive I might be arresting him. Or at the very least asking him to explain how his semen got on his half-sister's pants, that we found in his bedroom.'

'The woman in the Main Course?' Skinner exclaimed. 'That was his half-sister?'

'No, she was someone else. She assures us that she did her washing at home, and I believe her. But that's not why I'm calling, not directly. We want to put a name to Ayre's half-sister and find her if we can. The route to that is through another piece of clothing that we took from the house yesterday. The bar code information tells us that it was bought from a store called Bershka in Espai Girona, a shopping mall near where you are right now.'

'Near me?' he laughed. 'I can practically fucking see it from here! I know it too. Sarah dragged me off there one day last Easter.'

'Right,' the superintendent continued. 'What I'd appreciate is for you to use the police contacts that I'm sure you have out there to go to the store, and get them to find the holder of the card that was used in the transaction. We both know it'll get things done a lot faster than going through normal channels. I've got an image of the sales slip that I can send you so that you can brief the locals.'

'That sounds fine in theory, Sauce,' Skinner conceded, 'but for one thing. I'm the chair of a group that owns among other things the biggest daily newspaper in this city. As such the police like to keep us at arms' length. Now, I could go to the head of the *Mossos* in Barcelona and ask for strings to be pulled, but I don't want to do that because the people here might not take it too kindly.'

'So you're saying, Gaffer,' Haddock sighed, 'that I'll have to go through official channels.'

'Fuck no!' he laughed. 'I'm saying I'll do it myself. Send me what you've got and I'll go right now.'

Twenty-Nine

'Your daft granny was right, you know,' Noele McClair told her sleeping daughter. 'There is something to be said for working from home. Maybe I could attend crime scenes by video link and still function as a detective. It would do away with the smell and that would be a bonus. A lot of murders are smelly, Mattie. Like that guy in *Game of Thrones* said, "People shit themselves when they're killed." I'm pretty sure that in the not-too-distant future we'll be using artificial intelligence to help us process homicides, from the location all the way to prosecution, letting us avoid the nasty bits. Maybe AI will take over completely. Think about the manpower it would save if a suspect was able to say "No comment" to a computer programme rather than having to say it to a couple of expensive CID officers like me and Uncle Sauce. And then there's juries. AI won't be secretly prejudiced against anyone who winds up in the dock. It won't resent being forced to spend days in court listening to sordid details being spelled out in language that it doesn't understand. It won't rush to judgement just to get the hell out of there. And as for judges! They . . .'

Her diatribe was interrupted by her phone's soothing tone. She picked it up and saw from the country code that the caller was based somewhere in Spain. As she accepted, her assumption was that it was the man from the consulate, but a female voice proved her wrong.

'Detective McClair,' it said, 'my name is Núria Alabau. I am a manager of Banco Sabadell in Madrid. Senor Greaves from the consular department in the British Embassy called me about the account you are trying to trace.'

'Yes,' she exclaimed. 'Are you authorised to talk to me?'

'I am,' Alabau confirmed. 'It is not something I would normally do without an official request through the *Policia Nacional*, but Senor Greaves said that you are investigating a murder, so I am pleased to help in any way I can.'

'Thank you,' McClair replied. 'What I need to do is confirm the name of the account holder, and the contact details that you hold for him. The homicide victim is a man named Gavin Ayre, and he used this account to pay a bill, rather than the sterling account in Jersey that he normally used.'

'Then someone else paid that *factura* for him. The holder of the account you are asking about is Senor Gilbert Land. He is a Canadian citizen with *residencia* in Spain, with the identification number x1162323h. His *direccion*, his address, is *Masia Coll* in Riudaura, in the *comarca*, the district, of Garrotxa in Girona province in Catalonia. *Masia* means farmhouse, roughly, but that does not mean he is a farmer. It is a common name for a large property. I look at the account details and I can see an international payment to an entity called Lloyd and Price. That is the only item that I would call exceptional, but there have been large amounts paid recently to suppliers. From these I would say he has spent a lot on the property over the last few months. The rest is the normal, *facturas* for the local taxes, light, phone and wifi, and bills, supermarkets, shopping. He has one of our credit cards as well as his debit card, but that is hardly ever used.'

'Is there anyone else named on the account?'

'Do you mean does he have a partner? No, he is the only account holder, and the documents for the *facturas* are all in his name alone. What else can I tell you?' Alabau wondered. 'The account has been open since January, two weeks before he bought the property for two million euro. It was opened with a transfer of four million, from a bank in the Cayman Islands, and since then there have been further deposits totalling three million. The current balance is just over one and a half. But, Detective, none of this makes you any the wiser about your murdered man. All it tells you is that someone else paid one of his bills.'

'Maybe,' McClair conceded, 'but it does give us somewhere else to look. Senora Alabau, are there any other payments or transfers that might be significant?'

'None that I can see.'

'When was the last activity on the account?'

'The payment to Lloyd and Price,' the banker replied. 'That is on the account itself,' she added, 'but there was a small transaction on the credit card, two weeks ago.'

'Do you have a location for that?'

'Yes, it was a purchase in a shop called Bershka, in a place called Espai Girona.' McClair heard a soft gasp. 'That is funny,' Alabau murmured. 'I am looking at the activity on the credit card account and I see that someone else has been trying to track down the holder details.'

'They have?' McClair exclaimed. 'When?'

'Twelve minutes ago; but they did not get very far. The store requested more detail on the holder from the card management centre, but it's not clear why they did this. It may be the card was stolen and misused. Senor Land may have asked for details of the transaction. Who knows? You have competition, Detective, or you have another mystery on your hands.'

Thirty

'I didn't get far, I'm afraid,' Bob Skinner confessed. 'The store manager was very helpful, but all she could do was feed a request into the issuing bank's credit card department, but there's no guarantee it'll get a result.'

Sauce Haddock grinned at the frustration in his eyes, apparent even on the tablet screen. 'You couldn't expect anything else, Gaffer, not really. I mean some bloke walking in off the street speaking pigeon Spanish . . .'

'Fuck off, boy,' Skinner growled. 'My Spanish is better than your English. I did ask her if store security included video cover of the payment point. She said it does but she doesn't know how long it's kept. But, it's done by a contractor company, Servidor. As it happens, Servidor also provides perimeter security to the Inter-Media office building. I'll have someone talk to them tomorrow and see if they can help you out.'

The superintendent nodded. 'A happy coincidence, hopefully. And here's another. As for the holder of the credit card, I know that already.'

'How, in God's name?'

'Through Noele McClair. She pleaded with me to let her work on the investigation. She's been running checks from home and one of them threw up a lead, to another account used by Ayre to pay his architect. It's the same one that the Bershka credit card goes back to.'

'Well done, DI McClair,' Skinner exclaimed. 'How did she make that link so quickly?'

'Through the Madrid embassy and a very helpful banker. But,' he continued with a pause for emphasis, 'it's not Ayre's account. It belongs to a Canadian ex-pat called Gilbert Land, whoever the fuck he is. He lives in a big house in an area called La Garrotxa, close to a city called Olot.'

'I know it; it's out beyond Figueres. High country, quite spectacular.'

'Tomorrow, I'll have someone speak with the Canadian High Commission in London to see what they can tell us about him. And one other thing,' he added, 'a slight digression but one that might interest you. I told you about the clothing we recovered in Ayre's bedroom?'

'Yes.'

'Well, that indicates a close personal relationship between Ayre and its owner in more ways than one.'

'What are you saying?'

'That there's nothing like keeping it in the family!'

'Fuck! This case is full of surprises.'

'Too right. Anyway, Noele got a lot of info about Land's bank account. There's a few million in it, the source being a Cayman Islands bank. Tomorrow we'll talk to its manager as well as the Canadians.'

Skinner laughed. 'Who will tell you they've never heard of him. Sauce, pause and think about what you've told me. Gavin Ayre, the dead man with the false passport nobody knows any-thing about. Gilbert Land, who paid one of Ayre's bills. Ayre,

Land, both first initial G. I wonder if there's a George Ocean out there as well.'

'Billy.'

'What?'

'Billy Ocean. There's a singer called Billy Ocean. Forget the G and maybe he's the link. After all, when the going gets tough . . .'

'Fuck off, Sauce,' Skinner repeated. 'Red light spells danger.'

Thirty-One

'Is my dad going native in his new Girona apartment?' Alexis Skinner asked her stepmother.

Sarah Grace Skinner laughed. 'You might say that. He's becoming more Catalan by the week. You're right, he likes it there. L'Escala's too busy for him in the summer months. When we were there with the kids in July he spent most of his time on the golf course, because the town, he says, makes him claustrophobic. Plus, the rowdier element of the tourist population can push his buttons.'

'Tell me about it,' Alex said. 'When I was about twelve, he and I were down in the marina in a café, when a loud-mouthed English yob in a bunch of the same came out with some language. Pops told him to wind it down. The idiot got up, puffed out his chest and came out with "What you going to do about it, mate?" I remember looking at him, and actually feeling sorry for him.'

'I'll bet,' Sarah murmured. 'I haven't heard this one. What happened?'

'Pops picked him up and threw him off the jetty that we were on, into the sea. Quite far, too. Then he chucked a lifebelt in after him, turned to his three mates and asked if any of them could swim.'

'He hasn't changed,' her stepmother sighed. 'Worse, I think he's raising his son in his image. I'm trying to exercise a little influence. Jazz is his own man, well, he's his own boy, but I'm trying to teach him to take an extra second to consider his options, trying to lengthen his fuse.'

'And how's that going so far? Pops told me about the Yellow-craig incident.'

'Let's say it's a work in progress,' Sarah sighed. 'But,' she continued, 'speaking of men with slow fuses, how are you and Dr Jackson getting along on your first trip as a couple?'

'We're not a couple, Sarah,' Alex retorted. 'I know that everyone's too polite or too scared to ask me but, for the record, we are not shagging. I may post that on Facebook. He's my best friend and I'm his; we agreed a long time ago that it's not worth putting that at risk. Dominick is celibate by choice. At the moment so am I. If I want to change that I will make other arrangements, if you get my drift. As we are, when I get my tits out by the pool it doesn't bother him at all. I think I'd notice if it did.'

'I get it. I'll rephrase my question. How are you two friends getting along?'

'Very well, thanks. It's been good for us both. For Dominick especially. He's been to L'Escala before, remember, in another life when he was literally someone else. It's made him confront the man he used to be, and lay any last vestiges to rest.'

'That's good. I'm happy for you both.'

'Is that why you called?' Alex challenged, lightly. 'To satisfy your step-maternal curiosity?'

'Not entirely,' Sarah replied. 'I was wondering if you'd heard from your father.'

'Not recently, no. Why?'

'He called me a few minutes ago, asking if it was okay for him to spend another couple of days in Spain. He said he wanted to call in on you and Dominick. He said something about planning a trip in-country and wondering if you'd like to go with him.'

'How intriguing.' She paused, as her phone sounded an alert. 'Incoming call,' she exclaimed, 'and guess who it is? I'd better take it. Bye Sarah.'

Thirty-Two

'What does it mean,' Chief Constable Neil McIlhenney asked, 'this second identity that the man Ayre seems to have had?'

'As the late great David Francey may or may not have said during a Radio Scotland football commentary,' Mario McGuire, his deputy, replied, 'Fuktifano. But the first task is to prove for the purposes of the investigation that they are one and the same.'

'How are they going to do that?'

'We need a facial of Land to see if it matches with the body we have in the morgue. As a first step DI Noele McClair's been tasked with contacting the Canadian High Commission to see what they can tell us about Gilbert Land. Lowell Payne's people managed to establish that Ayre created his identity in the classic manner, by stealing it from a real child who died in infancy, through his birth certificate. It may be that the Land profile was done in the same way.'

'We don't actually have a Canadian passport in our hands?'

'Not yet. That's McClair's job. The link to Canada came through the Spanish bank. Noele's informant also said that he had residency in Spain, which obviously he couldn't get without showing proof of identity. Unless the banker was mistaken, he'll have a Spanish identity card too.'

'How easy will it be for McClair to access that?' McIlhenney wondered.

'A fucking sight harder than it will be for an InterMedia journalist making inquiries about a possible link between the holder and a murder in Scotland. If there's a photo on record, it'll do the same as the passport. It'll show us whether he's our man Ayre or not.'

'Jesus, Mary and Joseph and the wee donkey too!' the chief exclaimed. 'Are you telling me that Bob Skinner's involved in a criminal investigation?'

McGuire nodded. 'What did he teach us about doing what was expedient rather than just doing what the rule book says?'

'. . . as long as it's legal and won't land you knee deep in shit in the witness box. I seem to remember him adding that.'

'True, and this is. Look he's there, and he's got resources that we don't. I know you're hesitant about us being seen as too close to him, but remember another of his buzz words . . . pragmatic.'

'I never quite worked out what that meant.'

'It means, in Bobspeak, if it works it's okay. So let's thank him for his journalist's time, and for the access he's getting for us to the security footage of the store where that garment was bought, the one in Ayre's house.'

McIlhenney sighed. 'Aye okay. Thanks, Bob.'

'And for the other thing he says he's going to do.'

'What other thing? No, don't tell me! Here's one of my buzz words, mate . . . deniability.'

Thirty-Three

'Pops,' Alex said. 'Should I be worried about you?'

Her father stared back at her. 'No, why would you be?'

'You're not impulsive, normally. Your life's all planned out. It's not like you to turn up anywhere with only an hour's warning. You're not having a mid-life crisis, are you? You're spending more and more time in Spain with your job. Now, with buying the penthouse and everything, I'm wondering . . .'

'You're wondering whether I've got a bit on the side in Girona? Granted, I've got form in that respect, but no I haven't. I'm absolutely devoted to Sarah, having learned that I can't function properly without her. You're wondering whether I prefer living alone rather than in a house with a workaholic wife, four growing kids, a nanny and a dog? No, I don't; I love being surrounded by them. Darlin',' he drawled, 'I know guys in Gullane who catch the Heathrow shuttle on a Monday morning and fly back on Friday after working in the City all week. I do the same, only I'm away for a few days as a rule, plus I travel in much greater comfort. As for buying the apartment, everyone in the business got a commensurate performance bonus last year; I wasn't going to take mine, but Xavi insisted. I've always believed that property is the best long-term investment, so . . .' He turned to the third person at the poolside table. 'What do you think, Dominick? You're an eminent psychologist. Am I starting to unhinge?'

Dominick Jackson leaned back, his bulk straining the chair in which he sat. 'Mid-fifties,' he murmured. 'High pressure job in an industry that's still new to you, unexpectedly wealthy, naturally volatile; all the ingredients of a classic crisis profile. Only,' he added, 'I don't see any sign of it. You'd be having your crisis if you weren't doing all these things, if you were a retired senior police officer with nothing to do but play golf and read the *Scotsman* in the clubhouse.'

'I never read that fucking paper!' Bob interjected. 'Not since the independence referendum.'

'Okay, make it the *Saltire*, but you hear what I'm saying, and so do you, Alex. Your lifestyle gives you stability. Yes, it's perpetual motion, but that's what you've always known and it's what comes naturally to you.'

'See?' Bob turned to his daughter. 'Vindication.'

'You're still frustrated,' she insisted. 'This exercise, for example. You pitch up here with hardly any notice, demanding that we come with you on an expedition. But you haven't told us what it's about.'

'I was getting to that. Tomorrow morning I want to check out a property, an address that might be linked to the murder investigation that's going on back home.'

'You see?' Alex exclaimed, to the skies. 'Frustrated! You can't let go! You're still coming to terms with not being a cop any longer, and failing most of the time. Isn't that right, Dominick?'

'That's one interpretation,' the seated giant replied diplomatically.

'Fine,' Skinner declared. 'Are you coming with me or not?'

'Of course, we are,' she shouted back at him, then looked at Jackson. 'Aren't we, Dominick?'

'Well,' he said, slowly. 'I think it might be better as a father and daughter outing. You're a lawyer so you can advise him against doing anything that might be a shade illegal when you get there. If you fail and he goes ahead with it anyway, I couldn't be any-where near, for reasons I need not spell out. I'll have dinner ready for you when you get back . . . if you get back.'

Thirty-Four

Noele McClair was in Tesco, pushing Matilda in an adapted shopping cart, when her phone sounded. She thought about letting voicemail take it, then remembered how long it had taken her simply to leave a message at the Canadian High Commission. Tapping her earpiece, she accepted; at once she knew she had made the correct decision.

'Is that Detective Inspector McClair?' a crisp female voice asked. 'My name is Nadine Markle, vice-consul. You left a message asking for assistance with an on-going investigation, is that correct?'

'Yes, it is. We're trying to trace a Canadian citizen by the name of Gilbert Land. He overlaps an investigation into the murder of another man.'

'You mean he's a suspect?' Markle asked, caution in her tone.

'No, I don't, not at all. He's the holder of a bank account in Spain and he's said to be a Canadian citizen officially resident there. That's all we know about him for now. We're checking the Spanish end, but we also need to confirm his citizenship with you.'

'How much can you tell me?'

'Little more than the name. However, we're operating on the assumption that he would be in his early thirties.'

'That's all? A thirty-something male and you want us to find him among thirty-seven million people?'

'That's right,' McClair confirmed. 'But I should tell you that we believe the likelihood is that you won't.'

Thirty-Five

'Detective Superintendent Haddock?' the caller began.

Sauce frowned. 'Yes, but how did you get this number?'

'I was given it by my colleague, my boss really, Sir Robert Skinner. My name is Hector Sureda and I am the chief executive of InterMedia. Bob asked me to have one of our reporters check something out, and to pass the information straight to you when we got it.'

'Okay, thanks,' Haddock said. 'Understood and I appreciate it. What do you have for me?'

'Just this; confirmation that a man named Gilbert Land, a Canadian national, has been officially resident in Spain since October last year.'

'That helps, but . . . does his residency card include photo identification?'

'For *etranjeros*, no it does not. My reporter also tried to establish whether he had a Spanish driving licence. Legally he can drive in Spain with a Canadian licence and an international permit, but after that he would need the Spanish licence. That would have a photograph on it, but there's no record of him having applied for one. However,' Sureda added, 'he does own a vehicle. In Spain we pay our car taxes not to the State but to the community in which we live. In his case that would be the *Ajuntament de Ruidaura*, and there we found one listed to Land's address. The people there gave my reporter the number and she was able to match it with an SUV, a Nissan X-trail, bought from a dealer in Olot in April. That's as much as I can tell you for now, Senor Haddock. If you need anything else, let Bob know. However,' he paused for a second, 'you know him. It may be that he'll come up with some answers himself. *Adios.'*

As the call ended, Haddock frowned again: out of curiosity until he understood Sureda's inference. *Answers? Oh my God. He can't keep his hands off.*

Thirty-Six

'Are you sure you have enough charge?' Alex asked a little nervously as they drove quietly up the mountain road.

'Mr Musk says this model will give me five hundred kilometres,' her father replied. 'We have three quarters of that left.'

'Are you sure? I don't share your faith in electric cars.'

Her father laughed. 'I've had faith in you for over thirty years and you've never let me down.'

'Oh no? What about when you found out about me and Andy?'

'I never blamed you,' he replied. 'I blamed him. I still do; making a move on a friend's teenage daughter was never going to sit well with me.'

'Has it ever occurred to you that I might have made a move on him?'

'Did you? Make the first move?'

Her brow furrowed. 'I can't remember, truth be told. I think it was probably a case of us both having the same idea at the same time.'

'Doesn't matter; the principle's the same. He shouldn't have, end of.' He sighed. 'Actually, the person most to blame is me. I knew what Andy was like with women.'

'A bit like you, you mean? You and Alison Higgins were

together when you had your fling with Mia and my half-brother Ignacio got made.' Her sigh was almost a match for his. 'I liked Alison,' she murmured. 'I liked Mia too, but I could see from the start that she had a bit of darkness about her.'

'The widow McCullough, as she is now. And Sauce Haddock's stepmother-in-law. What a complicated tree we're growing.' He glanced at her sideways. 'Now that we're up here, alone, something I've been meaning to ask you. Have you got plans to add any branches? Short-term or long?'

'Christ, are you on about me and Dominick too? First Sarah, now you?'

'No,' he protested. 'I wasn't thinking about him, or about anyone in particular. It was a general enquiry.'

'Then the answer's no,' Alex insisted. 'You and Sarah keep producing babies for me to nurture, but I'm quite happy to leave them at the end of the day and go back to my place, or to Dominick's. I don't see it in my future, Pops.'

'These things can happen by accident. Just like Nacho did.'

'Not in my case. I might be living a quiet life but I'm still on the pill, just in case Dominick and I forget ourselves . . . not that we ever have,' she added. 'Aunt Jean calls him my "handbag", you now.'

'That sounds like her,' Bob said. 'For the record,' he added, 'I don't care if you do. You make a nice couple.'

'Have you told him that?'

'Hell no,' he laughed. 'However, you being with him should stop Andy Martin sniffing around again, should he ever think about it.'

'Don't be so sure. He called me when he was elected to the Scottish Parliament. Sir Andrew Martin, MSP, potential Tory leader. I'm not sure what he wanted really. A pat on the back or an invitation for dinner when the Parliament's in session . . . and he's on the other side of the country from Karen.'

'What did you tell him?'

'Congratulations but we won't be bumping into each other. That was pretty much what I said. I think I added that he'll be too busy on the Opposition front bench to have any leisure time.'

'Yeah,' Bob drawled. 'Maybe busier than he thinks. The political editor at the *Saltire* gave me a tip last week. After she lost her Westminster seat in the last wipe-out, Aileen is thinking about a comeback in Holyrood.'

'As in Aileen de Marco, your ex-wife? Wow! What will Sarah think about that?'

'Sarah won't spend a minute thinking about her.'

She stared at him. 'What fucking planet are you from, Pops? The woman split you and Sarah up first time around! Of course, it'll get her attention.'

'Then she needn't worry . . . if I even have to, I'll tell her that. Besides, as far as I know Aileen's still with Joey Morrocco, the actor, the guy she was seeing while we were married. Plus,' he added, 'if she does return, she'll be fully occupied undermining the current leader of the Scottish Labour Party. She'll want her old job back.'

'What did you ever see in her, Pops?' Alex asked. 'Apart from the obvious, that is.'

'Her eyes. That was the first thing I noticed about her. I thought they were honest and kind. But I ignored or I underestimated one fundamental: she was a fucking politician and they all work on looking honest and kind. It's part of the trade; being all things to all people.'

She grinned. 'You could say that about defence counsel too.'

'Maybe,' he conceded, 'but you're a prosecutor now. How does that work?'

'We work on looking severe. You know that from experience in the witness box. But,' she added, 'my stint in the Crown Office ends in a month. They asked me to stay on for another year, but I will probably say, "No thanks". I've been lucky so far, I never had to prosecute someone I believed was innocent. I'd have had trouble if that had . . .' She stopped in mid-sentence. 'Hey, that sign we just passed, didn't it say *Masia Coll*? Back up, Pops.'

Skinner did as she instructed for a hundred metres until they reached the sign she had spotted, on a post that was topped off by a post box. It was small, but clear: the address and an arrow, angled upwards beside a narrow opening that led into a *cami*, a narrow road without tarmac. 'Shit,' he murmured. 'Not the best surface for this thing. We should have brought the Jeep from L'Escala. Sorry, love, it could be bumpy.'

He drove carefully along the winding road, looking out for ruts in the rough roadway, but happy to find none serious enough to impede their progress. They climbed slowly and steadily for fifteen minutes, until finally they reached a thirty-degree bend at the end of which *Masia Coll* came into sight.

'My God,' Alex murmured, 'what a view.'

The house stood on a summit facing west, with an outlook across a spectacular wide canyon, rivalling its grand equivalent in America in its geology, if not in size. A low fence seemed to mark the boundary of the plot on which the *masia* was built but there was no gate, simply a point where the *cami* became yellow-dyed concrete. The Tesla cruised silently towards the red stone building, coming to a halt twenty metres from the heavy studded wooden entrance door, alongside a patio which opened out into a swimming pool. As they stepped out, Skinner glanced towards it; the water was dark, almost black.

'Nobody's been here for a while,' he observed, 'or the pool guy's doing a terrible job. The algae have taken over.'

'It feels deserted,' his daughter said.

'If I'm right about Mr Land, and the two names aren't just a massive coincidence, we know where he is.' He reached back into the car and blasted the horn, shattering the silence of the mountain top. 'If there is anyone around, that should fetch them.'

They stood by the car and waited. Each of them was dressed in the same way, shorts and a T shirt. The sun was at its highest in the sky, but the temperature was less fierce than it would have been at sea level.

'What are we going to do now?' Alex asked. 'All in all, I don't think I fancy a swim, so what's the grand plan, Pops?'

As she spoke her father straightened his back, his gaze bypassing her. She turned to see a white-haired, lean, leather-skinned man approaching. '*Ningu aqui,*' he called out. '*L'home fa dues setmanes que no es aqui. La dona durant deu dies.*'

'*Qui ets?*' Skinner asked him.

'*Josep, el vei. I tu?*'

'*Amics de la cuitat. Massa dolent, va dirque seria aqui. Ens refredarem una estona abans de marxar.*'

'*Be, adea.*' The man turned and shuffled off, disappearing into a small plantation behind the *masia*.

'Well?' Alex demanded.

'His name's Joseph; he's the neighbour. Says there's nobody here, hasn't been for a few days, since the woman left. The man's been gone for a fortnight. I said we were friends from the city, that we'd chill for a while then go.'

'I'm impressed,' she said, 'although "chill" isn't a word I'd have used. What are we going to do?'

'Have a look around. We haven't come all this way just to admire the view.' He set off, walking beyond the pool. The area beyond was flat, almost unnaturally so, as if the land had been levelled off or built up. She saw him stop, look around, then make a whirling motion with his left hand as he strode back towards her. 'That's a helicopter pad round the corner,' he said as he reached her, 'out of sight, with a big X for landing. I need to call Girona.' He stepped away once more as he took his phone from his cargo shorts. She saw him find then call a number, hearing a buzz as he made a connection. 'I've asked Hector to have our reporter find out if there's a chopper registered in Spain to Gilbert Land, and if so, where it is right now.'

'Maybe he uses an air taxi service?'

'If he does, we'll find it. Come on.' He headed for the *masia*'s front door.

'Pops,' she called after him. 'You're not thinking about breaking in, are you? Although we're in Spain, I'm still an officer of the court.'

He stopped and turned to face her. He was smiling. 'Of course not, but if this place happens to have a keypad entry system like the one in Scotland and I happen to know the code, I'll regard it as an invitation.'

'And does it?'

'Yes, what do you think that box is on the doorjamb?'

'And do you know the code?'

'No, but Sauce Haddock told me the one for the Scottish house. If Gavin Ayre and Gilbert Land are one and the same, how likely do you think he is to have two?'

'I don't want to know,' she moaned as he reached the door.

He took out his phone once again, checking the code that Haddock had texted to him, then entered the numbers slowly and carefully, smiling as he ended with 'two' and the door swung open.

As it did, Alex saw him stiffen, then hold up a hand. 'Don't come any closer!' he shouted, as the forerunners of a swarm of heavy black flies buzzed past him out into the open air. He closed the door firmly and took a step back. 'Got any tissues?' he called out.

'No, sorry. Pops,' she exclaimed anxiously. 'What is it?'

Skinner's mouth was a tight line, his face screwed up in the vain hope of expelling a foul odour from his nostrils. He stripped off his T shirt, used it to wipe every surface he had touched, each number on the keypad, one by one but out of sequence, then backed away until he was beside her.

'What?' she repeated.

He shuddered. It occurred to Alex that she had never seen her father so shocked, even though they had shared some bad moments in her lifetime. 'What do you think?' he murmured.

'Is it Land?'

'Could be, if he and Ayre aren't one and the same. It could even be the woman. From the very quick sight I had, I can't rule it out, but I don't think so. My instant impression was male. Who-ever it is, whatever it is, it's been there for days. There's no aircon running so the place is like an oven, even though the shutters are down. You saw the flies, but this is fucking Spain, so there'll be ants as well, millipedes and Christ knows what else. Come on,' he said, sharply. 'Back to the car. I need water and I need to gather myself. Christ, love,' he muttered as they walked, 'I must be going soft. I've seen people blown to pieces, like Alison, I've seen them burned to a crisp, like Jackie Charles's wife, I've picked bits of them off moorland after a plane crash, but nothing has ever got to me like that.' As they reached the Tesla, he pulled his T shirt back over his head.

Inside the car, they were silent for over a minute. Alex watched her father as he leaned back against the headrest, eyes closed, sipping water while he strove to regain his composure. It occurred to her that for the first time in her life she was seeing what he was, a man in his middle years, experiencing the first loss of confidence that ageing can bring, a man realising perhaps that he was no longer invulnerable. And then his eyes opened wide and he was Bob Skinner again.

'Right,' he declared. 'What are we going to do? One thing for certain, I never opened that fucking door. Agreed?'

'Absolutely.'

'Part of me is saying, let's get the hell out of here and let Sauce follow due process, ask the *Mossos* to check out the address, and let them discover that frightful thing in there, or what's left of it. Half of it will be in a fucking anthill by then, if it isn't already. I think he might have burst, from expanding gases.'

'He?' Alex repeated.

'Yes, I am sure it's a male. I'm back together; I know what I saw. If it is a man called Gilbert Land, he was older than our Gavin Ayre. The body was angled towards the doorway, so all I really saw was the head. White hair, although there was a dark streak that might have been blood. Left arm thrown out, right by his side. Short-sleeved shirt, that could have been blue at one time but it's stained now, as you don't want to imagine.'

'The blood,' she said. 'Could that have happened in a fall? Might he have had a heart attack, a stroke, or even a simple faint in the heat and hit his head on something as he fell?'

'If he crawled for a bit afterwards,' he conceded. 'He wasn't near anything that would have done anything like that. Watch,' he said, suddenly, 'he was wearing a watch, a gold Rolex Submariner. I'm sure of that; remember Eden Higgins? Alison's brother? He had one; the dead guy's was the same.'

'What are we going to do, Pops?' Alex asked. 'Get out of here like you said and toss it back to Sauce in Edinburgh?'

'I would, but . . . we've been seen here, by Joseph the neighbour. Sooner or later, somebody's going to talk to him and he's going to remember the friends who came to visit. So I'm going to make a call to my friend in Barcelona, the politician who oversees the *Mossos d'Esquadra*. I'm going to tell him that the Girona paper has been investigating a tip from an anonymous source about a resident ex-pat named Gilbert Land. Because I was in the area visiting you, I volunteered to check out the address. Now we're here, I find that the place is deserted, that the pool is black with algae and that there are signs at the back that someone's been trying to force an entrance.'

'So maybe they'd better check it out?'

'Exactly.'

'What about the signs of an attempted break-in?'

He grinned. 'Once I've made the call, I'll take care of that small detail. Meantime, you'd better call Dominick, and tell him we might be late for dinner.'

Thirty-Seven

'I'm surprised,' Nadine Markle told Noele McClair. 'My search for Mr Gilbert Land took hardly any time at all.'

You're right, the surprised detective thought. *I'm only just home from Tesco.*

'You found him?' she asked.

'My passport office did,' the vice-consul confirmed. 'In all of Canada, there is one passport held by a citizen of that name, just one. It's due to expire in nine months' time, but by then the holder may have expired himself. Mr Land is ninety-one years old. His listed address is number seven Acorn Hill, Oxbridge, Ontario. The rest I did myself. I found him in the online telephone directory and called that number. His granddaughter answered my call. Grandpa Land is a resident in a Toronto care home and has been for the last eighteen months. Does that help you?'

'It does,' McClair said. 'Very much. On the basis of that success can I ask you for one more favour? Can you check your death records over a period of let's say five years, with the midpoint thirty-four years ago, for an infant or childhood mortality with Gilbert Land on the death certificate?'

Thirty-Eight

'Why did you ever leave the police service, Gaffer?' Haddock wondered aloud, his voice crisp in the car speakers.

'Not again,' Skinner growled. 'I didn't leave it, son. It left me when it started serving the penny-pinchers rather than the people.'

'Maybe Andy Martin will take us back to the old set-up if he ever becomes First Minister.'

'There's more chance of Dean Martin doing that. Andy was the first beneficiary of the new system, the first chief constable of all Scotland, so he won't turn the clock back . . . not to mention that he's a Tory, and as such unlikely ever to be First Minister.'

'Who's Dean Martin?' the superintendent asked.

'Fuck me.' Reminded of his age, Skinner sighed. In the seat beside him, his daughter smiled. 'Never mind that,' he said, testily. 'Do you hear what I'm saying to you? If not, I'll repeat it. You need to make official, high level contact with the *Mossos d'Esquadra*, and tell them you have an interest in a resident ex-pat named Gilbert Land in connection with an on-going murder investigation. Give them the address and tell them that you got the details from Land's bank. Do not, whatever you do, mention

147

me. Your interest in Land should appear to be entirely separate from the local press interest.'

'You said you've made a call already,' Haddock pointed out. 'Won't that have made a connection?'

'No, it won't. My contact's a member of the Catalan government. He knows me only as the chair of InterMedia, an organisation he needs to keep on his side politically. Listen, on second thoughts, don't you make that request; get McGuire or McIlhenney to do it, chief to chief. The point is, sooner or later, the timing being dependent on the skills or the equipment of the responding officers who'll be on their way here right now, the house that we're sitting outside is going to be opened. When it is, all hell will break loose and a major criminal investigation will begin, one that I'm certain's going to overlap with yours. You need to be part of it, Sauce, from the start. You need to have a presence in that house, but it'll probably take somebody of chief constable or deputy rank to make that happen. Understood?'

'Understood.' They heard Haddock pause. 'You've been in there already, Gaffer, haven't you?' he ventured.

'I haven't put a foot over the door, Sauce, and that's the truth. But I do know what they're going to find. Don't ask any more, okay? You don't want to compromise either of us.'

'Do you want to phone the chief yourself,' the superintendent asked, 'and ask him to make the contact?'

'Fuck no, Sauce. Neil would wet himself. You do it, and do it now. I can hear sirens in the distance . . . these boys do like to let the world know they're coming . . . and I don't want to have to explain myself to a couple of junior plods, as they probably will be.'

'Okay,' the detective said. 'I'm just wondering who I should send out there,' he mused. 'If we do need to have feet on the ground, whose should they be?'

'They should either be yours or be attached to someone with enough seniority to get respect,' Skinner replied. 'If you're asking, I can think of somebody who fits the bill.'

'Tarvil?'

'No,' he chuckled. 'It's your decision but the person I mean has a much heavier tread than his.'

Thirty-Nine

'The Chief Constable's office passed on your request, Detective Superintendent,' Deputy Chief Constable Mario McGuire announced over the video link. 'The chief has no problem with it, but he's delegated the job to me. I speak fluent Italian and my Spanish is passable, so it makes sense.'

Haddock nodded.

McGuire grinned. 'Between you and me, Sauce, of the two of us, Neil and me, I've always been the fixer. Even back when we were plods, when they called us The Glimmer Twins after the Rolling Stones, mostly we made joint decisions, but it was my job to get things done. He used to say I was a better communicator than him, but it wasn't that, it was more that people found it easier to say "No" to him . . . apart from Olive, that is.'

'Who's Olive?'

'His first wife; the one who died. I brought them together, you know. I was going with a girl from an insurance company at the time and I asked her if she had a mate who might make it a foursome with Neil. He was reluctant; he was always a bit shy, but on the night it was as if me and Magda weren't there. When Olive went, I thought it might have broken him but Bob Skinner and I got him through it, us and his kids of course. I'm their godfather,' he explained. 'I couldn't take Olive's place, but I spent a lot of time with them after she went. Then Neil met Louise and the whole course of his life changed. She lived in a world that's basically driven by ambition, and it rubbed off on him. People who don't know, think of him as aloof but he's not: private yes, precious no.'

'How old are his kids now?' Haddock asked.

'Lauren's twenty-one, at university. Spencer's just about there too. That's if he doesn't get side-tracked by professional sport. He plays cricket; Scotland under eighteens. I'm trying to encourage him to go to Loughborough University, where he can combine sport and study. So, Sauce,' he squared his shoulders and straightened in his chair, 'what's the pitch I have to make to the Catalan cops?'

'In summary,' the superintendent replied, 'the Gavin Ayre homicide investigation has thrown up a link to an entity in Spain, a bank account from which one of the bills for the construction of the house in East Lothian was paid. The account holder is a man named Gilbert Land, allegedly a Canadian resident in Spain. The name by itself aroused suspicion, and we were able to establish very quickly with input from the Canadian High Commission that, like Gavin Ayre has proved to be, it's a false identity. The Spanish bank has been co-operative. As in Scotland, large sums of money have been deposited from abroad and invested in a multi-million-euro property. We believe that Ayre and Land might be one and the same, but without visual confirmation, we can't prove it. We hope to find that in the Spanish house, when it's opened, as it will have to be. The *Mossos d'Esquadra* need to be alerted to that link between Ayre and Land, and the fact that Ayre's been murdered, but they know already that Land's identity is questionable.'

'How do they know that?' McGuire asked.

'The Spanish media have been looking into him . . . following an anonymous tip-off.'

The DCC winced. 'Do I want to know which branch of the Spanish media?'

'Probably not,' Haddock murmured, his face dead-pan.

'Shit. Now you understand why I'm the fixer. Is there anything else that I don't want to know?'

'You're probably best to be unaware that a media representative checked out the property itself, and that as a result the *Mossos* are there now. They won't be able to effect an entry without specialist equipment and, I believe, a warrant from a judge, but my understanding is that when they do get in a criminal investigation will begin and will link very quickly to ours.'

'Therefore we need to be part of it? That's the case I make to the *Mossos* commander?'

'Yes, that there needs to be mutual cooperation. Spain gives us access and we do the same with them.'

'Feet on the ground?'

'Big feet, sir. I'm thinking DCI Mann. I know she isn't part of the Ayre investigation, but she can be brought up to speed.'

'Does Lottie speak Spanish?'

'I doubt it, but that would be their problem, just as it might be ours to provide a translator for anyone they send here.'

'Okay, Sauce. I've got all that. You are sure there's nothing else that I don't need to know?'

'That's all I know myself, sir.'

'If I didn't know better,' McGuire ventured, 'I might think that your informant might have done something that's slightly illegal and didn't want to involve you in it.' He frowned into the camera before adding, 'One more thing, Sauce, and this comes from both the chief and me. Why did you bring this directly to us? ACC Stallings is Serious Crimes' line manager. Why have you broken the chain of command? Were you told to?'

'With respect, sir,' Haddock said, 'I make my own operational decisions, whatever advice I might be given. In this case, I felt and still do that the chain needed to be as short as possible.'

The DCC nodded. 'Right answer, Sauce. It is too long and not only today; we appreciate that. ACC Stallings will be reassigned; from now on you report on all investigations directly to me. I'll make the call and get back to you. While I do that, tell Lottie Mann to pack her sunscreen, and . . . get her uniform out of mothballs. In my experience the police in Spain aren't big on plainclothes detectives.'

Forty

'We got out of there just in time,' Alex said. 'Rather than go back the way we'd come we took another route back to L'Escala. We were on the road for less than a minute when a *Mossos* patrol car went bombing past us going in the other direction. It had blues-and-twos full on even though it was open countryside and there was hardly any traffic apart from us.'

'What do you expect will happen next?' Dominick asked.

'Pops reckoned that there was no way those guys would get into that house. Even if they had a ram in the car, he said, it would never get that door open. They would need special equipment, or they would need the keypad code.'

'Which he had?'

'Yes,' she confirmed. 'It was the same as the code for Gavin Ayre's house that Sauce had given him. It sounds as if the security systems were identical in both places. Meaning for sure that Ayre and Gilbert Land are, or were, one and the same.'

'And Ayre is dead in Scotland?'

'Stone ginger; his brain's in a glass jar in Sarah's pathology lab.'

'Did your dad have any idea who that could really be in the house overlooking the canyon?'

'None at all; I'm certain of it.' She looked at him across the outdoor dinner table. Around the garden citronella candles burned, keeping the mosquitos at bay. Three places had been set, but only theirs remained occupied, Skinner having left for Girona as soon as he had finished the meal, which they had eaten in near silence.

'He sure as hell did not want to talk about it tonight,' Dominick observed.

'No, and not just because he didn't want us to know anything we don't need to. I'm sure that he didn't want what he saw in that house to get back in his head. I've never seen him so shaken. Christ, I've never seen him shaken at all. Should I be worried about him, do you think?'

Jackson shook his head. 'If what he saw was that gross, you should probably be relieved that he reacted in that way.'

'Will he be okay tonight?'

'If I thought he wouldn't I'd have persuaded him to stay. But he's still the toughest guy I've ever met. Okay, for the first time he's let someone else . . . other than Sarah, maybe, or your mother . . . see a chink in his armour, but he'll deal with that. He said that he expected another phone call and that it might be better if he was in Girona when it happened. I'd take that at face value.'

'Mmm,' Alex murmured. 'Maybe just as well he's gone,' she said. 'I couldn't do this in front of my father.' She rose from the table, pulled her ankle-length pale blue dress over her head, took four short steps towards the pool and dived in, naked.

'Oh bugger,' Dominick sighed. He stood, unbuttoned and discarded his shirt, and followed her.

Forty-One

'How are Alex and her friend?' Sarah asked.

'Tanned, relaxed and very comfortable in each other's company,' Bob declared. 'If you ask me, I'd say that I've never seen her as contented in all of her adult life. She's not chasing anything any longer; when she was with Andy Martin or any of her other flings, she was always restless, never able to take any time out just to be herself. She's content now, it's as simple as that.'

'And are you content? About her and Dominick, I mean? You know his back story better than anyone. Are you completely okay about the two of them together?'

'They're not together,' he protested, 'not in that way. You said it yourself, they're friends.'

'Granted, but don't you think they ever . . .'

'That's their business, end of story.'

'Have you ever asked her? Directly?'

'Of course not.'

'No, and why not? Because you know she can't lie to you, and you don't know how you'd handle it if she said yes.'

'Bollocks! I'd be fine with it.'

'You weren't fine with Andy.'

'That's different. Anyway, they're not. She told you so.'

'Yes, but she could lie to me, if she chose.'

Bob laughed, only to be interrupted by the sound of his entry system. 'What the . . .' he murmured. 'Love, there's someone downstairs. I can't think who it is, but I'll need to check it. Speak tomorrow.'

He closed his laptop and crossed the open living space to the door. The evening light was almost gone. Enough remained for him to see a male figure, but the features were indistinct. 'Yes?' he said, into the active microphone.

'Senor,' a voice replied. As its owner moved closer to the street camera, Skinner saw dark eyes and a neatly clipped beard. 'I am security for Senor Mateu. He is in Girona tonight and wondered if you are free for him to come up.'

Skinner's eyebrows rose. Manuel Mateu was the security minister in the Catalan Government, the acquaintance he had called to trigger the interest of the *Mossos d'Esquadra* in the Gilbert Land property in Riudaura. He was a smart politician and understood the value of a healthy relationship with the head of the autonomous region's most influential media group. 'He's welcome,' he told the minder. 'You and the driver as well, if you wish.'

'Thank you but no. We will stay on the street. You understand why.'

He did: the pro-independence Mateu was generally accepted as the real power within the ruling Catalan party, a man who was happy to be leader-in-waiting, for the time being. As such he was potentially a target for the extreme Right nationalist faction that had been growing in Spain. Skinner pressed the buzzer that unlocked the door.

He was in the lobby to greet the minister as he stepped out of the lift. Manuel Mateu was in his mid-forties, ten years younger than Skinner, of medium height, lean, tanned and with a black moustache. He had been a regional official at the time of the unilateral declaration of independence that had led to intervention by Madrid and the imprisonment of the Barcelona leadership. Mateu had been detained briefly himself by the *Policia Nacional* but had narrowly escaped prosecution, leaving him free to grow his influence and his personal power base. An economist by profession, his early career had included a few years in London with a merchant bank, making him the most fluent English speaker in his party.

'Good evening, Bob,' he said. 'I checked with your office that you were still in Spain. I was pretty certain of that from the location of your call this afternoon but it was always possible that you had stepped straight on to your private jet and got the hell out of town.'

Skinner smiled as he led his visitor to his sitting area. 'The private jet's in Italy, so that would have been a long step. Why would I have done that anyway?'

'Possibly to avoid being detained as a material witness?'

'A witness of what?'

'Of whatever is in that house you said I should bring to the attention of the Mossos. You chose your words carefully: "A member of your staff had checked the place and become suspicious," if I recall them accurately.'

'The location of my call,' Skinner murmured. 'You traced it, Manuel.'

'Of course we did; that's automatic. 'We don't have a secret service as such, but we do protect our Catalan national security from threats at all levels.'

'I'm glad to hear it. We do the same in Scotland, although we don't regard London as hostile.'

'Anyway,' Mateu continued, 'we both know that you were the InterMedia staffer who checked out that house. The fact that the commander of the *Mossos* had a call an hour or so later from your Deputy Chief in Scotland registering an interest in the same property, that suggests to me that you might know what my people will find when the judge allows them to go in there.'

'Would you like a drink?' Skinner asked, blandly. 'If you want a beer it'll have to be Corona, but I do have a decent Albarino.'

'Corona will be fine. You can skip the lime.'

He crossed to the kitchen area, returning with two bottles of the Mexican beer, one with a wedge of lime in the neck. He handed the other to Mateu. 'The most practical thing I can tell you is that the place appears to have the same entry and security system as a property in Scotland that belonged to a man named Gavin Ayre, whose murder is currently under investigation. The *Mossos* might want to check the entry code with them before they go knocking things down.'

Mateu swigged his beer, a thin smile playing with the corners of his mouth. 'Couldn't you just tell them?'

'Fuck off, Manuel,' Skinner chuckled.

'Who was he, this man? And how does he relate to the property in Riudaura?'

'The investigating officers would need to tell you that. My role in this has been . . . let's say peripheral. I've been something of a mentor to the SIO in Scotland; he still bounces things off me sometimes.'

'Hence your reporter's interest in the man named Gilbert Land? The owner of the Riudaura house?'

'Maybe.'

'Should the *Mossos* agree to Mr McGuire's request to second an officer to the investigation? Should we send one to Scotland?'

159

'Yes, they should. Has he given them a name?'

Mateu nodded. 'Mann. Detective Chief Inspector Charlotte Mann.'

Sauce can still read my mind, Skinner thought. 'I know her,' he said. 'A good choice. She tried to chuck me out of a crime scene once.'

'Did she succeed?'

'She might have if I hadn't been her acting Chief Constable. Lottie is, as we say in Scotland, as tough as fuck. She once insisted on entering a police boxing night; the only woman on the bill. Flattened her opponent inside a minute.'

'I'll warn my people to treat her with respect. What about us having someone in Scotland?'

Skinner shrugged. 'Up to you.' He frowned. 'Why are you so interested in this, Manuel? Okay, I reached out to you, but I didn't expect you to become so involved.'

'You tripped a switch,' Mateu replied. 'As I told you, we have our own security apparatus. We cast an eye over ex-pats with residency in Catalunya even though we're not part of the registration process. We've never been a major destination for foreign hoodlums . . . too cold, they all prefer the Costa del Sol . . . but we don't want to become one. So yes, Gilbert Land was on a list of people whose movements we monitored. When my people heard that your reporter was asking about him, we stepped up our interest. We're still waiting for confirmation of his identity from Canada.'

'You should be talking to his bank.'

'We are. So is a Detective Inspector McClair, I am told.'

'Is she indeed? Noele's on maternity leave, but she found the body of the Scottish victim. I guess she felt a personal connection, asked to be involved.'

'But what would send her looking for Land through his bank?'

'Again, that's something you should ask Scotland.'

'Okay, I'll pass that on. I'll make sure that Detective Mann is given a good reception and shown every courtesy.' Mateu finished the remaining half of his Corona in a single swallow. 'You'll keep me in touch?'

'With what?' Skinner asked. 'My former junior officers who're now in charge of the magic fucking roundabout that is our Scottish national police service, they like to be seen to be their own people. They keep me at arm's length . . . or they try to. I can understand why, for the same reason that the Girona *Mossos* are wary of InterMedia. We own the *Saltire*, the most influential newspaper in Scotland. They don't want to piss off the others by being seen to be too close to us.'

'I understand too,' the politician admitted. 'In fact that policy comes from me.' He stood. 'Time for me to go. My guys downstairs have homes to go to.'

'Yeah.'

They moved towards the door; as they did, Skinner said quietly, 'Manuel, it occurs to me. DCI Mann speaks fairly broad Glaswegian, but neither Catalan nor Spanish. You'll need two interpreters, not just one . . . unless . . . I could spend another couple of days in Girona. I'm good in both your languages, and I went to school in Glasgow. I could do the job, if you want.'

The security minister looked up at him. 'You old cops,' he murmured. 'I'll tell the *Mossos* that you're available . . . but not to mention it to Scotland!'

Forty-Two

'Are you packing your bikini?' Dan Provan asked.

The force of Charlotte Mann's glare threatened to set the curtains on fire.

'Maybe not then,' her partner laughed.

It was generally agreed that Dan and Lottie were the unlikeliest couple out of many whose lives had come together through their police service. He had been her detective sergeant, her supervisor, during her early years in CID. With no wish to rise above that rank he had stood aside, watching her pass him on the promotion ladder, then spending the final years of his career as her back-up. For most of that time, the years after his wife's departure and their divorce, he had been viewed as a dishevelled and slightly disreputable character and had been prepared to live down to that image. Then an extended break to visit his daughter in Australia had seen him taken to a clothing store other than Marks and Spencer, to a proper hairdresser and finally to her gym, where he had surprised himself and her by the underlying level of his fitness. The transformation in him was such that Lottie had not recognised him at first, when she met him at Glasgow Airport. Within a fairly short time she had realised that she liked the new model Provan in a way she had never imagined.

A few months later, she and her son Jakey had moved in with her newly retired sergeant and the Glasgow policing world had tilted on its axis.

He watched her as she folded her summer-weight uniform and laid it on the bottom of her case. 'Why?' he asked.

She shrugged and made a wry face. 'Because Sauce asked me to. He said the Spanish don't do plainclothes. Everybody's got to know who's a cop.'

'I know a couple of Rangers fans who found that out the hard way in Osasuna a few years back. Are you taking your equipment belt too?'

'He didn't say, so I'll take that as a "no". I doubt that I'll be pepper spraying anyone.'

'*Aerosol de pimiento*,' Dan exclaimed.

'What?'

'Spanish for pepper spray.'

'How the hell do you know that?'

'I've been studying Spanish on the QT,' he confessed. 'I've had this thought that when you've retired and Jakey's off to university we might move out there . . . that's assuming I've still got some mileage left by then.'

'Thanks for sharing,' Lottie said.

'I'm sharing now. What do you think?'

'Honestly? I've never thought about retirement. In my head, I haven't got beyond getting Jakey through university.'

'I can help with that.'

'His dad will help with that, or his rich parents will, the cu . . .'

Her partner looked at her from the bedroom doorway. 'It's none of my business,' he said, 'but . . . would it be in Jakey's interests to take a penny from those bastards?'

'Fair point,' she conceded. 'He'd probably be better off

without their hooks in him. Anyway, they've got another grand-kid now, thanks to Scott and his new woman; their pride and joy, I heard. Jakey never even got a card from them on his last birth-day.' She closed her case and secured it, using the combination lock. 'That's me,' she announced. 'Y *viva España*.'

'What time's your plane take off? You never said.'

'I'll be leaving early doors,' she sighed, wincing. 'Sauce promised to send a car for me, one way or another. It could be a taxi or it could be a patrol car, but whatever, I have to be ready for an eight o'clock pickup. They've got me on an EasyJet from Glasgow to Barcelona. I'll need to be at the airport for nine to check in the suitcase, even though the flight's not until eleven. That'll mean I'll be in Barcelona between two and three with the time difference. They'll meet me there; take me to the scene, I suppose.'

'To do what?' Provan asked. 'This has all happened so fast. What the fuck's it about?'

'There's an investigation in Edinburgh that Sauce has been overseeing,' Lottie replied. 'Dead guy on a beach, shot in the head: you might have read about it in the red tops.'

He nodded. 'I did, but there was precious little information there, not even a name. What have you been told?'

'Only that there's a possibility it links to an incident in north-ern Spain. Sauce said that's liable to be major and that we need a senior presence there from the start. He's sending me the file on his investigation; I'll read up on it on the flight.'

'Not tonight?'

'No, my love,' she said, shaking her head. 'I don't know how long I'm going to be away, so the rest of today is ours. Are you sure you'll be all right looking after Jakey? This is going to be a surprise for him when he gets in from football training.'

He smiled as he lifted her case from the bed. 'Why would I not be? We'll be fine, the pair of us. If you're still there come the October holiday week we'll maybe come out and join you.'

'Fuck me,' she cried out. 'It won't be that long, surely not.'

'I had that in mind,' he said, his grin widening, 'just in case. You never know with these international inquiries . . . especially now we're not in the EU. They can drag on.'

Lottie frowned. 'Sauce told me to pack for a week,' she admitted, 'but he did say he couldn't be sure how long the gig would last. Come on,' she said. 'Let's get downstairs and eat.' At the foot of the stair, she added, 'By the way, when I'm away, the two of you, you have to eat right. No Chinese takeaways; no pizza boxes in the recycling when I get back. No Tesco ready meals. Understood?'

'Understood,' Dan agreed, his fingers crossed behind his back as she led them into the kitchen. 'You'd better show me how it's done.'

She shook her head. 'Oh no,' she declared. 'It's your turn. Tuna steaks I believe, with broccoli. No garlic though,' she warned. 'Given your promise earlier on, I don't need that on your breath.'

He opened the fridge and selected the ingredients. 'I suppose,' he said, as he laid them on the work surface, '*el elefante en el cuarto* is you not speaking Spanish. How will you all cope with that?'

'Sauce said the *Mossos* would provide a translator. Their schools are still on holiday, so he guessed they might hire an English teacher.'

'Let's hope he or she can understand a fucking word you say. You can take the girl out of Maryhill and all that . . . What about accommodation?' he asked. 'Where are they putting you up?'

'I don't know that either,' Lottie admitted. 'In a hotel I suppose.'

'Won't they still be rammed in August?'

'I'll find out when I get there. As long as it's not a police barracks. I'd draw the line at that!'

Forty-Three

'*Gracias por venir, senor,*' the Servidor manager said.

'*De nada,*' Skinner replied. 'I realise that you're doing me a favour. It wouldn't have been reasonable to expect you to come to me. What do you have to show me?'

Linda Andreas frowned. '*Poco.* Very little. At the *tiempo,* the time, you gave, *la tienda,* the shop, *estaba muy occupada, pero* . . .'

Looking over her shoulder at the screen, he could see that it was indeed very busy. The throng was made up almost exclusively of teenage girls. Almost. There was one at the till who was older by at least ten years, probably more. The footage, which was monochrome and jerky, showed her proffering a card and touching it to a contactless terminal. The angle of the camera did not provide a full-face image; he could not judge whether there was enough to be run through facial recognition software, but she appeared to be fair, both of hair and skin tone.

'*Es todo,*' Andreas said. 'Is all. I can send to your phone, *Senor,* si *lo desea,* if you . . .'

'*Si, por favor,*' he said, nodding. '*Mi numero es quatro quatro* . . .' He recited the number slowly, then waited. A few seconds later successive beep tones told him that a WhatsApp message had arrived. He nodded. '*Muchas gracias.* I'll find my own way out.'

Rather than call Haddock from his car, he waited until he was back in his office. They were connected at the second attempt, by which time Skinner had forwarded the Servidor footage clip.

'How close is Girona from Riudaura?' the superintendent asked him.

'You wouldn't go there to buy groceries,' he replied, 'but if you were clothes shopping and were fussy, it's probably your nearest option. I know there was a woman living in the house; the one in that image is shopping with Land's bank card, so there's a reasonable assumption that it's her. You'll need to share it with the Mossos, but do it tactfully.'

'I know that much, Gaffer,' Haddock said. 'I don't want to come across as a smartarse, that's what you're saying. I've got Lottie on the way there as we speak; last time I checked there was a short flight delay but she should be in the air by now. What I don't need is to antagonise the *Mossos* before she's even touched down. So far we're good. I had a call from the commander, Major something. He expects the judge to give them authority to enter this afternoon. The plan is they open the place tomorrow morning. I've sent him an image of the entry system in East Lothian, and Ayre's entry code.'

'He'll be your friend if he finds it works.'

'If, Gaffer?'

'Of course. How would I know whether it does or not?'

'Yeah, right,' Haddock sighed. 'Do you know if they've found an interpreter for Lottie yet?' he asked.'

'Yes, they have,' Skinner confirmed. 'Not just that; he's going to meet her at the airport.'

Forty-Four

DCI Lottie Mann's suitcase was bright yellow and embla-
zoned with a large Saltire; unlikely to be taken by mistake from
the carousel, even by a totally colourblind passenger. However,
that carried no protection against it being the last to appear
through the hatch. Border control had taken fifteen minutes, followed by twenty-five in the baggage hall before the canary case
appeared. By that time, she was hot, irritable, and sending evil
thoughts in the direction of Sauce Haddock.

She wheeled her bag into the toilet and freshened up before
the mirror, wondering whether two uniform shirts would be
enough for her stay, as she slipped on her light cotton jacket, covering the sweat patches beneath her armpits. When she felt ready
to make an appearance, she stepped through the exit doors into
the sunny concourse.

Until that moment she had given no detailed thought to the
manner of her reception. Her assumption had been that she
would see a person in *Mossos* uniform, and had familiarised herself with its form by studying the website of the Catalan force; she
had not considered that she might be met by a taxi. There were
perhaps twenty people facing the doorway through which she
had emerged. She scanned them, looking for her name on a sign,

but saw nothing. She checked her watch. Her flight had landed ten minutes behind schedule. That, added to the delay in the baggage hall, meant that she was running an hour late, enough, she conceded, for her pick-up to have gone for a coffee or a comfort break, or possibly to have lost patience completely and given up.

Her forehead was ridged as she decided that the last of these possibilities was most likely. She reached for her phone, where she had stored an emergency contact number, and was about to locate it when she became aware of movement to her left, of a tall figure in shorts and a collarless shirt, with a takeaway coffee in each hand.

'Hello, Lottie,' Bob Skinner said. 'Welcome to Catalunya.'

Her frown disappeared as she gasped. 'Sir,' she murmured, 'what the hell are you doing here?'

He shrugged, handing her one of the coffee beakers. 'What does it look like I'm doing?' he replied. 'I'm picking you up. This way.' He took her suitcase, extending its handle and wheeling it behind him as he set off.

'That's good of you,' she acknowledged, feeling the heat instantly as she followed him out of the cool covered concourse, walking towards a small parking area around fifty metres away, 'but why? Are the *Mossos* that short-staffed?'

'Call me a civilian volunteer,' he told her as they walked. 'They're not short-staffed, but they're not rich in English speakers either. I said I'd be your interpreter and Major Teijero thought it was a good idea.' Actually, Skinner had no indication that was true, but he did know that a suggestion by Manuel Mateu was invariably taken as a directive.

Mann smiled. 'So do I,' she confessed. 'For how long?' she asked.

'A couple of days,' he replied. 'We'll see where we are after that.'

'Well, thanks but, sir . . .'

Skinner held up the hand holding his coffee, cutting her off. 'Look, you've got to get over that. I've given up trying to get Sauce Haddock to call me Bob, but I won't with you. I'm not a cop any longer: also I'll be helping you informally so let's keep it that way.'

'What does Sauce call you?' she asked. 'He's my boss now, so . . .'

'He calls me Gaffer. He reckons its Scottish for Guv'nor.'

'I like that,' Mann said. 'It works for me too.'

'Okay,' he conceded, 'but I don't know why it needs to work for either of you.'

'The fact that you don't makes it even more appropriate. Anyway . . . Gaffer . . . what I was going to ask was how you came to be involved in this?'

'Who says I am?' Skinner protested. 'I'm just doing a friend a favour.'

'Come on, I'm not buying that.'

'Okay, I offered Sauce a bit of informal help. It was mutual; my paper's getting a story out of it.'

'And the place we're going to?' Mann asked.

He replied with another question, 'You've been briefed about Gavin Ayre?'

'I read the file on the flight. It didn't tell me anything about a Spanish connection.'

He stopped beside a Tesla. She recognised it as a Model X; her son Jakey was a Tesla expert. 'The connection is a Spanish bank account that was used to pay one of Ayre's bills for his East Lothian house. The holder's a man named Gilbert Land. Before the *Mossos* got involved I had one of my reporters look into him.

The name connection is obvious, and the more we found out about him the less likely it became that it's a coincidence.'

'And this house that I've been told about?'

'We're going there tomorrow; you need to be there when the *Mossos* open it up.'

'So I've been told, but that's all. Why?'

'Officially? You're looking for photographic evidence, probably a Canadian passport, maybe a driving licence. Something that'll prove Gilbert Land and the late Gavin Ayre are one and the same.'

'And if they are? What's it all about, Gaffer?'

'That's anyone's guess at this stage, but mine is that it's about money. The best way to hide it as well as the best way to invest it is by turning it into property. If that's the case, the underlying question will be, what's the source?'

'Drugs?' Mann suggested.

'That would be the likeliest answer,' Skinner agreed opening the boot of the Tesla and stowing her suitcase one-handed.

'Where am I staying while I'm here?' she asked.

'Tomorrow we'll probably find you a hotel. Right now, we're heading for my place in L'Escala. My daughter and her friend are there, and she's expecting us.'

'Alex?' she exclaimed. 'That's great. It'll be good to see her again. I'm still grateful for the way she helped me when Scott and his parents tried to get custody of Jakey. "Her friend", you said?'

'Dominick Jackson.'

'The psychologist?'

'That's right.'

'Friend,' she repeated but with a question in her tone.

'That's what she tells me. If there are benefits involved, well . . .'

Mann smiled, eyebrow raised. Then her expression changed. 'You said "officially" about the place we're going tomorrow,' she observed. 'What about "unofficially"?'

He returned her gaze with a faint smile. 'Unofficially? You should stand well back when they get the door open.'

Forty-Five

'Is that the best they can do?' Jackie Wright asked as she looked at the printed image. 'It looks almost like an Identikit.'

'Compared with what I was sent,' Sauce Haddock told her, 'it's a portrait. It was taken off security footage from a camera that was a few years old. It's a bonus that we've got anything at all.'

The original had been digitally enhanced, with colour added, to produce a photograph of a woman, halfway between full face and profile, with a fair complexion and lustrous blonde hair; she was around thirty, the superintendent guessed, with a couple of years' margin for error in either direction.

'What do you want me to do with it?'

'Identify her,' he said.

The DS stared back at him, restraining laughter. 'That simple?'

'If possible,' he added. 'We have her in Girona, using the credit card from the account that links to Gavin Ayre. We see her buying a garment that was found in Scotland, but we don't have her wearing it. She may be an employee, sent to buy it for the woman who actually wore it, who we believe has a half-sibling relationship to Gavin Ayre. Or she may be that woman. If she is, she was in Scotland, leaving a DNA sample in Ayre's wardrobe.

All we can do is show the photo around Gullane, Dirleton, North Berwick, see if anyone recognises her. You and Tiggy, you do that.'

'How about the restaurant where Ayre was seen with his girlfriend?'

'Yes, there too. You should go back to Mrs Hornell as well, although it's a long shot.'

Wright nodded. 'Will do. That's a weird one right enough,' she said. 'His semen being found in his half-sister's pants.'

'You're making an assumption, Jackie,' Haddock pointed out. 'We only have a familial link to the bikini thong. We don't know for sure that the knickers belonged to the same woman. Hornell says they're not hers, fair enough, but Ayre could have had a pla-toon of girlfriends apart from her. The only thing that's certain is that the sister was there.'

'No, Sauce, if that's her in the photo and they've got the enhancement right, there is one other certainty.'

He frowned, puzzled. 'And what would that be?'

Wright grinned. 'It's right there in the lab report from the Crime Campus,' she replied. 'In common with ninety per cent of the woman I've encountered so far in my journey through life . . . she's not a real blonde!'

'In that case,' he laughed, 'you'd better show the photo in Boots and all the other chemists, just in case her roots started to show when she was here.'

Forty-Six

'He's a deep one, that Dominic Jackson,' Lottie Mann observed as Skinner turned on to the C31 highway, heading for Figueres. She had been silent since they left his house after a quick breakfast.

'Yes, he is,' he agreed. 'But the question is, do you like him?'

'Yes, Gaffer, I do. I doubt that I'd have liked the man he was before, but this version is calm, hyper-intelligent, thoughtful and caring. Also he worships Alex and the ground that she walks on, but he's careful not to let it show.'

'Why not, do you think?'

'Because he's got massive respect for you. Have you ever read *The Godfather*?' she asked.

He smiled at the unexpected question, glancing to his right, catching her eye. 'I've seen the movie, more than once. Why?'

'Because Jackson strikes me as Luca Brasi to your Don Corleone. You should read the book, don't just be happy with the film; it has more depth. The character is much more developed there. Don Vito is the man Luca respects more than anyone else in the world, the last man he would ever want to kill him. That's how Dominick sees you . . . it's why he hides his feelings for Alex.'

'Are you telling me that I'm a mafia boss?' he laughed.

'In another universe, you probably are.'

'And you? What are you in that universe? Chief Constable? First Minister?'

'Me? I'm a hudden doon big lump that stayed at home and kept house while her crooked husband walked all over her until he pissed off with a better prospect.'

'In consequence of which she put an axe in his head?' he suggested.

'Maybe,' she agreed, 'but not until her son was grown and able to fend for himself.'

'And Dan? Where does he figure?'

'He doesn't, not in that one. Dan only belongs here. He's a one-off, an intelligent, caring man who spent years pretending to be an apathetic idiot. I'm the real idiot for not seeing through the disguise before I did.'

'And in this one,' Skinner asked, 'what happens with Dominick and Alex?'

'How would I know, Gaffer?' she replied. 'I don't tell fortunes. I only deal with the present. Like, for example, I can see right now he's not a hundred per cent well.'

'What do you mean?'

'There's something about him, the careful way he moves. Did you notice the plaster on his finger last night?'

'Yes, he cut himself chopping the lettuce.'

'Yes, and not for the first time. When he and I shook hands, he winced. I saw another recent wound on another finger, and maybe another couple of scars. A wee bit later on I saw him on the move; for a second I'm sure there was a very slight tremor. I didn't say anything to Alex, though,' she added.

'No, best not,' Skinner agreed. 'Are you certain? I've never noticed anything like that. How come you did?'

177

'It's my job, Gaffer,' Mann said, 'noticing things. And I never switch off, I'm always on duty.'

'In that case,' Skinner sighed, 'you're a better detective than I ever was.'

Forty-Seven

'No,' the counter assistant said. 'I can't say I recognise her. Mind you, I don't serve everyone who comes in here.'

'Okay. I wasn't expecting any other response, really,' DS Jackie Wright acknowledged. 'The photo isn't the best, and I know how busy North Berwick gets in the summer.'

'Tell me about it,' the man sighed. 'Try parking here in the winter, let alone just now. Those exclusion zones in Edinburgh? They've got it all wrong; they should be starting out there.'

Wright expressed her sympathy with a nod; she was parked on a yellow line. She had left a 'Police business' card displayed, but even that did not guarantee protection from a parking warden intent on filling a quota of tickets issued.

She left the pharmacy, the last of the frustrating calls she had made in the seaside town. Seated once again in her un-ticketed car, she took out her phone and called DC Benjamin. 'How are you doing, Tiggy?' she asked. 'Any better than me?'

'No, Sarge,' her young colleague replied. Wright could hear road noise in the background and a hands-free echo. 'I've done everywhere in Gullane, the chemist like you said, both golf club-houses and all the bars and restaurants . . . including La Potiniere.

It might have helped if we'd had a photo of Gavin Ayre as well, but I doubt it.'

'We could have had,' Wright said, 'but there isn't one where he looks anything other than very dead. Where are you now?' she asked.

'I'm on my way to Dirleton, to the Castle Inn.'

'I'm ready to leave North Berwick, so I'll meet up with you once you've done that. It occurs to me that there's one place in Dirleton that I forgot to put on the list; the Open Arms. I'll see you there.'

The DS connected her phone to CarPlay, then eased slowly into the traffic, under the glare of a parking warden in a hi-viz jacket with an open notebook. Waving him farewell with her idle finger extended, she made her way steadily along the High Street in a line that was moving at well below the twenty-mile speed limit. It picked up a little pace after the traffic lights, but it was not until she reached the filling station at the outskirts of the town that she was able to put her foot down.

When she reached the Open Arms, Benjamin was waiting for her, standing by her car on the opposite side of the road beside the ruined castle, a monument that had been closed to the public by its own servants, on grounds of health and safety. Wright turned into the last available space outside of the hotel and waited for her young colleague to join her. 'This doesn't need the two of us,' she said. 'There's a café back there, where I came in. You go down there and get us a table. Mine's a flat white, by the way.' Benjamin rubbed her thumb and fingers together. The sergeant sighed and handed over a ten-pound note. 'And a slice of million-aire's shortbread if they've got it,' she added.

As the DC left on her mission, Wright entered the hotel, by the main entrance rather than the door that led directly into the restaurant. There was a reception area on the right; it was empty, but after a few seconds a man appeared, compact, neatly dressed and with a manner that said 'Welcome', without any need for the word to be spoken.

'How can I help you, Officer?' he began.

She stared at him. 'How did you know I was police?' she asked.

'When you've been in this business for as long as I have,' he replied, 'you just know. Plus,' he added, with a small shy grin, 'ten minutes ago I had a call from a business friend in Gullane telling me that a CID officer had asked him if he could identify a woman in a photograph. He thought you might be heading this way.'

She smiled back. 'That's an effective grapevine you have. I'm DS Jackie Wright, and this is the photo in question.' She produced the print from her pocket and held it in the beam of a ceiling light. 'I don't expect you'll have seen her, but we have to ask. She could be connected to a major investigation.'

He stepped closer to her, peering at the photograph, studying it for some time. 'You know,' he murmured, 'I may confound your lack of expectation. I think I may have seen her. Here. Yes. I have.'

'Are you sure?' she exclaimed.

'Yes.' He nodded. 'I am. The hair colour I'm not sure about, but it's the angle of her jaw that I recognise. She was here a couple of months ago; on June the twenty-second in fact. I remember because she and I had a discussion about whether that was the longest day of the year or whether it's the twenty-first. They ate in our Library restaurant, she and her companion.'

'Can you put a name to her?'

'I should be able to. It'll be in the book and it'll be the last on the list because they got the last table. Come with me, Sergeant.'

He led her through a lounge, into the restaurant she had seen from outside, and then to a small antechamber with a coat rack and a bar counter, on which she saw a large diary with the year engraved in gold on the cover. He picked it up and flicked through the pages, until he found the date he was seeking.

'Black,' he read. 'Geraldine Black, it says, table for two, Lib . . . short for Library. She was American.' He smiled. 'It doesn't say that, but she was.'

'Who paid?' Wright asked.

'He did,' the hotelier replied. 'If you're going to ask if I have a record of the transaction, well I do, somewhere, but it won't give you any more information. He paid in cash. Crisp fifty-pound notes, three of them. I remember that because he told the waiter to keep the change; the bill was about a hundred and twenty.'

'The man,' the sergeant ventured. 'Was he tall, fit, in his mid-thirties?'

He shook his head. 'No, you're way off the mark there. She was in her thirties but he was grey-haired, bulky, and least twenty years old than her, probably more. Old enough to be her father, I would say.'

Forty-Eight

'I'm beginning to regret having to wear this uniform,' Lottie Mann confessed. 'Your car's nice with its air conditioning, but I'm liable to melt when we step outside. That might not be a pretty sight.'

'You'll be fine,' Skinner reassured her. 'We're a few hundred metres above sea level here; that makes a big difference to the air temperature. Plus, it's late August; we're heading into autumn.' He glanced to his right. 'The uniform's about respect, Lottie; it saves explaining to everyone what you are, and those three pips on your shoulder tell them you're not to be messed with.'

'Do you wish you still had yours?' she asked.

He laughed. 'Why? I'm your driver and your translator, that's all. Anyway,' he continued, 'how many times did you see me in uniform back then?'

'Not very often, I'll grant you.'

'Like never,' he said firmly, 'in the brief period I was chief in Glasgow. In Edinburgh, only when the Queen showed up, God bless and keep her.'

'You said it was about respect. Didn't you want that?'

Skinner smiled, wistfully. 'Respect has to be earned among your peers, Lottie, for it to matter. It isn't something you wear.

183

You know that as well as I do. I like to think that when I was in the police I had some. I'll tell you this; any officer who disrespected me had limited career prospects, even the odd one who might have been senior to me at the time. There was a bloke called Jay in the Edinburgh days. Somehow he made it to chief super before I overtook him, but his sins found him out in the end. See,' he laughed, 'I'm flawed: piss me off and I take it personally. Ask me to hole a two-foot putt on the golf course and you've made an enemy for life'

'Luckily, I don't play,' she reminded him. 'What about here, in your new life? Is that different?'

'No, it isn't. The same principle applies. I have a sign on my office door in Girona that says I'm the *jefe*, the boss. It means eff all. I know that when Xavi withdrew from the chair and asked me to take over, the guys on the shop floor so to speak, the rank and file, had no idea who I was. They do now. Senior management? With one or two exceptions, no more than that, they thought I was just the boss's mate, drafted in to hold his jacket while he went for an extended toilet break. I had to prove to every one of them that I could actually do the job, that my time as chair of the UK subsidiary had counted for something. I had to prove it to myself too, although I like to think that if I'd had any doubt that I could do the job I'd have turned it down. Now, I'm settled into the chair; it fits me, my senior colleagues can see that, they treat me accordingly, and word has trickled down. And yet, it's still a temporary appointment, it could end tomorrow if Xavi chose to return. It's his company.'

'Will he? Choose to return?'

Skinner shook his head. 'I doubt it. He's happy as the supreme leader in exile, so to speak, like that old Chinese bloke was, the one after Mao. It suits him. His name, *Aislado*, in English that means isolated, alone, and it's always been fitting. No, he'll stay on the estate that his brother Joe left him, and I'll hold the fort until Paloma, his daughter, has enough experience to take over. And you know what?' he exclaimed. 'That suits me. I've grown into the job, Lottie, and to be completely frank, I want it to go on for a few years yet. Commuting is easy, so I can spend half my life in Scotland with the family and in the holidays they can come over here. I was at a loose end until this came up; now I have a future.' He gazed at the road ahead, as he took a corner and a long stone wall came into view. 'But back to the present,' he said. 'We've arrived.'

He turned the Tesla through an open gate and cruised slowly along the driveway. There was one other car parked in front of the *masia*. As he drew up alongside it, a woman in uniform appeared from the back seat. Skinner whistled softly. 'A *comissari*,' he murmured to Mann. 'The major's sent a deputy. This is being taken seriously.'

'Who?' she asked.

'Major Teijero is the commander of the Mossos,' he explained. 'I don't know this one, but her epaulettes say that she's a *comissari*, one level down from him. Come on.' He stepped out of his car, stretching to take the kinks out of his back.

'Good day,' the officer said in a crisp accent. 'I am Lita Roza. You must be Sir Robert. My boss said you had offered to give us assistance in this matter.'

'My pleasure,' he replied, turning as his passenger emerged. 'This is Detective Chief Inspector Charlotte Mann. She's a senior officer in the Serious Crimes division of the Scottish police service.'

'You think we have a serious crime here?' Roza asked.

'We know that the owner of this property is linked to one in

Scotland,' Mann responded. 'We think he might even be the victim,' she added.

'That is a big assumption, surely. Based on what?'

'Our dead man, Gavin Ayre, had a false identity,' she said. 'When your man, Gilbert Land, came up in our investigation, we looked at him and found that his is phoney too.'

The *comissari* nodded. 'So did we, after Senor Skinner's reporter started nosing around. We found the same.'

'Hopefully what's in that house will answer at least some of our questions. How do we get in?'

'Our forensic team are due here in the next three minutes,' Roza told her. 'I've been following their progress on Maps. In fact . . .' She paused, turning at the sound of tyres crunching on gravel.

A people-carrier pulled up ten metres behind them and an eight-strong squad emerged; two were in uniform . . . Skinner read their insignia; an inspector and a sergeant . . . the rest in sterile tunics. The senior officer moved to the door and pressed the entry buzzer. He waited for a full minute then repeated the process, to satisfy himself that the property was indeed empty.

'I can't imagine that you turn out at too many scenes like this,' Skinner said quietly to Comissari Roza, as they looked on.

'I don't,' she admitted, 'but when my boss gets a call from his boss and your name is mentioned . . . he has too much dignity to jump himself, so he sends his kangaroo.'

'I'd been wondering about your English accent. Am I right in what I'm guessing?'

She smiled. 'When I was a lieutenant, I spent two years on secondment in Sydney. The accent is all I gained from the experience, apart from a love of surfing that I brought home with me.'

'I don't imagine the surf's as good in the Mediterranean.'

'Very rarely,' she admitted, 'but my partner and I go to Morocco in the winter. Do you surf?'

'Only the internet. Are you going to open the house yourself?'

'No. I'll leave that to Inspector Avila, or one of the blue suits.' She issued an order in Catalan: the team moved towards the shuttered building. Roza, Mann and Skinner followed a few metres back; he stood behind the *comissari*, with a clear view of the entrance over her head.

He watched and listened as the inspector dictated a series of numbers to one of the SOCOs as they were punched in. He braced himself as the door swung open . . . to reveal a pristine cream-tiled floor where before there had been putrefying human wreckage.

What the f . . . he gasped inwardly. As the squad moved into the house, he moved forward without a thought for the two women. '*Luz*,' he barked, with such authority that the inspector turned on the lights instantly, flicking a switch by the door. '*Persianes*,' he ordered, and the powered shutters were raised, flooding the space with sunlight.

'Sir Robert.' Comissari Roza was by his side, 'is something disturbing you?'

He frowned at her, and at Mann, who was equally puzzled by his reaction. 'Look at the place,' he said. 'We know that there's been a very expensive refurb. We know it was lived in. But look at it,' he repeated. 'It's as if an estate agent's set it up to photograph it for sale. Look at that bowl. Is that fresh fruit? It looks like it. Look out there.' He pointed through a window to the pool. 'It's sparkling. Two days ago it was gone, almost black with algae.'

'How do you know?' Mann asked.

'I know because I was here, Lottie. I came with Alex to check it out. She'll vouch for the state of it.' He turned back to Roza. 'When I saw it just now, I assumed that the pool maintenance guy had been in since then. *Comissari*, I recommend that we all get out of here; then you get your top forensic team here . . . unless this is it . . . and go through this place. If they find a scrap of human DNA other than ours, I'll be amazed. I'm sure this place has had the cleaners in . . . and I'm not talking about people with squeezy mops and buckets, I'm talking about real cleaners, specialists, people who don't miss a thing.'

Roza stared at him. 'But why would anyone do that?'

'They'd do it,' he said slowly, 'because this was a crime scene.'

Forty-Nine

Sauce Haddock frowned. 'He said that?'

'Yup,' Lottie Mann confirmed, nodding in the direction of her phone camera.

'How did Comissari Roza react?'

'She was as taken aback as I was. But then he went on; he said that the owner of the house was known to have a false identity, therefore you could argue that it was a crime scene. Only he didn't say that. He said *"ergo"*. I don't know whether it's Spanish or Catalan, but I guess that's what it means.'

'I remember the Gaffer telling me he did Latin at high school. Some of it must have stuck. Where is he now?'

'He's gone back to Girona, to his office. I'm still at the house with Lita. She's taking me back there when we're done here. I don't need translation when I'm with her; her English is probably better than mine.'

'To where? Where are you staying'?

'At the Gaffer's Girona place for now. He's taken my case back there. Christ alone knows when we'll be done here, though,' she added. 'They're doing what he suggested, crawling all over the place looking for DNA traces.'

'Have they finished the search for documents?' he asked. 'Have they found anything that might show us Gilbert Land?'

'Yes to the first and no to the second. The house has been emptied, Sauce. There's nothing here. No personal papers, nothing in the fridge or freezer, no cutlery or plates or glasses, no table linen, no towels. Even the fucking toilet rolls are gone. The Gaffer's right; this place has been professionally sterilised. I can guarantee you right now, the forensic team won't find a single human trace in there. The DNA profiles that Dr Bramley sent them? They're useless because there won't be anything to compare them with.'

'What about Land's car? The Gaffer's colleague told me he had a Nissan off-roader.'

'That's gone too. The garage was empty when it was opened. Nothing, not even a set of spanners.'

'Did it have keypad entry like in East Lothian?'

'Yes,' Mann confirmed. 'Same code.'

Haddock's eyes narrowed. 'Were there any signs of forced entry? Either to the house or the garage.'

'No.'

'Is your *Mossos* friend Lita wondering how the cleaners got in? Has she got round to that yet?'

'I don't think so.'

'Then she should. Either they were able to override the code, or they knew it. If they did, how? It was set up by Lloyd, the architect. He told me, but I don't imagine that he shared it with too many other people. So, how did they know it?'

'Maybe somebody should ask Mr Lloyd,' Mann suggested.

'That's the first call I'm going to make once we're finished here,' the superintendent told her. 'The second will be to the installers, as soon as Lloyd tells me who they were. Are you close enough to the house to show me the keypad?'

'Yes,' she said. 'Hold on.' She walked the short distance from the poolside to the garage entrance, turned her camera and displayed the entrance system.

'It's the same,' he declared. 'Both systems were installed by the same Swiss firm, and yet as far as I know . . . although I'll have to check it . . . Lloyd wasn't involved with the Spanish property at all. Ayre just told him who to use on his. It makes me wonder . . . and again I'll check . . . whether whoever settled those invoices got the two accounts mixed up and there's a payment from Ayre's Jersey account going in the wrong direction.'

'Is that relevant?' Mann asked.

'We won't know until we find out, one way or the other. I'll contact the Jersey banker. Meanwhile, ask your colleague Lita if she can check who filed any necessary building applications in Spain. If there was an architect involved, maybe they can tell us what we need to know about the missing Senor Gilbert Land.'

Fifty

'This Ms Geraldine Black,' the Border Control official said. 'What's her nationality?'

'I think she's American,' Jackie Wright told her. 'I want sight of her passport, if that's possible.'

'I'm sorry, but there's no guarantee that she had her passport stamped. With a biometric passport US citizens can use the e-gates, as long as they aren't coming for business purposes. If they are, she'd need to have it stamped, and a record would be kept.'

'Would she have needed a visa?'

'No,' she smiled wryly. 'We're generous in that respect.'

'That means she could come and go and nobody need know about it.'

'Effectively, yes.'

'She wouldn't have needed a landing card?' Wright wondered.

'No, those were scrapped a few years ago. I'm sorry, Sergeant. If you were hoping I'd be able to pin this person down for you, that's not going to happen. You'll have to go to the airlines, and that's not a job you'll be able to do on your own. And that assumes,' she added, 'that Ms Black arrived by air. People arrive in the United Kingdom by land as well, through the Channel Tunnel or Northern Ireland. And by sea,' she added, 'officially or otherwise.'

The sergeant thanked her, sighing as she ended the call. She rose from her desk and walked across the squad room to Tarvil Singh's work station. He looked up as she approached. 'How are we for available people power on the Ayre investigation?' she asked.

'That depends on the importance of the job we're talking about,' he replied cautiously.

'A name's come up: Geraldine Black. The owner of the Open Arms in Dirleton identified her from the image that Bob Skinner got from his security firm. We believe she's the owner of that bikini bottom, the one we found in the Ayre house and traced to Spain. I need to check aircraft manifests for flights into Edinburgh before the twenty-second of June.'

'Why?'

'Because we need to find her,' she snapped, impatiently. 'Tarvil, we're short of living witnesses and she's one.' She took a breath, gathering herself. 'Plus, there might be another player. When she was in the Open Arms, she wasn't alone, she had a companion, and it definitely wasn't Gavin Ayre.'

Singh nodded. 'I'll give you two DCs in addition to Benjamin, for two days. If you haven't found her by then, you never will.'

Fifty-One

Nicola Tremacoldi looked up as his unexpected visitors entered his studio. Each was in uniform: one he recognised as that of the *Mossos d'Esquadra*; the other was unknown to him. '*Señoras, esto es una sorpresa. ¿Le puedo ayudar en algo?*'

'*¿Hablas inglés?*' the *Mossos* officer asked. '*Sería más fácil para mi colega.*'

'I have a little English,' he said. 'Not very good, but I can try. I am Italian,' he volunteered, as if that was an explanation.

'Mr Tremacoldi,' the other, larger, woman began, 'we believe that you were the architect on a project near a town called Riudaura.'

He nodded, scratching his light beard. '*Si. Masia Coll.* Yes, I am. I mean, yes I was. The project it is now finished. It was a real, how you say, challenge, to take a big important building that is almost two hundred years old and make it something for the new age, to blend together the old and the new. It was really a ruin, *un disastro*, we say in Italian. The client paid a lot of money, too much money, but now they have *una propiedad* that is worth millions.' He smiled. 'Is the first I ever work where there is a *helipuerto* in the *especificación*. I don't know if it will be used, but they want and the *terreno* allowed, so they have it.'

'Who supplied the entry system?'

'*Yo, lo hice.* I did it. The client wanted *alta seguridad,* top security. I know a *compañía* in Switzerland so I use them.' Tremacoldi grinned again. 'They like me now. The owner tell me they have *un otro pedido de Escocia,* Scotland, for the same system. Someone see it and they want exactly the same.'

'The client, Senor Tremacoldi,' the Catalan officer said. 'Gilbert Land. *Es importante que le hablemos.* We need to speak to him. Can you tell us where we can find him?'

The architect shook his shaven head, regretfully. 'No, I cannot. I have never speak to him. *Nunca lo he conocido.* Always when I meet, I meet with the lady. The lady American. *Su nombre es Black, Geraldine Black.* But I know he has been here. *Hace un mes,* a month ago, she call me to make sure that the *helipuerto* is safe and can be used. She say me it was important, *muy importante,* because Senor Land was coming.'

The other woman nodded. She moved towards the area of the studio in which photographs and models of Tremacoldi's work were displayed. 'There's nothing here about Riudaura,' she observed.

He sighed. 'That is true. *Me temo que nunca habrá.* I fear there never will. Always, I ask the client permission to display his property. Always they say "*Si Nicola.*" This time no. This time they say they need to *preservar la privacidad,* to keep it private. Is very shame, for it is work I have much pride in.'

He looked up as the Catalan woman raised a hand. 'The entry code for the property. *El código.* Do you know it?'

'Of course. *Naturalmente.* If I go there I need it.'

'Is it noted anywhere? Written? *¿Escrito?*'

Tremacoldi reached out and touched his iMac computer. '*Esta aquí,*' he said, 'and on my phone.'

'Okay, thank you. You have been a great help. *Usted has sido de gran ayuda*. I will call if we need to speak again.' She nodded to her companion and they left.

'They hacked his computer, didn't they?' Mann said, outside. 'To get that code. Whoever cleaned the place.'

'That would be a strong possibility,' Roza agreed. 'We need to focus on that helipad. A month ago, Geraldine Black, whoever she might be, was expecting a visit from Senor Land. A private helicopter transfer will have been logged. There will be a record and we will find it.'

'Let's do that,' the Scot agreed. 'Also, the Gaffer said something about an old neighbour showing up the first time he was there and being curious. The world is full of nosey old bastards, but they can be useful. Should we maybe have a word with him?'

Her colleague smiled. 'Indeed we should. I like working with you, Charlotte. I haven't been out of the office as much in years.'

Fifty-Two

'I have some news for you,' Sarah Grace Skinner said to her husband. 'Are you planning to come home in the near future so that I can share it? Or has InterMedia become your new family?'

'I'll be home soon, I promise,' Bob replied. 'Things have been happening here, that's all.'

She stared at her tablet's camera, unsmiling. 'Including your mystery trip to the mountains?'

'That's part of it. How did you know about that?' He paused. 'Sorry, damn silly question. You've been talking to Alex.'

'More like she's been talking to me. She called me after you got back.'

'I told her not to tell anyone about it,' he growled. 'We will have serious words, she and I.'

'No, you won't,' Sarah told him dismissively. 'You haven't had serious words with your daughter since you caught her nicking a Cornetto from the freezer when she was six. You made her cry, and then said you were sorry and you'd never do it again. She didn't say that; she kept on pinching them, but she was careful never to get caught again.'

He laughed, lightening the mood behind them. 'That's what she thought. She had a way of getting them out of the wrapper without tearing it. She'd put the top on and put it back in the box, empty, thinking that I'd never find out since I never liked the things. What did she tell you about our trip?' he asked quietly.

'That you took her up past Olot, to the area with the spectacular geology that you and I love. You found a big old house that had been restored, at Christ knows what cost. You went to the door and opened it, somehow. Then you shut it again, fast, and more or less ran back to the car. You did some poking around, then you made a phone call and hauled ass out of there.'

'Missing the cops by a matter of minutes? Did she add that part too?'

'No, she left that out. She did say she'd never seen you so badly shaken before, not ever, although you and she have had some shared experiences that would shake most normal people. Bob, what the hell are you doing over there? Is it dangerous?'

She saw him shake his head. 'Not any more, if it ever was. Don't press me, sweetheart. I'll tell you the whole story when I can but not like this; when I'm with you.'

'Then get with me!' she demanded. 'Get your ass back here.'

'When I can,' he promised. 'Did Alex tell you about Lottie Mann?'

'Yeah, some nonsense about her being flown in and you volunteering to act as her interpreter. You brought her to L'Escala for dinner and she stayed over, then the two of you went back up to that house to meet the Mossos.'

'That's true, that's what happened.'

'Where is Lottie now?'

'Investigating with a *Mossos* colleague, who speaks good English so I'm not needed.'

'Investigating what? Bob, what did you see?'

He frowned; in his eyes, she thought she read something she had never seen there before. Anxiety.

'Something gross,' he told her quietly. 'Something so bad I literally ran from it. I think I'm past my best-before date, Sarah. And yet when that house was opened today, there was nothing there. Now I'm actually asking myself, did I imagine it all? Did I open that door expecting the worst and, maybe for the few seconds it lasted, did I make myself see it?'

'Then you should come home,' she repeated. 'Withdraw yourself completely from this business, leave it to the police. Bob, my love, post-traumatic stress disorder can last for a long time, a lifetime in some people, and we both know that you are no stranger to it.'

'I will,' he agreed. 'Once a few things are taken care of.'

'What things?'

'Questions that are still to be answered. About the investigation and maybe about me. If you're right, love, and I have had a blast of PTSD, you above all others must know that I'll refuse to let it beat me, or make me run away from anything.' He paused. 'You said you had news for me,' he continued. 'Out with it. What is it?'

'I've had an offer,' she replied. 'A visiting chair in forensic pathology.'

'Where?'

'The University of Barcelona.'

He said nothing, only smiled, but she reacted.

'You knew, didn't you?' she exclaimed. 'You bloody knew!'

'Well,' he said cautiously, 'I was at this reception a couple of weeks ago and I was introduced to this university guy, a really intense bloke. He was prattling on about the need to improve the city's academic reputation, to have Barcelona thought of as something more than a tourist destination. He said that part of the strategy was to increase the number of visiting professors, and I told him, "You could start with my wife." He thought I was joking at first until I told him who you were. He said no more about it at the time, but I guess he took me seriously.'

Her expression was thunderous. He winced in the face of her sudden anger. 'What?'

'Everything has to go through you, doesn't it!' she snapped. 'Even my damned career. Well, I'll tell you what Senor Cazador can do, he can stick his visiting chair where it'll only ever be found at a post-mortem. And you! You'd better get your ass back here before I change the fucking locks!'

Fifty-Three

'You could delegate this, you know, Lita,' Lottie Mann pointed out. 'You're what rank? In my force you're the equivalent of at least an assistant chief constable, maybe even a deputy. We don't find those people out on the street. No, they stay in their offices and push paper, or send out emails to interrupt the troops on the ground.'

'So do I normally,' Comissari Roza agreed. 'To be honest, I don't have faith in the line manager who would normally be involved with you in this investigation, so I decided to side-line him. Also, I have the feeling that your friend Sir Robert is keeping an eye on everything we do, so I need to keep an eye on him in return since he clearly has influence with our political master.'

'The Gaffer isn't like that,' Mann insisted. 'Fact is, he used to be famous for hating politicians. Okay, he was married to one for a while, but that didn't last.'

'That may have been true of the man you knew as a police chief,' Roza countered, 'but the version we have here is very politically aware. In that way he's much more effective than Xavi Aislado, when he was chairman of InterMedia. Xavi was aloof, unreachable. Sir Robert is different. Since he took over, he has learned a great deal and it shows in the editorial profile of the group. He knows how the political balance is in Catalunya, and the group newspapers and radio stations reflect that. The same is true in the rest of Spain. InterMedia has much more influence in Madrid than it ever had. It's perverse but true; the government needs the support of the Catalans to stay in power. Therefore it needs the support of our media, of whom the most powerful are the InterMedia titles, printed, broadcast and online. Sir Robert, he knows this and he is using it. Since he became chairman, InterMedia have been granted eight new broadcast licences by the government, and its social media profile has gone from regional to national. Charlotte,' she said, 'I met him not long after he became chairman. Then he spoke what he called restaurant Spanish, even though he had a home here for twenty-five years before that. Now he's fluent and he speaks acceptable Catalan. Hector Sureda, the chief executive, runs the business on the ground and he is very good, the best. But the power, that is Sir Robert. I have a couple of friends who work for InterMedia. They tell me that he used to spend a couple of days a week here. Now, they say, he is more or less full time.'

'But he's a British citizen,' Mann pointed out. 'Is he allowed to spend that much time in Spain?'

'Yes. He bought his apartment in Girona for seven hundred thousand euro. Invest half a million in property in Spain, and you have a Golden Visa, that lets you live and work here as if you were a citizen. Actually, he didn't really need it. When he became chairman, Xavi Aislado covered him by getting him a business visa; that's another route.'

'I wonder if that's sustainable.'

'Perfectly,' Roza said.

'I meant domestically,' Mann murmured.

They were interrupted by the return of the manager of the

Banco Sabadell office in which they sat, a brisk little man whose status seemed to be emphasised in that he wore a tie, pale blue and white-striped. *'He mirado los movimientos de la cuenta que solicitaste,'* he announced. *'Ha habido tres retiros de efectivo recientes cada uno por cuatrocientos euros. El primero, hace quince días fue en Figueres. El segundo cuatro días después, en La Rambla de Barcelona desde un cajero automático comercial. El tercero fue hace siete días, en Sant Sadurni d'Anoia. Eso es todo lo que puedo decirte.'*

'There have been three cash withdrawals from the Land account over the last fortnight,' Roza translated. 'Figueres, Barcelona and Sant Sadurni: that's the place where most of the world's cava is made. That suggests Gilbert Land, or whoever is making them, is moving south.'

'¿Existen registros visuales de los retiros? ¿Alguno de los cajeros automáticos tenía una cámara?' she asked the manager. 'Did they catch anyone on camera?' she added for Mann's benefit.

'Si señora. Sí lo hizo el cajero de Sant Sadurni, y tengo la cara de la persona que usó la tarjeta. No parece ser el titular, Señor Land. Un momento,' he said as there was a rap on the office door and a woman wearing bank uniform entered, carrying a sheet of paper. She handed it to the manager who passed it immediately to Roza.

It was a print of a still from the security camera of an ATM. It was that of a woman, but not recognisable. She wore large sunglasses and a scarf was wound around her head and the lower half of her face, revealing only a single lock of blonde hair.

'Estás en lo correcto,' Roza told the manager. *'Seguro que no es Senor Land.* For sure that's not Land,' she repeated.

'No hay otro signatario en la cuenta,' he exclaimed. *'Debo cancelar la tarjeta de inmediato.'*

'No,' the *comissari* said, sharply. '*Necesitamos que lo mantengas abierto. Si se usa de nuevo, nos dirá dónde está esta mujer.*' She turned to Mann. 'He says he's going to cancel the card. I've told him not to.'

'¡*Pero señora, debo proteger la seguridad de la cuenta! Posee casi cinco millones de euros. Debo proteger al Senor Land.*'

'Did he say there's five million euros in the account?' the Scot gasped. Roza nodded.

'*No creemos que el Senor Land exista. Si lo hizo, creemos que está muerto. ¿Esto es el Señor Land?*' She signalled to Mann, who understood what was needed and displayed a post-mortem image of the dead Gavin Ayre on her phone. She thrust it towards the manager.

He shook his head, vigorously. '*No, ese no es el Senor Land. Es mucho mayor que ese hombre. Los detalles de la cuenta muestran que tiene sesenta y tres años.*'

'He's saying that according to his account details, Land is sixty-three,' Roza told Mann.

'Fuck,' she murmured. 'Then there really are two of them.'

Fifty-Four

'That puts a completely different complexion on things,' Mario McGuire told his junior colleague. 'You've been operating on the probability that the dead man Ayre and Land in Spain were one and the same. Now we know they're not, you need to focus on the link that we know exists between them.'

'And the money that's behind them,' Haddock added. 'Lottie says there's about five million euro in Land's account. There's slightly more than that in Ayre's. It all seems to be coming from countries that offer people banking secrecy. But who or what's behind it all? You would say that organised crime is a strong possibility. Yes?'

'Say what you like, Sauce, but it's a guess at this point. The Crown Office here and the prosecutors in Spain don't buy those. At the moment your problem is that you don't have any lines of inquiry. You need to find Geraldine Black, Ayre's supposed half-sister. From what you're telling me, Lottie seems to be your best chance of doing that. But at the moment that's all you've got.'

'We need to find Gilbert Land too,' Haddock pointed out. 'Could it be that he and Ayre fell out, fatally?'

'It could, but it's still guesswork. You need more than that. You and big Singh, get yourselves back out to Ayre's house. Search it again, see if there's something that you missed.'

Fifty-Five

'*No me importa que mañana te pierdas tu partido de golf del sábado por la mañana,*' Commissari Roza told the lieutenant in her Barcelona office. '*No me importa si tienes que trabajar todo el fin de semana. Necesito saber acerca de todos los movimientos de helicópteros en las coordenadas que le he dado, y necesito saber quiénes eran los pasajeros.*'

She ended the call. 'Get the message?' she asked Mann. 'Suppose he has to work all weekend, I want to know who landed here in a helicopter and when. Jose is a golfer, but sometimes he needs to remember that his job is more important.' She checked the time on her phone. 'We can get to Riudaura this evening to see the old man . . . or we can go and eat and leave it until tomorrow. What do you say?'

The Scot shrugged her broad shoulders. 'I say you're the boss. I'm only an observer here.'

'Do you need to report to Scotland? To Sauce, your boss? Where did he get that name by the way?'

'It's tribal,' she said. 'It would take too long to explain, and even then you probably wouldn't get it. I've got nothing to tell him after updating him on what the banker told us. Besides,

I know that he missed a golf game last weekend because of this investigation. If I called him and interrupted another, I don't think he'd take it nearly as well as your man Jose.'

Fifty-Six

'You're still in the office?' Sarah looked surprised.

'Yes,' Bob replied. 'There's a lot going on here. I'm about to knock off, though.'

'Your work or police work?' she asked.

'InterMedia,' he said. 'I've done all I can in the other thing. Lottie's being looked after and, I assume, progressing. Sauce hasn't called me in a while so I guess he's happy too.'

'That's good. Listen,' she continued. 'I'm sorry I was such a cow earlier on, it's just that . . . I've always been sensitive to suggestions that your career helped mine in any way, and when you said . . .'

He nodded. 'I know, and I get it. I should have kept my mouth shut; not at the event but when you told me. The fact is, you were already on a long list of possible invitees without anyone being aware of our connection, and you being you, you'd have made the short list very quickly, and beyond. Are you going to accept?'

'I need to clear it with the University here,' Sarah said, 'but subject to that formality . . . these things reflect credit on the institution as much as the individual . . . I will. I don't know how the schedule will be, not yet, but . . .'

'You could fly with me,' he suggested.

'Could I? Would that be acceptable to InterMedia?'

He grinned. 'I'll run it past the chairman, but I think he'll say it's okay.' He paused. 'What about Dawn? The other kids will be fine with Trish in charge but she's a toddler.'

'She'll come with me until she's school age.'

'You sure?' he asked.

'I wouldn't do it if I wasn't. It'll work for us both. I know you're struggling to balance your home and work lives. This will ease the pressure. In the holidays the family can live in Spain and I'll commute to Edinburgh.'

'You've got it all worked out, haven't you?' Bob laughed. 'Are you turning into a control freak?'

She gazed into the computer camera. 'Can you have two of those in one family?' She smiled. 'Go on, get off home. Enjoy your bachelor pad while you still can. Come back here as soon as you can.'

Fifty-Seven

'Do we even know what we're looking for, Sauce?' Tarvil Singh asked.

'No,' Haddock admitted, 'but when the DCC suggests something, "Why?" isn't something he necessarily wants to hear.' He looked at the open kitchen drawer, 'Eight of everything,' he said, 'everything in its proper place.'

'Same with the crockery through there in the sideboard. Wedgwood,' the DI added, 'Vera Wang lace gold. The mugs in that cupboard are Wedgwood too, and the coffee cups and saucers.'

The superintendent stared at him. 'Eh?'

'My mother,' Singh explained. 'Wedgwood's her passion.'

'How about the cutlery?'

'That there? Oh, that's just bog-standard IKEA. But there's a Viners canteen in the sideboard. And William Morris placemats. I wonder if Ayre ever had a dinner party for eight. If he did, it was without napkins. I didn't see any of those.'

'From what we've learned of Mr Ayre so far,' Haddock ventured, 'I doubt that he hosted any dinner parties in the short time he lived here. As for his sister and the man we now believe, thanks to Lottie's Spanish banker, to have been Gilbert Land, they seem to have eaten out when they were here.'

'Does the big man have any thoughts about that development?' Singh asked. 'I mean, he found Black, didn't he, through that security firm?'

'For which we thank him, but I haven't spoken to him since then. It's been made clear to me that the Chief is keen to keep him at a distance.'

'And Neil McIlhenney's not a man to mess with,' the DI observed.

'Not unless you're Mario McGuire. Come on, Tarvil, we're done here. Let's take another look at the stable and the garage and that'll be us done.'

The two detectives moved outside. Steady rain was falling as they made their way to the out-building, making Haddock hurry to key in the code and fail at the final digit.

'Come on, Sauce,' Singh complained. 'We're getting wet here.'

'Give us a minute, fucksake.' He tried again, and the door clicked open. He smiled. 'Patience, Tarvil, patience.'

The only change from their previous visit was the light film of dust that had settled on the vehicles. 'You do these,' Haddock said. 'I'll check the stable.' He crossed the open area, passing the stall that had housed Ayre's horse, wondering how it was faring in its new lodgings and what its fate ultimately would be. Perhaps the mounted unit would adopt it; he made a mental note to suggest that to McGuire. He moved into the changing area, opening the wardrobe as Singh had done on their earlier visit, surveying the riding gear and seeing nothing there. He opened the first of the two smaller compartments, finding towels that appeared to have been disturbed, by the clumsy DI, he assumed. He took them out, thinking to fold them more neatly, and saw a small box, with a clip, but no lock to secure it. He opened it, revealing two tangled iPhone cables, several keys and a black rectangle, less than three inches long, less than an inch wide. 'Hey,' he called out, holding it up for Singh to see. 'What about this?'

'I saw it before,' the DI replied. 'It's a storage disk but it's old. It's a USB connection. It wouldn't fit the computer in the house.'

If that's so, Haddock thought, *it's the only thing in this whole place that is old. That's curious.* He rummaged in the box and found, beneath the tangled cables, a square foam casing. Wedged within was a small device, no more than three centimetres long. He freed it with his thumb and help it up. 'And this?' he asked.

The DI crossed the room to join him, peering at the black plastic. He took it from Haddock, extended the connector of the memory stick, and joined the two together. 'Oops,' he murmured. 'My bad. I never saw that last time. It's an adaptor. Now, it'll fit the computer.'

Fifty-Eight

Scientists were still working on the house when they arrived. Mann was astonished to recognise among them, standing outside having a water break, a tall figure with strands of ginger hair escaping from his sterile head covering.

'Paul Dorward,' she exclaimed. 'What are you doing here?'

'Much the same as you, DCI Mann,' he replied. 'With a potential connection between the two scenes, the wise ones decided there should be a presence here, so I got stuck on a plane at fuck o'clock this morning. I flew to Paris then on to Perpignan, and got here three hours ago.'

'Have you found anything significant?' she asked.

'Nothing, and that's what's significant. It's as if no human being has ever set foot in there.'

'So the Gaffer was right,' she murmured. 'Somebody put the cleaners in.'

'Did they ever,' Dorward confirmed. 'They've even pumped out the septic tank.'

'Who could have done that?'

'Not your average fussy estate agent, that's for sure.' He drained his water bottle. 'I must get back in there. We have one room to do and that's it.'

'You speak Spanish?' Mann asked.

'Catalan,' he replied. 'I studied in Girona for two years. That's why Jenny sent me.' He frowned. 'I think I might stay if they'll have me.'

Mann left him to his thoughts and re-joined Roza, who was waiting by their car. After she had been updated on the team's progress, the *comissari* frowned. 'From what you tell me,' she said, 'we may have trouble keeping Madrid out of this. Come on, let's go and find the old neighbour.'

They set off down the light slope, stepping carefully on the rough track by the side of the road, too far from any town for there to be any paving. They had walked for less than half a kilometre when a house came into view. It was as modest as *Masia Coll* was grandiose, a single storey, with a balcony facing west towards the setting sun, but also with a view of the side of the rear of the big house on the hilltop, the area, the officers cal-culated, where the helipad was located. An elderly man sat there on a rocking chair, beside which stood a telescope on a stand. Mann thought he might be asleep until, without warning, he pushed himself upright and turned to face them.

'*Les tomó un tiempo a los policías venir a hablar conmigo,*' he called out.

'He says it's taken us a while,' Roza translated. 'I think he feels neglected.' She turned to face him again. '*¿Eres Josep?*' she asked.

'*Sí, le dije al grandote hace unos días.*'

'He says he told the big guy a few days ago.*¿Que mas le dijiste al grandote acerca de el hombre que es dueño de esa masia?* What else did you tell him about the man who owns that place?'

'*No es un hombre, es una mujer. El hombre solo estuvo aquí una vez. Llegó en helicóptero.*' He raised a hand and made a whirl-ing motion above his head. '*Hizo un ruido infernal.*'

'Not a man, a woman,' she repeated for Mann's benefit. 'The man's only been here once. He came by helicopter and made a hell of a noise. *¿Cuando?* When?'

'*Hace dos semanas.*'

'Two weeks ago. *¿Lo viste salir?*'

'*No, pensé que todavía estaba allí, hasta que el tipo grande vino a buscarlo. Dijo que era un amigo, pero no le creí.*'

'He hasn't seen him leave. He thought he was still here until the big guy came. He said he was a friend but he didn't believe him. *¿Y la mujer?*' she asked.

'*Se fue dos días después de que llegara el helicóptero. La vi alejarse en el auto.*'

'The woman left a couple of days after the man flew in. By car.'

'*Lo he visto antes,*' Josep volunteered.

'*¿El tipo grande?*'

'*No, hombre del helicóptero. Hay joder todo que hacer aquí, pero miro la televisión, así que lo hago mucho. Lo he visto en la televisión, pero no recuerdo cuándo.*'

'Wow,' Roza whispered. 'What he says,' she told Mann, 'is that there's fuck all to do here but watch TV, so he does that a lot. He says he's seen helicopter man on television, although he can't remember when.'

215

Fifty-Nine

'That, last night,' Dominic Jackson said gravely, 'that wasn't supposed to happen.'

'No,' Alex agreed, 'but it did. It was good, it was spontaneous and it was something that's been on the cards for a long time, whatever we've both been telling people. You are my best friend, Dominick, the best I've ever had, and you always will be. I've had terrible taste in men before, made terrible choices: Andy Martin, Griff Montell, a couple of blokes I've met on nights out whose names I don't even remember. There was one, I told him who my father was and he was dressed and out of there inside five minutes.'

'I don't blame him,' Dominick said. 'Are you going to tell your father?'

'Why should I? The fact that you and I finally got round to having sex doesn't change anything between us. It wasn't a proposal of marriage. You have your professional life and so do I. We don't live together and there's no reason why we should. I'll only make you one promise and it's this. You're exclusive. There won't be anyone else from now on, not ever.'

'I made that same promise to you quite a while ago,' he confessed. 'I never told you, that was all. The living together part,' he continued. 'Did you mean that?'

'Yes. I like my own space and so do you. You had years of solitude preparing you for it.' She paused. 'Why? Have I got that all wrong? Do you want to?'

'I want what you want,' he promised. 'I hear what you say and I agree with it. Equally, I've enjoyed being here with you for the last ten days more than I've enjoyed anything in my life.'

'We can do it again any time you like,' she told him. 'Here, or anywhere else we choose. We can take time out each year and go off together, go on cruises, stuff like that, without telling a bloody soul.'

'Not even your dad?'

'Especially not my dad! Although I'm sure he knows how we are, and I'm sure he's happy about it because . . .' She hesitated, trying to find words to express her feelings '. . . because for the first time in his life he really doesn't have to worry about me.'

'He trusts me to keep you safe? Is that what you're saying?'

'More than that,' Alex replied. 'He trusts us to keep each other safe. For all your spectacular shared history, you're like a brother to him.'

'As he is to me,' Dominick said quietly. 'If it wasn't for him, I doubt that I would still be alive.'

Sixty

Bob Skinner had never minded working long hours. He was a positive thinker, one whose glass . . . or bottle if he was drinking Corona . . . was always half full, and one of the benefits of being last to leave the office was freedom from the constraints of commuter traffic. He winced as he recalled his time as the last chief constable of the dying Strathclyde Force, a job he had never coveted but which had been forced upon him by a significant event. Then he had commuted from Gullane to Glasgow. Even in a police car with a driver and instant communications, he had found the slow grind along the intercity motorway arse-breaking, and boring. The distance between the InterMedia headquarters and his Golden penthouse, as he thought of it, was relatively short, but Girona was a regional hub with town-sized streets that could become grid-locked, a circumstance he had learned to avoid.

He smiled as he thought of the amicable outcome of his discussions with his wife. He knew that he should have greeted her excited announcement with feigned surprise and was relieved that the damage had been short-lived. Since then, he had been considering the rebalancing of his business and family lives, and how it could be achieved positively. His private discussions with

Xavi were pointing to him being in post for up to nine years. Paloma Aislado Craig, his eventual successor, was twenty-one years old. She was on course for a first-class honours degree from the London School of Economics that would be followed by an MBA, at Harvard rather than Edinburgh, her father's original preference. That summer she was working as an intern in Inter-Media's Italian division to improve her languages as well as her understanding and experience of the group. When her education was complete in three years, her intention . . . Paloma had declared from the outset that she herself would plot her career pathway . . . was to spend a total of five years working in each area of the business, learning how it worked overall. That would be followed by a year shadowing Skinner, before taking over the chair and coming into her birthright.

With his own future linked to hers, Skinner had been aware of the consequences for his lifestyle, and for his family. Money had never been an issue, although the job had raised him to a new level of wealth. He could have walked away, but his commitment to the company had become total. Beyond that, he had made a promise to a friend. For the future, the main question was his children's future, their education and their happiness. Mark, their adopted son, was on the verge of early entry to Cambridge University. Jazz and Seonaid were at different stages of school, and Dawn would be starting nursery in a year or two. Could he be an absent father through the week? It would be tough on him. Would it be fair to them? Boarding school was not an option . . . his Lanarkshire roots and upbringing ruled that out . . . but his research had found that there were four international schools in Girona, each one teaching in English and Spanish. Paloma had been educated at one of them but Xavi had assured him that they were all equally good. The apartment was big enough to accommodate them all, but if the kids preferred to live in L'Escala by the sea, as they did in Scotland, the distance to any chosen school was not great.

He frowned as he approached his apartment block, imagining the conversation he would have with Jazz. How would his son feel about being uprooted? Seonaid, he knew, would not need a separate discussion; she worshipped her brother and would follow his lead. The jet was ready for him and he was ready to return to Scotland the next morning. He would gather the family together and make his pitch.

The frown was replaced by a smile as he drove through the automatic entrance gateway and down into the garage that served the apartment owners. He had made his own mental commitment and he was confident that his son's sense of adventure would sweep him along. He eased the Tesla between the concrete pillars that supported the structure above and reversed into his parking place. He checked the battery level, as he always did on returning home. It was still high from its charge the night before, and so he switched off the electric motors and stepped out, hearing the street door close automatically above him as he closed the car. He walked towards the exit door, beneath the *Sortida* sign, opened it and stepped through; to be confronted by two men, facing him and blocking his route to the elevator. One was white-skinned, one was black; each was tall and each wore a dark suit, white shirt and dark tie. Each had a small badge in his lapel.

'Fuck me,' Skinner exclaimed, with a mix of curiosity and rising anger at any intrusion into his space. 'It's the Men in Black: my favourite fucking movie too. You'll be K,' he said to the man on the left, 'and you,' he nodded to the other, 'you must be Will Smith. Agent J. I promise you guys, I might be an alien but I'm not an extra-terrestrial.'

'Sir,' the latter murmured. 'We need you to come with us.' The accent was American; Skinner felt the dawn of understanding.

'We all have needs,' he replied. 'But it would be a sadder world if they were all fulfilled. Now get out of my way, lads. You're trespassing on private property, you're acting illegally, and you're covered by security cameras.' The third claim was untrue, but Agent K reacted, glancing upwards.

'We need you to come with us, sir,' his colleague repeated. 'Refusal is not an option.'

Skinner smiled, restraining a laugh. 'In that case does "Fuck off" work? Look,' he said, 'you might be twenty-five years younger than me, and I'm sure you're trained in stuff, but you've never met me. I'm not going with you, I'm going to that lift and you're not going to stop me.'

'Not so, sir.' The third voice came from behind him; it was female and it coincided with a sudden pain in his back, and a tension that sent shudders through his body. He had heard of neuromuscular incapacitation but had never expected to experience it.

You must be Agent L, he thought, as the two men gripped him on either side, as the hypodermic needle went into his neck, and as he faded to black.

Sixty-One

'There is nothing like motivation,' Lita Roza exclaimed as she ended the call. 'Jose can play his golf tomorrow morning after all.'

'He's got a result?' Mann asked, her expression registering surprise.

'He has,' the *comissari* confirmed. 'There are lots of helicopter taxi companies in Catalunya, but he got lucky. He prioritised air traffic control rather than go through them individually, in the hope that a flight might have been logged in, because not all of them are. Just over two weeks ago a company called Helibar gave notice of a taxi trip from Barcelona Airport to Riudaura. The flight was tracked and was uneventful.'

'How many passengers?'

'We'll need to check with the company to find that out,' Roza grinned. 'I could have told Jose to check it out tomorrow morning, but I took pity on him . . . and his golf partner. I said I would do it tomorrow.'

They were in the *comissari*'s car, in Girona. The journey back from La Garrotxa had been uneventful but it was late in the evening. 'Do you want to go for a drink and some tapas, or will I drop you at Sir Robert's place?'

'Much as I'd fancy some *patatas bravas* and a couple of meat-balls,' Mann said, 'I don't feel comfortable going anywhere in this sweaty uniform.'

'Okay, we'll stop off, you can change and we'll go somewhere.'

'Don't you have to get back to Barcelona?' the Scot wondered.

'No, I have a cousin in Caldes de Malavella. I'm staying with her tonight. I often do when I'm working here. My partner knows that.'

'Fine, the Gaffer's it is.'

Roza told Maps to guide her to Skinner's address, following the instructions as the app obliged. As they reached their destination, she spotted a parking place in the street and headed for it.

'Did you see that?' Mann asked suddenly.

'What?'

'A drunk, I think; on the other carriageway. Two guys were huckling him back to their car. The bloke looked completely out of it.'

'That's very unusual in Spain,' Roza admitted. 'You will rarely see a drunk on the street. It can only be a tourist.'

'He was in a white shirt and cargo pants but the guys carrying him didn't look like tourists. They were in black suits. Do you want to do something about it?'

'Hell no!' her colleague snorted. 'That's way below my pay grade, and anyway, it's a job for the locals, not the *Mossos*. Come on, let's roust Sir Robert. Maybe he'll come out with us.'

They made their way to the entrance to the apartment block. Skinner had given Mann a key, but she pressed the entry buzzer; whether as a courtesy or a warning, she was not sure. She waited for a time, but there was no answer. She tried again with the same negative outcome. Finally she reached for the key. 'He must be working really late,' she guessed.

They rode the elevator to the top floor. Mann let them into the apartment; as they expected it was in darkness, with all the shutters lowered against the daytime heat. 'Gaffer,' she called out, against the outside chance that her host had been tired and had gone straight to bed. There was no response; from the hall she could see that his bedroom door was open.

'Call him,' Roza suggested. 'Tell him what we're planning and ask if he wants to meet us.'

Mann nodded, retrieved the number from her contacts, and called it. She held it up for the Catalan to hear the ring tone repeat and repeat and repeat. 'Bob Skinner not beside his phone?' she murmured. 'That is not usual.'

'Could he have gone to his daughter?' Roza suggested.

'He could, but he didn't say anything about it earlier. He definitely said he was going to his office. "See you later", he said. I remember it.' Nevertheless, she called the L'Escala landline number that he had given her before her arrival as a precaution. Alex picked up on the fifth ring; she was less than her usual crisp self; sleep was in her voice.

'Sorry,' Lottie said. 'Did I wake you?'

'No, we were dozing beside the pool, that's all.'

Her years in CID made her doubt that, but she let it pass. 'Your dad wouldn't be there, would he?'

'No, he's still in Girona. He called me about an hour ago to wish us a good flight home. He said he was just leaving the office. He'll be at the apartment by now, Lottie; must be.'

'No, he's not. I'm there and there's no sign.'

'In that case he's probably gone to eat. Check the garage; if his car's there, that's what he'll have done.'

'Will do. The only thing is; he isn't answering his phone.'

'It may need charging,' Alex suggested. 'God knows he's on

it often enough; and he did say the battery was starting to degrade; you know that one, Apple's cute way of making you buy a new phone. When you find him, Lottie, let me know,' she asked, the first trace of anxiety creeping into her voice as she disconnected.

Frowning, Mann pocketed her handset, nodded wordlessly towards the lift and headed for it, with Roza on her heels. They rode it down to the garage and stepped out into a passageway that was dark only for as long as it took a sensor to register their presence and turn on the lights. There was a fire door at the other end with an automatic closer above. It took a little strength to open it but when she did, the garage was illuminated also. She could see Skinner's car in its space.

'That's it,' she called out. 'He's gone for a meal or a drink, or more likely both. I'll take a look in the car; he might have left his phone in it. Probably he has done.'

'Lottie.' Roza's voice came from the other side of the fire door. As Mann turned, it opened. The other woman was holding a pale blue cotton jacket; one that Lottie knew she had seen before.

'This is his, isn't it?' the *comissari* murmured. 'It was on the ground behind the door. You didn't see it when you opened it.' She held it up and explored its pockets. 'His wallet,' she said, as she withdrew it. 'His car keys,' she added. 'He hasn't gone anywhere. He's been taken.'

'By a small army maybe,' her colleague replied. 'Jesus,' she whispered. 'That guy, the one I thought was drunk. Lita, that must have been him. Not drunk, unconscious. It's the only way they'd have managed it.'

'But not through the front entrance,' Roza pointed out. 'That would have been too public. This way, come on.' She headed for the garage entrance. Beside it, separated from the road by a railing, was a curving pathway leading up to a pedestrian exit marked *Sortida* like the internal door. It opened onto a side road that led to the twin carriageway at the front.

Mann pointed. 'It was over there!' she called out. 'That's where they took him.' She looked around then pointed to a street lighting column, one of a line in the space separating the two roadways. 'Is that a camera? If it is you need to access it and get to the footage. Lita, can you do that?'

'Yes,' she replied 'but on a Friday night God knows how long it will take. It's run by a private company.'

'We need sight of that car,' Mann yelled. 'Big and dark, possibly black, that's all I can tell you about it. But there must have been a third person behind the wheel, on the other side. When they pushed him into the back seat, one of them got in there behind him, and the other jumped into the front passenger seat. You need to call this in now!' she insisted.

Roza was ahead of her, firing instructions into her phone in Catalan. '*Immediatament!*' she ended. 'Done,' she said. 'Officers will access the camera footage as a matter of urgency. Meantime, every big dark car on every highway within fifteen minutes of here is going to be pulled over.'

'Who would do this?' Mann asked her. 'I mean, what the fuck?'

'I don't know,' the *comissari* confessed. 'I have no idea. But Sir Robert is the chair of InterMedia, which has taken a strong editorial stand against the extreme Right across all Spain. Those are not people you mess with; I can only hope it's not them, otherwise we'll find him in a ditch.'

'Or them, when he comes to,' the Scot said, grimly optimistic. 'Meanwhile, I've got another problem. Do I phone Alex now, and if so, what do I tell her?'

Sixty-Two

'Dad's been kidnapped? Are you kidding me, Dominick?'

' "Abducted" was the word she used, but yes, that's what Lottie said,' he confirmed. 'She got my number from Sauce Haddock. She thought she should call me rather than break it to you over the phone, and she was right.'

'Kidnapped?' Alex repeated. 'How, in God's name?'

'They think he was waylaid in the garage of his apartment block, drugged and driven off. Lottie and a Catalan officer found his jacket there when they went to look for him and later the police first-responders recovered a hypo.'

'Even so,' she said. 'My dad? He's never lost a fight in his life.'

'Don't I know it,' Dominick murmured. 'They reckon there were three of them.' He paused, concerned about her reaction, but continued. 'Lottie said that when she and the other cop arrived at the building, they actually saw someone being loaded into a car but from that distance they couldn't see who it was. They assumed it was a drunk. It was only later, after they found the jacket, after she'd called you, that the penny dropped.' He went to the fridge, took out a bottle of Vichy Catalan sparkling water and handed it to her. 'Drink this, breathe deeply and be calm.'

'It's okay,' she assured him, 'I am calm. I've had worse nights than this with him. That time he was stabbed, for example; Sarah and I were told it was odds against him surviving.'

'What time?' he exclaimed. 'I never knew.'

'Why should you? You were away. Now he never talks about it and neither do we. The kids don't know: Jazz was a baby at the time, Mark hadn't come into the family and Ignacio . . . we didn't even know he existed. "One night in Paris",' she sang, smiling softly. 'Only in his and Mia's case it was Davidson's Mains.'

'You have quite a family,' Dominick observed.

'Get used to it. You're part of it now.'

'That's a nice thought. I've never had a family before.' He smiled rarely. When he did, she thought it lit up the room. 'Are you saying we're official?'

'We are what we are, best friends. The fact that we sleep together, that's our business. I'll make that clear to Dad when I tell . . .' She stopped, the sentence hanging in the air. She looked up at him. 'Did Lottie say what the police are doing?'

'Everything you'd expect. Road-blocks on the highways out of Girona, door-to-door around the apartment block, looking for witnesses who might have seen the abduction. They're also recovering street camera footage; with luck they'll have some video.'

'Suspects?'

'Lottie didn't say. I doubt that there are any.'

'It has to be business-related,' Alex said. 'Back home he's made a lifetime's worth of enemies, but here he only has a business profile . . . a high one at that. What about the Basque nationalists? Are they still active?'

'No, they're not. They disarmed years ago, and even if they hadn't, latterly their policy was not to stage active operations . . . assassinations, in other words . . . in Catalunya as it was in the same situation as they were, an autonomous region seeking independence. The Catalans themselves, they've never been violent, not to that extent.'

'And the new Right?' she suggested.

'They'll be considered, I'm sure,' Dominick conceded. 'But I wouldn't subscribe to that. They've been steadily increasing their profile in the Madrid Parliament. I don't see them risking that by targeting individuals in that way.'

'Then who could it be?'

'I don't know,' he admitted, 'but one thing. I hope they're going to find the truth of an old adage.'

'What's that?'

'Be careful what you wish for.'

Sixty-Three

'I've been awake pretty much all night,' Lottie Mann confessed. 'I expected him to walk through that door at any minute.'

She and Comissari Roza were seated on stools at the breakfast bar in Skinner's apartment, contemplating the two croissants that remained of the six that the Catalan had brought with her. Mann broke the deadlock by reaching out and taking her third. 'Another coffee?' she asked.

Roza nodded. 'I'll do it.' She stepped down, rinsed the cups that they had drained and placed them under the nozzle of the bean-to-cup machine. 'None of your capsules for Sir Robert,' she observed.

'No,' Mann confirmed, swallowing a mouthful. 'When he was in the police, even in his few months in Glasgow, he was famous for having a coffee machine on the go all the time in his office. The word was that his wife had ordered him to cut down, so he drank hardly any at home. Then it was just filter stuff. He's gone up-market now.' She paused as her colleague took a call, watching the narrowing of her eyes, listening to the tone of her brief responses.

The *comissari* stayed silent when it was over, focusing on the coffee cups as the milk frother did its work. She carried them back to the breakfast bar and resumed her seat. 'They've ruled them out,' she said.

The Scot gasped. 'What?'

''It wasn't the extreme Right,' Roza told her. 'Our security branch reached out to them, to their people in Parliament. They promised us that the only interest they have in Sir Robert is in persuading him to have InterMedia adopt a more neutral line editorially. They are realists; they know that isn't going to happen, so their real focus is on the rest of the Catalan media . . . good luck to them with that.'

'Do you believe them?'

'Yes, I have to. If they turned to violence it would give the moderate majority in the Cortes an excuse to crush them. They know that.' She paused, eyeing the last croissant but deciding to leave it for Mann. 'But there's more, much more. Our scrutiny of the street cameras was able to pick up the moment of the kidnapping. There is a verifiable image of Sir Robert, so there is no doubt. The vehicle is a Cadillac Escalade. Footage shows that it went through two roadblocks, then joined the autopista heading south.'

'Hold on,' Mann insisted. 'How did it go through two roadblocks? They were told to stop big dark vehicles. Lita, cars don't come any bigger or any blacker than a Cadillac fucking Escalade. Were they all asleep?'

'No,' her colleague replied. 'They were wide awake, enough to know that they could not stop it, because it had diplomatic plates: red, code two seven. That's American, Lottie. They have him. They've snatched a UK national and a major Spanish business figure from the streets of Spain. Fuck! On my watch!' She sighed and sipped her coffee. 'Last night . . . I will never forget this . . . I said he was way below my pay grade. Now, he is way above it. I must take this to Major Teijero, my boss, in Sabadell. I guarantee that he will shit himself . . . maybe literally. He will certainly take it to Manuel Mateu, the Catalan security minister. And he is a friend of Sir Robert, so he will take it to Madrid.'

'And what about InterMedia?' Mann asked. 'Its chairman's been snatched off the street. Who's going to tell them? Who's going to tell Xavi Aislado?'

'Not me,' Roza said firmly. 'If your old boss was looking at this situation objectively, looking at his own abduction, the way it was done and who did it, what would he do? Would he go public? Would he break the biggest international scandal in years? Tell me. You know him, Lottie, I don't.'

Mann gazed at the last lonely croissant, took pity on it and picked it up. 'As a man called Mick Herron would put it,' she murmured, 'this stuff is straight off Spook Street. The Gaffer's more than fifty per cent spook himself, always has been. I'm pretty sure he'd say to sit on it for twenty-four hours and see how it plays out.' She wrapped the croissant in paper torn from a kitchen roll, and stepped off the stool. 'Come on, let's go to Barcelona and see your bosses. I'm not a spectator here; he's my translator, remember, so I have an interest. I feel that I'm representing him, and his family and everyone back home. I need to be part of what happens next.'

Sixty-Four

Awareness returned to him slowly. He was lying on a firm surface, his head on a cushion. At first he thought he was in a dream. Minutes went past as he anticipated his awakening, but he was still disconnected from time and so. for all he knew, they could have been days. His name, he thought, was Bob, but he was not quite certain of this.

Surgery. The word swam into his head and lodged there. A random knife attack, blues and sirens, then a gurney and bright lights, people in gowns and masks, and then nothing but dark thoughts and visions. So why, he wondered, did he still have twin pinpoints of pain in his back and an ache in the right side of his neck, just below the jawbone?

'Is he still out?'

The voice seemed distant and yet close, all at the same time. Familiar too. His father? Couldn't be, with that accent. His father was from Motherwell, not Minneapolis. And come to think of it, his father was dead.

'Zonked,' a second voice said, one he had not heard before. 'Maybe we gave him too much. Fried his brain.'

'That would be unfortunate,' Agent K said. 'It might cause difficulties.'

Agent K? he thought. Where had that come from? And then he remembered the movie, how suddenly he was in the middle of it. Although . . .

Bob Skinner lay there, on the firm surface, cushion under his head, and waited for his memory to reassemble itself fully, taking care to keep his eyes closed as he anticipated what would happen when he decided to awaken. *Zappy thing*, he promised himself, would be the least of their worries.

Sixty-Five

Lottie Mann was not, as a rule, a nervous passenger but there was something about the curves of the southbound AP7 towards Barcelona, the density of its traffic and above all the speed at which they were travelling, that scared her witless. Okay, they were in a police car to which normal speed limits did not apply but nothing, not the decals on its sides, not the blue lights, not the screaming siren sounds, put it beyond the reach of the laws of physics and their consequences, most of all those of hitting an immovable object at upwards of a hundred and seventy kilometres an hour. When the ringtone sounded on the car's hands-free system and Lita Roza slowed down to take the call, she breathed an audible, thankful, sigh of relief.

'*Diga me.*' Mann had come to recognise 'Talk to me', as the Catalan way of taking a call.

'*La companyia d'helicòpters va tornar a trucar. Hi havia un passatger en aquell vol. Un canadenc anomenat Gilbert Land.*'

'*Gràcies.*'

She turned to Mann as the call ended. 'Did you get that? The helicopter taxi company responded. The passenger they took to the Ruidaura *masia* was Gilbert Land.'

'That begs a big question, doesn't it?' Lottie looked ahead, holding back a smile as she saw that the traffic ahead was grid-locked. 'Where is Mr Land now?'

'Yes,' Roza agreed. 'And one more. Where is the *mujer*? Where is Geraldine Black?'

Sixty-Six

She seemed gaunt as she gazed at the screen, taking in what she had been told. 'I knew it was too good to be true,' she sighed. 'Everything was falling into place for us yesterday; we had a heart-to-heart and at the end of it we were ready, both of us, to commit to Spain, with me building my work life around his. Now, it's all falling apart.' Her hand went to her mouth. 'Oh God, that sounded so selfish. Alex, I didn't mean it like that; it's such a shock, what you've told me, is all.'

'We know, Sarah,' Dominick Jackson replied. 'It's a huge shock, we appreciate that. Alex reacted to it by having a swim. You reacted to it with guilt, where there is none. So, let's all think rationally, all three of us. Agreed.'

She looked back at them, drinking in the reassurance that his calmness offered; his arm was around Alex's shoulders, as if he were holding her together.

'Are we afraid for him?' he asked. 'Yes, we are. It takes power to snatch Bob Skinner from his own home. Do we have confidence in him? Yes, we do. Do we expect to see him again? Yes, we do, once he's sorted out his present situation and made the people involved feel very sorry indeed.'

Sarah realised that she was smiling. 'I expect they'll need counselling afterwards,' she chuckled.

'If they do,' Dominic said, 'they can find their own counsellor. This one won't be sympathetic.'

Alex kissed the back of his hand, taking her stepmother by surprise. She offered a shy smile and shrugged. 'That was then,' she murmured. 'This is now.'

Sixty-Seven

'Is this verified?' Major Teijero asked.

'It is,' Roza assured him. She had asked him to speak in English, for Mann's benefit.

'The Americans have done this, in Catalunya, without asking permission?'

'Without asking permission of the *Mossos*. That's all we can say for certain. If they asked the security ministry in Madrid, do you think they would tell us?'

'I would hope they would,' the major replied. 'But if they chose to keep the circle of knowledge very small one might understand it.'

Mann had abandoned restraint. 'This one might not,' she snapped. 'Sir. If it was the fucking Russians, we'd be sending drones over Moscow, not making exculpatory noises.'

'You might,' he said, stiffly. 'We might not. I am only in effect a regional official. I have no power.'

'In that case why am I wasting my time talking to you? I'm trusting Spain to sort this out, not you, but that trust's vanishing by the second. Either you put me in a room with someone who does have power, or I'll do what I might get the sack for not having done earlier, that being, phone my boss in Scotland, my big boss, the chief constable. He's a quiet man, but Bob Skinner's one of his closest friends. If this goes wrong and something bad happens the shite that flies off the fan will fucking engulf you and you will be kissing your career goodbye.'

Teijero stiffened; beneath his summer tan his face had turned chalk white. 'Ladies,' he hissed, 'if you will leave me for a few minutes, I will make a telephone call.'

'"Ladies",' Roza muttered, once they were outside. 'Sexist little fuck! Did you mean that?' she asked. 'The threat to phone your boss?'

Mann smiled. 'Do you think I'm crazy? I called him last night, then again as soon as we knew about the Americans being involved. He's given me full authority to act on his behalf, as you've just witnessed. I have a big arse, Lita, but I make sure it's covered all the time.' She nodded towards the major's closed door. 'What do you think he's doing now?'

'Covering his,' the *comissari* said, 'although it's a lot skinnier than yours.'

As she spoke, Teijero's door reopened. 'Please remain here, ladies. I have called the minister and told him what has happened. I expected to be summoned to Barcelona, but no. He is coming here. Particularly, Chief Inspector, he wishes to see you.'

Sixty-Eight

Skinner lay as still as he had been lying since he recovered full control of his senses, and of his memories. His eyes were closed, but he was aware of all the movement around him. He knew that there were two men in the room, no more, and he knew who they were.

Finally, he allowed himself to stretch out his arms and to shift his position, accompanied by a grunt and a sigh. He opened his eyes, looking around as if in surprise, but in reality scanning the room for cameras. He saw none, only a table with two chairs, one occupied by Agent K.

Agent J stood over him. 'Sir, you're awake,' he said. 'We've been worried about you. Here, let me help you stand. You need to get the blood circulating again.'

'Thank you,' Skinner whispered, as the American took his arm and raised him to his feet. Agent K came across to help, but he shook his head. 'That's better,' he murmured, clenching and unclenching his fists several times. 'What drugs did you use on me?'

'Propofol and pentobarbital,' Agent J told him. 'We were maybe a little too heavy on the propofol.'

'Maybe, but it's the best sleep I've had in years. Are you left-handed?' he asked.

'Yes, sir, I am. Why do you ask?'

'It means that you're the one that stuck the needle in my neck.'

Skinner's smile vanished. He seized the man by the lapels, lifted him off his feet, drew him close and, as he did so, head-butted him between the eyes as hard as he could, hearing the satisfying crunch of a breaking nose. He threw him across the room and in the same movement turned to meet Agent K as he came to his colleague's aid. He feinted to the left, inviting a punch, and grabbing the man's arm as it came. Spinning him round, he jerked upwards, dislocating K's shoulder and elbow in the same movement, and drawing a scream. It had taken five seconds.

Moving fast, he took a firearm from K's hip holster. J was semi-conscious, in danger of choking on his own blood. As Skinner removed the pistol, he turned the man on his side. Holding both pistols he stepped across the room. When the door opened and Agent L rushed in, taser brandished, he was standing behind it. He pressed a pistol to the back of her head with his left hand. 'Bang,' he murmured, 'you're dead.' With his right hand he took the stun gun and shot her, point-blank.

'Well, children,' he said as he surveyed the carnage. 'Look how your day's turned out. If I had the zappy thing like you guys had in the movie, I'd erase your memories. But I don't, so you'll have to remember this for the rest of your lives.'

He walked over to the table and laid down the weapons then waited. A few seconds later, a woman appeared in the doorway. She was white-haired, leaner than she had been when they had met years before but still unforgettable.

'Merle bloody Gower,' Skinner exclaimed, with a widening grin. 'I might have known.' He looked down at the three casualties and sighed. 'Are these the best you could find?' he asked. 'I think I feel a little insulted.'

Sixty-Nine

Lottie Mann peered at her watch, her eyes wrinkling as she tried to focus on the hands. 'A present from my other half,' she explained. 'It has a mother-of-pearl face, which makes it bloody difficult to see when it's got light reflecting off it, but it was expensive and he was really chuffed with himself when he gave it to me, so I have to wear it.'

'What does your husband do?' Lita Roza asked

'Dan was a cop. We worked together for years. He's retired now but he lectures part-time at one of the police colleges. But he's not my husband; we have this Scottish word, "bidey-in", that you won't find in too many dictionaries. I'm his.'

'But he isn't yours?'

'We moved in with him, me and my son. His house was bigger.'

'Does that make you feel secure?' the Catalan wondered.

'With Dan, always. I'm protected in his will.'

'But if you break up? I have two woman friends; each of them was in a long term relationship that broke up and he kept the house.'

'We won't. Dan and me, we're like Alex Skinner and her new fella. We're solid, we're for life.'

'But if you did?'

'I never sold my old place. It's rented. That's all the answer I can give you.' She frowned at her watch again, gave up and checked the hour on her phone. 'He's taking his time, this minister of yours. The major said he was on his way.'

Roza smiled. 'Don't take the major literally; Senor Mateu will be here as soon as he can, and as soon as the Barcelona traffic allows. Nobody is exempt from that. It's one reason why our headquarters are here in Sabadell and not in the . . .'

There was a rap on her office door. '*Entrar*,' she called; it opened and a sergeant stepped into the room. Quickly and quietly he gave her a message; he spoke too quickly for Mann to grasp any of it.

'Progress,' the *comissari* announced, as he left. 'The car that is registered in the name of Gilbert Land has been found. It's gathering bird shit and parking tickets in a town called Ribes de Freser in the *comarca* of Ripolles in the north of Catalunya. It's a pretty little place, almost a kilometre above sea level. It's a tourist centre but for many it's only a junction on the way to somewhere else. We have officers checking the hotels and hostals. When we are finished here, we will go there.'

'Hold on,' Mann exclaimed. 'What about the Gaffer? He's my priority.'

'There is nothing that you and I can do for him, Lottie,' Roza pointed out, 'other maybe than finding Gilbert Land, or whoever else was driving that car.'

Mann was unconvinced. 'I'll need to think about that,' she murmured, as the door swung open again, and a lean tanned man stepped into the room.

Instantly, Comissari Roza sprang from her seat and saluted. '*Ministre*.'

'Ssh,' the newcomer said. 'Let's not be formal.' He turned to Mann, who was in the act of rising. 'Chief Inspector, I am Manuel Mateu. I'm the security minister of Catalunya and as such I am in charge of the search for my friend Bob. Sit back down and let's talk about what has happened. Major Teijero gave me a brief explanation, but I need to hear it from you, and from Comissari Roza, whom I have never met but of whom I have heard important things.'

'Shall I ask the major to join us?'

Mateu shook his head; Mann thought she saw a small grimace. 'No, that will not be necessary. He has other duties. One of those is to consider why he failed to mention to me the fact that Madrid had told him the Americans would be conducting an off-the-books national security operation in Catalunya.'

'Madrid knew about it?' Roza repeated.

'Yes, that much I know, but that is all. How much they knew, that's another matter. Major Teijero doesn't know any more himself, of that I am sure. He was told by his opposite number in the *Policia Nacional* so that his officers might not interfere in any unorthodox situations that might arise. That's how he put it.'

'By which they meant,' Mann growled, 'if they see a man being drugged and kidnapped, they should look the other way?'

'I don't like that any more than you do, Chief Inspector,' the minister said, glancing at her. 'That's why the major declined to tell me; he knew I would raise hell. Bob told me about you, by the way. He said you were a good choice for this assignment, formidable. I can see why he thinks so.'

She suppressed a smile and said nothing.

'I know that you are here because of a link between a homicide investigation in Scotland and a man called Gilbert Land, in whom we also have a certain interest. He owns a house near a town called Riudaura and I know that Bob was there. Did he tell you anything about it?'

'No,' she said. 'But he was there when it was open and his reaction was . . . interesting. That's the word I would use. Would you agree, Lita?'

Roza nodded. 'Yes, I would. I would say that what we found when we went in there was not what he expected. But what we've found since then, that's exactly as he predicted; the place is unnaturally clean, and absolutely empty.'

'The swimming pool was sparkling too,' Mann added. 'His daughter was with him when they checked the place and she confirmed that it was almost black with algae.'

'Is she still in Spain? His daughter? Does she know about the kidnap?'

'Yes, and she does. So does Sarah . . . that's Sir Robert's wife.'

'Anyone else?'

'My chief constable. Everyone's agreed to keep it secret, for his sake, but now that we know that it's the Americans . . .'

'Now that I know,' Mateu said heavily. 'This is Catalunya; we might not be independent, yet, but we do have autonomy. Now that I am in the picture I will make the decisions about how this appalling situation is handled.'

'In that case, Minister,' Mann suggested, 'can you make them before the Gaffer winds up in fucking Guantanamo!'

He smiled grimly. 'An unlikely eventuality, but yes, I will intervene.'

As he spoke, the sound of a mobile's vibration alert came from his pocket. He frowned as he produced it and stared at the screen. Roza could see it from her angle and read, as he did, 'Número ocult'.

'Not many people have my number,' Mateu murmured. 'My opposite number in Madrid, perhaps. She is among them. Whoever it is, I must take it.' He clicked *'Aceptar'*, and put the phone to his ear.

Seventy

Sarah was staring at her fifth mug of coffee since midnight when her older son came into the breakfasting kitchen. 'Mum,' Mark said. 'Are you all right? Scratch that, silly question; you're not all right. What's the matter?'

She shook her head. 'Nothing, darling, honestly.'

'Mum, please, give me some credit. I'm sixteen years old, I'm an adult near as dammit. It's bloody obvious you're upset.'

She shrugged and offered a weak, unconvincing smile. 'Menopause, that's all.'

'Unlikely,' he countered. 'You're a month short of forty-three. You'll need a better story than that.'

She felt tears come. 'I can't tell you, love, I really can't.'

'Does it involve Dad?'

She nodded, clutching her mug.

'Are you splitting up?'

She gasped, eyes widening. 'God no!' she protested.

'Then what? Is he ill? Has he had an accident?'

'Something like that,' she offered. 'Please don't ask me anything else, because that's all I can say.'

'In that case do us . . .' he said, gently, 'do us all a favour and go back to your room before Seonaid or Jazz come down and see

249

you like this. She'll just cry and he won't rest until he's got the whole story out of you.'

She nodded. 'You're right,' she murmured. 'You're a good kid, you know, Markie. And you're adult enough for me right now.' She tightened the belt of her dressing gown and headed for the door. She was halfway there when her phone rang in her pocket; she snatched for it, spilling her coffee. Mark stepped forward and took her mug from her as she pressed 'Accept'.

'It's me,' a familiar, if slightly hoarse voice said, 'I'll explain everything later but I'm all right. For now, please let everybody know who needs to, and I'll call again when I can. Love you.'

For the first time in her life, Sarah Grace Skinner fainted.

Seventy-One

'Where will they be taken?' Skinner asked, looking from a window as the private ambulance drove away, three casualties inside.

'Don't know, don't care,' Merle Gower sighed. 'The Embassy will handle all that. It'll be a private hospital somewhere near here, then back to the US for evaluation. Fucking Secret Service!' she exploded. 'They think they have no operational boundaries. I didn't want them for this mission but they were forced on me.'

'You got my phone?' he asked brusquely. 'There's a call I must make.'

'Yes, it was in your back pocket.' She took it from her jacket and handed it over. She waited as he called his wife. 'Bob, I'm sorry,' she said when he had finished. 'That was never meant to happen.'

'But it did,' he said, 'and now you're going to tell me why.'

'Looks like I have to,' Gower acknowledged. 'You've got all the guns.'

'I have more than that,' he told her. 'I have influence. Never mind the firearms; they'll be fine where I put them, in the freezer . . . although you'd better not forget them when you check out of here. Where the hell are we, incidentally?'

'We're in a house near a village called Rupia. It's the US Consul General's summer place. It was made available to me for the purposes of this operation. Those three were meant to invite you to meet with me, to explain a certain situation. I told them to be polite and to mention my name if you had a problem or needed assurance that it was legit. I did not say anything about drugging you and dumping you into a diplomatic vehicle, I promise.'

'I like to think you'd have known better,' Skinner observed. 'Are you going to feed me before you explain what this is all about? I reckon I'm two meals down. The freezer seemed well stocked when I put the guns in there.'

'We have burgers if you'd like . . . with a vegan option. I can do some on the Foreman grill. Those three could have done with Big George earlier on,' she added, with a wry grin.

'Nah.' He shook his head. 'These days he's too old, too fat, too slow. You can shove the vegan option,' he continued. 'I'll have meat, and some eggs if you have them.'

She led him to the well-appointed kitchen, where she took four thick burgers and half a dozen eggs from the fridge.

'And coffee,' he added, as she switched on the grill.

'Naturally.'

He watched her as she set to work. 'How long's it been, Merle?' he asked. On several occasions in his police career Skinner had interfaced with US Federal agents, in the UK and in America. Merle Gower had been one of those; initially they had clashed, but a mutual respect had grown.

'Very,' she replied. 'I moved on from the London Embassy a long time ago. My life's changed since then, as has yours, obviously.'

'What are you now? Still FBI?'

'National Security Agency. I don't have a title or a job description as such. If I did, "Troubleshooter" would cover it.'

'The trouble in this case being . . .?'

'A Presidential directive; from the man himself and his Chief of Staff. There is a matter that he wants to disappear before it washes all over him. Ever heard of Russell Silver?' she asked.

'Of course, I've heard of him,' Skinner laughed. 'I'm a fucking media magnate with interests in the USA, remember?'

'What do you know about him?'

'He's a declared candidate in the upcoming presidential election. A self-made man who's running as an independent with a very clever platform. He's cashing in on the increasing polarisation of the major parties, with the Republicans in the grip of the right and the Democrats edging further and further to the left, with young people in office and one or two older mavericks who're not afraid to call themselves socialists. That's creating a big gap in the centre, with millions of electors, across both traditional parties, feeling disenfranchised. They're the block that Silver's chasing, under the slogan "Make America Care Again", and the polls are showing him gathering enough support to be a threat to the President and to his main opponent, whichever nutjob the Republicans pick. How am I doing so far?'

'You're doing very well,' Gower conceded. 'But you didn't say anything about the supervision of campaigns by the Federal Election Commission. How much do you know about that?'

'You didn't ask me,' he pointed out. 'The FEC has six members, three from each main party, usually rendering it toothless when a complaint's investigated.'

'That's harsh, but more or less true. However, that goes out the window when a serious independent comes along and starts to gather significant campaign funding. Silver's been doing that, from legitimate sources, and the Republicans have been crying "Foul". Maybe it's sour grapes, probably is, but the Commission is starting to take an interest. Meanwhile, Silver's campaign is building. He's never going to win but the polls, public and private, are saying that the greater part of his support is coming from Democrats, to the extent that if the election was tomorrow, with him on the ballot paper, the President would be defeated. Without him, he wins.'

'Understood,' Skinner said. 'But how does any of that bring you and me here, and how did it lead to me getting a needle stuck in my neck by the People in Black?'

'That started when the President began to consider the unthinkable: offer Silver the vice presidency and bring him onside. Until very recently that was the preferred option. However, the President's a cautious man; before going public with the idea, or even floating it in-house among his Cabinet, he asked my Agency to look at Silver and subject him to the most extreme positive vetting you have ever seen.' Gower stopped in mid-tale. 'Medium or do you want them burned?'

'They should be fine for me right now.' He watched as she took the burgers from the grill and laid them on plates, three for Skinner, one for herself, each with two fried eggs. 'Bring the coffee,' she instructed. He obeyed, taking the jug from under the filter and a carton of milk from the fridge, and following her back to the other room.

'I repeat,' she said as they began to eat, 'I am sorry for what happened.'

'I get that,' Skinner replied, 'and I accept it. But if you want me to apologise for the broken toys, forget it.'

She shrugged. 'They're collateral damage. You want me to go on?'

He nodded.

'Okay. When the vetting began, it didn't take long to establish that Silver was up to something. Big chunks of his campaign money were being banked illegally, in Liechtenstein and the Cayman Islands. Of the three hundred million dollars he'd raised, approaching fifty million was no longer visible. But Silver's hands weren't on the transfers. They were authorised by one of his aides, a man called David Allen, a Canadian, born in Mississauga, Ontario, thirty-four years ago. When we went looking for Allen, he was out of town. His staff, a band of interns working for peanuts, couldn't tell us where he was.'

'I think I might be able to,' Skinner murmured, his mind racing, 'but we'll leave that for now. What about Silver's background? Was that phoney as well?'

'No. He made his money, a decent amount of it, a few million in real estate. He married when he was thirty, had a child, but it didn't last. His wife left him, they were divorced and he kept up the alimony payments until she died six years ago.'

'How about his political activity?'

'He was a registered Democrat into his thirties. Then, out of the blue eight years ago, he ran for Governor of Kansas as a middle ground independent like he's doing now. He finished third and everyone forgot about him until he surfaced again a couple of years ago, this time with an effective team run by Allen, and started raising money.'

'When you couldn't find Allen, what did you do?' Skinner asked, mopping up some of the runny egg yolk with a chunk of burger.

'We put Silver under twenty-four-hour surveillance,' Gower replied. 'Three weeks ago, less a couple of days, he took an internal flight from Kansas City, where he'd held a campaign rally the night before, to O'Hare, in Chicago. He never left the airport. We thought he might have got off the aircraft before it took off, but he was logged as arriving. We thought he might have changed to another internal flight, but we couldn't put him on any. It took us ten days to uncover images of a man boarding a flight to Madrid: it was Silver, but he was using a Canadian passport in the name of Gilbert Land.'

He nodded. 'You reported back to the President, and he said "Find him and bring him back, or . . . find him and don't bring him back?"'

'Only the first; this President isn't that sort of man. I was tasked with the recovery, and given a Secret Service team. I'd have preferred special forces but I was overruled by the Chief of Staff. It took us five days to track him to Catalunya, that long for his name to come out of the property register. But it did. We went to the house in Riudaura. We got in and we found him, dead. I don't want to see that again.' She glanced at Skinner across the table. 'I don't imagine you do either.'

Skinner frowned and shook his head.

'We were watching the place from a distance, Bob. When you and the woman arrived we were there, waiting for a clean-up team to get there,' she said. 'Who was she, by the way? The woman?'

'That was my daughter Alex,' he replied. 'I'm surprised you don't know that already.'

'Identifying her wasn't a priority,' Gower countered. 'I only wanted to clear up the mess and get out of there, nothing more complex than that. When the *Mossos* came I thought that was done for, but they left before dark, rather than keep the house under guard. By that time the clean squad was ready; it went in after dark. We got the remains out of there and worked all night to remove all traces of Silver and anything else human. Once it was done, I knew that I needed to talk to you, to explain what had happened, and to ask you to use the influence that I know you have in Spain to keep a lid on it. And that's why I sent the team to invite you to come here. Idiots!' she exploded.

Skinner grinned. 'Surely, Merle, with all your resources, you could have come up with my fucking phone number! A quick call, "Hi it's me, a blast from the past. Can we meet for a coffee?" That would probably have done it.'

'I don't exist here,' Gower countered. 'I couldn't take the risk of you blowing me.'

'You might want to rephrase that . . . Okay,' he continued, 'that's all history, for my memoirs or yours. What did you do with him?'

'Body bag; he's been flown back already to Dover Air Force base,' she replied. 'It has the biggest military morgue in America and it's very closed. We don't do our casualty repatriation in public, like you Brits do at Brize Norton.' She frowned, her tight grey curls shining as a shaft of morning sunlight, filtered by trees, shone through the window. 'I would expect the Silver campaign team to make a formal announcement of a sad sudden death whenever Mr Allen returns. If he doesn't . . .'

'If he doesn't, what will happen?'

'Then I imagine that his family will break the news. There's a brother somewhere and we know there's a daughter too.' She paused, watching him as he finished his third burger, using the last segment to mop up what was left of the egg yolk. 'Earlier,' she continued when he was ready, 'you said you might be able to help with Allen. What did you mean by that?'

'Do you have an image of him?' Skinner asked.

'Hold on.'

In the moment that she stepped out of the room, his phone sounded. 'Alex,' the screen read. He took the call.

'Pops!' Her voice was hoarse. 'You're okay?'

'I am, some others, they're not so good. Darlin', I can't speak now. You and Dominick catch your flights. We'll talk when you're home.'

'No way! We're not leaving here until I've seen with my own eyes that you're all right. Isn't that right, Dominick? He says the same. When will you be here?'

'I'll know better once I've sorted a couple of things out,' he replied. 'I must go now; one of those things has just come into the room.'

He ended the call as Gower returned; she was carrying a laptop. 'My daughter. She's a criminal prosecutor: you should be thankful you're not in Scotland.'

'I hope never to go there again,' she assured him. 'Too cold.' She opened the laptop and chose a file, from which she extracted an image, then turned the screen towards him. 'David Allen,' she said.

Skinner gazed at the full-face photo. 'Known in Scotland as Gavin Ayre,' he murmured, 'current residence cold storage in the mortuary in Edinburgh, where he's been for just over a week. My wife did the autopsy and removed a sniper bullet from his skull. From what I know of the scene and the circumstances, even Lee Harvey Oswald would have struggled to make that shot. Merle, are you sure you're in full possession of all the facts here?'

She stared at him. Alarm registered as she considered his question. 'Are you suggesting that I've been sent here to pick up the pieces?' she asked.

'That is what you're doing. The question is, who's been leaving those pieces behind? Is it an agent of your state, or is it someone else?'

'Is that a question that I should even ask?' she wondered. 'If it was you, Bob, in my shoes, what would you do?'

He closed the laptop and gazed out of the window, as if he was deep in thought. Finally he looked back at her and responded. 'In my long career, I have learned two things about our nations, yours and mine. One is that there really is a dark side in each of them. The other is, don't fuck with it unless you're prepared to go all the way. You're not, Merle; you don't have it. Potentially you're expendable. You're here, playing secret games in a friendly country where you have absolutely no locus, and you are out of your fucking depth. Should you ask that question? Absolutely not. You should pack up and sneak off home.'

'But can I do that, Bob?' Gower countered. 'I'm here with presidential authority and with the approval of the Spanish state. I don't think I can tell the White House, "Sorry, I'm out of here."'

'You're here with the knowledge of the Spanish state, but that doesn't mean its approval. Someone here might have given the nod, but you are still utterly deniable. My friend, I could put one in your head right now and walk out of here. Inside two hours I would be in my house in L'Escala having lunch with my daughter. What would happen? Nothing. Eventually the mess would be cleared up by the same people who sterilised the *masia*, and nothing would ever have happened. They wouldn't even fly you to Dover; you would just go up a chimney somewhere. The ground's too hard here in August to dig a grave; that's why the Spanish mostly bury their dead in catacombs.'

Then he smiled. 'It's just as well we're friends, isn't it?'

'Will that do me any good if it was my side that took out Silver and Allen? If it's so, you'll leave here and I'll be someone who knows too much.'

The smile became a laugh. 'In that event, it's just as well you kidnapped a fucking media magnate, isn't it?'

'Won't they go after you too? The dark side?'

'Me?' Skinner exclaimed. 'A public figure in a European nation? A NATO member state? I don't think so.' He topped up their coffee from the jug, 'However,' he continued, 'on the basis of what I know, I don't actually believe that your side did it. There's somebody else involved, another player in the game, one that the Catalan and Scottish police need to talk to. Does the name Geraldine Black mean anything to you?'

Gower frowned. 'Geraldine Black?' she repeated. 'No, should it?'

'If your people were any good at their jobs it might. Not to blow my own trumpet but I found her with one casual enquiry . . . and I'm only a humble journalist these days. However,' he continued, 'let's cover all possibilities, and keep you safe. To do that, I need to speak to the man who can do that.'

He picked up his phone from the table and called Manuel Mateu.

Seventy-Two

'I know already what I will do, Bob,' Manuel Mateu said. 'I will communicate directly with the *Presidente del Gobierno*, the Prime Minister, and I will tell him that my department has discovered that US Secret Service agents have been operating illegally in Catalunya, without my knowledge but with the approval of the Security Minister in Madrid. I will tell him of my outrage that an important business figure was forcibly abducted by these people and detained. I know how he will react: with horror, because this is not something he would ever have tolerated. The security minister will be fired today. I won't even have to murmur the threat to withdraw the support of Catalan members in the Cortes for this to happen, but I will insist that the three people who took you are expelled from Spain immediately and returned to the USA under police guard.'

'That's fine, but what about Merle Gower?' Skinner asked. 'Are you going to throw her to the wolves too? I have to tell you that I wouldn't like that. If you need to, you can tell the *Presidente* that her safety is the price of my silence.'

'I won't need to. I'll protect your Ms Gower in another way. Bring her to the *Mossos* headquarters; that's where I am now. We'll be photographed together at the entrance to the building, and I'll issue a bullshit press release about her being on an official visit, at my invitation, to demonstrate the commitment of the Catalan Government to maintaining the security of American visitors to Barcelona, their number-one tourist destination. I'll even back it up by ordering the *Mossos* to crack down on the pick-pockets on *Las Ramblas*. You'll carry that on InterMedia's channels, yes?'

Skinner had made the call in speaker mode. He saw Gower's eyes widen; she nodded vigorously. 'I'll ensure it,' he promised, 'and I'll feed it into our US outlet too. What about the late Gilbert Land?'

'We've never heard of him. His name will be wiped from the records of the *Mossos*; he'll continue to exist as the owner of the Riudaura property. We'll work out what to do with it later.'

'What about Geraldine Black?' he wondered. 'DCI Mann and her colleagues in Scotland have an interest in her; she might connect to the Gavin Ayre, scratch that, David Allen inquiry.'

'There,' Mateu replied, 'we may have movement. I will fill you in on that when you get here.'

'Rupia to Sabadell, give it two hours and Ms Gower and I will be there. There's a stop I must make before I go south, although Ms Gower will have to stay in the car.'

Seventy-Three

'What happened? You have to tell us,' Alex demanded.

'I can't do that,' her father said, pulling on the jacket that he had collected from his wardrobe after he had showered and changed into fresh clothes, 'not now and maybe not ever. I'm here to prove to you that I'm alive and well, and not one of those holograms that Markie keeps going on about. Look, I have to be somewhere else very soon. You two still have time to catch that evening flight, and I want you to do that, so that you can put Sarah's mind at rest. I've spoken to her and I will be with her as soon as I can, but it won't be today. Do it for me, please.'

She nodded. 'If you insist. Can you run us to the airport?'

'Sorry, no, I don't have time for that either. Send our friend Stan a text; he'll get you there if he can. If not, he'll know someone.'

He turned to Jackson, who was standing by the window. 'Dominick,' he said, 'look after her, and Sarah too.'

He nodded. 'I will, Bob.' He nodded towards the street. 'What's that you're driving?' he asked.

'A Cadillac,' Skinner replied. 'The guys who snatched me were driving it, but they don't need it any longer.'

263

'What happened to them?'

'Bad things.' He smiled. 'They probably thought the worst was over, but they're going to find out quite soon that there's more to come.'

Seventy-Four

'David Allen,' Haddock repeated.

'That's what the Gaffer said,' Mann assured him.

'Where did he get that?'

'It was the security minister who passed the message on. He didn't say, but I assume it was from the Americans.'

'The same Americans who . . .'

'No, from their chief, from what Senor Mateu said. I don't think those ones are saying much of anything just now.'

'What do we know about him? Allen?'

'He's Canadian, born somewhere in Ontario that I confess I can't pronounce, aged thirty-four. That's all I've been told.'

'Could that be yet another false identity?'

'It could, I suppose.'

'I'll look for it anyway,' Haddock said, 'although it'll probably be Monday before anything can be done. What about Gilbert Land? Was anything said about him?'

'By the minister to me, no. By the Gaffer to the minister, I have no idea. They're playing secret fucking squirrels, Sauce. All I can do is act on what I'm told. At the moment we have one live lead, and that's the Geraldine Black woman.'

'That's if she is,' Haddock observed grimly. 'Alive, that is. I've

265

got Jackie Wright looking for her here to see if she's left any traces since that sighting in the hotel. So far she's had no luck.'

'She's been invisible in Spain for a few days, but there may be progress on that. A car belonging to Gilbert Land's been sighted in a town up in the mountains. Comissari Roza and I are going there once we've seen the Gaffer. He's on his way here now.'

Seventy-Five

When Bob Skinner walked through the door, Lottie Mann experienced a wholly unprofessional urge to hug him. She dismissed it, instead rising from her seat and calling out across the room, 'Gaffer, you took your time getting here.'

He grinned. 'Sorry about that, DCI Mann; I had to call in at L'Escala to pick up another jacket.'

'You're good though?' she asked.

His smile widened. 'I haven't felt better in a long time, truth be told. A night's sleep and a strenuous work-out; that always does you good.' A quick frown showed on the face of the white-curled woman who had entered with him.

In fact, the attack of the night before had taken its toll on him. The drugged sleep had not been restful, there was an ache in his neck and he had pain in his back where the twin barbs of the taser had pierced his flesh. He wanted nothing more than to get back to Girona, to the paracetamol in his bathroom cabinet washed down by a couple of beers and some proper recuperation, before he saw Sarah.

'*Comissari*,' he said, turning his gaze towards Roza, 'this is Ms Gower, an old friend from the US who's paying a flying visit to Spain. I believe that Senor Mateu is expecting her.'

267

'Yes, Sir Robert, he is,' she replied. 'He is in the major's office with a member of our media team.'

'He said he'd brief me on a Geraldine Black development,' Skinner said.

'Lottie will do that. Ms Gower, if you will come with me. The minister has limited time. Sir Robert, there's a car outside and a driver; he'll take you back to Girona.'

'Thanks, that's appreciated. *Hasta la vista*, Merle,' he called out as they headed for the door. 'You're always welcome, but I'd rather be forewarned next time.'

She glanced back towards him with the hint of a smile.

'So, Lottie,' he began as they left, 'what have you got for me?'

'For openers,' she replied, 'I've got your other jacket and your wallet.' She reached back and took the garment from a hook on the wall. 'The people that took you,' she asked as she handed it over, 'what about them?'

'One needs a new nose, another won't pick his for a few months, and the third might think twice before shooting anyone else in the back with a stun gun, now she's had the experience herself. But that's between you and me; the whole thing never happened. They'll be on their way back home before the day's out.'

Mann jerked a thumb towards the door. 'You seem on good terms with her, all things considered.'

'Merle and I go way back. She assured me that her people exceeded their authority.'

'Do you believe her?'

'I choose to,' he said. 'She owes me and she knows that at some time in the future I'll collect the debt. Now, what about Black?'

'Land's car's been found in a place called Ribes de Freser. Lita and I are going there as soon as we can. It may be that she and Land are together, but . . .'

'They're not.'

'How do you know that, Gaffer?' she asked.

'Don't ask me, just believe it. Gilbert Land doesn't exist . . . and as for Black, well, the name meant nothing to the Americans. If she's in Ribes, then I'm pretty sure I know where she's headed and what she's planning to do, and I have no doubt that the *comissari* will figure it out too. Do me a favour; keep me in touch when you get there.'

'Aren't you going back to Scotland?'

'The plan is I go back soon. But there's another possibility I'm considering. And Lottie,' he added, smiling as he headed for the door and his waiting driver, 'I hope you enjoy the train journey.'

Seventy-Six

'We have a Geraldine Black listed on our service from Barcelona to Edinburgh, on Thursday the week before last,' the Irish voice told Jackie Wright. 'We had two flights on that day. She was on the first; it landed early afternoon. It was a last-minute booking, purchased online the evening before the flight was due to depart.'

'What about the return leg?' the DS asked.

'There wasn't one,' she answered. 'It was a one-way booking.'

'Did Black actually catch the flight? Was she actually on it?'

'Yes, she travelled. And before you ask, it would have been her; our Barcelona agents are scrupulous about ID checks.'

'How did she pay for it?'

'The only way possible, with a card; this one was linked to a PayPal account. If you want to trace it, that won't be easy.'

'She must have logged passport details, Donna, yes?'

'Yes, she did. She's a Singaporean national.'

'Singapore?'

'Yes. And she's thirty-one years old. I can text you the passport number, Sergeant, if that'll help.'

'Yes, do that please,' Wright confirmed. 'Thanks.'

She ended the call and crossed the squad room to DI Singh's

work station. 'This Black person,' she began. 'I have her arriving here on a flight from Barcelona on the day before the man we now know as David Allen was murdered. That's a new twist, Tarvil.'

His eyes widened with surprise. 'Too right,' he agreed. 'But,' he cautioned, 'if we're thinking of her as a suspect, that only puts her at Edinburgh Airport. We need to establish a presence at or around the scene. How would she get from one to the other?'

Wright frowned. 'Any number of ways,' she conceded. 'She could have got on the airport bus, even the tram, and gone on from there, by bus or train to North Berwick. Or she could have taken an airport taxi.'

'Or she could have pre-booked,' Singh added, then paused. 'I seem to remember reading one of the early statements where there was a taxi firm mentioned, picking up the victim and his girlfriend from a restaurant.'

'That's right: AJ Private Hire, the owner told Inspector Hill. It's by no means a certainty but if he used them and there's a connection, maybe so did she. It's a medium-to-long shot, but it's worth taking before we start on scattergun calls.'

'Okay,' the DI said. 'You do that and I'll brief Sauce.'

Seventy-Seven

'We're changing cars,' Roza told Mann as they emerged from the *Mossos* headquarters. 'Where we're going, it'll be better to have an all-wheel drive vehicle.'

'We're going off-road?' the Scot asked.

'Probably not, but it will be a climb and towards Ribes de Freser the road isn't exactly straight.'

'How high is it above sea level?'

'Not far short of a thousand metres; three thousand feet in your measurements.'

'Bloody hell,' Mann gasped. 'That's the height of a Munro.'

Roza stared at her. 'What's a Munro?'

'It's our name in Scotland for a mountain peak over three thousand feet high. We've got two hundred and eighty-two of them and they're my eccentric partner's new craze. He wants to climb the lot. That said, "climb" is an exaggeration. We're not talking crampons and ice axes here; you can walk up most of them.'

'How many has he done?'

'Since he got the bug, we,' she said with emphasis, 'have done forty-seven; he keeps a ledger. I must admit, I enjoy it. It's worth it when you get up there; there are some beautiful views . . . that's when you can see anything. Dan doesn't wait for sunshine; if it isn't snowing and the temperature's not too far below zero, we're off. Jakey's old enough to come with us; he loves it.'

'And you?'

She smiled. 'I'd never admit this to Dan, but so do I. There's a sense of achievement when you get to the top and see another one scored off in the book. This place we're going to . . . Ribes de Freezer . . . what is it?'

'It's a tourist spot. More a base for hikers than a resort. Small but pretty, surrounded by the mountains.'

'What does the name mean in English?'

'Nothing that makes any sense: I can't translate it from either Catalan or Castellano. Ah, here's our vehicle.'

At the forefront of a rank of cars and people-movers all bearing *Mossos* insignia, a Mercedes G Class, was parked. Two officers stood alongside, a sergeant and a constable; they saluted as Roza and Mann approached, a gesture acknowledged by the former.

'We're not driving?'

The *comissari* smiled and touched her epaulettes. 'Lottie,' she said, 'if Major Teijero was incapacitated, or even fired, I'd be in command of this force. I only drive when I want to.'

Seventy-Eight

Wright met the taxi-driver in the reception area of the police building. Tall, lean, fair hair mixed with grey, at first he seemed familiar until she realised that he bore more than a passing resemblance to Bob Skinner.

'Thanks for coming to see me, AJ,' she said, as she led him to a seating area behind the front desk. 'You've saved me a trip.'

'Not at all,' he replied. 'I've just dropped a customer at the Western General, so this is handy for me. Besides,' he added, 'my dad had a long association with this building, but I've never been in it.'

'Was he a cop?' the DS asked.

'Not exactly.' His smile could only have been described as mysterious. Wright decided not to press the point.

'This is about the Gullane homicide inquiry,' she told him. 'We understand that the victim was a client of yours.'

'Gavin, yes, he was. It's a real stunner, what happened to him.'

'Did he use you often?'

'Any time he didn't feel like driving. Usually that meant to and from restaurants, or to dinners at Witches Hill. I'd pick him up at the airport too, when he flew in.'

'We're interested in someone else in his circle,' Wright continued. 'A woman. Her name is Geraldine Black.'

'Geraldine? Yes, I've carried her several times. She was a fairly regular visitor once the house was habitable, and before, come to think of it. She turned up with Gavin on an inspection visit in February. They stayed in the Watchman Hotel in Gullane for a couple of nights. Then she was here again in June . . . Gavin was away that time . . . with an older guy, in his sixties. I think she called him Gilbert, but he never spoke a word. I know they stayed at Gavin's. I picked them up from the airport and took them there. Same trip, one of my drivers took them to the Open Arms in Dirleton.'

'When was the last time you saw her?'

'The week before last,' AJ replied. 'I had a short notice call for an airport pick-up.' He searched his memory. 'Thursday afternoon it was, the day before Gavin died, now that I think about it.'

'And you took her to the house?'

'No, that was the strange thing. She put the fare on Gavin's account . . . with which I might be stuck,' he added, 'but she said she didn't want to stay there.'

'Why do you think that was?'

'She didn't say and I didn't ask. I pick them up and I drop them off, that's it. Discretion's important in my business. In her case, I took her to the Castle Inn in Dirleton. She assumed she'd just walk into the Open Arms or the Watchman in Gullane, but they were both full. As it happens, I know Jim Dobson, the manager of the Castle; I called him and he had a room spare.'

'And when she left?' Wright continued. 'Did you pick her up?'

'I haven't seen her since,' AJ said. 'As far as I know she could still be here.'

Seventy-Nine

The constable driver took the most direct route north. Following it on Maps, Mann saw that it was a C road, until they passed a municipality named Ripoll when it became part of the N trunk road network. The climb was steady, but less dramatic than she had expected, and the views as they drew nearer to the mountains were spectacular.

'We're nearly there,' Roza said as they closed on a small town. *¿Dónde nos reunimos los ripollanos?*' she asked the sergeant.

'*Hotel Los Cacadores, senora.*'

'We're meeting the team from Ripoll at a restaurant. Lunchtime,' she added with a grin.

'What are *Cacadores*?' Mann asked.

'There are two translations. The polite one is "Hunters". The other, you do not want to know; it would take too long to explain.'

'Okay, but maybe one night before I go back we'll have a couple of drinks and I'll teach you some Glaswegian.'

The hotel and its restaurant were in a narrow one-way street on the edge of the small town; Mann would have called it a village. A lieutenant and a corporal, both male, were waiting outside beside their car, beyond which another parking place was vacant. As they approached, the corporal removed a red

276

cone and waved them in. Once they were installed, he opened the rear door for them and stood to attention as they emerged. It occurred very quickly to Mann that the lieutenant, who introduced himself as Josep Prat, was exceptionally deferential to Roza, and by extension to her. *This is like me chumming Mario McGuire in Scotland*, she thought. *That's how senior she is and she's been chumming me.*

The restaurant offered a three course *Menu del Dia*, but Roza said that all she wanted was tomato bread and anchovies. '*Eso es normal para mí, teniente*,' she assured him. 'It's okay.'

'And me,' Lottie added.

'Do you speak English?' the *comissari* asked Prat, once the waiter had taken the order. The other three uniforms had opted for sandwiches in the bar. He nodded. 'Then we'll speak it. What have you done so far?'

'First, I have impounded the car. When the alert for the number came to my office, I passed it on to all the municipal police. One of them spotted it but only after he had put three tickets on it. He called it in; it's still there. It will be no small matter, towing it out of this place.'

'Has it been opened?'

Prat smiled and touched his nose. 'With a key no, because we don't have one, but one of the locals is old school. I had a look inside . . . wearing gloves,' he added. 'There is nothing there; apart from the documents and the insurance, as you would expect.'

'And Geraldine Black? Have you looked for her?'

The lieutenant nodded. 'We have checked every hotel. She has never spent as much as a night in any of them. But that's not the end of it. In this tiny little place there are fourteen Airbnb's; we're going to have to check them all.'

'If we have to, we have to,' Roza said, 'but there may be other places where she left a trace.'

'*Comissari*,' Prat ventured, 'are we certain that she was the driver of the car? The documents show that the owner is some-one else, Senor Gilbert Land. Could it have been him?'

'No,' she assured him. 'It was her, for sure. How many shops are there in this place?' she asked.

'Not many. Food stores, a tabac, tourist places where they sell guide books and days-old French and British newspapers. It takes that long for them to get here, and the locals don't bother any more. They get their news from TV. I saw one other shop,' he volunteered, 'in what looks like the main street. It sells activity gear; things for tourists and for winter sports. It's open, but I don't know how it survives in the summer. People who come here on walking holidays surely bring their own equipment.'

'Nevertheless, we will check it.' She looked up. 'Hey, here comes our lunch.'

Eighty

'I'm staying here into next week, Sauce,' Skinner said. 'I'm personally invested in this thing both here and at home, but there's too much going on in Girona right now for me to leave it. Instead, Sarah's flying here tomorrow, for a few days. She has things to sort out in Barcelona; she might as well do it now.'

'You are okay yourself, yes?' Haddock asked, solicitously.

He laughed. 'Are you wondering if she's coming here to do my autopsy? I'm fine, son, just fine. I wasn't for a bit, but I'm over it now. How about you? What's happening at your end?'

'Jackie's got a lead,' he replied. 'We've discovered that Geraldine Black flew into Edinburgh the night before Gavin Ayre's murder. There's a coincidence for you. We're trying to find her.'

'A double coincidence,' Skinner told him. 'So are the *Mossos d'Esquadra*, and, from what I hear, with more success than you. Lottie's bang in the middle of it, so she might not have had a chance to update you. If you keep on following that trail, you should join up and a single pattern emerge.'

'What about the Gilbert Land person? He crosses over with Ayre too, and we know he was here last June.'

'He's not there now, that's all I can tell you.'

'Where is he?'

Skinner sighed audibly in his friend's ear. 'That's all I can tell you,' he repeated. 'Get it?'

'Are you withholding information, Gaffer?' Haddock murmured.

'Yes,' he said blandly, 'and you've known me long enough to let it lie. You'll never hear that name again, and you should remove it from the record wherever it comes up. That's what the Spanish are doing at the very top level.'

'But he exists, Gaffer.'

'No, he doesn't, and he never did. Just as the cadaver in Sarah's mortuary was never actually Gavin Ayre.'

Eighty-One

'She was a strange woman, Ms Black,' James Dobson, the manager of the Castle Inn volunteered. He had been dealing with a beer delivery when Jackie Wright had phoned the hotel, but had returned her call quickly. 'Some guests don't stick in the mind,' he said, 'but she did. I had a call from AJ, from the Gullane taxi firm, asking me if I had a room that night . . . Thursday, week before last. I told him she was in luck, but only for that night because I had a group of golfers from Greenland coming in on the Friday.'

'Greenland?' Jackie Wright repeated. 'Seriously?'

'Yes, they're regulars, they come here twice a year. There are a few Danes among them, but mostly they're Greenlanders. They love it here; as you can imagine they don't have too many courses there. In fact, I think there's only one in Nuuk. They showed me photos once; where we have rough, they have rocks. Anyway, Geraldine Black: yes, a strange woman, as I said. American by the sound of her, but her passport said she was from Singapore. I'm a stickler for that with overseas guests,' he added. 'I always insist on seeing the passport.'

'In what way was she strange?' the detective asked.

'She was agitated, nervous. I asked her if I could help her find accommodation for the weekend but she said she didn't know how long she'd be staying. "Family emergency." That's right, she said that. Truth is, I thought she might be the emergency herself. I did wonder about her mental stability. I mean she'd just come off an international flight, with nowhere to stay, but booked a local taxi driver and headed for East Lothian. That's not normal, is it, Sergeant? If I'd been full, she'd probably have had to sleep on the beach, only she'd hardly any luggage, just a cabin bag.'

'When did she check out?'

'I don't know; I never saw her again,' Dobson replied. 'She paid in advance, dinner, bed and breakfast; I gave her a deal, ninety-nine quid, so it was a contactless transaction. Breakfast ends at nine through the week and she was late. I thought I might have forgotten to tell her, so I went up and knocked on her door. There was no answer. I admit, I panicked a wee bit. A few years back I was in another place and I had a guest hang himself in his bathroom. She'd been so flaky I thought she might have done something similar, so I used the master key and went in. She was gone: the bed had been slept in and there were damp towels in the bath, but she was off. Why are you looking for her, Sergeant? What's she done?' He paused, but before Wright could feed him the standard 'Routine enquiries' reply, he exclaimed, 'Here, it was the next morning that bloke was found murdered on the beach at Gullane. She wasn't involved in that, was she? Is that it?'

'Routine enquiries, Mr Dobson,' she said, although the same thought had been in her mind. 'Just routine enquiries.'

Dead fucking end, she thought, frustrated, as the call ended. And then, to her surprise, she saw that she had voicemail. It would be from no one in the office; everyone on duty was in sight, including Sauce, deep in conversation with Singh in his glass-walled room. She dialled the three digits to retrieve the message.

'DS Wright, this is AJ. I told you that, as far as I knew, Geraldine Black could still be here. To double check that I asked my other drivers if any of them had picked her up without letting me know. Nobody had, but one of them who'd driven her before told me that he'd seen her. Early afternoon, on the Friday, the day after I picked her up. She was boarding a bus, the Edinburgh-bound X5, at the stop past Dirleton Toll at the entrance to the Archerfield Estate. It looks like it was a short visit, for she was carrying her cabin bag.'

Smiling, Jackie walked into Haddock's office. 'Listen to this,' she said, and played the message again.

'She arrives the night before,' she told her senior colleagues, 'books into a hotel that's walking distance from Gullane, has dinner and isn't seen there again. Next morning, Gavin Ayre is murdered. A few hours later, she boards a bus and leaves town. Have we got a prime suspect?'

Her colleagues gazed at each other for a few seconds. Finally, Haddock nodded. 'We have a prime person of interest, let's put it that way. What about the murder weapon, Jackie?'

'She's been here before. She could have planked it then, and disposed of it afterwards. She was with Gilbert Land. They could be in it together.'

'No, Land's no longer in the picture.'

'Okay,' she conceded, 'on her own.'

'The shot was Olympic class,' Singh pointed out.

Wright bristled visibly. 'Are you saying a mere female couldn't have pulled it off? Don't go sexist on me, Detective Inspector. We know nothing about the woman; she could be an Olympian herself.'

'But most likely not,' he countered. 'That's all I'm saying.'

'Children,' the superintendent chuckled. 'Come on now. Okay, Jackie, she's prime, let's agree that much, and we need to track her down. I happen to know that the Spanish are doing exactly the same, as we speak. Let's see if we can manage it between us. Step one, I know it's Saturday, but you and Tarvil get on to East Coast Buses and find out who was driving that X5 on that day. If you have to drag the CEO off the golf course, so be it. This'll be the second competition I've missed in as many weekends, so nobody else is using that as an excuse.'

Eighty-Two

'Did you like the tomato toast?' Roza asked.

Mann nodded enthusiastically. 'Yes, indeed. Do you always have it with anchovies?'

'No, they're an optional extra.'

'What's on it, apart from tomato? Is there a knack to it'

'There is a very specific way. First, toast the bread, obviously, then you rub on *ajo*, garlic. Next you halve a tomato and rub it all in. Then drizzle on the oil. The anchovies come last. Some restaurants will bring everything to the table and let you do it yourself. It's very simple, very basic, but of course the most important thing is that the bread is strong enough.'

Lottie nodded. 'I can see that. It's not going to work with Asda own brand sliced wholemeal, that's for sure.'

'If we eat together tonight, I will introduce you to our national dessert,' the *comissari* promised. 'Crema Catalana: it's like crème brulee, only it involves a blowtorch. Come,' she continued, rising from the table, 'let's check out the sports shop. Lieutenant Prat, lead the way. The uniforms can stay here, otherwise we'll look like an invading force.'

The presumed main street was no more than sixty metres away, through a narrow passageway. All of the shops, with the exception of the tabac, were closed for lunch, but as they approached their target the shutter over the display window was rolled up from within. A few seconds later, the door was unlocked and opened.

The store was called *País Alt*, 'High Country,' Prat explained, although the visitor had worked that out for herself.

Roza gave him a tiny nod as they approached, indicating that he should lead. 'Again, three of us, the shopkeeper might be intimidated.'

'Plus,' Mann volunteered, 'this place likely has its social media newsgroups like everywhere else these days. We're probably on them already.'

'We may be,' Prat agreed. 'But all they'll be able to say is that we're looking for a woman. We haven't given a name anywhere that we visited, simply showed the image.'

'Which isn't great,' the Scot observed, 'so maybe this whole exercise is a waste of time. She could have been here but not be recognisable from that. It's the best we've got, though, so good luck, Josep.'

He stepped into the shop, leaving his colleagues to window-shop. 'Dan would love this,' Lottie said. 'Those boots, those walking poles. Personally, I think they look daft, but he's always on about getting a pair.'

'You should buy him something from there,' Lita suggested.

'I'll do better. I'll bring him here next summer; Jakey'll want to go to a beach, but he won't be given a vote, not this time.'

Her planning was interrupted by the return of Lieutenant Prat. His expression was animated, his eyes lit by the glow of a result. 'She was here,' he announced. 'She bought a pair of hiking boots, a backpack and a heavy jacket. The owner says she's going to the top of the mountains; he says that only somebody doing that would buy a thing of that weight at this time of year. What do we do, *Comissari?*' he asked.

'You know what we do,' Roza told him. 'We go up to Vall de Núria; it's the only place she can have headed.'

Mann looked at them, puzzled. 'What's Vall de Núria?'

'It's a resort and a centre,' Prat replied, 'hiking in the summer, skiing in the winter. It's a very significant place for Catalans. Our Statute of Autonomy was written there almost a hundred years ago, in the Sanctuary of the Virgin of Núria.'

'I don't imagine she's gone to pray, so why?'

'There can be only one reason,' Roza said. 'She's planning to cross into France and disappear. We may be too late already but we need to get up there.' She looked at her colleague's footwear. 'Lottie, go in there and buy yourself a pair of boots, or at the least shoes as solid as mine.'

'Okay,' she agreed. 'I see now why you wanted a four-by-four vehicle.'

The *comissari* laughed. 'Ah, we don't go there by road; there is none past Queralbs. Other than on foot, which would take a while because it's a thousand metre climb that's almost vertical in places, there's only one way to get up to Núria, and that's on the *Cremallera*, the rack railway.'

'Jeez,' Mann murmured. 'That's what the bugger meant. The Gaffer,' she explained in answer to Roza's puzzled frown. 'He said to enjoy the train journey. Is there anything that man doesn't know, or can't guess.'

'He didn't know he was going to be shot in the back with a taser,' her friend countered. 'Josep,' she added, looking at the lieutenant, 'you didn't hear that. Bring your car and the

287

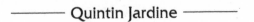

corporal, to take us to the station. My guys can stay here and look after the G Class, or it might have been stripped for parts when we get back. While you're doing that, I'm going to call Sabadell and have a helicopter sent to Núria. We may well need it before this is done.'

Eighty-Three

Davie Cobb was looking forward to the second home game of the season. With all the summer transfer movement, and the distraction of frustrating European qualifiers which involved the curtailment of player holidays for unpredictable away ties in places he had never heard of, it was usually into September before he could make a realistic assessment of Hearts' prospects. He was still uncertain as he left the Diggers, but his confidence was renewed by the time he neared Tynecastle Stadium. Third place was a certainty and if either of the big two faltered or, whisper it, both did, then a bloke never knew. As he moved towards the turnstile gate, reaching for his season ticket, he was buzzing.

'That's him,' the steward said. 'That's Davie.'

A constable stepped forward, blocking his way. 'Mr Cobb,' he enquired, with excessive politeness. 'If you can step over here, please?'

'Are you serious?' The exclamation was close to a wail. 'They're about to kick off.'

'Can you step over here please, sir?' The politeness gauge had fallen by at least three points.

'Okay, but just for a minute, mind. If I miss anything Pilmar'll hear about it, I'm telling you.' He stepped out of the queue and towards the PC . . . who stood aside, to allow a woman to step forward.

'Mr Cobb, I'm DS Jackie Wright, Serious Crimes.'

'I havenae done anything,' Davie protested.

'I'm not suggesting that you have,' she assured him, 'but there's something I need to talk to you about, about a route you drove just over a week ago.'

'How did you know where to find me?'

Wright weighed up her response. If she told the truth, that his wife had told her, would it go badly for Mrs Cobb? She thought not; the man seemed amiable enough. And yet she chose caution. 'Colleagues,' she lied. 'Mr Cobb, Davie, I need to talk to you about a passenger we understand you picked up on the North Berwick to Edinburgh X5, early afternoon on the Friday before last. It was at the Archerfield stop, between Dirleton and Gullane.'

He frowned theatrically, his face twisting in a show of serious consideration. 'A woman?' he said at last.

'That's right.'

'American?'

'She may have sounded so, yes. Can you remember anything else about her?'

'Absolutely. She was in a . . .' He stopped abruptly as a collective moan erupted in the stadium. 'Shite,' he muttered, 'that's us one down. Aye sorry, she was in a right state. She asked for Edinburgh; I asked her where; she said, "As far as you go." Then she tried to pay with a card but the machine either couldn't or wouldn't read it. She tried again, same no result. I told her I could take cash, but she said she didnae have any. In the end I took pity on her on. That's something I wouldn't normally do, but I had this feeling that she was running away from something or someone. "Battered wife?" I asked myself. I think she might have been.'

'Did she say anything else?' the DS asked.

'Not until we got to Edinburgh. She took the single seat behind me, out of the mirror's line of vision so I never saw her until she got off. When she did though, she asked me where the airport bus left from. I was pulled up in Frederick Street . . . that's where the X5 starts and finishes . . . so I told her she'd be as well walking down into Princes Street and getting a tram. I hope her card worked there, mind; those monstrosities have got no soul.'

Another collective moan, louder than the first, exploded within the stadium. 'Aw no,' Davie sighed. 'Two down. I think I'll go back to the Diggers.'

Eighty-Four

'How long has this been here?' Lottie Mann wondered aloud, as the rack railway climbed upwards on its single track towards the Vall de Núria.

'Over ninety years,' Lita Roza said, 'and it has always been powered by electricity. These days it's solar generated; before, it was probably hydro. Sustainability, that's the buzz word now. As well, for it carries over a quarter of a million people every year.'

There were rock faces on either side but on the right, very close to the track, there was a ravine with a sheer drop. Lieutenant Prat had a window seat facing the two women: his eyes were closed, tight.

'From Ribes de Freser to Núria the track is twelve kilometres long,' Roza continued. 'Over that distance we rise another of your Munros above sea level. If you like you can add two more to Dan's record.'

'He'll want to do it himself,' Lottie said. 'My worry is that he might want to walk up the other road.'

They were silent for the rest of the way, until the train entered a tunnel cut through rock. 'Almost there,' Prat whispered, with evident relief.

After a minute or so they emerged into sunlight; unexpectedly, on the left, there was a lake. 'A reservoir,' he volunteered. 'You can do everything here; ski, hike, canoe, even fish, I guess.'

Finally, the train rolled up to the buffer at the end of the line. As they stepped out of the carriage, at least fifty people were waiting on the platform to take their places on the downward journey.

'Follow me,' Roza commanded, leading the way out of the station. In the open air, she looked around the wide green valley. 'The fucking helicopter is not here yet,' she complained. 'I told them it was a priority. Never mind; for now we will check the hotel.'

'Is that the only place she could have gone?' Mann asked. She would have liked a moment to take in her surroundings but she understood the urgency.

'No, there's a hostel not far away, but we're here so we'll do this first. I'm hoping that she stopped at all. She could have got off the train and just started climbing.'

The hotel and station were part of a single complex, essential in the depths of winter, Lottie assumed, when days would be short, the snow deep and temperatures sub-zero. It was a large four-storey building, with its imposing entrance overlooking the lake.

'Lead on, Josep,' Roza said as they entered the reception area. 'You're on a roll. Let's see if your luck holds.'

Roza, Mann and the corporal stood back as Josep approached the counter. As he did so they heard the sound of an approaching helicopter, drawing a sigh of relief from the *comissari*. They looked on as Prat engaged with a balding man behind the reception desk. He seemed to have a habit of nodding at everything that was said to him. It continued as he moved to a computer screen, studying it with apparent concentration. 'His head's on a spring,' Mann muttered. It was only when the nodding stopped that he showed any sign of resolve, his mouth tightening into a line. Abruptly he turned, reached behind him and handed the lieutenant a key. Prat took it, shook his hand formally and returned to his colleagues.

'When I get back to Ripoll I am buying a lottery ticket,' he exclaimed. 'You were right, Comissari Roza, I really am on a lucky streak. Geraldine Black is here, and has been for three days. At this moment, she's hiking, but the manager says she told him, "See you later" when she went out an hour ago. He gave me her key; she's on the third floor.'

You're a lucky boy, Mann thought. *The second-in-command arrives in town and you get to show off. Great for your career prospects.*

As they climbed the stairs, in the absence of a lift, she was aware of the clumsiness of her new footwear, and reminded of the cost. Hiking boots from a shop with no local competition were never going to be cheap, she had realised, but it had been teeth-sucking.

The third-floor corridor was forty metres long; Black's room proved to be all of that distance away. Prat unlocked it then stood aside, allowing Roza and Mann to enter. There was only a sheet and a light cover on the bed; they were crumpled, a sign that the housekeepers they had passed outside were moving in that direction. The *comissari* opened the wardrobe; only one garment hung there, a dark red jacket. Leaving it on the hanger, she felt each of the pockets in turn but they were empty. She was about to close the door when something caught her eye. On the inside of the right sleeve, near the cuff, there was a mark, a smear. She took the jacket from the rail, crossed to the window, and held it up in the light.

'Lottie,' she said, 'what would you think this is?'

Mann emerged from the bathroom and took it from her. Awkwardly she took her phone from her pocket, switched on its torch and focused its beam on the blemish. She whistled. 'Blood's a real bastard to get off, isn't it?' she murmured. 'You do your damnedest but it never quite goes away. It's worse than red wine. You can run on all the white vinegar and Fairy Liquid you like, but it never quite goes away.'

She returned the garment and began to open drawers. 'Empty,' she announced. 'Every one of them. We assumed she'd be travelling light but this is invisible.'

'Where's her cabin bag?' Roza asked. 'The shopkeeper in Ribes mentioned it to Prat.'

'There,' Mann replied, pointing to the luggage space beside the door.

'Then where is her rucksack? The one she bought.'

'Not here. Lita, she may have said "See you later" to the hotel guy but I don't think she's coming back.'

'And this may prove it.'

She turned, and saw Roza holding out a metal bin for inspection. An attempt had been made to burn the contents but it had not been completely successful. Among the ashes were a plastic rectangle, melted and distorted by the heat but still recognisable as a bank card, and something else, scorched, light red in colour, bearing a crest, two lions flanking a shield. She took it out and flipped it open. The crucial page was still legible. 'Geraldine Black's in that bin,' she said. 'She's destroyed the identity and she's running.'

'No,' the *comissari* countered. 'Not running, she's climbing. And if she left only an hour ago, we may still catch her. Come on, Lottie, we need to get into that helicopter and go after her.'

Eighty-Five

'Wait here till I get back, Marcia,' Jackie Wright told the driver of the patrol car as it pulled up in front of Edinburgh Airport, 'and take no shit from anyone who tries to get you to move, not even our guys.'

She stepped out of the passenger seat and bustled into the terminal building. Looking around, she saw a general information desk and headed for it. She flashed her warrant card at the smartly dressed man on duty. 'I'm looking to trace a passenger we believe flew to Barcelona from here on Friday of last week. She may have had a ticket or she may have bought one here.'

'That's most unlikely,' the young attendant said. 'People nearly always have a ticket when they turn up here. It's not a bus station, Detective Sergeant.'

'But it is possible?'

'Yes,' he conceded, 'but . . .'

'Let's just stop at Yes,' she sighed, forcing a smile. 'Who flies to Barcelona from here?'

He paused, then seemed to commit himself to being helpful. 'Just about everyone, madam, if you don't need to fly direct. BA will take you there via London, Air France via Charles de Gaulle, KLM via Schiphol, Lufthansa via Frankfurt . . . you don't want to do that, though. I did, and it was a terrible experience. Only Ryanair fly direct from Edinburgh, but they can route you through other cities as well. Start with them and see how you get on.'

'Thanks for that.'

The Ryanair desk was a few yards away; an obviously anxious couple with a small child were having a heated discussion with the blue-blazered man behind the counter. As Wright moved across she picked up the end of the conversation. 'There's a pass for family fast-track security,' the attendant said. 'Leave the item with me and I'll make sure it gets on the flight.'

'Can you do that?' the father asked.

The man smiled and gestured behind him, towards a young woman in airline uniform. 'Yes,' he replied, 'because my colleague here's one of your cabin attendants. She'll take it on to the aircraft and give it to you on board. Now go on, catch your flight.'

As they hurried off, looking only marginally less stressed, he turned to Wright. 'Don't tell me. You've had security problems too.'

'I like to think I am security,' she said, grinning as she showed her police identification. There was something familiar about him, but she could not pin him down.

'Ah,' he murmured, archly, 'that sort. Can I assist with your enquiries, if that's the correct phrase?'

'It'll do. I'm trying to trace the movements of a person of interest. Friday before last, I believe she came to the airport. She'd have been looking for a flight to Barcelona. If she came here would you have any record of it?'

The sudden curve of his eyebrows made her warm to him even more. 'I can do better than that. I remember her. Late afternoon, it would have been; woman thirty-one years old, American accent. She came up to the desk all in a flap trying to get on a flight to Barcelona that had left ten hours earlier. She was in a proper state, poor soul; a family emergency, she told me. Someone close had died and she had to get back; she was babbling about the Spanish giving you forty-eight hours after a death to have the funeral.'

'But you couldn't help her,' Wright said. 'Did you see where she went next?'

'Ah, but I did help!' He beamed and she placed him; he had a striking resemblance to Alan Cumming, the Scottish Broadway star. 'I was able to route her to Barcelona Girona, through London Stansted. She was able to fly to Stansted that evening. She probably had to sleep in the airport but she'd have been in Girona before ten next morning. Okay, that isn't actually Barcelona itself . . . it isn't even Girona . . . but there's a connecting bus service.'

'Excellent, Mr . . .'

'Cumming,' he replied. He sighed at her instant reaction. 'I know,' he said. 'I get it all the time.'

'You wear it well,' she told him. 'Just to confirm,' she continued, 'was this her?' She showed him the store image that Skinner had sourced. 'Bad picture, I know.'

He nodded. 'That's her. Her passport photo wasn't much better.'

'A Singaporean passport, yes?'

He stared at her, frowning. 'Why would you think that? No, it was American. I remember everything; she was definitely a US citizen and her name was Ruby Goldstein.'

Eighty-Six

Mann stated the obvious, shouting above the engine noise as the helicopter rose from its stance, the downforce from its rotors rippling the grass beneath. 'Those are big mountains up there. How are we going to find her in all that territory, even if we are in a chopper?'

'We're going to have to get lucky,' Roza yelled back, her voice crackling through the headset, 'but we have some on our side. She can only be going to France,' she continued, her voice modulating as the aircraft gained height, 'and that's on the other side of that ridge. If she's just climbing blind, with the compass on her phone, she'll head due north. But if she does that she could be in trouble. The terrain is treacherous and it's a stiff climb. It's much more likely that she'll take a hiker route. They're marked on all the maps. The nearest and the most logical is the *cami* leading to Puigmal. It's the highest peak on the ridge, but it's accessible. Once she's past it she's on French territory and I can't go after her. The EU open borders only count for so much. There's a ski resort no more than twenty minutes away. Even at this time there will be people there. She'll get a taxi and be gone, maybe for good.'

'She's had an hour's start,' Mann said. 'Are we stuffed?'

'No, because it's like the railway; uphill all the way. Puigmal is three kilometres high; she has another Munro to climb.'

The Scot looked upward through the helicopter's window, towards the mountain. 'That thing's more than two Ben Nevises high? Will I get to stand on it?'

'If we spot her, we'll have to, or pretty close to it. There's no helipad up there.'

They hung on to their seats as the helicopter soared due north towards France before turning in a great sweeping arc, heading westwards for Puigmal. They had been flying for fifteen minutes when the pilot's voice sounded in their ears.

To Mann it was unintelligible, but Roza was elated. 'He can see her, about four hundred metres short of the peak. He'll put us down as near the top as he can."

'But he can't land, you said!'

'Ladder descent. You'll have to drop a few feet.'

'Fuck!'

The side door of the aircraft slid open. Clinging to a bar, Roza kicked a rope ladder that lay on the floor, sending it tumbling. She grabbed it, secured her foot in a rung and slid through the exit.

A few days later, Lottie told Dan, 'I had no time to be afraid. If I had, I'd have been scared shitless.' In the moment she followed the Catalan's example.

'Let go,' Roza called from below, 'it's only a few feet. I'll catch you.'

Good luck with that, she thought, and let go.

She landed on one foot and rolled sideways, her bulk taking the other woman with her, but the pilot had chosen a good spot for the evacuation. Within seconds they were both on their feet.

The person formerly known as Geraldine Black was fifty

metres below them on the *cami*. 'You realise,' Mann whispered, aware suddenly of the oxygen deficit at their altitude, 'that if she runs, you're going to have to fucking catch her, because I'll be no fu . . .' She stopped to catch her breath.

Roza nodded. 'That thought had occurred to me,' she gasped, 'which is why . . .' She drew her Glock from its holster and held it in the air.

The threat, or rather the gesture, for that was all it really was, proved unnecessary. Their quarry had removed her rucksack, sat on the sloping ground and buried her face in her hands.

'I hope you've got some energy left after that nice walk,' Mann said as they reached her, 'because unless our pilot can find a flat piece of ground big enough to land on, we're going to have to walk all the way back to Núria.'

That photo did her no justice at all, the Scot thought. *She's very attractive; half dead from exhaustion, but very attractive.*

And as for you, Dan Provan, her oxygen depleted mind declared as she thought of a call she would make in her first minute alone, *arresting someone at nine thousand feet? You'll never top that, sunshine.'*

Eighty-Seven

'They have her, Bob,' Manuel Mateu announced. 'I thought I should let you know.'

'Well done the two Ls,' Skinner replied.

'The two Ls?'

'Lita and Lottie,' he explained. 'Where did they find her?'

'A very short distance from France, in the mountains. It involved a helicopter, which is now flying them and their detainee back to *Mossos* headquarters in Sabadell. She'll be detained there overnight and interviewed tomorrow. Teijero wanted to do it but I told him, "No chance." Comissari Roza has earned this one, as has Chief Inspector Mann.'

'And what about Merle Gower? Or have you sent her back to Washington to dig herself out of trouble.'

'Far from it,' Mateu laughed. 'She's my government's honoured guest in a very fine hotel overlooking *Las Ramblas*. As long as she is in Spain, she's a weapon I can use against the weasels in Madrid. You know me well enough to understand that I will never forget what they did to Catalunya. I'm not saying I want to bring this administration down, for the next one might be much worse, but I want to use the situation to screw as much out of them as I can.'

'Don't tell me anything else,' Skinner pleaded. 'As a quasi-journalist, I'm compromised as it is.'

'If that's so, I guess you'll reject my informal information to sit in on the interview of Ms Geraldine Black tomorrow.'

Skinner laughed. 'Why would I do that? I pretty much know everything she's going to say. As long as I'm free to pick Sarah up from the airport at three o'clock tomorrow, I'll be there . . . with my cop's hat on, only.'

'But you're not a cop any longer.'

'You're kidding, Manuel, aren't you? With a foot in both camps, I'm even more effective.'

'Jesus, you are too. You know everything she's going to say, you claim. How can that be.'

'Well,' he replied, 'an hour ago I had a call from my friend Sauce in Edinburgh. He was very chuffed with himself because his team had uncovered Geraldine Black's real name. He told me what it is and I did a little digging myself. It wasn't hard at all, such is the power of Wikipedia if you know how to analyse its source material. Now, I don't just know who she is, I know what she is and how she fits in. I might be proved wrong tomorrow, but somehow I don't think so.'

Eighty-Eight

The interview room in the *Mossos* headquarters might have been acquired from a film set. Bob Skinner had always been amused by the idea that there had to be a one-way mirror to protect observers from the malevolent eyes of suspects and from potential retribution. Why bother, he wondered, when video cameras had been around for years? They could have been watching in another part of the building. They could have been watching in Madrid. He wondered for a few moments whether faceless people were doing just that.

His presence in the viewing gallery alongside Manuel Mateu, Merle Gower and Major Teijero brought to mind a similar situation, one that he had chosen to avoid. Years before, he had been invited by a lawmaker in Florida to witness an execution. 'To show you how we handle things over here,' the man had said.

'Why would I want to do that?' he had replied, containing his anger with an effort. 'I've had no connection to the investigation and no connection to the victim.'

'You'd be an official observer,' he had been told. 'We have those. There are people out there who've witnessed dozens of executions, as volunteers.'

'I'd love to see their psych profiles,' he had growled. 'A man

I know, and like, has a doctorate in that subject, but he's not available because he's currently doing life for murder. If he was American they'd probably be strapping him to a gurney by now, with the ghouls and the self-righteous salivating on the other side of a window.'

That image was with him as the door of the interview room opened, but it vanished as soon as the woman formerly known as Geraldine Black stepped through it, ushered in by a *Mossos* lieutenant. She was dressed in a pale blue sleeveless dress with a high collar. Her golden hair shone and was perfectly arranged, as if by a stylist; she wore make-up but it was minimal, eye-liner and a pale lipstick that emphasised her tan. Her appearance was in stark contrast to that of the officers who awaited her, seated at the obligatory desk. Roza and Mann seemed crumpled in their uniforms; they had spent the night in the police headquarters, and looked the worse for it.

The unconventional nature of the situation was emphasised by the seeming deference of the lieutenant as he ushered his charge to her chair, before retiring to a seat beside the door. As she arranged herself, calm and composed as she faced her inquisitors, Skinner realised that the dynamic had changed. Behind the blacked-out glass he leaned towards Gower seated next to him and whispered, 'You've done a deal, haven't you? He gave you access to her and you've carved it up. She talks, she walks and nothing ever happened.'

She allowed him a tiny smile.

'If that's so, have you told Comissari Roza and DCI Mann?'

Almost imperceptibly, she shook her head.

Skinner smiled. 'In that case,' he murmured, 'we could be in for some fun.'

'Good morning.' Lita Roza's voice filled the room. 'You look better for a night's sleep. I hope you will agree that you have been well treated.'

'For the tape? Yes, I have been.'

'There is no tape, this interview is entirely informal. If it was otherwise you would have a lawyer present.' She paused. 'You know who we are; we told you when we met yesterday. Perhaps you can begin by telling us your name; your real name, the one on your birth certificate.'

'Sure, I'm Ruby Goldstein, a citizen of the United States and I'm thirty-one years old.'

'Ms Goldstein,' the *comissari* continued, 'you were apprehended yesterday trying to cross from Spain into France. A search of the room you occupied at the Vall de Núria hotel found the remains of a Singaporean passport, bearing your image, in the name Geraldine Black. There was also a half-melted bank card linked to an account in the name of Gilbert Land. The man who used that name was found, a few days ago, in a house in the district of La Garrotxa. He had been dead for some time.'

For the first time a small flicker of doubt showed in Goldstein's eyes.

Lottie Mann read it and saw the same truth as Skinner. 'You weren't told that, were you, Ruby?' she exclaimed. 'You were told that we found the place empty when it was opened, and that the problem you were running from had gone away. That's true, we did, but we weren't the first to open that door. Listen, and believe me that whatever deal you've done with the woman on the other side of that window counts for nothing with us. You don't leave this room, lady, not even to piss, until you've told us the whole story, all of it. Isn't that right, Comissari Roza?'

Her companion squared her shoulders. 'Oh yes,' she agreed. 'You can tell us informally, or we can wrap this up and ship you out to the women's wing in Barcelona Prison for a couple of days to let you brief the lawyer you will undoubtedly need. What's it going to be? Does Lieutenant Prat put you in handcuffs or do you come to terms with the reality of your situation?"

Ruby Goldstein stared at the mirror window. If she hoped to see Merle Gower it was in vain, for all that came back was her own alarmed reflection, emphasising her situation. 'Where do I begin?' she sighed as she conceded.

'The beginning is always best.'

'Okay. The man you thought was Gilbert Land; his real name was Russell Silver. He was a declared independent candidate for the presidency of the United States and he was attracting a lot of support.' She stopped to look at the window once again.

'Russell Silver was my father,' she said. 'He and my mother split when I was a small child, and she and I moved to Wisconsin. I grew up using her name; I didn't even know what his was. She never spoke about him and I never saw him until, six years ago, she was watching TV news and a piece came up about a guy who was running as an independent candidate for the Governorship of Kansas, and making a decent fist of it. She pointed at the screen and said: "That's your dad." She was dying then; I suppose she thought that she had to tell me. I offered to bring them together, but she wouldn't have it. I had enough going on in my life then . . . I was just coming out of a failed relationship . . . so I let it lie. When she passed away, I found records of all his alimony payments through the years. I had Mum's executor contact his bank to stop them, but I never actually told him that she was dead. It would have felt like a betrayal. You see, by that time, I had discovered why she hated him.'

'Why was that?' Mann asked.

'Because he was a crook,' Goldstein snapped. 'He had a

reputation as this self-made millionaire real-estate dealer. The truth was, it was Mum who was wealthy. His business was based on her family money, but as he managed her affairs, she never knew until he'd blown a big chunk of it and my trustee started to get worried.'

'When did you contact him?' Roza asked.

'Two years ago, after he'd emerged as a presidential candidate and had started to draw attention. I went to his campaign office one day and told him who I was. Not unnaturally, he shit himself. He assumed I'd come to expose him for what he'd done to Mum. I can't deny it, I had that in mind, but when I met him . . . well, he was a charming guy, and at the beginning and end of the day he was my dad.'

'What did you do?'

'I joined his campaign team, but only after he'd persuaded me that nobody should know who I was, nobody at all. If it came out, he said, so would all the unpleasantness between him and my mother. His whole pitch, he said, was based on his personal integrity as the champion of the middle ground. He really did believe that he could win the presidency . . . and so did the people who were backing him with tens of millions of dollars in donations. That was then; as he gathered momentum, it was into the hundreds of millions.'

'Who was in charge of the campaign apart from your father?'

She looked directly at Mann. 'David,' she replied. 'A very charismatic man called David Allen. He had come from Canadian politics, a different arena but one where the same principle applies . . . tell the majority what the majority wants to hear and make them believe you'll deliver. And, believe me, he could do that.' Her expression softened. 'We had such momentum, and we had so much money in donations that we really did begin to believe. And so did the White House . . . not that we could win, but that we could take a decisive chunk of their vote. David heard very early that a VP offer might be on the table. And he saw the danger just as quickly, that scrutiny would expose Dad's weaknesses.'

'Who came up with the property plan?' Roza asked. Goldstein frowned at her. 'We know that's what this was all about: laundering campaign money through property.'

She nodded reluctantly. 'David. Dad didn't have the brains for that. David said we should siphon off as much cash as we could, and the safest way to do that was through property in proxy names.'

'Land, for example.'

'Yes. And Ayre. And me.'

It was Roza's turn to frown. 'Excuse me?' she murmured.

'Jesus,' Goldstein chuckled. 'Never heard of the Black Sea? Geraldine Mediterranean would hardly have cut it, would it? I did suggest Saragossa, but David said that was too showy.'

'When did you begin?'

'Eighteen months ago, when David first had a very tentative approach from the White House, and when the President practically hugged Dad at the correspondents' annual dinner and bigged him up in his speech. Even I wondered, "Why's he doing that?" Way back then, David began to create the false identities, by stealing the names of the dead and getting passports in their names. Then we bought the properties. Scotland, because the land was relatively cheap and we could build quickly. Spain, because it was remote and Gilbert Land would be just another exile. Singapore, because there are so many opportunities there. Italy, because it's corrupt. Dubai, because nobody would notice Gavin Ayre among all those golfers and millionaire sportsmen.

Russia . . . yes, that was a mistake. And you know what? We did it under the noses of the Federal Election Commission, which spends so much time making a pretence of over-seeing the big parties that it can't even see the rest. But when the White House interest firmed up and Vice President Silver's name began to be aired on the cable news channels, we knew that involved a different level of scrutiny. So, David and I began to spend more time as our alter egos. He began to create a presence in Scotland, buying a horse, joining a golf club. I did the same in Singapore. We watched the properties being built, or adapted, and one time Geraldine Black visited with Gavin Ayre in his seaside palace. That's when it happened.'

'What happened?'

'David and me. We'd worked very closely together, worked very hard, so hard that we never had time for anything else . . . until we had that down time together in his place. I had been to Spain to inspect and sign off on the work there. I knew that David was in East Lothian, so I decided to break my journey there on the way home. And that's where we had sex. No big deal,' she said, 'we just had sex, like friends do these days. And that's when I got pregnant.'

Silence fell over the interview room; in the viewing gallery, Mateu gasped.

'So?' Roza asked.

'So,' Goldstein continued patiently, 'some weeks later, Dad and I went to Spain. He panicked. He decided that the Secret Service scrutiny was about to reveal everything and that he would be busted. He wasn't bright enough to realise that by that time the President couldn't let that happen. It would have been hushed up more likely than not, but he didn't get that. So Russell Silver got on an internal flight and Gilbert Land flew to Spain. As soon as I found out I . . . unmistakeably overdue by that time . . . went there to bring him back, to tell him he was blowing it. To tell him that he'd fucking done it and the vice president's mansion would be his after the election, which jointly they would surely win, and to get his ass back home before they came looking for him. I found him in Riudaura, and that's when he did the big reveal: the secret he'd been keeping from both David and me.' She smiled, with incredible sadness that even drew a moment's pity from Skinner.

'Just as he hadn't told David that I was his daughter, he hadn't told me that David was his son; when he did, in that fucking place, he was telling me that I was pregnant by my own brother. I went crazy, I picked up a big pottery vase and hit him with it.' For a few seconds the interview room and the gallery fell silent.

'I didn't kill him,' she insisted. 'I didn't even knock him off his feet. But a minute or so later, he collapsed. He fell forward, hit his head on a table, shuddered for a few seconds, and then he died. I didn't kill him,' she repeated. 'Agent Gower told me last night that they've done an autopsy in the US and that's how it happened. He died from natural causes, and that's what it'll say on the press statement that I'll issue when I'm back in Washington . . . which I've been promised will be within forty-eight hours. There,' she challenged. 'Is that enough for you?'

'Hell no,' Mann replied. 'You've missed the best part of the story: the bit where you disappeared and then turned up on a mountain top a couple of weeks later.'

'I panicked,' Goldstein replied, 'like I told Agent Gower, I just panicked. I got in the car we'd put there and I drove south. In case anyone came looking for me I made cash withdrawals that suggested I was heading south, but actually I was going in the other direction. You worked it out. My plan was to leave

Geraldine Black in Spain for good, cross untraceably into France and go on from there as Ruby Goldstein, back home to face the mystery of the missing candidate. As,' she said heavily, 'I still intend to do. You've seen enough of Agent Gower to know that none of this will ever be shared with the American public. If it is, the Republicans get back in for sure, and darkness falls. And that's it, ladies, that's all I'm saying. Now, Agent Gower, please get me out of here as agreed.'

In the viewing gallery Manuel Mateu leaned forward. 'Do it, Comissari Roza,' he sighed, his order sounding in her earpiece.

'No,' Skinner boomed, his voice so loud that on the other side of the glass the three women and the lieutenant reacted. 'Manuel, that can't happen. Ms Goldstein's a suspect in a homicide investigation in Scotland. You have to hold her for extradition by our courts.'

The minister frowned, then sighed. 'Bob, I can't do that. There's an agreement.'

'Not with Chief Constable Neil McIlhenney, there isn't. Not with the Lord Advocate in Edinburgh. And not with the chair of InterMedia, right here in this room, who has his own reason to be interested in the outcome. There's no privilege here; you can't gag me and you won't. Lottie,' he shouted, 'you might not have the power of arrest in Spain, but you need to act as if you had. Minimum, you have to caution her.'

Through the glass he saw Mann rise to her feet. Through the speaker, he heard her say, 'Ruby Goldstein, I am arresting you under Section One of the Criminal Justice (Scotland) Act on suspicion of the murder of . . .'

'All right!' Goldstein cried out. 'Stop! I just want all of this to go away. You don't have to extradite me, you don't have to shackle me with you. I'll come with you to Scotland for as long as it takes. But I don't know why.'

'Yes, you do!' Mann barked. 'From the moment Lita and I stopped you on that mountain, you haven't asked the obvious question: what the hell am I, a Scottish detective, doing here? You haven't asked, Ms Goldstein, because you bloody well know.'

Eighty-Nine

'How did it play after that?' Sarah asked.

'It's still playing really,' Bob told her, 'but very soon Ruby Goldstein will be on her way to Scotland as a suspect in the murder of David Allen, formerly known as Gavin Ayre. Once everyone had cooled down, she accepted that and so did Mateu, the Catalan minister. The deal is, subject to it being signed off by our Lord Advocate, that the Scottish investigation will make no reference to events in Spain.'

They were on the terrace of their Girona apartment; to the west the sun was heading for the horizon but there was still enough daylight for Sarah to survey the view. 'Bob, what are those?' Still holding the monocular to her eye, she pointed south. 'Those jagged things on the skyline?'

He took it from her, and looked for himself. 'Those are the Mountains of Montserrat, a holy place. There's a monastery up there that houses *La Moreneta*, the Black Madonna. I've heard that in Franco's time, it was the only place where Catalan people could be married in their own language. We should visit, since we're going to spend more time here.'

'Yes, when you have a business-focused life and aren't being pulled off the street by rogue agents. Speaking of whom, what about the Merle Gower person?'

'She's not happy, and from what she told me before she left neither is her boss.'

'Which boss?'

'Her big boss, the President himself. He was getting used to the idea of Silver as his running mate; now that's gone and he's trying to keep the lid on a scandal. He's also got to keep the existing VP on-side. It's not too late for her to run against him for the nomination.'

'I hope she does,' Sarah declared. 'It'd serve him right for allying himself with a chancer. Is Gower's job on the line?'

'I doubt it; she knows too much. But there are three Secret Service agents who may find themselves chasing currency forgers for the rest of their careers.'

'That's unless they sue for compensation for workplace injuries!'

'I'd counter-sue for assault.' He grinned. 'It's a thought, you know. If I told Merle that I want a pay-off for the inconvenience, say five million dollars . . .'

'Please don't,' his wife retorted. 'It would be cheaper to have you shot!'

Ninety

'Are you good, Lottie?' Haddock asked his colleague.

Mann saw herself nod in the smaller of the two windows on her screen. 'Yes, but I'm glad to be out of that uniform. Part of the deal that assured Goldstein's cooperation is that she won't appear to be under police escort on the flight back tomorrow. Have you made the arrangements at your end?'

'Yes, I have. She won't be detained as such; instead she'll be given a room in a hotel with a plainclothes officer on guard, and she'll be escorted to and from interviews by Jackie Wright. Before that, she has a job to do as soon as possible after she lands: the Crown Office needs a formal identification of David Allen's body, and she's qualified to do it. I've made contact with the Canadian High Commission, by the way. They have the right to know that one of their citizens has been murdered.'

'Will they want to be involved in the investigation?' she wondered.

'Tough on them if they do, because that is not going to happen. There's been no request, though. I'm more worried about the Americans. Should I be?'

'They have a continuing interest,' Mann said, 'but I doubt that the Embassy's been told about it.'

'What do you think of Goldstein as a suspect?' Haddock asked.

'I'm trying to keep an open mind, Sauce. Bear in mind too that I haven't been part of your investigation, only what's been happening in Spain. What have you got that I don't know about?'

'We can prove she was in the area at the time, one hundred per cent. There's other stuff too that doesn't look good for her, but I'll tell you about that before we interview her.'

'We?' she repeated.

'Yes, you and me.'

She frowned. 'Not Singh? Not Wright?'

'No,' he replied, 'I don't want her to see two strangers. One will be quite enough.'

'That's good,' Mann declared, 'because I've been thinking . . . we've got a massive duty of care towards this woman, Sauce. She's lost her father, she's lost the half-brother she didn't know about and by whom she's pregnant.'

'Is she going to keep the baby?'

She stared at Haddock's on-screen image. 'It's not my place to ask her,' she said firmly, 'nor is it yours, but she is vulnerable and, as I say, we've got a responsibility to her and to her unborn child.'

'How do we exercise that?'

'It'll be your choice, but my view is that before we sit her down and caution her, we establish that she's emotionally fit to be interviewed.'

'We should get her a psychological evaluation, you mean?'

'Yes, I do.'

'Okay, we will,' Haddock said. 'And as it happens I have someone in mind who could do it . . . provided that he and Alex Skinner are back from Spain.'

Ninety-One

Detective Sergeant Jackie Wright was entitled to time off for weekend work. Her partner Kate had insisted that she take a full day rather than a couple of hours, warning her that the relationship would be in danger if it took second place to her work.

And yet there she was at her desk on Monday, just before midday. Her face was lined and craggy, but she was there, because the job was not yet finished. 'They're bringing her back today?' she asked Tarvil Singh.

'She's here now; they've parked her in a hotel as part of the deal to avoid extradition,' he confirmed. 'Lottie Mann brought her back. She's in with Sauce now, giving him a full briefing on what happened. That's why his blinds are closed. Oh, he wants you to be Goldstein's minder, by the way.'

'Do I have a choice?'

'Always,' the big DI said. 'Between CID and back in uniform.'

'Seriously?' she gasped.

'No, but has Sauce ever asked you to do anything you didn't think was reasonable.'

'No,' Wright admitted. 'It's just that I'm under pressure at home, and . . .'

'Jackie,' Singh exclaimed, 'you don't have to sleep with her.

I told you, she's under guard in a hotel. All he wants you to do is take her to and from interviews that you won't be involved in, while she's still just a person of interest. The first one's this afternoon. Sauce has arranged a psych eval session with Dominick Jackson at his place down in Leith. You'll be home in time for dinner, don't worry.'

'That doesn't sound too arduous,' she agreed. 'Tarvil, the fact is I'm not worried about Kate. "Me or the job?" is a dangerous question to ask, especially if you're taking the answer for granted.'

'And is she? Your other half?'

'What do you think?'

'Ah,' he sighed. 'You know best. I hope it works out okay for you.' He smiled. 'Meanwhile, we've got a task.' He held up a small device. 'Sauce and I took this from the dead guy's house. It needs checking for content, and this being a major investigation that means corroboration. Let's have a look at it.'

He turned his computer round to inspect the inputs: it was an older model, and as such he was pleased to see that it was compatible with the memory stick. He plugged it into the rear, then clicked on the file image that appeared on screen.

The contents were a single document, an Excel spread sheet. The sergeant watched as the screen filled with line after line. 'What is it?' she asked.

'I don't know,' he murmured, 'but there's lots of it. Jackie, go away; don't get yourself involved in this. It's going to take hours of analysis. I'll probably end up doing overtime. I'll get a uniform to sit with me. You're deep enough in the shit as it is; I'm not going to pull you further in.'

She took him at his word and went back to her desk.

Ninety-Two

The balcony of Alex Skinner's penthouse apartment had been designed with two people in mind, but when one of them was Dominick Jackson, it was a tight fit. She squeezed past and into the chair next to his and handed him a beer.

'I love this view,' he said, gazing up at Arthur's seat and the high slope known as the Radical Road. 'It defines Edinburgh.'

'Yeah, only don't look left,' she suggested. 'The Parliament building's controversial at the best of times, but the back end wins no fans. Plus, you never know who you might see sneaking out the back door.'

He smiled. 'Your ex, you mean? Sir Andrew?'

'I was thinking of a former First Minister,' she laughed, 'but yes, him too.'

'I see he's making his mark already. Shadow Justice Secretary, no less.'

'That was bound to happen. Andy didn't stand without an assurance behind the scenes that he'd go straight on to the front bench.'

'And his marriage? Heard anything about that?'

'Karen's taken him back; her boyfriend's job took him back to London, so there was a vacancy.'

Dominick shot her a sideways glance. 'That sounds pretty cynical,' he remarked.

'It is,' Alex conceded, 'but it's on the mark. They've always been well matched, him and Karen. He's politically aware and so is she. She'll be thinking that being Lady Martin won't do her police career any harm. She may well be right,'

'Why did you split up the first time? I know I asked you that before and you wouldn't tell me, but now, now . . .'

She grinned and squeezed his arm. 'Now we're shagging, you were going to say?'

'Not in so many words, but essentially . . . yes.'

'It was actually boring, being engaged to Andy,' she confessed. 'He made me feel diminished, as if I was part of the furnishings of his life. So, I had a casual fling with someone else and I got caught. By my dad, no less. Pops never really approved of Andy and me, you know. He went batshit when he found out about us. In the end he only tolerated it for my sake. Things were never quite the same between him and Andy afterwards.'

'Bob would never have shopped you to Andy, though: for your affair,' he said, with certainty.

'No, but he did make me take a look at myself. I think it made me grow up.'

'How does he really feel about you and me?' Dominick wondered.

'One hundred per cent good. If he didn't, you'd know by now.'

He shook his head. 'I'd have no chance in a rematch. Three Secret Service agents, really?'

'He didn't say, but that's what Sauce told me; hospital cases. He got it from Lottie Mann.' She paused. 'Want another?'

'Not if I'm driving home.'

She rose and left the balcony, returning less than a minute

later with two more bottles of Estrella. 'How did your afternoon go?' she asked. 'Your short notice appointment?'

'Patient confidentiality, Alex,' he reminded her. 'I can't talk about that.'

'Ah but, Doctor Jackson,' she countered, 'if I go back to private practice I might wind up defending the woman. On the other hand, if I decide to sign up for another stint in the Crown Office as an Advocate Depute, I might wind up prosecuting her. That would make me privileged, wouldn't it?'

'If it did, you've got a problem either way,' Dominick replied abruptly. 'I was asked to determine whether the subject is vulnerable in any way, before they interview her tomorrow in connection with a homicide inquiry. I wasn't told which one but it's blindingly obvious. What I think I can tell you, privileged or not, is that I've rarely met anyone less vulnerable.'

'If I could choose which side to be on . . .'

'Are you really thinking about staying on as a prosecutor? Might be a good idea.'

Ninety-Three

'Have your feet touched the ground yet, Lottie?'

Mann smiled faintly. 'Just about,' she replied. 'I managed a decent night's sleep for the first time in a week. At the end of the trip I did wind up sleeping in a police barracks, of a sort, although the overnight accommodation in the *Mossos* HQ is pretty comfortable. Better than Glasgow, that's for sure.'

'You don't have overnight accommodation in Glasgow,' Haddock said.

'We do,' she countered, 'but the doors are heavy, the beds are hard and there's a steel toilet in the corner. We're ready to go then?' she asked.

'Yes, Jackie Wright is with her, waiting for us. She's the only one who knows who the woman is, by the way. Not even Tarvil has the name. I've put her in what was the Gaffer's office when he was DCC, back in Sir James Proud's day.'

'Kid glove treatment?' Mann suggested.

'Yes, but the steel gauntlets are under the table.'

'How was the psych eval?'

'According to Dominick Jackson we're more at risk than she is,' the superintendent replied. 'A controlling personality, he reported, likely to be dominant in any relationship, and calm under pressure.'

'In Spain she said that she panicked and ran for it when her father collapsed.'

'I know,' Haddock acknowledged, 'and that claim was relayed to Dominick before the interview. He dismissed it out of hand. You were right to ask for an evaluation, Lottie, but not for the reasons that you thought. This is no victim of circumstances we're about to interview. Come on, let's get to it.'

They left his office and were passing through the squad room when Tarvil Singh called out. 'Boss, I'm finished with what's on that memory stick. I need to go through it with you, and probably with DCI Mann as well.'

'Laters, big man, laters.'

They kept moving, out of the south block of the complex towards what had been the command suite in the days when Edinburgh had been the centre of its own policing world. Skinner's former office had become a conference room, but it was one that was rarely used. They were in the anteroom and about to enter when Haddock paused. 'By the way,' he said, 'before you got here I had a call from the Gaffer's friend, the American spook woman.'

'I'm not sure she's his friend any longer,' Mann remarked. 'If she ever was.'

'Be that as it may, she asked me for regular updates on our interviews with Ms Goldstein.' He smiled. 'She said that the President has an interest in a speedy conclusion. I told her that if he presided over the Scottish Parliament I might start to give a shit, but until then I won't.'

'Don't underestimate her, Sauce.'

'I won't. I called the DCC and reported the approach.'

'What will he do?'

'He could call the US Embassy and make a formal complaint. Or he could route it through the Lord Advocate. Or he could play really rough and call the Gaffer. One word from him and the story's on the front page of the *Saltire*, and beyond. He was always influential as a cop, but now he has serious power of his own.'

'I wonder how his psych eval would read?' Mann mused, as Haddock opened the door and stepped into the conference room.

'Thanks, Jackie,' he told Wright, who had risen from her chair. 'We don't need you for this part. You might like to grab an early lunch, or whatever. I'll text you when we're done.'

As the sergeant left, he turned to Ruby Goldstein. She was seated at an oval conference table that he was sure was a relic from the Skinner era. He and Mann took their places, not directly opposite, but slightly offset, deliberately so on his part, to make the setting appear less confrontational. He looked at her; she wore no makeup at all and her hair was slightly disarranged. '"Manipulative", Dominick Jackson's report had read. "She will be aware of every situation and will adapt to it accordingly. She may appear anxious, even distressed. She will be neither; she will always have planned and she will always seek to control, offering only what she deems to be in her best interests."

He checked his watch; it showed five minutes before midday. 'Good morning,' he began, 'just. DCI Mann you know already. I am Detective Superintendent Harold Haddock. Most people call me Sauce, but you can call me Detective Superintendent Haddock. This is an informal interview, to which you have agreed, but I have my limits. There's no recording device on the table and I can assure you there are no hidden cameras. However,' he reached into his pocket and produced a small device which he slid towards her, 'if you wish, you can use this, keep it afterwards and I'll use my phone. In fact, I'd like us to do that, for your protection more than ours.' She nodded and switched on the recorder; he chose the voice memo facility on his phone.

'Ms Goldstein, you're here voluntarily, following a chain of events that began in Spain. I've only got peripheral interest in those. Primarily, I'm tasked with investigating the murder of a man who was known to us as Gavin Ayre. In that regard I do have an interest in you. If you were under caution, you'd have the right to a lawyer; you're not, but if you want one regardless, that can be arranged.'

Her right eyelid flickered; a nervous, seemingly involuntary action.

Very impressive, Mann thought, *being able to fake that.*

'No,' Goldstein said, 'I don't need one.' She hesitated for a moment before adding, quietly, 'I am hungry though; and herbal tea would be nice.'

She'll flicker her fucking eyelashes next, the DCI growled, inwardly. 'Bacon rolls all right?' he asked, then paused. 'Oh sorry.'

A brief smile appeared. 'Don't let my name fool you,' she said. 'I'm not practising, although I'd prefer tuna mayo on rye if that's okay.'

'I'll put them on order,' Haddock told her. He fired off a text to Wright. 'It'll be about half an hour,' he announced. 'Rather than wait that long, let's begin. Ms Goldstein,' he continued, 'can you describe your relationship to the person we knew as Gavin Ayre?'

'I knew him as a business associate,' she replied. 'That's until a very short time ago, when I was told by my father . . . my late father . . . that he was in fact my half-brother from an extra-marital affair that Dad had hidden from everyone.'

'What was his real name?'

'David Allen. But I really did not know until Dad told me. I didn't know that it was a false identity. If I had . . .' she exclaimed, with apparent fear in her eyes, 'it would be a crime in Scotland, wouldn't it? Buying property under a false name.'

Mann shook her head. 'Not really. In Scotland you can call yourself anything you like. You can even choose between Janet and John. But entering the country with a false passport, that's a whole different plate of sandwiches.'

'How did you feel when you discovered the truth about David?' Haddock asked. 'Did you feel he'd betrayed you?'

'I was afraid,' Goldstein whispered. 'I was afraid that we'd broken the law.'

'Can you explain that?'

'I'd slept with him. To discover that he was my brother . . . it's a crime, isn't it?'

'Actually, it's not,' the superintendent said. 'If you could prove that you were unaware of the relationship, you couldn't be charged under Scottish law.'

'Not even if I was pregnant? You know I'm pregnant, don't you?'

Mann shrugged. 'We're aware that you claim to be, Ruby. I heard you say so in Spain, yes. But there's no evidence of that.'

'Okay,' she retorted, 'bring me a test kit with the sandwiches and I'll prove it to you.'

'It could only be his?'

She stared back at Haddock. 'What do you take me for?' she snapped. It was as if a very fine crack had appeared in a smooth surface.

'I'll get to that,' he murmured. 'Your first reaction when you found out was fear, you said, fear of consequences. Consequences of what? Of conceiving a child with a man without knowing of the relationship between you? Consanguinity, we call it in Scotland. That's regrettable, no question, but in the circumstances it's fixable, whatever you want the outcome to be. Let me lay my cards on the table, Ms Goldstein.'

Before he could deal his hand, the door from the anteroom was pushed open and Wright appeared, carrying a tray laden with half a dozen rolls, and three closed beakers. She set it down, picked up one of the beakers and handed it to Goldstein. 'Lemon and honey,' she announced. 'Tuna mayo in wholemeal rolls. The best I could do; no rye bread in the canteen I'm afraid.'

Haddock kept his annoyance hidden as he thanked the DS; he had no choice but to allow Goldstein to regroup and gather her thoughts as they ate.

'Better now?' he asked, solicitously, as she finished. She nodded, wiping her mouth with a napkin. 'Good. Let's get back to consequences. If I were to suggest that you were afraid of the consequences of the unexpected death of your father, that would be true, wouldn't it?'

She gazed back at him, her mouth set more tightly than before.

'With him gone, your embezzlement of campaign funds and your laundering it into international properties was liable to be revealed. Isn't that why you vanished?'

'I admitted to that in Spain,' Goldstein pointed out.

'Yes, you did,' he agreed. 'Your plan to lure any pursuit south while you were heading north, destroying the identity of Geraldine Black to re-emerge as Ruby Goldstein, naïve, innocent and bereaved daughter. But, and here's the thing, we know that you omitted to mention the quick trip you made to Scotland. Disclosure: we know about it. We've tracked you from arrival to departure . . . and this is where it gets sticky . . . including your night in the Castle Inn and your very early departure. Talk us through that, Ms Goldstein; David was at home; you knew that. You could have gone straight there. Why didn't you?'

'I was still panicking,' she replied, 'still afraid, after my father's death, after what he had told me about David. My father had sworn that David didn't know about me being his half-sister. I had to believe that, I needed to believe that, but I felt that I couldn't just burst in on him at night. I wanted to choose my moment. So, my plan was to go there in the morning, to be there after he came home from his morning ride on Winalot. And I was. I left the Castle Inn early, before anyone was up, and I walked to David's place. It's not far. I used the code, let myself in, and I waited. After an hour, I thought, "He's late." After another thirty minutes I checked the stable in case I'd got it wrong and the horse was there, but he wasn't. The box was empty and David's phone was on the bench. That's when I started to worry. I took his car, I drove to the car park on Gullane Bents, and I parked. Then I saw a police vehicle at the far end of the park. I thought nothing of it until I walked down to the beach and saw activity there. I knew then, I just guessed that it was him. I went back up to the car; there was a parking ticket on it already. I ripped it off and threw it away, and I got out of there. I put the car back in the garage, did my best to remove any trace of my presence, walked the long way to the bus stop and got myself back to the airport, got on to a late flight, as Ruby, not Geraldine. I guess you know that part already?' she asked.

'Yes,' Haddock confirmed. 'Your story's plausible. But we have another version.'

'Do tell?' Goldstein drawled. The false vulnerability was gone; the real personality had come to the surface.

'You'd been there before,' he said, 'not just when David was there, but with your father, in June. Our hypothesis is that even then you perceived David as a threat. He'd become too comfortable in Scotland. The horse, the golf club, the girlfriend . . .' Her eyebrows rose; for half a second, but he saw it. 'Yes, he had a girlfriend . . . at least one that we know of. You were afraid that sooner or later he would give himself away, so you decided that he had to go. Our thinking is that somehow on that visit you acquired a firearm, and you hid it for later use. When it all blew up with your father you had to act. You flew to Scotland, did everything you said, only you left the hotel really early, retrieved the gun, lay in wait for him where you knew he'd be, and you took your shot. Then, you went back to the house, along the shore line; disposed of the firearm in the sea, weighted down at low tide, then did all the stuff you've just described.'

'A dead shot, am I?' she challenged.

Haddock smiled. 'Well yes, you are. My colleague DI Singh, he really has checked on you, Ms Goldstein, all the way back. One of the things he discovered was that when you were twenty-two, you joined the Wisconsin National Guard. You served in a tactical unit, where you were a sharpshooter. You even served six months in Afghanistan.'

He nodded. 'We're going to look for that firearm. The tide's exceptionally low just now, lower than it's been for months. We might even find it. When we do, we'll be having this discussion again in different surroundings.'

Ruby Goldstein drained her lemon-and-ginger tea, looking each detective in the eye. 'I'd like to go back to the hotel now,' she said. 'You have nothing; your theory sucks. As we all know, I came here voluntarily. Tomorrow, I'd like to go back to the US to deal with my father's death.' She smiled, with force. 'National Guard, huh? Tell your hotshot detective to check again.'

Her confidence seemed unshakeable. Inwardly, Haddock

sighed, as his own evaporated. 'I will,' he promised. 'For now, yes, you can go.' He texted Wright. They waited in silence for the sergeant to return. When she appeared, his orders were curt and clipped. 'Back to the hotel, Sergeant. Ms Goldstein,' he warned, 'don't make any travel plans.'

He waited until they had left, then called Singh, handsfree audio so that Mann could hear. 'Tarvil,' he said, 'Goldstein's service record. How did you get it?'

'Through the Embassy in London; I was surprised they came up with it so quickly. I said as much to their guy. He laughed and said the US defence department never sleeps, but apparently it was accessible because of her service overseas with the regular forces.'

'Get back on to him right away and check that it was fully awake when it came up with that information. There's something wrong; she pretty much laughed in our faces when I dropped it on her.'

'Will do, Sauce,' the DI promised. 'Are you and DCI Mann ready to come and see what's on this spreadsheet? I don't understand all of it but the bits that I do are very interesting.'

Ninety-Four

'You're kidding me!' Skinner exclaimed.

'Nope,' McGuire said. 'I've just been told.'

'Bloody hell! I would love to be in the room when that breaks.'

'Best not,' his friend retorted, as he ended the call.

He sat back, smiling; until his ringtone played again: his grin vanished when he saw the incoming ID. It was a US mobile number. At that moment there was only one likely caller. 'Merle,' he sighed as he accepted. 'Where are you now?'

'Edinburgh,' Gower replied. 'I need to stick as close to Ruby Goldstein as I can. I'm keeping a low profile: only the Chief Constable and his deputy know I'm here.'

'When was your profile ever high, Merle? A word of advice: don't imagine you can pull any rank with either of them.'

'I'll bear that in mind. If I have to ask them for anything my cap will be in my hand.'

'Wise,' Skinner said. 'What might you be asking them for?'

'Ruby Goldstein. We need her back home to make the story of Russell Silver's sad death plausible. The President still feels exposed because of his courtship of Silver as a running mate.'

'I wish I could get excited about that, but I can't.'

'Your journalists can, though; your group has White House

accredited correspondents. If we don't put a lid on this damn soon, it will blow. The *Washington Post* asked the Press Secretary yesterday whether Silver was away working on his acceptance speech for VP, since he seems to have paused his own campaign. It was laughed off, but in the absence of anyone in his office to explain his absence, and David Allen's, it's only a matter of time.'

'Maybe I should instruct our people to ask the question,' he suggested.

The words hung in the air. 'You fucking wouldn't,' Gower murmured.

'You owe me, remember. Merle, we've known each other for years. You've had a few roles in that time, but every one of them has had a running theme: you're a law enforcement officer. We both know this woman's guilty of a serious crime yet you're talking about whitewashing her. I don't know if I can let that happen, seriously.'

'Bob, don't get me wrong,' she countered. 'If the Department of Justice could prove that Silver and his crew, his kids, embezzled campaign donor funds, the President would likely throw them to the wolves and claim all the integrity points that were going, but they can't. Allen's been very clever: there is no trail.'

'If proof was given to you,' he asked, 'what would you do with it?'

'Me, I'd burn them,' she replied, instantly. 'And,' she added, 'I'd use it to get the best deal for myself. I'm highly placed now, Bob, but I've always wanted one of the top jobs to round off my career. Director of the FBI, Head of the National Security Agency. Either of those, I don't care.'

'Watch this space,' he said. 'So long, Merle.'

Ninety-Five

'This is a pleasant surprise,' Ruby Goldstein said as Jackie Wright showed her into the conference room. 'I expected to be back here, but not this soon.' She paused as she realised that four people awaited her, rather than the two that she had seen before. One of the newcomers was Merle Gower, whom she had met in Spain, but the other was a stranger. He was a massive man, wearing a black suit that seemed to suit his appearance, thick black hair, curls flecked with grey, heavy eyebrows and dark eyes. *Italian?* she wondered.

Whoever he was, the young superintendent still seemed to be in charge; she made eye contact and gave him a confident smile. 'I guess this means I don't have to spend another night in that hotel: it isn't the best, and the two goons on the door don't add to its charms.'

'Sorry about that,' Haddock said. 'Our hospitality budget's limited; as for the officers, it's our duty to keep you safe. Your guess is correct though; you won't be going back there.' He broke off. 'Introductions: Ms Gower you know; the other is my boss, Deputy Chief Constable McGuire.'

The dark man nodded. 'Purely a courtesy visit,' he said in a deep Scottish voice. *Not Italian*, she decided, *and yet . . .*

'The courtesy is appreciated,' she replied. *But what the hell is the NSA woman doing here?* she wondered.

'I need to update you on our discussion this morning,' Haddock continued. 'We left it hanging, just a little. We're always eager to please, so we acted upon your suggestion. It took a little while, but DI Singh was finally able to access your National Guard records at state level. And as I'm sure you knew he would, he discovered that you were discharged from the Guard three years ago, after a head injury that you sustained in a cycling accident left you with severely compromised vision in your right eye. You were no longer fit for active duty in the Ranger squad of which you were a part, so they kicked you out. Bottom line, our hypothesis that you assassinated the victim, your half-brother David Allen, falls at that hurdle. You couldn't have taken the shot because you can't see well enough.'

She smiled. 'Finally,' she said, 'you got there.'

The superintendent shrugged. 'We persevere. We can't take a flawed case to court, so we look at it from both sides. We'd have got there in time, without your help. There's something else,' he continued. 'We checked with the East Lothian parking enforcement people and found an outstanding parking ticket issued on Gullane Bents to the car registered to Gavin Ayre, issued around the time you said you were there. It's pretty clear that if by some miracle you had hit him from that distance, you wouldn't have been revisiting the scene of the crime.' He nodded, with a faint smile. 'With these new factors taken into account, Ms Goldstein, I thank you for your voluntary cooperation and I confirm that you are no longer a person of interest to our investigation.'

'Well . . .' she began but his raised hand cut her off.

'However,' he continued, 'there is the matter of entering the UK under a false name and with a false passport. Enough of that survived the fire in Spain for it to be identified as yours. Even better, it was stamped at Border Control and that page was intact too.'

She glared at him, then at Mann, then Gower and then the impassive McGuire. 'Lawyer,' she murmured.

'You don't need one,' the DCC said. 'We're not going to report you for prosecution. That would only get in the way.'

'Of what?' she challenged.

'Of this.' He held up a small device: a memory stick. 'We found it at your brother's house. We've examined it and also consulted with Ms Gower; she confirms that it appears to be a detailed record of all the money that you embezzled from your late father's campaign fund, and of how it was spent. There are annotations there; initials, GA, GB and GL. I'm new to this investigation but I know what they stand for and so do you.'

'The fuck!' she hissed. 'Why would . . .?'

'Why would he do that?' the DCC finished the question. 'I don't know, but I'll take a stab at it.' He showed the stick once again. 'I'd say this was a bargaining chip; it's an attempt at protection for himself in the event that the fraud came to light. You can see it, can't you, Ms Goldstein? You're all caught, he cooperates with the Department of Justice and a plea deal is struck. He does a couple of years; you and your father do thirty. But now, it's in our hands.'

'It's numbers,' she countered, rallying, 'that's all. How can you tie it to me?'

McGuire's smile was dazzling, flashing white teeth and gleaming eyes. 'Because there's more in there than just a spreadsheet. There are JPEG files of written notes, in two different hands. He photographed them and he stored them. Guesswork again: one of them is your father's and the other is yours.'

336

It was over; everyone in the room knew that as her brick hard resolve crumbled before them. 'What's next?' she sighed.

'Next,' he said, 'in a fine example of international co-operation, I do this.' He handed the memory stick to Merle Gower.

'And I,' she said, 'in my capacity as a sworn US Federal Marshal, am arresting you, Ruby Goldstein, to be returned to the United States to face trial.'

'Seriously?' she retorted, recovering some of her venom. 'How long do you think it'll take to get me back there?'

'Extradition?' Gower replied. 'That would depend on how long you could drag out the appeal process, but bear in mind that you'd be in custody for all that time. Actually, it would be easier for the Scots to try you for the passport offences, then deport you as a criminal, after you'd served half your jail sentence here. Isn't that right, Detective Superintendent Haddock?'

Sauce nodded. 'It is,' he confirmed. 'I've spoken to the Crown Office. On the basis of the evidence we have, you'd be charged under indictment; the maximum penalty would be fourteen years, and our judges aren't known for their leniency.'

Beside him, Gower nodded. 'I can vouch for that,' she confirmed. 'However, I have a feeling that it won't come to that.' She drew a deep breath.

'I have a once in a lifetime offer, Ruby,' she said. 'It comes from the President through me . . . although,' she added, 'I really fucking hate having to make it. The deal is that you and I will take a flight home, tonight. In Washington you'll announce your father's death. You'll attribute it, tearfully no doubt, to the shock of discovering that his campaign manager, his son, was guilty of a huge embezzlement. In other words, you throw David under the bus that you're driving yourself. You go home to Wisconsin and raise your baby like any other single mom. The President, he makes a public statement about what a great man your father was and how his death is a great loss to the nation. Me? I'm being quietly sick in the corner of my brand new office, wherever that is.' *Because, like McGuire, I will also have copied the contents of the memory stick,* was left unsaid.

'This all sticks in my throat,' she concluded, 'and I'm sure in the throats of every cop in this room . . . who are now here as witnesses incidentally . . . but it's politics, it's expedient and, unless you're feeling suicidal, it's what is going to happen.'

Ninety-Six

'Could you not have squeezed me into the room,' Singh sighed. 'I'd have loved to have seen all that.'

Haddock laughed. 'You and McGuire in the same room? The size of you two, there'd have been no oxygen left for anybody else. Tarvil, I'm only telling you what happened in there because you know what was on that storage device. It's locked away forever in your box of secret knowledge, all right?'

'It goes with me to my grave, Sauce,' the DI promised. 'Speaking of graves, and that of Gavin Ayre . . . what happens to his body, by the way? Has anyone thought about that.'

His colleague nodded. 'Now that we know who he really was, yes. His mother's his next of kin; Tiggy Benjamin's established that she still lives in Mississauga, where he was born. She's married with one other kid. Someone will reach out to her, maybe our High Commission in Ottawa, or possibly the Americans. When Goldstein makes her stay-out-of-jail announcement, the world's going to know the secret that the poor woman's kept for over thirty years . . . who fathered her son. It's also going to hear that her boy David was a major league fraudster. I hope the White House is up to managing her reaction.'

'Mmm, me too. Do you think they'll tell her she's going to be a granny?'

'Would you?'

'Not a chance.' He gazed at Haddock. 'You know the next thing that's going to happen, don't you? We're going to hear from her, wanting to know who killed her boy.'

'Yes, we are,' he agreed. 'And we're no nearer finding out than we were on the day he died. Back to square one, Tarvil. Everything we know about everyone involved, and renew the public appeal for witnesses.'

'Of course, boss,' Singh said, 'but, we're getting stretched. We've got an armed robbery in Dundee on our books and there was a multiple-victim knife crime in Leith last night that will come to us. We're struggling for manpower.'

'I appreciate that, Tarvil; our resources are spread thin and I will take it up with the DCC, but for the meantime we have to balance what we have as best we can. Look,' he murmured. 'Noele McClair's been helping out on her maternity leave, doing stuff on the phone. Ask her if she's up for carrying a bit more of the load.'

Ninety-Seven

'That's how it's playing out?' Sarah asked. 'In a cover-up?'

'That's power for you,' Bob replied.

'Does it have to?'

'No, but it can be seen as the best outcome available, the most pragmatic. If the right wing got hold of the truth, imagine the consequences; there could well be a landslide and God knows what would happen.'

'What about InterMedia's interests? You know the facts. Doesn't it tweak your conscience to go along with a lie.'

'I know a version of events, love,' he countered, 'but ultimately the facts are what you can prove, and I can't.'

'You could if Neil McIlhenney gave you access to the files from the memory stick?'

'Could I? It would still be only one version of events. This too; if I blew the story we'd lose our White House accreditation. Worse, we'd be hailed as heroes by people we oppose, philosophically and in every other way. No,' he said, 'there's only one alternative to the White House strategy, and it's one that I've suggested to Merle Gower. Do nothing at all: let Ruby Goldstein announce her father's death and leave it at that: leave every fucking stone unturned. Do that and there's only one other loose end to be tied off . . . and that's the real reason why Neil called me. The Canadians will need to be told about David Allen; his mother will need to be told. You're holding the body in your mortuary; they're going to want it back when the Crown Office is ready to release it. Until then, it's yours. They'll want to see the autopsy report, of course; they might even want to do one of their own . . . although I doubt that; there are few things more clear and obvious than a bullet in the brain.'

'And what about Gavin Ayre?' she challenged.

'Who's Gavin Ayre? Sauce Haddock never released that name. The Secret Service has already searched David Allen's office in Washington and recovered his genuine passport. By now there's probably a record of him entering the UK and using an e-reader at Border Control.'

'Will Gower be able to sell your strategy to the White House?'

'If she buys into it herself, yes. I think she will; she'll know that if everything is dumped on Allen, his family could become a problem.'

'What about the properties? The stolen money?'

'Who says it was stolen? Why can't it have been a longterm investment strategy by Silver? The property market was down internationally at the time. It's recovering already. The houses and the land can be sold at a profit.' He grinned. 'Maybe Cheeky and Sauce can buy the Ayre place. It's handy for the golf course, and the baby could learn to swim in the pool!'

Ninety-Eight

'I know that my colleague, Inspector Hill spoke to you a few days ago, Mrs Wayne,' Noele McClair told the stable owner. 'However, it's standard practice at this stage of an investigation for us to re-interview witnesses, to see if their recollections have changed.'

'Is that police speak for "we've made no progress", Detective Inspector?' Marion Wayne asked.

'Pretty much,' McClair admitted.

'In that case, this might be your lucky day . . . although not very lucky,' she added. 'My recollections have changed, as it happens. When your inspector chap called and told me about the fatality on the beach, I told him I couldn't think of anyone who fitted the description he gave me. I can now: Mr Ayre, his name was. He approached me looking for occasional accommodation for his horse. He said he had a stable block in his house, but he was single and travelled so he needed temporary cover while he was away; someone had recommended me, he said. He seemed like a nice chap, until he told me that he called his horse Winalot, would you believe? That takes bad taste to a whole new level. Poor animal, I was almost glad that I had to turn him down. Instead, I recommended a friend in Kingston, John Barley;

343

I believe that he took him on. Was that him?' she asked, suddenly. 'The dead man? Mr Ayre?'

'That was him. Do you know anything else about him?'

'Nothing, but John might. I'll give you his number: save you looking it up. Hold on.'

McClair waited; a few seconds later, Mrs Wayne dictated an eleven-digit mobile number. 'Try him,' she said. 'He might be able to fill in some of your blanks.'

The detective inspector thanked her, then keyed in the number on her phone. Her call was answered almost instantly. 'Yes?' a gruff voice barked.

'Mr Barley?'

'That depends. Who are you?'

'I'm the police,' she shot back. 'DI Noele McClair, Serious Crimes Unit.'

'Ah,' his tone changed. 'I'm sorry, I get so many junk calls. How can I help you?'

'I'm making enquiries,' she began, 'about a man that I believe might have been a client of yours, Gavin Ayre.'

'Ah,' Barley repeated. 'You're using the past tense. Are you going to tell me that what I've suspected is the case? That the dead man on Gullane beach was Gavin?'

'Yes, I'm afraid I am,' she confirmed.

'What a bloody shame!' he sighed. 'The police statement implied that he was murdered. That's the case, is it? I mean, bloody hell, what was it, yobs? I've known of people who've set their dogs chasing equestrians. Was that what happened, something like that?'

'I can't go into detail, I'm afraid,' McClair replied, 'but I can tell you it wasn't that. How well did you know Mr Ayre?'

'He was a client, so I knew him on that level, maybe a bit

better. God!' Barley exclaimed suddenly. 'What's happened to Winalot? Is he . . .'

'The horse is fine,' she assured him. 'He's in a police stable for now.'

'As a witness, I . . .' He cut short his black humour. 'What a bloody stupid thing to say, John,' he murmured. 'Inspector, if you're looking for a home for him, I'd take him like a shot, and make whatever financial arrangement is necessary with Gavin's family.'

'We'll bear that in mind,' she said, 'but it's not a priority; he's fine where he is for now. Right now, we're trying to find out as much about Gavin's life as we can.'

'I see.' Barley fell silent for a few reflective moments. 'I can't really tell you much,' he confessed eventually, 'even though we did talk. Thinking about it, I told him a lot more about me than I got out of him. He was vague about what he did; said something about international property and asset management, whatever the hell that might mean. All I really I know is that he was a novice golfer. He bought himself into Witches Hill rather than go on one of the interminable waiting lists for membership that we have around here. It's handy if you have the means to do that,' he mused. 'I was his guest there a couple of times: it's a lovely layout. Best course around here, after Muirfield and Gullane One.' He sighed. 'That's closed off to me now, I suppose, not having silly money. Sorry, Inspector,' he murmured, 'I'm rambling. What else do you need to know?'

'Anything that I don't know already,' McClair replied, 'which basically means anything, because we know nothing right now. Mr Ayre's vagueness wasn't accidental; there was a reason for it. We do know that he had a couple of casual dates, but that's all.'

'No, more than casual,' Barley corrected her. 'The last time we played Witches Hill Gavin told me that he was seeing a lady, and that they were planning to get together, once some complications had been worked out. His words: I don't know what he meant and I didn't press him.'

'Did he say anything about her?' she asked, thinking through everything she had been told about the man's life. 'For example, could she have been a work colleague?'

'No, I don't think so. I believe she was from around here. Come to think of it, she must have been,' he murmured. 'He told me they met on horseback. I assume that he meant here. Does that help?'

'It might,' she told him. 'Thanks, Mr Barley. Should we need a formal statement, we'll be in touch.'

She ended the call and opened the hard copy of the case file that had been delivered to her, scrolling through it until she found the page she was after. She scanned it and then called Jackie Wright.

'It's Noele,' she said when they connected. 'I'm looking through the transcript of your interview of Claire Hornell. She definitely described her affair with Gavin Ayre as casual, yes?'

'If that's what it says, that's how it happened,' the sergeant replied, abruptly.

'Of course,' McClair continued quickly, 'but I've been told it might have been more than that . . . in Ayre's eyes at least. We need to go back to this woman, Jackie.'

'If you say so, I'll do that,' Wright responded.

'No, I'm not asking that. It's something I can take on, but I want to eyeball her when it happens. See if you can set up a meeting with her, time and place of her choosing. I'll get my mum to mind Mattie if necessary.'

Ninety-Nine

'Are you still in Spain?' Merle Gower asked.

'Yes,' Skinner replied. 'I'm in the office. Sarah's in Barcelona, at the university, sorting out the details of her visiting chair. And you?'

'I'm in my nation's capital, failing to sleep at five o'clock in the morning. I was with the President until midnight . . . not the Chief of Staff mind, POTUS himself . . . talking through the Russell Silver mess. He's bought your low-key solution: Ruby Goldstein will announce her father's death at midday and will leave it at that. Nothing beyond it, nothing about missing funds, and nothing about David Allen.'

'What if she's asked about him? He was the campaign director, after all.'

'Was,' Gower emphasised. 'With Silver dead there is no campaign. It becomes a family matter. If she's asked, she'll say that he went off a couple of weeks ago to reflect on progress and plan future strategy. She doesn't know where he is and can't contact him. When it emerges that he's a murder victim in Scotland, that's a separate issue. By that time Goldstein will be home in Wisconsin managing her developing pregnancy. If the FEC ever asks about the missing money . . . well, as you pointed out, one, it will all have been written off against tax, two, the major donors all have to live in the real business world, not the one that Silver might have brought about. They all donated discreetly and they'll want to keep it that way. It's all going away, Bob, all of it. As far as you're concerned, you have the President's personal thanks, and his assurance that when InterMedia launches its Hispanic cable news channel, you will have no regulatory problems, none at all.'

Skinner smiled. 'That's nice. Nice for him too,' he added. 'Latinos are the fastest growing ethnic voter group in the US; they'll be our viewing audience and he'll have our support.'

'He knows.'

'And what about you, Merle?' he asked. 'What's the outcome for you?'

'Me?' she replied. He could sense the tiredness in her voice. 'I'm now Assistant to the President for National Security Affairs. I have direct access and I attend meetings of the National Security Council. I've also been told that the Director for National Intelligence is standing down after the next election and that I'll replace him. Cabinet post, Bob. Fuck me, InterMedia's well connected,' she chuckled. 'You should get a bonus.'

He laughed. 'I'll tell Xavi. Funnily enough, Sarah and I were talking about a new property last night . . . it might even be going cheap.'

One Hundred

'Are you comfortable with us doing this here?' Noele McClair asked.

Claire Hornell glanced to her left and right. They were the only customers in the farm shop café and their table was far enough away from the rest to give them reasonable privacy, should others arrive. 'I'm good,' she confirmed. 'It suits me. I can pick Poppy up from nursery when we're done.' She reached out and touched the pram by McClair's side. 'How old is Matilda?'

'A couple of days short of two months,' the detective replied. 'I'd have left her with my mother, but she and her fella have a lunch date.'

'Is she your first?'

'No, I have a son at primary school; Harry.'

'Shouldn't you be on maternity leave?' Hornell wondered.

'Officially I am. But our team's stretched, so I volunteered to do what I can from home. This counts as "home", by the way. I live only a mile away.' She paused as the waiter arrived with a tray, bearing a pot of tea, a latte and two pieces of Rocky Road.

'So,' Hornell said, as McClair poured tea into her cup, 'DS Wright said you were reinterviewing witnesses. Does that mean you're no closer to finding out what happened to Gavin?'

'We know what happened to him,' the DI told her, 'but we're no closer to finding out who did it.'

'How can I help you do that?' she asked.

'You probably can't but we have to be sure that everything in our case file is one hundred per cent accurate. And that's why we're here. Claire, you told my colleague, DS Wright, that your relationship with Gavin was casual, yes?'

'Yes,' she replied, quietly, 'I did. Why?'

'Well, the thing is, we've been told by someone who knew him that he confided in this person that he was in a relationship that was going to become permanent once, in Gavin's words, some complications had been sorted out. From something else that he said, we're thinking that his potential new partner might have been you. Are we wrong in that conclusion?'

The tall coffee cup trembled in the woman's hand. She replaced it on the table, picked up the confectionery and took a bite. As McClair gazed at her, she shook her head.

'No,' she murmured, when she was ready. 'It's true what you were told. I was planning to leave Eddie and move in with Gavin. I'm sorry, I should have been honest with you. Am I in trouble?'

'That's not for me to decide,' McClair told her, 'but I doubt it in the circumstances. With you being that close,' she continued, 'did you know that Gavin Ayre wasn't his real name?'

Hornell stared at the DI. 'What do you mean?' she gasped.

'It was an identity he used when he commissioned his property,' the detective explained, 'but his real name was David Allen. I'm telling you this in confidence for now, Claire. It will become known at some stage, probably quite soon, but for now it can't be repeated.'

'Good heavens,' she whispered. 'You're saying I was about to commit my life, and my daughter's, to someone I didn't know?'

'Let's assume he would have told you when he was ready,' McClair said, gently. 'There were reasons why he might have chosen not to, but I can't go into them. Let's just assume that was one of the complications he referred to with his friend.'

She smiled weakly. 'That's kind of you. It helps. The other complication, of course, would be Eddie, my husband. He was the main reason why I was less than frank with DS Wright. Eddie's a lovely man, I want you to know that, but he's become a stranger to me and to Poppy. The Royal bloody Navy's the real love of his life, not us; it was bad enough before when he was on destroyers, but since he was promoted and transferred to that anachronistic aircraft carrier . . . its deployment lasts for months at a time, I mean like months. And never close to home either: if he was in the Med, say, Poppy and I could fly somewhere near to him, but he's always in the Far East, trying to impress the Chinese or the North Koreans. When I met Gavin that day in the woods, I was at my loneliest and he was kind, and even more than that, he was bloody there!'

'What are you going to do now, Claire?' Noele asked her.

'I don't know,' she confessed. 'I don't know where I stand, or what I'll do. Go back to my parents, maybe, that's a possibility.'

'Or just carry on with Eddie as if Gavin never happened?'

She shook her head. 'Too late for that, I bloody told him, didn't I?'

McClair's antennae twitched, but she kept it from her expression. 'When?'

'About three weeks ago. I decided I had to be honest with him, so I called him on WhatsApp. We had a decent video connection for once . . . normally he calls me and it's audio . . . and I broke it to him.'

'How did he take it?'

'Calmly, as I knew he would. Eddie's submissive by nature. I'm not saying he's a wimp but . . . fuck it, he's a wimp. There was one time a couple of years ago, when he was still on destroyers and closer to home, we were out for a bar meal in a place in Haddington and a guy was really rude to me. In fact, he made a pass at me, even though I was pregnant with Poppy at the time. When Eddie told him to stop it and go away, the fellow squared up to him. And my husband, he just turned his back on him. It could have been very nasty but the guy's mates dragged him away. He took some dragging, I can tell you. Welsh; on a rugby trip, I think. He was a real archetype: his pals called him Clive Boyo, I remember. I thought he was full of wind and piss, but he scared Eddie. He got the bill and we left straight away. I was angry with him; when we got home, I went straight to bed.'

She frowned. 'He was much the same when I broke the news about Gavin, mild and submissive, afraid of any confrontation. He just said "Fine, if he's what you want; as long as I can see Poppy when I'm home." I felt like a heel; I still do. Maybe I can pretend it never happened and, like you say, just carry on. The trouble is, I don't think I want to. I wanted Eddie to be furious; I wanted him to fight for me but he didn't. I don't know if I can ever get past that. I have a couple of months to decide, though. The carrier's still near the Philippines.'

One Hundred and One

'Check it out, please, Jackie,' McClair had said. 'It's niggling away at me. When I was made station inspector at Haddington I went over all the open incident files. I'm sure that there was a missing person among them, a drunk Welshman who went off to answer a call of nature when he and his pals were on their way back to their hotel and was never seen again. I deployed uniforms to take another look within a one-mile radius, in case he'd choked to death on his own vomit and was still lying there, but there was no joy.'

'Yes,' Inspector Ronnie Hill confirmed. 'That's still in my pending tray, still listed as a misper. I reviewed it last week in fact. His name's Clive Sullivan, and he's from Pontypool. He and his three pals were up for a rugby international at Murrayfield. The four of them had one ticket between them. They were going to draw straws for it on the day of the game, and this was the night before. When Sullivan went off for his dump in the bushes he had it in his back pocket; when he vanished, so did the ticket. His pals decided that he was so drunk he'd decided to stiff them by walking all the way to Murrayfield, either to use it himself or sell it for as much as he could get. Next day they waited for him outside the ground, but no sign, then or ever since. Their rugby club knew the seat number; we went as far as to check but it was never used.'

'And it's still an open case?' Wright asked.

'Yes, but according to the file, Sullivan was massively in debt; credit card bills, car finance, mortgage payments. The likeliest explanation is that he simply ran away from it all and chose that as his moment.'

'Do you buy that version?'

'In the absence of anything else, yes,' Hill said. 'He was a big unit just to make vanish.'

'Ronnie,' she countered. 'Not so long ago there were human remains found a few feet from the John Muir Way on the coastline; a murder victim. They'd been hidden there for years without being discovered. Vanishing's been made to work before.'

'I suppose so,' he conceded, 'but, Jackie, what do you want me to do about it?'

'It's your division, but if I had your bars in my shoulders I might get the file out of the pending tray and search again, but with a wider circle this time, say three miles initially, and with cadaver dogs if you can get them.'

'Okay,' he agreed grudgingly, 'but with minimum manpower, mind.'

Wright ended the call and turned to the second task that McClair had delegated. She had to wait ten minutes for her call to the Ministry of Defence, naval staff section, to be answered. When it was, the voice was crisp, female and authoritative, but it took a further three minutes to identify herself to its owner. Finally, the detective sergeant framed her request: 'I want to confirm the service status of an officer, Lieutenant Commander Edward Hornell, and the current and recent location of his vessel, HMS *Prince William*.'

'Give me a number and I'll get back to you, Sergeant.'

'It's okay,' she said, 'I can hold on.'

'Give me a number,' the voice repeated, slowly.

'I can hold on,' Wright growled. 'Look dear,' she regretted 'dear' as soon as she had said it, but it was too late to back down. 'I'm the police; I've got authority.'

'I'm the Royal Navy,' the woman countered. 'I've got authority too and I think you'll find it's bigger than yours.'

One Hundred and Two

The photograph that Noele McClair had sourced was three years old. Therefore it showed Edward Hornell in the uniform of a lieutenant rather than a lieutenant commander, but it was recent enough for her purpose. She printed it out then placed it in the investigation file, after that of his wife. Looking at it she understood what Claire had said: this was the man who had sand kicked in his face in the old Charles Atlas ads she remembered from her grandfather's collection of boxing magazines.

She turned as the door opened and Sue, her mother, came in, followed by her son. There was a sparkle in her eyes. 'It was coming up on quarter to four when I left Duncan's,' she volunteered, 'so I thought I'd pick this one up from school.'

'I thought you were going out for lunch,' Noele said.

'When did I say that? I had lunch at Duncan's.'

And the rest! she thought. She was still coming to terms with the notion of her mother having a sex life; and a little jealous of her, truth be told.

'Whatever, you're just in time. I have to see to Mattie. Can you get Harry started on his homework?'

'Of course.' Sue followed her grandson into the living room, but paused at the table, where the file lay open. 'What's this?' she asked.

'It's what we used to call the Murder Book,' her daughter replied. 'The case file.'

'What's he doing in it?' She pointed at the photo of Edward Hornell.

Noele frowned. 'He's the husband of a witness.'

'Is he? That's a coincidence.'

'Why, Mum?'

'Because that's the birdwatcher. The camper we met just before you saw the poor man's body. That's him: I'm sure of it. And there were two sleeping bags in his tent, I remember. Husband of a witness, you say? It looks as if they both were.'

One Hundred and Three

'She's certain?' DCC Mario McGuire asked.

'Noele says she's pretty certain,' Sauce Haddock assured him. 'Not a hundred per cent but damn sure. Noele can't swear to it herself, because she was carrying the baby. She was heading for a seat and didn't pay the man too much attention, but Sue stopped and had a chat with him. He was cooking breakfast on a stove, she said. She could see inside the tent and saw two sleeping bags; he even told her that his partner had gone to find the showers.'

'Are you saying the wife's a suspect too?'

'Noele doesn't think so,' Haddock replied. 'and she's met Claire Hornell.'

The computer camera picked up McGuire's frown. 'I'm sorry, Sauce,' he said. 'I don't buy it. She has to be mistaken. From what you're saying, the photograph Noele used for the file was, what, three years old? There's room for error in that. But much more than that: the guy's exec officer on an aircraft carrier and it's on patrol on the other side of the world. He couldn't just nip out for a couple of days to shoot his wife's lover and then get back on board.'

'So what do I do, sir?'

'Put the wife under surveillance for now, to give me time to think about this. Wright's spoken to the MoD, you said?'

'Yes, she's waiting for feedback.'

'Okay, we'll wait too. As I said, let me think about this and get back to you, but I'm not pushing the panic button on the word of a woman with stars in her eyes.'

'Okay, sir. I'll get the surveillance in place and wait to hear from you.' Haddock closed the call.

As the computer screen went black, the DCC leaned back in his chair, its protests squeaking in his ears. He made two mental notes; the first was to ask office supplies for a replacement, and the second was to lose weight.

'What would Bob have done?' he whispered.

As he waited in vain for an answer, his desk phone buzzed. He picked it up, and heard the voice of the assistant he shared with the chief constable. 'Sir,' she said, 'I have a call for you from a Major Hitchin, Ministry of Defence. He says he'll only speak to you.'

One Hundred and Four

'Seriously?' Tarvil Singh exclaimed. 'Surveillance for a single woman with a young child?'

'That's what the DCC said,' Haddock replied, 'so that's what we'll do.'

'What's the purpose? Is she a suspect?'

'We've got a suggestion from a source that she was at the crime scene. The same person claims that the woman's husband was there too. It's questionable on two counts; one, her husband's ship is somewhere in the Pacific, two, she told Noele that she was leaving him to go off with the victim.'

'Who's the source?' the DI asked.

'Never mind that, Tarvil. Let's act upon it for now like our boss says. Discreetly though. Use Tiggy Benjamin, in an unmarked car, just to keep an eye on her. From what I'm told her routine's pretty simple: her kid's at nursery and when she's there sometimes she goes out on her pony. You do that and I'll get Jackie to check out something else.'

He left Singh to brief Benjamin and crossed to Wright's desk. 'Jackie,' he said, 'I've got a task for you; it may be nothing, it may be everything.'

'Yes, Sauce, but can I get in first? I spoke to Inspector Hill in

360

Haddington yesterday afternoon, about an open missing-person file in his area, a Welsh rugby fan who had a run-in with Claire Hornell's husband a couple years ago, after he tried it on with her in a pub. According to her, the husband chickened out and took her home. I suggested that he take another look; he's just called me to say that a cadaver dog has found skeletonised remains covered by a gorse bush a couple of miles from where the man disappeared. They're male, clad in what looks like a rugby shirt; you can still make out "Pontypool" on the chest, above the badge. He's got the scene taped off, awaiting CID response.'

Haddock whistled. 'Thanks, Jackie. Brief Tarvil; ask him to call out a crime scene team from the Crime Campus. We'll get out there once I've told the DCC. Meanwhile . . . I'd like you to call East Lothian Council and ask whether there are any security cameras near the toilets on Gullane beach.'

One Hundred and Five

'Mr McGuire? Gareth Hitchins, Major, Ministry of Defence. I'm told you're the main man in Scotland on security matters.'

'After the chief constable,' the DCC replied, 'yes, I am. What's your interest, Major?'

'Same as yours,' the soldier responded. 'Security. I've been told that one of your people, a Detective Sergeant Wright, has been making enquiries about a naval officer, Lieutenant Commander Edward Hornell. I'm afraid she's run up a red flag.'

A faint anticipatory smile showed on McGuire's face. 'Talk to me,' he murmured.

'What's your interest in Hornell?' Hitchins asked.

'My officers need to eliminate him as a person of interest in an investigation. That's the formal way of putting it. Informally, his wife had a lover until just under two weeks ago, when someone put a bullet in his head. Our information is that Lieutenant Commander Hornell is executive officer on HMS *Prince William*, and that he was on patrol in Far Eastern waters at the time of the crime.'

'If I can confirm that you'll have no further interest in him?'

'Not necessarily, Major,' McGuire countered. 'There are such things as contract killings. We'd still need to vet him, discreetly.'

He paused, distracted by an email as it flashed up on his computer screen; it was from Haddock and it bore a priority marker. 'Excuse me for a moment,' he murmured, then studied its contents. 'And something else,' he continued, when he was ready. 'We now need to confirm from his service records that he was on leave two and a half years ago, at the time of the Scotland/Wales rugby match in Edinburgh, early March from memory.'

'I see.' McGuire heard a breath being drawn, as if a response was being weighed. 'I can confirm,' Major Hitchens said. 'That HMS *Prince William* is on patrol in the South China Sea as part of a group of NATO and Australian vessels. I can confirm that Lieutenant Commander Edward Hornell is its executive officer of record. I have his full service record in front of me. He is an exemplary officer with the potential to reach flag rank . . . should he choose to follow that route.' He stopped; something in his tone made the listener hold his breath.

'I say that, he continued, 'because he's not currently on board the *Prince William*. He remains on the crew list for reasons of personal security.' He paused. 'Before I go any further, Mr McGuire, can you assure me that our conversation isn't being recorded and that there's nobody listening in? Nothing personal,' he added, 'it's something I'm obliged to ask.'

'You have that assurance,' the DCC responded, his calmness belying the tension he felt.

'Thanks. For your information only, for the last two years Lieutenant Commander Hornell has been seconded to the Special Air Service. Three years ago, he applied to join, as any officer in any service may. He was accepted for training and he completed the courses in Wales and in Brunei; he was the top graduate in each. At the time you mentioned, two and a half years back, yes, he was on leave, having just completed his hot weather training and was ready for deployment. Why? What happened then?' Hitchens asked.

'He was out with his pregnant wife,' McGuire replied, 'when a drunk, for want of a better word, propositioned her. She told my officer that Hornell backed away from confrontation and took her home. The man disappeared that same night, but the two incidents were never linked until now. The missing person file's been lying open since then, until yesterday when we took another look at it in the light of the new information. We've just found a body we believe to be his. Any thoughts?' he asked.

'Unofficially?' the major responded. 'If Hornell decided to kill the man, then he was as good as dead. He's the best, simply the best, to quote dear old Tina, God bless and keep her.'

'Does his wife know he's SAS?'

'Not unless he decided to tell her,' Hitchens said. 'Many SAS personnel choose not to: when they're on duty they use live social media to communicate. If Mrs Hornell thinks that her husband is still a sailor, and in international waters, that's quite feasible.'

'And if he decided to shoot her lover, from a distance?'

'The same as I told you before: goodnight. Hornell is second in command of the CTW, a specialised squadron; he has sniper skills.'

'Two weeks ago, where was he?' McGuire asked.

'Let me look,' the soldier murmured, and then he whistled. 'He was on leave. He booked off for ten days. He left on a Friday and reported back the following Monday.'

'Jesus. Major, would it have been possible for him to take a weapon with him?'

'I'd love to say no,' Hitchens replied. 'But if his unit wasn't operational, and it couldn't have been if he was on leave, yes, it probably would.'

'If I had my lab send you an image,' McGuire continued, 'of the markings on the bullet taken from our victim's skull, could you match it?'

'It might take a while, but I'm sure we could.'

'Thanks, I'll order that at once. Major, I have grounds to hold Lieutenant Commander Hornell for questioning, with the probability of charging him with at least one murder, possibly two. He's one of yours: will the Military Police do that?'

The silence on the line chilled the police officer. 'We would, DCC McGuire,' Hitchens said, 'if he was in Hereford. But we, you, all of us, have a big problem. Hornell is on leave again; he checked out two days ago, citing a family emergency. I'm sure we're both thinking the same thing; that you may need to protect his wife. But I'd go beyond that; I advise that you shouldn't put your people at risk. The MPs have specialist units to handle this contingency. I will get one to you soonest. Until then, for God's sake be careful. This might be the most dangerous man you've ever met.'

One Hundred and Six

'I'm limited in what I can tell you,' Haddock said to his team, gathered around his meeting table, 'but Edward Hornell is now the main person of interest in the Gavin Ayre investigation, and in another suspected homicide. You've all been issued with an up-to-date image of the man. It's not certain, but it's very possible that he's in the area. If he is, the best assumption is that he's planning to make contact with his wife. If so we don't know why, but he hasn't just turned up at the house, that's for sure; so let's assume that he has bad intentions. I've had eyes on Mrs Hornell since this morning. She dropped her child at the nursery at nine thirty and then went straight home, since when she hasn't left.'

'Isn't the wife a possible suspect too?' Noele McClair asked. Her voice came from the superintendent's computer, where a Zoom link was active. 'My mum is still adamant that she saw two sleeping bags.'

'We believe that's what any passers-by were meant to see,' he replied. 'Jackie's established that there's a camera overseeing the new toilet-and-shower block at Gullane Bents, to guard against vandals. There are sightings of Edward Hornell over two days, but none of his wife. Not just that, her drop-off times at the nursery are a matter of record. I'm disregarding her as a suspect. Instead we have to consider her as a potential target.'

Singh raised a hand. 'Is the husband likely to be armed?'

'Not in the same way. The DCC and I think we know where he got the weapon that killed Ayre. It's one among many but, once test firings are done, we hope to be able to identify it.'

'What's the next step?' the Sikh asked.

'I've told Benjamin to maintain discreet surveillance, but not to expose herself.' A young DC's sudden grin froze on his face and vanished under Haddock's glare. 'If Hornell does show up at home, she's to withdraw and we surround the place with an armed team . . . and a negotiator.' He paused. 'People, we're not alone in this. Hornell's a serving officer, so the Military Police are involved. That said, it'll take them a while to get here.'

'How about the MoD police,' Wright asked. 'They guard the nuclear power station at Torness, and they're armed.'

He shook his head. 'No, we need specialist MPs. But, until they get here we're alone on the ground. To back us up, I'm . . .'

Haddock stopped as his phone sounded. He checked the screen and took the call, handsfree. 'Tiggy, you're on speaker,' he told her. 'What do you have?'

'Mrs Hornell's on the move,' the young DC said. 'I'm following her at a distance and I think she's taking me to a riding stable.'

'That would be part of her routine,' McClair volunteered. 'She exercises her pony, then picks up the kid.'

'Alone?'

'Not sure,' Jackie Wright answered. 'I think it depends on whether anyone else is there or not.'

'I've just passed two other women,' Benjamin advised. 'Heading back towards the stable.'

'Then we assume she'll go out alone and be in the open. We

have to get out there. Tiggy, we'll join you as quickly as we can. Meantime you're on your own. If you have a chance, stop her and get her out of there whether she wants to go or not. If you can't do that, keep her in sight and keep us advised of her location.'

'Sauce,' McClair intervened, 'this is my community: I have a feeling I know where she'll go. If she does, it's where she'll be most vulnerable. I'm no more than a mile away. If I could leave Maddie with a neighbour . . .'

'No!' Haddock exclaimed brusquely. 'Noele, you're back on maternity leave and no arguments. The rest of you, let's get moving.'

One Hundred and Seven

'The Military Police investigation branch have turned something up,' Major Hitchens told McGuire with a hint of professional pride in his voice. 'They've established that Lieutenant Commander Hornell caught a train at Hereford yesterday morning. He bought a ticket at the station on a service to Edinburgh, changing at Crewe, and arriving just before three yesterday afternoon. That's as far as they've traced him but the map tells me it's not far from his home. The MP unit is on the way to you by road, as fast as they can, but the earliest they can get there realistically is late afternoon. Can you cope until then?'

'We can,' the DCC said. 'Are you still confident that he isn't armed?'

'The headquarters arsenal is all accounted for: I can confirm that but he wouldn't be the first soldier to have brought a private firearm back from a foreign posting. Take nothing for granted and, remember, he has special skills.'

'I'm not likely to forget it,' McGuire retorted. 'I was shot myself once so I'm even less likely than most to put my officers at risk. We have eyes on his wife and reinforcements, including armed officers, are on the way to her location. The plan is to take her into protective custody as quickly as possible, but if he shows up and offers even a sight of a gun, he's going down.'

'That's understood,' Hitchens agreed. 'Our people will have the same orders when they arrive. But Mr McGuire, that may not be your only problem. I'm afraid that I've just had some rather worrying intelligence from the armourer at regimental headquarters. In the light of that, you may decide to shoot him on sight.'

One Hundred and Eight

'The old railway line,' Noele McClair told Haddock, on handsfree, as his car sped eastwards with Jackie Wright seated beside him and Tarvil Singh in the back.

'It's exactly that; a single track that left the main line just after Longniddry, stopped at Aberlady, then carried on to Gullane, with a request station at Luffness golf club. It stopped carrying passengers ninety years ago but it took coal into the villages for thirty years after that. The track itself is long gone, and the section within Gullane's either overgrown or built on now, but the rest of its land is still a sort of walkway. People use it a lot, dogwalkers and horsey folk like Claire. It's okay in the open but . . .' She paused. 'Sauce, I can see her now, on her pony. I'm on a hillock across from my house with binoculars and I have a clear line of sight. She's past the farm, starting to head back towards the stables. I can just see Tiggy too, but she's trying to follow on foot. She's got no chance of catching the woman before she crosses the Peffer Burn and goes into the woods. That's where she'll be at her most vulnerable; if her husband's lying in wait for her that's where he's most likely to be.'

'We've cleared Aberlady,' Haddock shouted, 'what's the quickest way to the location?'

'If you turn into the Luffness golf club car park,' she replied, 'and go as far as you can past the clubhouse, that's as close as you're going to get. You'll see the woods from there. If you're lucky you'll be able to stop her before she crosses the burn. Where's our armed team?' she asked.

'We're ahead of them, Noele. Hornell may not even be there, but . . .'

'Sauce, even if you scare him off and he escapes, the priority is to protect Claire, yes?'

'Of course. Where is she now?'

'I'm sorry, I can't see her any longer. Listen,' McClair said urgently, 'has anyone tried the obvious and called her mobile? Jackie has the number, I know that.'

'Yes,' Wright called out, 'but she's not picking up. I doubt that she's got it with her.'

'Noele,' Haddock intervened, 'we've got to go, we're there now. You call Tiggy, tell her to stand down.'

He turned off the road and into the golf club. The car park was informal, a flat grassy area, and it was full. *Midweek medal*, he guessed, taking McClair's advice and driving between the clubhouse and the first hole, startling a three-some who were ready to tee off, and carrying on across what he remembered from a playing visit was a practice area rather than the course itself. He pressed on but the way forward came to an end when they reached a fence, with a banked ridge on the right. Sauce stopped, letting the car brake itself as the trio jumped out.

They could see what had to be the old railway track on the other side of an uncultivated field, little more than a hundred yards away. They could see Benjamin, bent double, trying to catch a breath. And they could see Claire Hornell, her eyes focused on the track ahead as she pushed her pony into a trot, gathering pace as she neared a bridge, on the other side of which the woodland began.

'Claire!' Tarvil Singh's basso profundo boomed across the space between them, reaching the trees and stirring a murmuration of starlings from their branches, but the rider carried on looking only straight ahead.

'Fucking AirPods,' the eagle-eyed Wright shouted. 'She's wearing fucking AirPods!'

'We need to get into the woods to cut her off,' Haddock ordered. 'Be careful, but get to her one way or another. The first one to catch her stops her; we worry about him once she's safe.'

He led the way, leaping over tufts of grass. As he ran he remembered a time, six months before, when he had been humiliated in a footrace by Jazz Skinner, a twelve-year-old monster, but he was still ahead of his companions as he reached the woodland. Claire Hornell was still in sight as he splashed across the shallow Peffer Burn; she had slowed the pony to cross the bridge, but it was still moving briskly. In the corner of Haddock's eye, he was aware of Jackie Wright becoming entangled in the wire of a broken fence and falling, splashing and cursing. He had no time to rescue her; all he could do was press on, his cries of, 'Claire! Claire!' still bringing no reaction.

The wood seemed to thin a little as he pressed on, and the pony's pace seemed to slacken a little. He had given up shouting, but was closing in on his objective when . . .

An object, a black, flying, whizzing, shapeless object, caught the pony on the side of the head. Frightened, it reared up, whinnying and throwing its rider to the ground. Still running and almost upon her, Haddock looked to his right to see a figure approaching, a man of medium height and build. As he came towards them steadily, he tossed a catapult into the bushes. His gaze was focused totally on the stricken woman, as if Haddock was invisible, or dismissed as no threat at all. The pony regained its footing and galloped away, perhaps towards what it perceived as safety, an abstract notion for the detective in that moment.

Sauce had seen the military photograph of Edward Hornell; in life it occurred to him that he bore a close resemblance to the younger brother in the TV series *Succession*, but this was a much more deadly version of Roman Roy: not merely because of his bearing, nor because of his undoubted close combat skills, but because inside his green jacket Hornell was wearing what was very obviously a suicide vest.

His wife's ankle was twisted beneath her; she was motionless, staring up at him in silent terror as he stood, little more than ten yards away. 'Give me a hug, baby,' he said, reaching out a hand as he took another step towards her.

Haddock was further away but he did all he could; he started to run again, towards the scene, to do what he knew not, other than die. He knew that would have been inevitable, even if he had chosen to flee, having been shown the effects of an Improvised Explosive Device on a training course. As he moved toward his death he thought of Cheeky and Samantha. And he thought also of his friend and colleague Stevie Steele who had opened a door in a country cottage to find an IED on the other side. He hoped that he would be as relatively unmarked as Stevie had been, but he feared that his identification would be by DNA. He was ready to close his eyes, hoping he would reopen them in Heaven, when . . .

A massive figure burst from the treeline. He was clad in

a muddy black suit, strewn with twigs and leaves, and he was moving inconceivably quickly for a man of his size as he enveloped Edward Hornell in a vast embrace and slammed him face first, with the boom of a contained explosion, into the ground.

One Hundred and Nine

'What's the last line of *Some Like It Hot?*'

'How the hell should I know?'

'"Nobody's perfect",' Tarvil Singh revealed with a huge grin. 'He wasn't, and am I glad of that. The best fucking operator in the SAS he may have been, but because he had one loose wire in his suicide vest, it was useless.'

The bomb squad leader had told Haddock that the force with which the massive DI had hit Hornell had shaken that wire loose. 'A miracle,' he had said. 'It was only your colleague's size that saved him. If you or I had tackled the subject, it would have stayed intact, the device would have detonated and everyone within thirty yards would have been dead.' That was information that the superintendent had decided to keep to himself, for ever.

'Where is he now?' Singh asked, sitting further up in his hospital bed.

'The Military Police have him and they're keeping him. The DCC's been co-operating with a guy from Ministry of Defence security with the agreement of the Crown Office. I interviewed him this morning with their lead investigator, a captain. When you swallowed him up and decked him, as well as knocking yourself out cold on a tree root, you managed to fracture his collarbone, four of his ribs and rupture his spleen. He was on morphine and post-operative sedation so he was cooperative. He confirmed everything that we knew; his wife had told him she was leaving him for someone she'd met. He didn't argue with her, didn't plead his case; he decided to eliminate the opposition, simple as that. He took some of the leave from Hereford that he'd been due . . . Hornell could have spent weeks longer at home than he did, but he was too happy killing insurgents . . . hired a car and drove up to Longniddry. Then he pitched his camp by the beach car park and put Claire under observation. He saw her meet up with Ayre on the second day; she went to his home in the morning when the child was at nursery, and of course he had followed her. That same day Hornell moved his camp to Yellowcraig and switched his attention to Ayre. He watched him for three days until he'd established his routine, the early morning ride and then home. With that done, he pitched his tent where Noele and her mother encountered him, and waited for an opportunity to take the shot. And yes, the second sleeping bag was indeed for the benefit of curious middle-aged ladies, like Susan McClair and other passers-by.'

'What if an opportunity hadn't come up?' Singh wondered.

'We asked him that. He said he'd probably have waited until the next time she went to Ayre's place and taken them both out. But at that stage, Hornell didn't really want to kill his wife,' Haddock said. 'It was only when he'd done the job on Ayre and was back in Hereford that he decided that their life, his and hers, could never be the same, so he made his plan to end it. Obviously, we saw what that was: wear the suicide vest, grab her and detonate it. And that's what would have happened had it not been for you, you fucking big lunatic. If it had gone wrong, I swear I'd have had it carved on your stone.'

For the first time, Singh's smile left him. 'My family don't have to know about it, do they? About what happened?'

The superintendent shook his head. 'They know you suffered a concussion apprehending a suspect. That's all they need to know. How it happened, they'll never hear from me, I promise you that. The Chief's coming to see you, by the way. He doesn't know whether to write you up for a medal or bust you back into uniform for your own safety.'

The DI rubbed his head, where a swelling was still obvious. 'Whatever way that goes,' he said, 'I've made one decision. From now on, I'm wearing my turban on duty.' He looked at Haddock. 'What happens to Hornell now?'

'He's a serving officer, so it'll be treated as a military matter. That and also the murder of the Welshman; he coughed to that as well. The Crown Office have signed off on it all but they didn't really have a choice. Given Hornell's SAS status, he can never be brought to open court. It'll be a military trial, a court martial in private, and he'll get life in a civilian prison.'

'And his wife?'

Haddock shrugged. 'I guess she and Poppy will go home to daddy. I doubt that she'll ever want to ride along the old railway line again.'

One Hundred and Ten

'They won't tell you?' Sarah exclaimed. 'McIlhenney and McGuire, the Glimmer Twins, your protégés, are actually keeping a secret from you?'

'They are,' Bob confirmed. 'All they're prepared to say is that the Gavin Ayre slash David Allen investigation is closed. The Crown Office has released the body and the Canadians will ask you for it on behalf of Allen's mother as soon as they've made arrangements to fly it home.'

'Don't you want to know the whole story?' she asked.

'Of course,' he conceded, 'but if I did I'd be one up on Lowell Payne, and he's head of the security branch in Scotland.'

'You asked Lowell?'

'Of course, I did. If I knew the truth I'd also be one up on Dame Amanda Dennis. I asked her too.'

'MI5 don't know?' Sarah gasped. 'She must have been lying to you, surely?'

'If she was, she never has before, and she and I go back a long way.'

'I thought you told me Amanda was retiring.'

He smiled. 'I did, because I thought she was, but the Home Secretary won't let her, nor would the two before her.' He paused.

'And speaking of retiring,' he added, 'someone else who isn't: Aileen de Marco. My ex.'

'Didn't we know that?' she suggested. 'She's going back to Holyrood, isn't she?'

'She was,' he conceded, 'but my political editor on the *Saltire* tipped me off that she's taken a look at the numbers and changed her mind. She doesn't want to be First Minister again; she'd rather be Prime Minister. With that in mind she's found herself what should be a safe Labour seat at the next Westminster election: our constituency, no less.'

'She won't get my damn vote!' Sarah exclaimed.

'Nor mine, I promise. Anyway, we might not vote there: at least I might not. Now we've taken the decision to move the family base out here for a few years, there's a case for only voting in local council elections.'

'I can see that.' She looked up at him, as the last of the sun died behind the hills. 'Have you told Alex we're going?'

He nodded. 'We had that discussion this afternoon. She said she's pleased for us. She added that it'll be good not to have me tripping over her career every so often.'

'And she and Dominick? Are they going to live happily ever after, do you think?'

Bob Skinner sighed. 'Fuck me, I hope so.'

One Hundred and Eleven

'Vall de Núria,' Dan Provan read from the laptop screen. 'Yes, I fancy that. When do you want to go? The website says it's all year round. How about the school October week?'

'Nah,' Lottie said. 'That's too near winter; that high up in the mountains it might snow. That would make hiking difficult, and you'll never get me on a ski slope. No, I'm thinking of next summer; the weather will be beautiful, but not too hot at eight thousand feet, and by that time Jakey will be a year older and able to come with us on all of the hikes.'

'Even up the peak and into France?'

'Maybe; it would be good to try it without a helicopter.' She frowned. 'That was one fit wumman that Lita and I chased up there. On foot we'd never have got near her. In fact, if she'd had just a wee bit of energy left and went on in a different direction, we'd just have watched her disappear.'

'Was it all worth it in the end?' Dan asked. 'All that effort to bring her back?'

'Probably not,' Lottie admitted. 'Pure fuckin' politics is what it was in the end, but we weren't to know that at the time . . . even if Skinner bein' kidnapped by the Secret Service might have given us a clue.' She laughed. 'Those poor sorry bastards. Did I tell you he's moved to Spain, by the way?' she added.

'No, you didn't.'

'A mix of business and family reasons, Sauce said to me when he told me that they'd folded the Ayre investigation. That was hardly surprising given that Ruby Goldstein was their chief suspect and I saw her on Sky News two weeks ago announcing her poor father's death.'

Provan leaned back in his chair. 'Lottie, my love,' he said. 'I never liked the idea of some things in the job being above my pay grade, but the fact is, sometimes they are, even for you. Move on, and focus on breaking in this new DS of yours. What's his name again?'

'I told you. Another John, to follow his predecessor, Cotter. This one's called Stirling, same as the city. But he's from Perth, to confuse me further.'

'That's right. Do you want me to talk to him and explain the realities of life with DCI Charlotte Mann?'

'Hell no! Let him find out for himself.'

Fifteen minutes later she was helping her partner in the kitchen when they were interrupted by her ring tone. 'Stirling', the screen read. She sighed and then, against her better judgement, accepted.

'John?' she began, forcing herself to sound patient.

'Boss.' The DS sounded appropriately nervous. 'I know you're off, and normally I wouldn't bother you, but I've just had a call from CID in North Ayrshire. They're standing beside a camper van in a new housing development in Irvine. It's got a wheel clamp on it and it's been there for a while. The neighbours reported it because they said it was starting to smell bloody awful. According to the CID at the scene, they're absolutely right. It smells like death, they say.'

Skinner's Elves

By Quintin Jardine

A Bob Skinner Christmas Story

'Twas the night before the Night Before Christmas, 2041 . . .

For all my father's distinguished career in the police service, and in several situations beyond it that he has always been reluctant to discuss, even with me, he has never been a devious man. Invariably what you see is how it is; I doubt that he has ever nursed a hidden motive. No, James Andrew, there can be no doubt; the word 'ulterior' isn't in his vocabulary.

He was never the type of detective who laid traps for the unwary. He achieved his clear-up rate, and it was formidable, by observing, asking, analysing, and eliminating until he was left with only one possible solution, and no mere suspects, only those he knew for sure, and could prove, were guilty.

In short, he's never surprised me. Or he hadn't, not until last Christmas, when he came back from the land of the dead.

None of my siblings would challenge that view, and I have a number of those, five to be precise. There's my beloved half-sister Alex, Alexis to give her the name on her birth certificate; she's a King's Counsel, President of the Scottish Society of Solicitor Advocates, and number one name on the emergency call list of those our father spent half his life locking up. She's twenty-two years older than I am . . . I thought she was my aunt until I was four years old . . . from another mother who died in a mangled car when Alex was four herself, leaving her to be brought up by Dad, with occasional visits from a succession of ladies, most of whose names she no longer even tries to recall.

One she does remember is Mia Watson, or Mia Sparkles if you prefer, the professional name she still uses on her occasional foray into oldies' commercial radio. Mia and Dad were ships that passed in the night, just one night, so Alex told me, but they passed sufficiently close by for him to dock, and leave her with my half-brother Ignacio, a secret that Mia kept until he was going on twenty and in the sort of trouble that not even Alex could make disappear completely.

When Ignacio did come into my life he was twice my age, and I was privately resentful of anyone who upset the equilibrium that Dad and Mum had worked so hard to maintain . . . not always successfully, I must admit, as witness a brief and unhappy stay in the US, Mum's home nation. (My late mother, Professor Sarah Grace, was a forensic pathologist. Her stated ambition was to perform her own autopsy, a feat she achieved, effectively, with the aid of state-of-the-art scanning, allied to the 3D printing of an exact replica of the inoperable brain tumour that killed her the year before last, one day before my thirty-first birthday.)

Mum was a great woman; she treated Ignacio as if he were her own, ignoring my undisguised resentment, and was every bit as proud as Mia, and every bit as fearful, when he was chosen as chief scientific officer on the international mission to develop Stage Two of the Martian Colony. He's been there for two years now, and there is no word on when, if ever, he'll be back. Dad never mentions him, but he knows exactly where Mars is in the dark sky, and on a fine night in the summer, those walking on Gullane Bents may hear one half of a conversation as they pass our garden.

My sister Seonaid took Mum's death personally. She's a medical research scientist, whose obsession is to develop a process by which the brain can heal itself and regrow cancerous or degenerated tissue, as can be done now by all other major organs. The project was her obsession before Mum's diagnosis. She almost went crazy trying to find the missing pieces of the puzzle in time to save her, but they eluded her, as they still do. It was all that I, Dawn, my youngest sibling, and Dad could do to keep her together as Mum's illness progressed to its inevitable conclusion. He and I couldn't have managed it on our own. Dawn is special; she's a healer. Not the conventional kind, but holistic, working one-on-one with those who are emotionally damaged or deprived. Her technique with the autistic and with Asperger's sufferers is so moving that when BBC screened a documentary on her in the summer, there wasn't a dry eye in our house, or, I'm sure, in many others. She's only failed with one patient as far as I know; I'll get to him shortly.

With such a record of fecundity, it would be reasonable to imagine my father being knee-deep in grandchildren, but that's not exactly the case. If it wasn't for me and for my adoptive brother Mark, he wouldn't have any. Mark is what they used to call a geek. He is the least physically co-ordinated person I know. When we were kids he was crap at football, worse at golf, and he flat out wasn't allowed to play rugby. But sit him in front of a games console and he is a killer. That's how he met Luisa, fourteen years ago at a geeks' convention in Tokyo. Yes, she was one too, still is; it was love at first sight, a marriage made in virtual reality and in a combination of two unique talents. Mark had been working on the principles of holographic gaming, but was growing frustrated because no matter what he tried, he couldn't get the blood to look realistic. Luisa showed him how; then she told him that he was wasting his talent, and that not everything had to be interactive and voice-controlled. Instead of games, between them they started to make movies, 3D hologram dramas, comedies, romances, you name it, with stars who cost nothing at all, for they were self-generated within the family. That's right, they used us as the models for their heroes, heroines and villains. They took the old-fashioned graphic novel and used it as the basis for their own art form. They've gone beyond virtual reality, contained within a headset, and developed a lifelike experience that can be enjoyed by groups of people. Holo-halls are popping up around the world, and their beauty is that they require little or no set-up investment.

Mind you, they'd still be dirt poor without me. Technically they may be creative geniuses, but they are completely lacking in imagination and in commercial know-how. I fill both those gaps: I write the screenplays, I run the sales platform, and I promote the product, globally and beyond. The Lunar City, which has grown exponentially over the last ten years, after a hesitant first decade, is one of our biggest markets. It's quite a place, half of it on the surface and half in a network of caverns that the Japanese discovered back in the Teens; Priti and I were blown away when we visited it two years ago.

Priti? My wife, and our musical director, when she's not being a reconstructive orthopaedic surgeon. She and I met in hospital, once she'd put me back together again . . . with a little added value . . . after an unfortunate outcome to a mission in Montenegro. I got rather too close to an old-fashioned RPG in an old-fashioned combat situation, one of the very few these days that brings opposing forces into the same kill zone.

'It's always the fucking Balkans,' Dad growled, as I emerged from the anaesthetic. 'It always will be the fucking Balkans. They tore the EU apart like they've torn themselves apart for centuries.'

'Tore me apart too,' I whispered, remembering my last sight of the remnants of my right leg.

He nodded. 'Yes, but you're back together. Your surgeon completed all the neural connections to your prosthesis in one go, and married the real bone to the synthetic one.'

Behind him, Mum nodded. 'It had to be done in a hurry, while the nerves could still be linked; there were only three available and they took the best match. You won't have a limp, but you will have one foot larger than the other for the rest of your life, which, thanks to Ms Makela here,' she glanced to her left at a tall brown-skinned woman in a blue uniform 'will run its full course.'

'But not in the military,' Dad said.

'No?' I frowned. 'One of my company has a prosthetic arm. Don't write me off yet.'

'Not in the military,' he repeated. For a second I thought I saw tears in his eyes, but I was still well zonked, so I could have been mistaken. Whatever, I knew there was no point in arguing. Even if I had defied him and reported back for army duty, my father has powerful friends, not least among them my one-time stepmother, who was Prime Minister for twelve years. I had no doubt that if I did try to return I would fail the inevitable medical. And so I sat quiet and lived with it when they promoted me to Major, gave me a medal and, a couple of months into my leave of absence, discharged me.

That happened four years ago. For a few weeks after my surgery I had no idea how I was going to spend the rest of my life. Dad, always looking for a return on his investments, offered to find me something with InterMedia, the group of which he's been a director since he left the police service, where I could use the degree in business studies that he insisted I take before I joined the army. I declined as gracefully as I could, telling him that I wanted to make my own way. His mind must have blanked that out, for in the next breath he offered to have a word with Chief Constable Harold Haddock, his one-time protégé, and ease my path into the national police force. I laughed out loud at that one; no way was I going to spend a career failing to live up to his legend.

Instead, after a few weeks of therapy and mobility work, I went home on leave to await the inevitable, back to Gullane where I'd grown up. I moved into the apartment above the garage that had been created when Ignacio joined the family; yes, a twenty-eight-year-old war veteran occupying a space designed for a teenager. Happily it was big enough for two, because in the first months I had a regular weekend visitor, until she secured a move to an orthopaedic reconstruction unit in Edinburgh and moved in permanently. My surgeon had taken a keen interest in my rehab, as I had in her, to the extent that after three weeks she had to recuse herself from my care. We found that we had shared interests; music, art, crime novels, the theatre, fine dining, travel, and sex, of course.

It was Priti who ordered me to write; she wanted to make a case study of me, and it would be a hell of a lot easier, she said, if I drafted something out myself. I took her rather too literally. I began with an account of the first day of my basic training, and three weeks later I presented her with a full narrative of my service career, ending on the day I walked out of hospital in Birmingham. My draft was no use for her purposes, but she enjoyed it so much that I changed all of the names and most of the locations, since many of my company's operations had been officially deniable, then self-published it as an e-book on every available platform, under a nom-de-plume, Jazz Morgan, a combination of the childhood moniker that's followed me ever since, and Dad's middle name.

It made me a small fortune and nobody in the Ministry of Defence caught on that I had danced around the Official Secrets Act, not then, not ever. That surprises me as I dedicated it to Priti, but the people who run our armed services have never been famed for their joined-up thinking.

I didn't even mention my work to my siblings, but the name was a dead giveaway to Mark when he spotted it while trawling on Amazon. He's a tight sod, so he made me send him and Luisa a freebie. They read it. Mark winced all the way through, but Luisa's eyes just got wider and wider, she told me, as she saw its possibilities . . . and holo-theatre was born.

My story was their first production, from the start to its gory conclusion. I did the script, and found screen-writing to be no great hassle; my story was full of dialogue and taking it further wasn't difficult. The music was a bonus; Priti's played the sitar since she was twelve, and had written several original pieces for that twangy instrument. One of them was perfect as the theme, re-scored and played on a synthesiser.

Three years after that successful launch, and on the back of nine feature productions that followed, we decided to mark the event by gathering the family together . . . apart from Ignacio, obviously . . . for Christmas in Dad's house in L'Escala in Spain. In truth it was more than that; we were all still mourning Mum, Dad deepest of all, so deeply that we were afraid he would follow her, way before his time.

I say 'we decided' but there was no discussion involved. Alex decreed, and that meant it was a done deal. Okay, Dad put up a token protest, but he hasn't been able to overrule her since shortly after her thirteenth birthday. The clincher for my brother and I, and our partners, was the fact that it would bring our two children together. That happens rarely since Mark, Luisa and Roland, who is four, are in London, while Priti and I and our two-year-old, Alexandra, moved from living near Alex in Edinburgh to take over the Gullane house after Mum's death, at Dad's insistence. He refused to go in there, declaring it haunted. Instead he moved into the apartment, indifferent to my hope that eventually he might occupy a small bungalow that would be built on another part of the plot.

The Spanish house isn't big enough for us all but, so that Dad would always be close to his grandchildren, Mark and I rented a villa three doors down, with the same view across the bay, for our sisters. Those three are all single, although only Alex is resolutely so. She has never had a relationship that's lasted longer than three years, although her first, with one of Dad's detective crew, was an on-off-on-again and finally off-for-good affair that occupied half of her twenties, and left her handicapped, maybe even crippled, emotionally. Seonaid has no such hang-ups, and plenty of boyfriends, but declares herself too busy to share her life. Dawn is gay, but waiting for the right woman to come along.

The rental property was no more than a dormitory. Yes, we set up a small fibre-optic tree against the chance of visits by Roland, who took a keen interest in Christmas, and Alexandra, who was beginning to catch on that presents and a fat bloke with a beard and a red suit were involved, but the focus of the gathering was at Dad's place. Auntie Alex would have taken charge of everything, but for once Dad surprised us by stirring from his melancholic apathy.

In the aftermath of Mum's death he had been able to focus on only one thing. She's buried in the cemetery just outside Dirleton and, after the funeral, he would walk there and back, a four-mile round trip. He could have driven, he could have used his bus pass, but no, he walked, hail, rain or shine . . . no snow; we haven't had snow at sea level in Scotland for fifteen years.

The rest of his time was spent in isolation. He shut himself away in the apartment with his memories, his misery and with too much booze. He grew a beard. His hair became thick, shaggy, and tousled. He took to dressing in jeans, and T-shirts with logos of all the places he and Mum had visited. That was against the golf club dress code, but since his clubs lay untouched in their locker, it made no difference. He rarely answered phone calls: friends and former colleagues, notably Maggie Steele and Mario McGuire, rang me frequently, anxious, and asking how he was. Any business he did for InterMedia was over a video-link, for he never went into the office in Edinburgh that he had maintained for over twenty years. Xavi Aislado, his friend, had given him indefinite leave of absence from InterMedia, but he had decided that he would resign from the board altogether rather than face the monthly trip to Spain for its meetings. Nothing I could say deterred him; it took a full-scale bollocking from Alex to make him change his mind.

Worst of all, though, he took little or no interest in Alexandra. Eventually Priti and I stopped taking her across to the apartment; although her skin is darker she has a strong resemblance to my mother. My fear was that looking at her was only adding to his pain. Mark's fear was that he would lose all interest in Roland, since he has no biological connection with the boy. And our overriding fear was that one day his grief would prove too much for him; one of my nightmares saw me staring at the apartment door for a few days before breaking it down and finding him behind it, the booze, the pills, the note . . . no, maybe not the note; Dad never was one for stating the obvious.

He was pathetic, that's the truth of it, in his behaviour and in his obsession. 'You don't care about the rest of us!' I heard Alex screaming at him one night when she visited him, more or less forcing her way across his threshold. 'Keep this up and we may stop caring about you!' She was in tears when she left, slamming the door shut behind her.

Maybe it was that exchange that made him think twice about refusing to come to Spain. He did make a pass at it though; 'Your mother will miss me,' he pleaded to Seonaid, Dawn and me. It was Dawn, the youngest of us, who squashed that. 'Alex was a part of your life before Mum or any of the rest of us,' she pointed out. 'She's missing you too, and she's still alive.'

He made a show of glaring at her, then sighed. 'Okay, I surrender. I'll come.'

It was the start of his re-emergence, although it didn't happen overnight. None of us relaxed completely until we boarded the hyperloop that took us to London to meet up with Mark, Luisa and Roland for the rest of the journey to Figueres. 'We used to drive down to Spain,' Alex said, as she strapped herself into the pod for the second leg. 'Remember, Dad? Just you and me.'

'Uh-huh,' he grunted. 'I'm surprised you do,' he added. 'Most times you slept most of the way. Pee-ed yourself once or twice.'

He didn't say another word until we were in the terminal in Spain. Even then he ignored the rest of us, speaking only to the grandchildren he was holding, safe in the crooks of his arms. He'd had his hair cut, but the beard was still there; Alexandra was running her fingers through it, tentatively, for it was thick

'When we came down here, Granny used to make me fly to Barcelona,' I heard him tell them, and I knew it to be true. She couldn't stand the hyperloop; we didn't know it at the time but it was the start of her illness. 'There's a hotel she likes there,' I winced at the present tense 'on a big square, the Plaça Reial. Coming this way's much faster, but I liked the old planes better. I even liked driving better, with Auntie Alex.'

'Even though she pee-ed herself?' Roland ventured. Kids, they soak up everything.

'Even though. It wasn't too bad; she'd grown out of doing that by the time she was ten.' He said it deadpan, but I realised that it was the first time in a couple of years, since Mum was diagnosed, that I'd heard him venture anything resembling a joke. That's if it was; my father has always maintained that his favourite comedian is an old-timer called Chic Murray. Since I was a boy, he's made me watch his stuff on YouTube, and with his archaic Scots vocabulary sometimes I can't tell if it's a gag.

When we got to L'Escala there was nothing to do but drop off our luggage and go out to eat, in a restaurant called La Caravella on the sea-front. Dad seemed to relax there just a little, but even then his focus was mainly on Roland and Alexandra, making sure that they flanked him at the table and helping his granddaughter wolf down her macaroni.

He stayed there after we left, he and Alex. I don't know what they talked about, but when he came in he was calm, and sober. He even kissed Priti and Luisa good night before going to bed.

Next morning, when he emerged for breakfast, the beard was gone, and he was clear-eyed, with an air of purpose. 'I have decided,' he declared, as he rubbed tomato and garlic into a thick slice of bread, that I had brought in earlier 'that my grandchildren and I are going on a mission, if that's all right with their mothers.'

'What sort of a mission?' Priti asked.

'Secret. We're going to my friend Xavi's estate outside Girona. He's shown off his grandkids to me for long enough, and now it's my turn.'

The two women exchanged glances, then nods. I was less certain, but for the first time in a while, the man before me was someone I recognised, someone I'd always trusted absolutely, and so I kept quiet as he loaded the kids into the big SUV that lives in the garage out there. The two of them were as high as kites when they set off, as their parents strove to conceal our nervousness.

That grew with each passing hour, five of them, until they returned . . . with a bloody enormous tree lashed to the roof rack, and boxes of decorations in the space at the back. Our worries had been needless; the children were as excited as I'd ever seen them.

So was Dad. It was as if he had decided to step back into the world.

My secret dread, as I passed through my teens and into my twenties, had always been that one day my parents would diminish, fade with age, become mere shadows of what they had been. Mum had forestalled that by dying in her prime, her early sixties, something my worst dreams had never foretold. But in the months that had followed her passing, I had watched my resolute, rock-hard, immutable father begin to grow old before my eyes.

It had scared me, no question; as well as my fear that he might end himself. I woke up more than once in the middle of the night, wide-eyed from a vision of him sitting in a window of the village care home. And so, when the old Bob Skinner jumped out of the SUV, laughing and full of life, with a wriggling armful of Roland as he unclipped Alexandra from her car seat, I felt light-headed, positively dizzy.

I must have looked it too, for he grinned at me, eyebrows raised with the old scar above the bridge of his nose becoming deeper and more obvious as it does when he smiles. 'My God, Jazz,' he boomed. 'What a face you've got on you! Cheer up, son; get that tree off the car and bring it inside. It's bloody Christmas, for God's sake!'

He left me to it as he followed the kids indoors, past Alex, who had emerged to see what the fuss was about. 'What the hell?' she gasped when they were gone. 'Has he been drinking?'

'If he didn't have the kids with him, I might have thought that too,' I confessed. I shrugged. 'Come on, let's get this monster unpacked. There are boxes of Christ-knows-what in there.'

As I lugged the tree into the hall, I heard Priti's voice from the kitchen. 'Bob, have the children eaten?'

'Of course, they have!' he retorted amiably. 'Paloma fed them fries and fish while Xavi and I were cutting the tree. It came from his plantation; it's a beauty, isn't it? They are expecting hot chocolate and marshmallows, though. It's their reward for helping me pick the decorations. They're from Girona,' he added.

He left the two mothers to calm their over-excited children and re-joined Alex and me, Seonaid, Dawn and Mark. He had been working on the design theme of a new production . . . my brother is a workaholic . . . only to have his concentration shattered by the noise of our dad's return.

The tree was too big to fit in the house, but we were able to secure it in a big garden tub, and position it between the front terrace and the pool. We had a hell of a job decorating the thing; I'm six four and I needed the set of steps from the garage to fit the fairy on top. Dad, to Dawn's unspoken annoyance, had ignored the British Twenties-Thirties trend towards gender-neutral fairies; his . . . it was Alexandra's choice, he said, but none of us believed him . . . was blonde, with a sparkly dress, wings and a star-like wand.

As I secured it to the highest branch, he related his story of how the first fairy came to be on top of the Christmas tree. Although I had heard it before, when he reached the punch line, failing as always to contain his laughter at his own joke, my prosthetic leg betrayed me; Mark had to steady the steps or I would have fallen into the pool.

When we were done, and night had fallen completely, Roland and Alexandra were given the task of switching on the lights, flashing LED in red and yellow . . . the colours of the Catalan flag, Alex pointed out, although it wasn't lost on any of us. Dad never allows us to forget that in the crisis of Twenty Seventeen, InterMedia kept its corporate and physical base in Catalunya, and championed editorially the right of its people to determine their own future in the face of threats from the Madrid government to remove the broadcasting licences it held across Spain.

With the children in bed, we dined as a family on the terrace, within the heated glass enclosure that makes it habitable in winter. We weren't short of power; the solar roof had been charging the storage batteries throughout the year, with minimal use in our absence. Alex had hired kitchen staff for the duration of our stay. Her plan was that the only main meals we would cook for ourselves would be on Christmas Day and *Cap d'Any*, that's Hogmanay to us Jocks. She also had a sommelier choose the wines. She'd have paid for it all too, but Mark and I vetoed that. Alex is at the top of her profession, but Dad told me that she earns less in real terms than she did in her twenties as a partner in a corporate law firm, before she switched to the Criminal Bar.

I watched Dad carefully through the meal, looking for any sign of a return to his dour depression. He was quiet, reflective, as were most of us, I suppose, given the imaginary empty chair at the table, but there was a softness in his eyes and the faintest of smiles at the corners of his mouth and they reassured me. On the few occasions when we had dined together in the immediate aftermath of our awful bereavement, he had eaten too fast, drunk too much and become more and more withdrawn, until finally rising from the table and stalking off. Happily, and to my great relief, on that first in-house Spanish gathering he savoured each course and praised it, and studied the descriptions of the wines with which we were served, rather than thrusting a glower and an empty glass at the waiter, as he had done on one fraught evening at Greywalls Hotel, for which I had felt the need to apologise to the management next day.

I held my peace until the dinner service was over, and the staff had left us with the coffee, the petit fours and a range of liqueurs. I knew that Alex had been studying him as carefully as I had, and so I waited, deferring to my big sister. When her mother had died she had been a pre-school child. If Dad had reacted in the same way to his first widowhood she would have been oblivious to it, although everything I had been told suggested that he had been forced to contain his grief, and remain functional for her sake.

She said nothing, though, nor did anyone else. Maybe she was waiting for him, maybe we all were, but he kept as quiet as the rest of us, gazing through the glass at the tree outside, his smile more obvious than it had been.

'Come on, Dad,' I said eventually. 'Say something; a toast, a eulogy, whatever, but out with it.'

He looked at me. Those eyes that had been so cold for so long were warm again, as they had been throughout my childhood, throughout my life.

'There will be no toast,' he declared, raising his glass in apparent contradiction 'and no more eulogies. We've all mourned the past enough. It's time to embrace the future that is Sarah's legacy to us all, and to do nothing but celebrate it, and her. I've been immured in my self-pity for long enough, for far too long. Today I realised that, and I was ashamed of myself, of how I've been to you all. I'm the fucking patriarch of this family.' He chuckled, at the notion, I assumed, then looked around the table making eye contact with every one of us.

'As such, I apologise to you all,' he continued calmly. 'I should have been helping all of you to handle your grief; instead I've been making it worse. I should have been reminding all of you of a fundamental truth, simply this. Our parents are meant to die before we do, it's the natural order of things. Mine did, now it's your turn.'

He paused again, for a second or two. 'But you know what?' he ventured. 'This isn't more of my self-pity, it's just a fact. You're all luckier than I was. My mother was an alcoholic, and my father was a sad man so affected by things that happened to him in the Second World War that he was withdrawn and oblivious to her problems and to the other issues in our dysfunctional family. You lot, you've all had Sarah to bring you up,' he glanced at my older sister 'aye, even you, Alexis, although you were at university when she appeared on the scene. I hope you know how lucky you've been.'

'Amen to that,' Mark murmured, mistily.

'You know what knocked the scales off me?' Dad continued. 'Spending today with my two grandchildren. Listening to them in the back of the car, enjoying their chat, realising finally the opportunity I have. When I woke up, even this morning, I had no ambition left in my life. Well, more fool me, for now I do.

'Something I never told any of you,' he continued. 'I had a medical for InterMedia early last year in the Trueta Hospital in Girona, just before Sarah got ill. It had something to do with a key man insurance policy that the company maintains on its senior people, even those as old as me. They gave me treadmill tests, blood tests, urine tests, shit tests, a full body scan, the lot. And you know what? The consultant who supervised the show said that physically I'm twenty years younger than my passport says I should be. There's a lot of mileage left in my engine, and I intend to put it to good use. I'm not just going to be Granddad to those kids, I'm going to be their mentor, theirs and any others you lot may produce. That doesn't mean I'll get in your way as parents, but as they grow, I will be there for them, unless God disagrees, right through to the day they graduate from whatever universities they go to. It's a duty, it's a challenge and it's a pleasure, all rolled into one. By God, we're going to have fun, them and me!'

'Did you tell them this when you were away today?' Priti asked him.

'Nah,' he replied. 'I thought I'd leave that to you lot. Besides, we were too busy on the trip talking about other things.'

'Such as?' Seonaid peered at him over his shoulder from the seat on his right.

'Santa,' he announced. 'Alexandra isn't really up with the concept, being two . . . at least I thought she wasn't, but Roland is, and as his parents' son he is quizzical, even at four. He's a real child of the Forties. "Is Santa real, Granddad?" he asked me. "Of course, he is," I replied.' He made an involuntary chortling sound. 'Little bugger said he didn't believe me. "I think Santa's really you," he said. I had to think fast, and I did. "No," I told him, "but it is a very big world and, realistically, Santa has to delegate a lot of the practical stuff, so he can do his job after you've all gone to sleep on Christmas Eve. That's where us Granddads come in; we do his leg work. Think of me as Santa's agent." And that's where Alexandra blew my mind. From her seat in the back, she pipes up, "Papa, can Roland and I be your elves?"

'I tell you all, I nearly put the car in a ditch. "Absolutely, my darling girl," I declared. "From this day on you and your cousin are Skinner's Elves, my personal assistants in everything related to Christmas, and anything else you like." That's a solemn promise that I intend to keep.'

'Awww!' Dawn exclaimed, as she reached for the decanter. 'You deserve another drink for that, Dad.'

He held out his glass. 'Too damn right I do. My inertia is over. Tomorrow I go back to work, right across the board . . . in a very literal sense. Today Xavi asked me if I would return as Chairman of InterMedia while Paloma takes some maternity leave. I accepted and it will be announced tomorrow. As that happens, I'll be reversing a decision I took two days ago, if it's not too late, and accepting an offer I've had from the Scottish National Party to be its candidate for the Presidency in next year's election.'

'You what?' Alex gasped.

'You heard me, girl,' he retorted. 'You may wind up being First Lady. But before any of that, I'll be going back to my old job, detecting, for I find myself facing another challenge right here.'

In the seat on his left, Luisa gazed at him. 'What's that, Pops?'

'You've been staring at it all night,' he said, grinning again, 'all of you, and none of you have noticed. Look at the tree.'

We did, and I got there first. The gauzy, sparkling, old-fashioned sexist fairy that I had fixed in place, at risk to life and remaining limb, had disappeared.

'How the hell did that happen?' I called out, pointing at the branch where it had been.

'I don't know,' Dad admitted. 'It's what we refer to in the trade as a Mystery. But tomorrow, I will set up an investigation, and be assured,' he gave a quick sidelong glance at Dawn 'with Skinner's Elves to help me, the culprit will be found.'